MELTWATER

Michael Ridpath spent eight years as a bond trader in the City before giving up his job to write full-time. He lives in north London with his wife and three children. Visit his website at www.michaelridpath.com.

Also by Michael Ridpath

THE FIRE AND ICE SERIES

Where Shadows Lie

66° North

MELTWATER

MICHAEL RIDPATH

First published in hardback, trade paperback and E-book
in Great Britain in 2012 by Corvus Books,
an imprint of Atlantic Books Ltd.

This paperback edition published in Great Britain in 2013 by Corvus,
an imprint of Atlantic Books Ltd.

9 8 7 6 5 4 3 2 1

A CIP catalogue record for this book is available from the British Library.

Paperback ISBN: 978 085789 847 0
E-book ISBN: 978 0 85789 682 7

Printed in Italy by Grafica Veneta S.p.A.

Corvus
An imprint of Atlantic Books Ltd
Ormond House
26-27 Boswell Street
London WC1N 3JZ

www.corvus-books.co.uk

for Mary

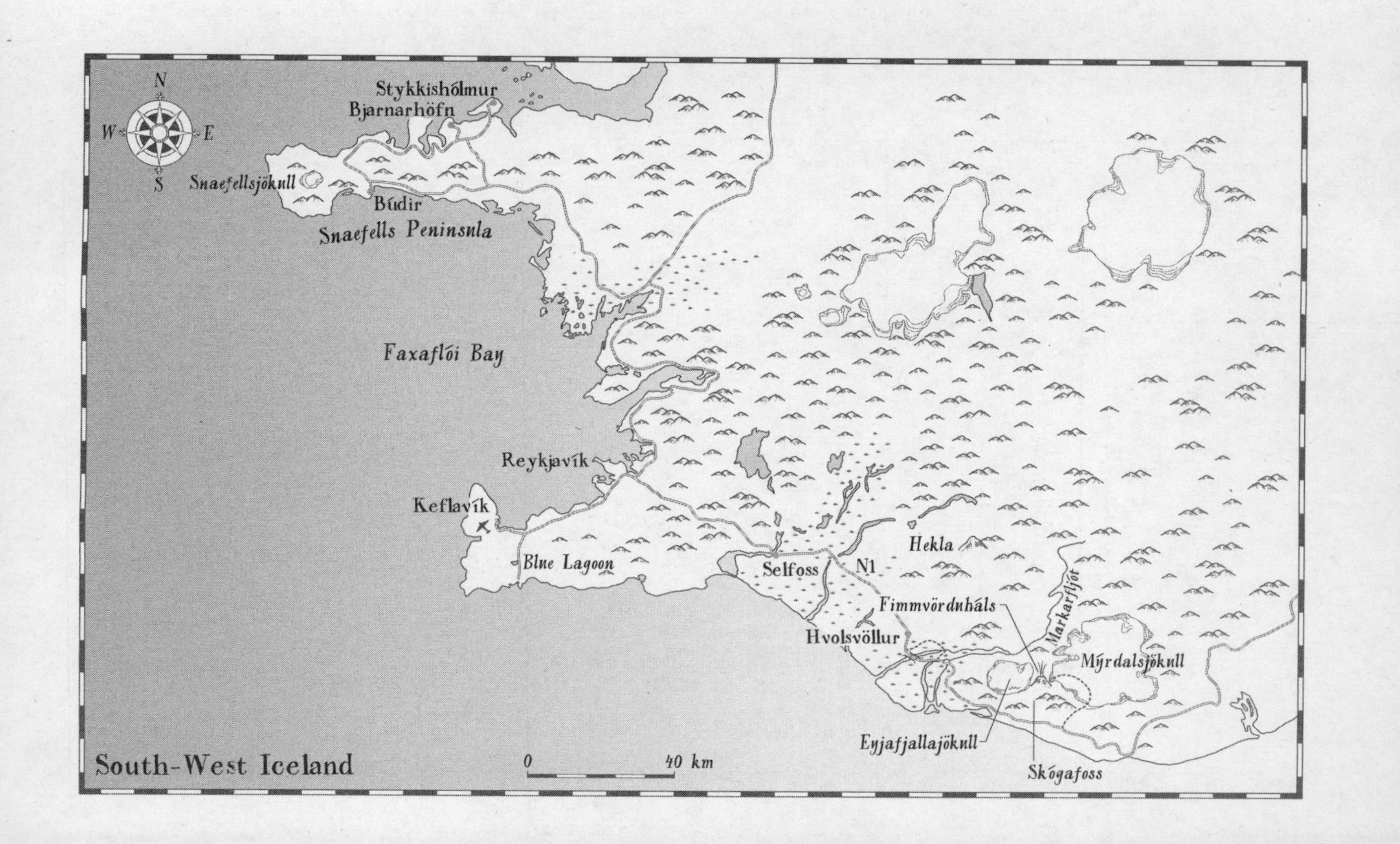
South-West Iceland
N
W
E
S
Stykkishólmur
Bjarnarhöfn
Snaefellsjökull
Búdir
Snaefells Peninsula
Faxaflói Bay
Reykjavík
Keflavík
Blue Lagoon
Selfoss
N1
Hekla
Fimmvörduháls
Hvolsvöllur
Markarfljót
Mýrdalsjökull
Eyjafjallajökull
Skógafoss
0
40 km

Gunnar of Bjarnarhöfn

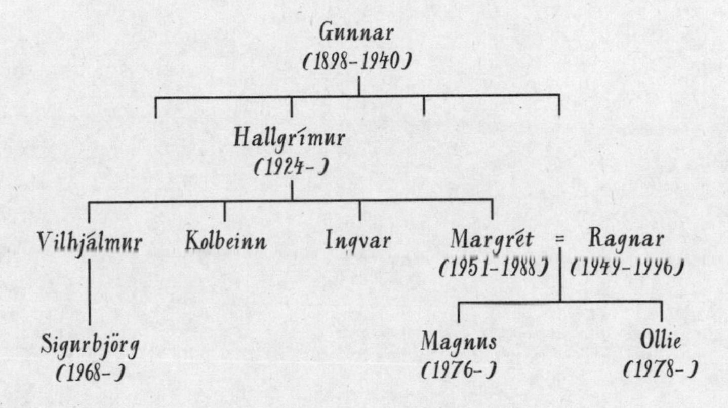

Jóhannes of Hraun

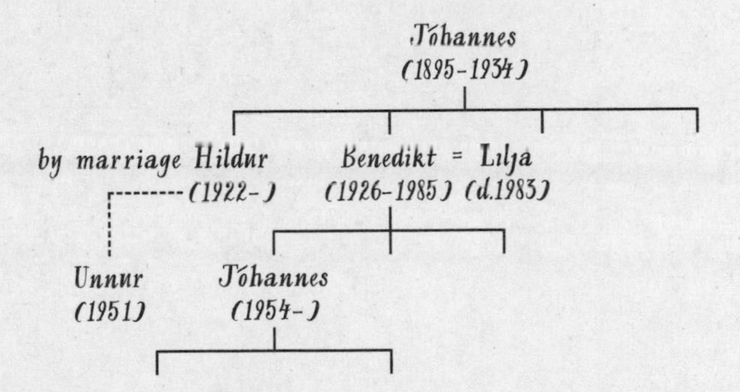

CHAPTER ONE

Saturday 10 April 2010

DEATH CAME FRAME by frame, in grainy black and white.

Erika stared at the screen of her laptop. It showed the tatty rectangular roofs of a poor Middle Eastern city. In the centre of the screen a white box hovered over a truck upon which the letters 'UN' could clearly be seen as it manoeuvred down a narrow side street. A burst of rapid speech in a language Erika didn't understand zipped through her earphones. The truck came to a halt and about half a dozen people dropped out of the back. Another burst of chatter, more urgent this time. And then one word.

Esh!

There was silence for a second and then little spurts of dust erupted around the feet of the group and the figures crumpled.

Esh!

More spurts. The bodies were motionless on the ground now as bullets slammed into them.

Chatter. A laugh. Erika wanted to close her eyes, look away, look anywhere but at the screen, but she couldn't. She had to watch. Someone had taken enormous risks so that she could see this.

The perspective changed as the helicopter circled for a better look. The shaky rectangle grew wider as the camera zoomed.

One of the bodies began to move. Miraculously a figure climbed to his feet and, stooping, shuffled towards the shelter of a building, a leg dragging in the dust. Climbed to her feet. The figure had long fair hair, light grey in the image.

A curse. Chatter.

Esh!

The spurts of dust danced around the flailing body for several seconds, a period as long as the first two bursts combined. Then the body was still. The white frame lingered over it as radio reports were passed back and forth in the impenetrable language. The helicopter must be hovering, waiting, explaining. After a minute Erika could bear it no longer.

She clicked 'Pause' and turned away from the screen. Outside, the last of the daffodils nodded through the railings of the London square in front of the hotel, dingy yellow in the light of the streetlamps. It was five a.m. and still dark. She turned to check the bed where the renowned Greek-American professor of strategic studies she had met the night before was lying. Asleep. Definitely asleep.

The previous evening she had taken part in a public debate on the subject 'Information Has a Right to Freedom' at the Royal Geographic Society. There were three speakers on each side: she, of course, had been in favour of the motion. It had been one of her best performances. The Greek-American strategic studies professor had put up a good fight, but the audience had overwhelmingly agreed with her. So had he in the end. After dinner and a few drinks back at his hotel.

She had still been feeling the glow of victory four hours later when she crept out of bed to open up her laptop and check her e-mails.

The glow was gone. It was replaced with horror and disgust.

And anger.

These were supposed to be her people.

She turned back to her laptop and pulled up Jabber, the encrypted instant-messaging service. They were all online, waiting for her response.

Erika: *hi guys.*

Nico: *hi erika.*

Apex: *hi.*

Dieter: *hi.*

If she had to guess Dieter was up late and Nico up early. As for Apex, who knew? He never seemed to sleep. A bit like Erika herself.

Erika: *have you seen it?*

'*yes*' came the response, from all three.

Erika: *is that woman who i think it is?*

Dieter: *it's tamara wilton. for sure.*

Apex: *it's her. the date on the video tallies with the day she was killed. jan 14 2009.*

Erika: *i know it's war but i can't believe people do that kind of thing. it makes me sick to my stomach.*

Nico: *wait till you hear what they are saying. do you understand hebrew?*

Erika: *i'm not that kind of jew.* As she wrote those words, Erika wondered exactly what kind of Jew she was. That was something she would have to figure out pretty soon. *did you get a translation?*

Nico: *i sent it to an israeli volunteer. she is sending me back a full transcript. i'll pass it on as soon as i get it.*

Dieter: *please tell me you didn't send it to israel!*

Nico: *yeah, but through tor.*

Apex: *nico, you have to leave that kind of thing to us! anything going into israel is vulnerable.*

Erika: *cut it out guys. nico, did the volunteer give you any idea what the israelis are saying?'*

Nico: *yeah. the controller tells the helicopter that some hamas fighters have just fired an anti-tank missile and jumped into a un truck. the helicopter finds the truck and asks for permission to engage. it's given. then you see the shooting.*

Erika: *what about tamara wilton? can't they see she's a woman?*

Nico: *just as they are firing, the controller tells the helicopter they've found the truck with the anti-tank unit. it's a different truck. the pilot sees the woman moving and tells the gunner to shoot her. they can tell she is a woman. the gunner questions this, but the pilot says they don't want witnesses, and besides, the united nations are a bunch of interfering bastards. then in the chatter afterwards the helicopter tells the controller that the people getting out of the truck were armed and one of them escaped with an anti-tank missile launcher.*

Erika: *but no one escaped!*

Nico: *precisely.*

Erika: *i remember this. it was supposed to have been investigated by the israeli authorities. i'm pretty sure they cleared the soldiers of any blame.*

Dieter: *how can they have done that! these guys are murderers. it's that simple.*

Erika: *and that's what we will tell the world. we'll ream them with this.*

The screen was still as the four of them digested what Nico had said. Behind Erika the professor of strategic studies grunted and rolled over in the hotel bed. Disturbed by her furious tapping on the keyboard, perhaps.

Nico: *what do we do?*

Erika: *we publish, of course! but we do it carefully. this is one of those situations where the cover-up is as important as the crime itself. the israelis will want to quash this, and if they can't quash it they will discredit it. we'll need full transcription, analysis, verification. release the video online and the transcript through selected newspapers. the washington post. the guardian, maybe der spiegel. are we sure it's genuine?*

Apex: *not yet.*

Erika: *okay we'll have to check that out. we need to be one hundred per cent.*

Dieter: *it's going to be difficult to do this remotely.*

Erika: *yes. we should meet somewhere. just for a few days. get a team together. just like we did last year in stockholm for the zimbabwe arms leak.*

Nico: *this is bigger.*

Dieter: *so where do we go?*

Apex: *i'm not coming.*

Erika: *okay apex.* Apex never came anywhere. He stayed in his room somewhere in a time zone a long way away. None of them had seen him apart from Dieter, and that was almost twenty years before, and no one even knew his real name. Erika had spoken to him on a voice link over the Internet frequently; he had a rapid Australian accent. So, no, Apex wouldn't be coming.

They were waiting for her to suggest somewhere. Technically she was nothing more than the Spokesperson for Freeflow. The organization had no hierarchy, at least in theory. Most decisions were taken by the four of them: Apex and Dieter were the technical guys; Nico did finance and general organization.

In practice Erika was the leader. They all followed Erika. Anywhere.

Erika: *what about iceland?*

Dieter: *but that's the middle of nowhere.*

Erika: *when I went with nico in november they were really friendly. they treated us like stars. and they seem dead serious about protecting the press.*

Nico: *iceland might work. we have some good guys there we can trust.*

Dieter: *yeah duddi is good. i rate him.*

Nico: *i'll organize it. hey you know there's a volcano erupting at the moment?*

Dieter: *cool. i've never seen a live volcano.*

Nico: *i did my masters in geology. i'll give you a guided tour.*

Erika: *guys we won't have time for any sightseeing.*

Nico: *you're no fun erika. so when do we go?*

Erika thought a moment. It was Saturday morning. She could work on the transcript and do some background research in London over the weekend. There were people she could stay with whom she trusted in London, the man in the bed behind her not being one of them. There were people she could stay with in lots of cities.

Erika didn't really live anywhere. Her few possessions were strewn all over the globe: in her parents' place just outside New

York; with Dieter in Cologne; some with Nico in Milan; some of her most personal stuff with her grandmother in Queens. But most of what she needed she kept in her small backpack. And in her computer backed up and encrypted remotely in several servers dotted around the world.

She would need to borrow a warmer coat for Reykjavík.

She resumed typing: *when can you get things ready nico?*

Nico: *tuesday?*

Erika: *monday.*

Nico: *monday.*

Erika: *great. see you all in reykjavik on monday. and we need a name for this project. see what you can come up with.*

Monday 12 April 2010

Erika emerged through the double doors of the arrivals hall and scanned the dozen or so people waiting. She knew Nico would have arranged for someone to pick her up, but she had no idea who it would be.

There were a couple of signs in the hall, and one of them had her name scrawled on it, with a smiley face. She approached the young woman holding the scrap of cardboard. 'Hi, I'm Erika.'

The woman smiled and held out her hand. She was thin with short dark hair, pale skin and big blue eyes. She was wearing jeans and a thick tan coat. And a clerical collar around her throat.

'Ásta,' she said. 'Welcome to Iceland.'

The woman led Erika out of the terminal to a beaten-up old Peugeot, which needed a wash. Erika wasn't entirely surprised by her host – Freeflow's volunteers came in all shapes and sizes – but this was the first priest she had come across. Certainly the first female one. Erika checked to see whether anyone was following them; she didn't think so, but it was hard to tell.

'I'll take you to the house,' Ásta said in flawless English. 'It's right downtown. A great location.'

'I doubt we'll be going outside much,' said Erika. 'Who does it belong to?'

'The owners live abroad. We've rented it for a couple of weeks.'

'We won't need it that long. A week at most.' Ásta eased the Peugeot out of the car park and on to the road to Reykjavík. Forty-six kilometres, according to the yellow road sign.

'You speak very good English,' Erika said.

'Thank you. You'll find most Icelanders speak English, especially the younger ones.'

'Yeah, I remember that from last time I was here,' said Erika. 'Do you always wear that thing?'

'What thing?'

'The dog-collar thing.'

'Oh, no. But I want to while I'm helping you out. I think what you are doing is good. There should be more openness in Iceland, and more in the Icelandic Church. I guess I'm making a point. Christians believe in telling the truth.'

'So do Muslims and Jews,' said Erika. 'And atheists. Or the majority of them do anyway: their governments are a different matter.'

Erika was wary. All kinds of people tried to win Freeflow over to their cause. But independence was everything. Independence from any one country, any political ideology and any religion.

Ásta smiled. 'Oh, don't worry, I won't try to influence what you are doing. I saw you on *Silfur Egils* when you were here last year, by the way. I was impressed. A lot of people here were.'

Silfur Egils was the biggest TV chat show in Iceland. Erika had used her appearance to encourage the Icelanders to set up a haven for free information. The idea seemed to have gone down well. 'I'm glad you remember it,' Erika said.

'I might have something for you,' Ásta said.

'About the banks?' Freeflow received information from all over the world, some of it big, some of it small. It had published the details of one of the Icelandic bank's loans several months before, but had also received several pieces of unsubstantiated gossip that it had left unpublished.

'No. About the Church here in Iceland. Certain things that happened here in the past.'

'OK,' Erika said. 'But, Ásta, if you do decide to leak something to us, you should do it anonymously. Upload it to our website or mail it to us on a CD. We go to great lengths to protect our sources, and the best protection is if we don't know their identity ourselves.'

'But if you don't know who they are, how can you tell if they are reliable?'

It was a common criticism of Freeflow, but one Erika had answered many times. 'We are very careful to check and double-check the information we are given. That works much better than a subjective judgement on whether a source is reliable or not.'

'I see,' said Ásta.

They were out on the highway now, a long straight strip of black through the barren lava field that separated the airport at Keflavík from the capital. Checking behind her, the only vehicles Erika could see were two large trucks: not the vehicles of choice for surveillance teams. No trees anywhere, nor grass. Grey sea on one side; black mountains beyond the lava on the other. A small mountain rose up ahead in a perfect cone. Bleak. A sign to the right pointed to the Blue Lagoon and Erika saw steam leaking out from behind a fold in the lavascape a few miles in that direction. Erika had seen the posters at the airport: she could use a long soak in the geothermally heated pool.

The middle of nowhere, as Dieter had said. A long way from Israel.

'Nico showed us the video,' Ásta said. 'It's going to make quite a splash when it gets out. There was a lot of coverage here when Tamara Wilton was shot. It was a big deal.'

'Yes, it will make a splash.' Tamara Wilton was an ordinary British student who had decided to spend six months after graduating from university with the United Nations High

Commission for Refugees in Gaza doing her bit for the Palestinians. Except she wasn't ordinary – she was a pink-cheeked, fair-haired English-rose type in the mould of Princess Diana. The world knew that because she had an identical twin sister Samantha, who looked just like her and who turned out to be not just cute, but articulate and angry as well. Samantha Wilton had been all over the papers and TV, not just in Britain, but also in the rest of Europe and even the States. The story of her sister had touched all kinds of people, even Erika, who saw something of herself in the idealistic young woman willing to go to dangerous places for what she believed in. It had been a public-relations nightmare for the Israelis, which they had fought hard to contain.

But until now no one outside the Israeli Defence Force had actually seen it happen. More importantly, no one had heard it happen.

Erika had spent Saturday and Sunday holed up in an activist's flat in East London going through everything she could find on the death of Tamara Wilton. The Israeli Defence Force investigation had been a whitewash. The recent Goldstone Report, instigated by the United Nations to examine human rights abuses by both sides in the Gaza war of the winter of 2008–9, had found no evidence to question the IDF's version of events: that the helicopter crew's assumption that the UN truck contained a Palestinian anti-tank unit was reasonable, as was their action to destroy it.

There were doubts, accusations, but no proof.

Until now.

As she looked out over the broad expanse of brown and grey rubble that had been spewed out of a volcano several thousand years before, Erika felt the excitement build inside her. The Icelandic priest was right, this *was* big. This was very big.

In the three years of its existence Freeflow had published many important leaks: it had started by exposing international inaction in Darfur, then corrupt arms deals in Africa, cover-ups in Belgium, political shenanigans in Italy and dodgy loans in

Iceland. This video would cause the biggest stir. Which is why they had to make it objective, hard-hitting and above all unimpeachable.

This time their target was Israel.

Erika had always known that at some point Freeflow would have to publish a leak concerning Israel, and she had no doubt that this particular leak deserved to be published. But she also knew what her family would think of it. What Erika was doing would be a step too far for them.

She took a deep breath. Too bad.

CHAPTER TWO

THEY PASSED THROUGH the newly built suburbs of Reykjavík into the city centre, a warren of small, brightly coloured houses with corrugated iron roofs. Ásta drove up a hill towards the tall smooth swooping church spire that Erika remembered from her previous visit to the city. From the summit by the church she could see over the roofs towards a broad mountain ridge dusted with snow to the north and sea to the west.

'That's Mount Esja over there,' Ásta said. 'It looks different every time you see it.'

They descended a pretty residential road, a little wider than the others, with small leafless trees and cars parked on one side perpendicular to the sidewalk. She caught sight of the street sign: Thórsgata. Ásta drew up outside a yellow concrete house with a metal roof. Lights glimmered behind drawn curtains. 'Here we are.'

Inside, the house was buzzing. The ground floor was open-plan, essentially a large living area full of computer equipment, wires, folding tables and chairs, and people.

'Hey, Erika, great to see you!' Nico, tall, with shaven cranium and unshaven jaw, kissed her on both cheeks. Dieter looked up from a nest of cables and waved absent-mindedly.

Dúddi, a young Icelandic computer-science student, came over holding out his hand. Erika ignored it and kissed him on the cheek. 'Hey, Dúddi. Great to see you again. How's it been?'

Dúddi grinned. 'It's been good. It's great to have Freeflow here.'

'Let me introduce you to the other two,' said Nico. He was wearing black designer T-shirt and jeans, and the familiar diamond earring in his left ear.

The two volunteers in question were Zivah, an Israeli student who would act as translator, and Franz, a Swiss video and sound guy. They were both in their early twenties and, like Ásta and Dúddi, full of enthusiasm.

Freeflow claimed that it had an army of volunteers all around the world. This wasn't strictly true. People certainly put themselves forward to help, but most of them soon faded away when given the simplest tasks. Erika hoped that these two would prove more reliable.

'Thanks, everyone, for giving up your time,' she said. 'You've all seen the video. You've all seen Tamara Wilton and the four other aid workers in that truck die. You might think that that is what happens in war: that's certainly what the Israeli Defence Force will say. But it shouldn't be like that; it doesn't have to be like that. International treaties have been signed in The Hague, in Geneva, in Rome to prevent actions like these.'

She lowered her voice. The little gathering strained to hear her. She knew the importance of converting her allies to the cause before she tried to convert anyone else.

'What we saw on that video was a war crime, pure and simple. And governments all over the world will suppress evidence of war crimes if they can and if the people let them. Not just bad governments, but good governments too. Freeflow cannot prevent these war crimes from happening, but it can ensure that when they do happen the world knows about them. We can shine a bright light into those dark corners they don't want us to see. It's something we have done in the past and something we will do in the future until governments around the world finally realize they can no longer cover up these obscenities against all that our civilization stands for.'

She fell silent for a few moments, letting her words sink in. She scanned her listeners. She'd got them.

'Freeflow is in a unique position in history. The Internet has given ordinary citizens such as us enormous power. It is not the power to oppress or censor, but the power to set information free. Someone has risked a lot to get this video to us; possibly committed treason in their own country. We owe it to that person, and to humanity as a whole, to make sure that this work will have the maximum impact.

'This is possibly the most exciting leak Freeflow has been involved with. We're going to have to work hard over the next few days, but it will be worth it, I promise you. What you do this week will be noticed throughout the world.'

'Way to go!' said Franz, the Swiss guy, with a cheer.

The Icelanders Dúddi and Ásta looked impressed; the Israeli student a little anxious. Erika didn't blame her.

'So let's get to it!' She turned towards the big man standing in the middle of the tangle of cables, his matted fair hair and scrappy beard streaked with grey. 'Hey, Dieter, don't I get a hug?'

Dieter grinned as he extricated himself from the wires. He wrapped his arms around her and squeezed. He was a German computer security consultant, and he and Erika had been through a lot over the last three years. They had first come across each other on the *Save Darfur* website. It was Dieter who had suggested setting up a separate secure site to publish leaked UN documents exposing the diplomatic dithering over the massacres of refugees in Darfur a few years earlier, and so Freeflow was born. His technical expertise and Erika's crusading drive were at the heart of the organization.

'How close are we to getting started?' Erika asked.

'We'll have all the machines hooked up in another hour or so,' said Dieter. 'But Apex has a security issue.'

'Not again?' said Erika. Apex always had security issues. Erika was never sure whether they were real, or whether Apex was just paranoid. 'Does he know who it is this time?'

'He's pretty sure it's the Chinese.' Ever since 2008, when Freeflow had published a list of websites blocked by the Chinese government, its network had come under attack from China.

'He doesn't want us to transfer the video across until he is sure everything is secure.'

'Do you think he's overreacting?' Erika asked.

Dieter shook his head. 'No. It's a real intrusion.'

'OK. How long?'

'Tomorrow morning at the earliest.'

'Damn.' Erika glanced around the room. 'Where's Gareth?'

Gareth was a British security analyst, a former employee of GCHQ, the British government department responsible for collating and analysing electronic intelligence. His expertise would be vital for interpreting the video and for assessing its authenticity.

'He can't come until Wednesday,' Nico said.

'Wednesday! You're kidding?'

'He's doing some freelance work that he can't get out of. But he will be able to analyse information we send him.'

'Can we do that securely?' Erika asked Dieter.

'Yes,' Dieter said. 'We can use Tor once Apex has given the all-clear.' The Tor network allowed encrypted data to travel through a virtual tunnel between two computers that was extremely private. It was Dieter and Apex's favourite system and at the heart of Freeflow's operations. When layered with PGP or 'Pretty Good Privacy' data encryption, information was just about as safe as it could be. 'It'll be better than nothing for a couple of days. It's not ideal, though,' Dieter added.

'No, it's not,' said Erika.

'Erika?' Nico was giving her his most charming smile. It put her on her guard but she couldn't help warming to it. He was an Italian in his late thirties who used to run a hedge fund in London and had made himself several million before quitting. He had approached Freeflow the year before, offering help, both financial and organizational, and after proving himself over a three-month trial period, he soon became a vital member of the team. He claimed he didn't think like a finance guy, and he didn't dress like one, but it was thanks to him that Freeflow hadn't run out of cash months ago.

'Yes?' Erika couldn't help returning his smile.

'Given this security hiccup, we could go and see the volcano. This afternoon.'

'We're not here to sightsee,' Erika said.

'Of course not,' said Nico. 'But this is a once-in-a-lifetime opportunity. It would only take a few hours. I told the people we rented the house from we were Internet journalists here to report on the volcano. It would be good for our cover if we actually went to see it. And it would be an excellent way for the team to get to know each other.'

Erika glanced at Dieter. 'Are there not things we can be doing in the meantime?'

'Some things, maybe. But it would be safer to wait until Apex is sure the system is secure. And the volcano would be cool.'

It would. Erika had arrived at the house desperate to get going, but she knew that waiting for Apex to give the all-clear would be painfully frustrating. A few hours wouldn't make much difference. And Erika never underestimated the importance of the team's morale. She would have preferred a trip to the Blue Lagoon, but . . .

She nodded. Nico's smile broadened, almost like a little boy's. It was kind of cute. 'How do we get there?'

'Dúddi's father has a superjeep. Dúddi can drive us.'

'OK,' said Erika. 'We'll leave in an hour.'

'I'll arrange it,' said Nico.

'I have a feeling, Nico, that you have already have.'

'Is that it?'

Erika pointed to a dome-shaped mountain whose snowy cap was glimmering in the sunshine. They were driving through a flat flood plain covered in brown grass. The 'superjeep' was basically a Ford Super Duty on giant wheels, and it held the seven of them comfortably: Erika, Ásta, Zivah, Franz, Dieter, Nico and Dúddi, who was doing the driving.

'No, that's Mount Hekla,' said Ásta. 'It's one of Iceland's most active volcanoes, but it's quiet at the moment.'

'So where is it, then?' asked Erika. 'Can we see it yet?'

'Straight ahead,' said Dúddi.

Ahead the brown plain met the foot of a long mountain ridge. The ridge itself was hidden in clouds.

'Oh,' said Erika.

'Yeah, there are two glaciers up there, Mýrdalsjökull and Eyjafjallajökull. The volcano is on a ridge called Fimmvörduháls just between them.'

'In the clouds.'

'Yes, in the clouds,' said Dúddi. 'For the moment. But this is Iceland. Clouds come and clouds go.'

'Are we going up on the glacier?' asked Franz, the Swiss guy.

'We sure are. That's why we need the jeep.'

'Is it safe up there?' Zivah asked.

'Of course it's safe,' said Dúddi. 'I went up there in this with my dad last week. It's an awesome sight, believe me.'

They drove on; to their right lay the Westman Islands, volcanic cubes of rock scattered like dice across the sea. They crossed a broad river and skirted the southern edge of the mountain range. Farms nestled in the shelter of the ridge, and horses dotted the meadows that lined the road. They passed a waterfall, a broad curtain of white slipping off a cliff edge, before turning off the main road and heading upwards on a track. Soon they were on ice. The glacier.

It *was* cool, Erika thought. It was also cloudy. In a moment they were in something close to a whiteout, snow beneath them and white water vapour all around them. Dúddi slowed down. He appeared to be following the dozens of tyre tracks spreading across the ice.

'Do you know where you're going?' Erika asked.

'Sure,' said Dúddi. 'I just follow the tracks. But I've got my GPS here.' He tapped the instrument mounted on the dashboard.

Every now and then headlights would appear out of the mist, as a jeep made its way past them down the glacier.

'Do they know something we don't?' Erika asked.

'I guess the visibility's not too good up there,' Dúddi said.

'Did you check the forecast?' Ásta asked.

'Er, no,' said Dúddi. His confidence was crumbling.

'Shouldn't you check the forecast before you drive up a glacier?' Erika asked.

Dúddi slowed and turned to his passengers. Erika liked him; he was one of a small group of students who had taken it upon themselves to invite her to the University of Iceland the previous year to speak at a conference on Internet censorship. He was a good-looking kid with an open, honest face that combined innocence with intelligence. And doubt. 'Look, it's not guaranteed we'll get good visibility,' he said. 'There's a chance we might be wasting our time. But the clouds do come and go in the mountains. And believe me, it's worth it. Do you want me to turn around?'

'Let's go for it,' said Nico. 'We've come this far.'

'Yeah, let's go for it,' said Franz. 'This rocks.'

Erika was beginning to wish she had never agreed to the jaunt. And Franz's grasp of American college-kid slang was beginning to irritate her. But if they turned back now, it would be disastrous as a morale-building exercise. Better to get up there and see nothing than not to try and never know what they had missed. 'No, keep going, Dúddi,' she said.

They drove on. The wind was picking up; loose snow skipped across the tracks in front of them. They almost hit two snowmobiles that shot out of the mist towards them.

'Hear that?' said Nico.

Over the roar of the jeep's engine and the swish of snow, they could hear a distant crashing, which grew steadily louder.

The volcano.

'Blue sky!' said Franz, craning his neck against the side window of the vehicle to look upwards. It was true; above them rips in the cloud revealed patches of blue, darkening now that afternoon was slipping into evening.

'We might still get lucky,' said Dúddi. 'We're nearly there. Look at the snow.' Patches of brown rock were emerging from beneath the snow and ice. 'It's the heat from the volcano.'

The cloud thinned ahead of them to reveal a flat section of ice and rock on which a lone four-by-four and a couple of snow-mobiles were parked. Dúddi eased his superjeep next to the other vehicle. A man and a woman were sitting inside staring upwards into the mist.

The team got out of the jeep. It sounded as if an angry monster was thrashing about just out of sight in the clouds. It was cold; the wind was biting. Everyone zipped themselves up in their snow jackets and they walked as a group towards the bottom of a pile of rubble; Erika was very grateful for the coat Dúddi had borrowed for her from his sister. Despite the wind, she could smell sulphur in the air.

Then the curtain lifted.

Erika looked up and saw the most astounding sight of her life. About three hundred yards ahead the monster was revealed: a churning mass of orange and red fire, spitting, exploding, pouring up into the air with a steady rhythmic crash. It had eaten out the top of a small dome, creating a bubbling bowl of magma, over the rim of which a dribble of super-hot lava spilled, an orange river burning its way through the ice of the glacier down to the side. Steam spewed out of the cauldron, and from fissures in the ridge all around them where smaller fires of stone burned.

'Wow!' said Erika.

'This is so cool!' said Franz.

Dúddi smiled.

'Amazing,' said Nico, his eyes alight with excitement and the orange reflection of the volcano. 'Can we get closer?'

'Of course. We can climb up there.' Dúddi pointed to the pile of rubble ahead of them.

'Are you sure?' asked Erika. 'Isn't that lava?'

'It is, but it has cooled. Last time I was here it was crowded with people. Look! There are a couple of guys up there now.'

It was true: there were two people silhouetted against the orange of the volcano.

They all followed Dúddi up the slope. Erika could feel the warmth beneath her feet. She picked up some of the stone in her gloved hand. It was warm and it crumbled. She was a little nervous that the whole slope would slip away underneath her, but it seemed to hold. The wind was still blowing, but Erika didn't notice the cold.

'I told you it would be worth coming,' said Nico, grabbing her hand.

They reached the top and the view was even better. The volcano itself was only a hundred yards away. They couldn't get any closer: the lava was too soft.

'It looks powerful from here, but this is actually a small eruption,' Nico said. 'It's what's called an effusive eruption. They're the pretty ones. Basalt lava gets thrown up into the air and then flows down the side of mountain.'

'What's the other type?' Erika asked.

'Explosive eruption. That's when the magma explodes into ash and is flung way up into the atmosphere. They are nasty: you don't want to be anywhere near one of those.'

'My, aren't we the expert?'

'Told you,' said Nico with a smile. 'They say there's a chance that Katla will blow, that's a big volcano under the Mýrdals Glacier back there. If it does there could be a real mess – massive floods.'

'Floods?'

'Yeah. The eruption melts the ice in the glacier, and the meltwater surges down the mountain in a series of powerful flash floods. *Jökulhlaup*, I think the Icelanders call it – "glacier leap". You really don't want to be in the way of one of those.'

They stared at the convulsions of the volcano in awe.

'You know what? I've thought of a code name for this Gaza video project,' said Nico. '*Meltwater*.'

'Not bad,' said Erika.

They stared a bit longer. 'It's amazing to finally see an eruption for real,' Nico said. 'Come on! Let's take a closer look at the lava flow.' He led Erika along the rim.

*

Ásta was impressed. She had seen Hekla erupting before from a great distance, but she had never seen a volcano this close. She had meant to join the thousands of inhabitants of Reykjavík who had flocked up to Fimmvörduháls over the previous three weeks, but had just never got around to it. Although she thought Dúddi was an idiot to drive up on to the glacier without checking the weather, she was very glad she had come.

As she watched the volcano thrashing and writhing in front of her, she thought of the line in Genesis: 'In the beginning God created the heavens and the earth.' Well, that was what she was witnessing: God creating the earth. You could do that here in Iceland. And it was a magnificent sight.

It was beginning to get dark. The setting sun slipped behind the volcano, blushing pink across the whiteness of the Mýrdalsjökull behind them and stroking the underside of the cloud just above it. A few flakes of snow bit into her cheek.

She was excited to be working with Freeflow. She liked the look of Erika. It was good to meet another woman who believed in something and had the energy and drive to make a difference. To Ásta's disappointment, there weren't many people like that in the Icelandic Church.

She could learn from Erika. She would need all the inspiration she could muster if she was to go ahead with her own plans to shine light into dark corners.

The snow thickened ahead of her, horizontal flakes obscuring the volcano. The sun had disappeared. She turned to Dúddi. 'Do you think we had better get back?'

A blizzard on a glacier was a really bad idea. Especially at night.

Dúddi nodded. 'Time to go, guys. Where are the others?' The visibility was deteriorating rapidly. Dieter, Dúddi, Zivah and Ásta were all in a group together, but the other three were out of sight.

'I think Nico and Erika are just along there,' said Dieter, pointing along the rim. 'Don't know about Franz.'

'Can you get Nico and Erika and tell them to come down?'

said Dúddi. 'The rest of you, follow me. We'll keep an eye out for Franz.'

They could no longer see their jeep below them. Scrambling down the pile of cooled lava was unpleasant: the wind seemed to be blowing harder and colder and the stones slipped underfoot. It was a relief to get back to their vehicle, and to find Franz waiting inside. The jeep they had parked next to was gone; only the two snowmobiles remained, as far as Ásta could see.

They piled into the car and waited for Dieter and the others. Dúddi switched the engine on: the warmth and the shelter from the wind was a relief. Ásta saw two figures climb on to the snowmobiles and zoom off. The mess of tyre tracks was still visible, but it wouldn't be long before they would be covered in snow. She hoped Dúddi knew how to operate his GPS.

They could no longer see the volcano, save for a fuzzy orange glow through the whiteness. But they could hear it.

'Come on,' muttered Dúddi to himself as he sat in the driver's seat. 'We can't hang around much longer. I'm going back to get them. You wait here.'

He climbed out of the jeep and Ásta watched him bend into the wind towards the slope of lava.

'I hope they're OK,' said Zivah, nervously.

'Of course they are,' said Ásta.

'You don't think they could have fallen into the volcano or anything, do you?'

'No,' said Ásta, peering into the bitter white gloom. 'Don't worry. They'll be fine.'

CHAPTER THREE

SERGEANT MAGNUS JONSON sipped from his bottle of Viking beer and stared at the wall of his studio apartment. He was still tingling from his after-work swim, and the soak in the geothermally heated hot tub at the Laugardalur baths. He had been in Reykjavík nearly a year now, had graduated from the National Police College five months before and was now well into the routine of the Violent Crimes Unit of the Metropolitan Police. That afternoon, he had investigated a suspected domestic violence case: a woman had supposedly fallen down the stairs, bruising her shoulder and getting herself a black eye. Magnus had goaded her hung-over but abusive boyfriend, hoping for an opportunity to slug him, but Vigdís, a fellow detective in the unit with a bit more patience than Magnus, had defused the situation. Bummer.

His room was right downtown in Reykjavík's 101 district, on the first floor of a small house on Njálsgata owned by the sister of one of his colleagues. Through his window Magnus had a great view of the sweeping floodlit spire of the Hallgrímskirkja. But he wasn't looking at the church.

He was looking at the wall.

He had only started sticking up the photographs when his girlfriend Ingileif had disappeared to Germany five months before. He had felt a little self-conscious at first, and he knew she would have laughed at him. But he was a detective, a detective with an unsolved crime. He had tried hiding from it for years, but he hadn't succeeded. So he pinned it up on his wall.

He had started with just photographs, but now there were copied pages of reports, newspaper articles and multicoloured Post-its. He would occasionally rearrange everything to look at the evidence from different angles. Sometimes the fiddling revealed a new insight, but it had never revealed the solution. At least not yet.

At the moment his father, Dr Ragnar Jónsson, was smiling down from the top left section of the wall. Beneath him were photographs of Duxbury, Massachusetts, the town outside Boston where Ragnar had been stabbed to death fourteen years before in 1996. The photograph had been taken by Magnus in the back yard of the house there where Magnus, his brother Ollie, Ragnar and Magnus's stepmother had spent a month that summer. Beneath it were notes about the case, many scribbled by Magnus when, as a twenty-year-old student, he had tried to figure out what had happened. One page, highlighted, described how his father had been stabbed once in the back and twice in the chest.

On the far right of the wall was a cutting from a newspaper showing a photograph of the famous Icelandic novelist Benedikt Jóhannesson, and another describing his murder in the winter of 1985 at his house in Reykjavík. Next to it was a photograph of Hraun, the farm in the Snaefells Peninsula a couple of hours north of Reykjavík where Benedikt had been born. Underneath was a photocopy of the forensic pathologist's report describing how he had died: a stab wound in the back and two more in the chest.

In the middle of the wall, connecting these two murders in some way as yet unknown to Magnus, was Magnus's family, or more specifically, his mother's family.

There were two photographs of his mother. One of her in her twenties, leaning against his father, sitting in a café on holiday somewhere in Italy, looking relaxed, happy and beautiful: light tan, blond hair falling down over her eyes, warm smile. The other, taken ten years later, of the same woman only different: puffy eyes, lined face, pursed lips. That was a couple of months before she drank half a bottle of vodka and drove herself into a rock.

Also in this section of the wall were photographs of Bjarnarhöfn, the farm on the Snaefells Peninsula just a couple of kilometres from Hraun where Magnus's grandparents lived, and where Magnus and Ollie had spent the four most miserable years of their lives. There was a photograph of Hallgrímur, Magnus's grandfather and the farmer of Bjarnarhöfn, who had made the two boys' lives so miserable. They had been sent there after their father had moved to Massachusetts, leaving their mother, swiftly becoming an alcoholic, in Iceland. She couldn't cope and so the boys had been sent to their grandparents' farm. It was a time Magnus wanted to forget and his little brother Ollie had blanked out entirely.

So what linked the family in the middle with the unsolved murders on the left and the right? Magnus didn't know.

No matter how long he stared at the wall, he didn't know.

There were clues.

A promising line of inquiry had emerged the previous autumn, when Magnus had called up the old file on Benedikt's murder and discovered that the writer had died in exactly the same way as his father. He had also discovered there was a feud between Benedikt's family and Hallgrímur's. And Magnus knew, of course, that Hallgrímur hated Magnus's father, although apparently the old man had been happy to see his son-in-law leave the country and Magnus's mother.

Magnus was a detective; he wanted to investigate. Ollie, his brother back in America, begged him not to.

Magnus had flown to Boston for a couple of days in January. Visited Duxbury, spoken to the detective who had worked the case fourteen years before, stayed with Ollie, tried to talk him round, but with no success.

For the sake of his damaged little brother, Magnus had held off asking more questions in Iceland. He had felt a sense of duty towards Ollie ever since they were kids together at their grandparents' farm, a duty that had only increased after their father had died. And Ollie had needed Magnus's help many times over the years as he had got himself into trouble with women, with drugs and with money. Magnus was happy to give it: he didn't really hold his brother responsible. If anyone was to blame, it was their grandfather Hallgrímur.

But for once Magnus had decided to put his own interests before his brother's. Ollie was coming to Reykjavík to stay with him in a couple of days and this time Magnus would insist that he carry on digging.

He took a swig of his beer, hauled himself up out of his armchair and examined the photos of Ollie lying on his desk. There were two: one of Ollie, or Óli as he was then known, taken at Bjarnarhöfn: a curly-haired blond kid in Iceland, a nervous smile under anxious brows. The other picture was of Ollie as a thirty-year-old failed real-estate investor, hair a little darker but still curly, smile cocky. Magnus picked up the second print and examined the wall.

He never knew where the hell to put Ollie.

His phone rang.

'Magnús.'

'Hi, it's Vigdís. There has been a murder in the Hvolsvöllur district. Niccolò Andreose, thirty-eight, Italian national. They want our help. I'm coming to pick you up with Árni.'

Magnus's pulse quickened. Murders in Iceland were few and far between, unlike his old beat in South Boston where every week brought several. But most homicides in this country were quite straightforward to solve: one drunk hitting another too hard. The role of the detective was merely to get the paperwork right. He had been transferred to Iceland from the Homicide Unit of the Boston Police Department at the request of the National Police Commissioner to help out the local cops with the more complex big-city crimes that the Commissioner feared would become more common. Magnus had worked the odd interesting case in his first year; perhaps this would be another one. 'Are there any suspects?'

'Not yet,' said Vigdís. 'They've rounded up the witnesses at the Hvolsvöllur Police Station. That's where we're going now.'

'What about the scene of the crime?'

'That's a little inaccessible at the moment. It's on the rim of the Fimmvörduháls volcano. And there's a blizzard blowing.'

It was past midnight by the time they reached Hvolsvöllur, a small agricultural town on the broad floodplain to the south-east of Reykjavík. With Magnus were two other detectives from the Violent Crimes Unit: Vigdís, one of the few female detectives in Reykjavík and certainly the only black one; and Árni, who was young, keen and error-prone. It was Árni's sister who was Magnus's landlady. Vigdís had left her car outside Magnus's place and the three of them had piled into Magnus's Range Rover, which was better suited to the terrain outside Reykjavík. Magnus was glad he had only had a few sips of his beer; it would have been a shame to miss the case because he had had a skinful.

The police station was a square modern building opposite the Saga Centre on the edge of town. Inside, lights were on.

They were met by Chief Superintendent Kristján Sveinsson, a neat, dark-haired man of about forty, displaying the three yellow stars of his rank on his black uniform. Although a chief superintendent, Kristján – whatever their rank or title Icelanders always called each other by their first names – had only nine officers reporting to him. For serious cases such as a murder, he needed reinforcements from Reykjavík.

Kristján showed the three detectives into his office, small but modern and tidy.

'What happened?' asked Magnus.

'A group of foreign journalists went up to see the volcano with a couple of Icelanders. The weather was bad; there weren't many other sightseers up there. Two of them – Nico the murder victim and an American woman named Erika – wandered away from the others. They were attacked by a single assailant and Nico was stabbed.

'Erika ran away, with the assailant chasing her. Other members of the group came back to look for her and Nico.

When the assailant saw them, he gave up the chase and disappeared.'

'Anything at the scene?' Magnus asked. 'Murder weapon?'

'The assailant took his knife with him. The crime scene is a blizzard. I have two men up there now, but I doubt we'll find anything. Forensics will come out from Reykjavík first thing in the morning.'

'And the body?'

'Still up there waiting for the forensics guys.'

Magnus grunted. Normally, you wanted crime-scene investigators at the scene as soon as possible, but Magnus understood why it didn't make sense to crawl around a volcano with a pair of tweezers in a blizzard in the dark.

'I pity your guys,' Magnus said.

'They're used to it,' said the chief superintendent. 'We've spent all our time up there over the last three weeks, trying to control the sightseers. I feared someone would get killed at some point. But not like this.'

'Witnesses?'

'The group are all here in the station. Four journalists and two Icelanders. One of them is a priest.'

'A priest? Really? What was he doing there?'

'It's a she. And we haven't interviewed them in any depth yet.'

'Good,' said Magnus. 'What about other witnesses?'

'We're looking. They say there was a couple in a jeep and two snowmobilers up by the volcano. They passed other vehicles coming down on their way up the glacier, but the weather was so bad by the time they got there there was scarcely anyone around.'

'We should appeal for witnesses to come forward. A press conference first thing in the morning.'

'I can arrange that.'

'OK, Vigdís, you interview the Icelanders,' said Magnus. Vigdís didn't speak English. 'I'll interview the foreigners with Árni. Can you lend us a man to join Vigdís?' he asked Kristján.

'I can do it if you like?'

Magnus almost laughed. In Boston a chief superintendent would never have offered to sit in as an assistant to a mere sergeant detective, but this was Iceland. This guy was clearly smart, and he wanted to be helpful.

'Sure. Please do. So where are these people?'

Kristján showed Magnus through to a kind of common room where half a dozen figures were huddled miserably around a table, drinking coffee in silence.

Magnus addressed them in English. 'Hi, my name is Sergeant Magnus Jonson of the Reykjavík Metropolitan Police,' he said. He used the American form of his name. Since his father was Ragnar Jónsson, he had been born Magnús Ragnarsson. However, when he had joined his father in Boston at the age of twelve, that had all become too complicated, so he had lost the accent on the 'u' and taken an Anglicized form of his father's last name.

He introduced Árni and Vigdís. 'I know you have all been through a terrible experience, and you must be very tired, but we will have to interview all of you now. As soon as we've finished you will be free to go.' Magnus turned to the chief superintendent. 'Is there a hotel in town?'

He nodded. 'I'll find them rooms. If the hotel is full we'll find somewhere for you.'

'Thanks,' said Magnus. Then, turning back to the group, 'Erika Zinn?'

A thin, pale woman in her thirties with shoulder-length black hair looked up. Despite the fatigue, her brown eyes were piercing. It took Magnus aback. 'Can we start with you?'

CHAPTER FOUR

THE STATION HAD a small but comfortable interview room. Árni and Magnus sat opposite the woman.

'All right,' Magnus began. 'Let's start with some basic details. What's your full name and address?'

'Erika Sarah Zinn.' She gave an address in Chappaqua, New York. Árni wrote it all down.

'Profession?'

'I'm a journalist.'

'Do you have your passport?'

Erika dug the blue document out of her bag. Magnus glanced at it – the name checked, and the place of birth was given as New York, USA. It was thick: extra pages inserted and nearly every one of them stamped. Erika liked to travel.

He handed it back. 'Here to cover the volcano?' he asked.

She nodded.

'So, what happened?'

Erika told Magnus about the trip up to the volcano and how they had climbed up to the rim.

'Did you see anyone else up there?' Magnus asked.

'We did notice two people right up by the volcano when we got out of the jeep,' Erika said. 'I don't remember seeing them when we were up there.'

'These were the snowmobile riders?'

'I guess so,' said Erika. 'There were two snowmobiles parked down at the bottom, I remember that. And there was a couple, a man and a woman, who climbed up the lava bank after us.

They had been waiting in their car for the weather to clear. But I don't think they stayed at the rim for as long as we did.'

'Can you describe any of these people?'

'No. Wait, the woman had a bright blue woolly hat.'

'And the snowmobilers?'

'No – I didn't get a good look at them. I was looking at the volcano. It really was amazing. One of the most incredible things I've seen in my life.'

'Of course. So what did you do at the top?'

'We gawked. Nico told me some stuff about volcanoes. Then he and I went to look at a stream of lava flowing down over to the side. It had just started to snow.' Erika was concentrating hard, making sure she told her story clearly. 'I don't know where the man came from. I didn't see him at all, but Nico did. He shouted something like: "Hey!" I turned to see this guy swinging a rock towards my head. He would have hit me too if Nico hadn't dived for his arm.'

'Then what happened?'

'The guy dropped the rock and jumped back. Nico lunged at him. Then Nico kind of jerked and gave a little cry of pain. Not a scream or anything. I saw his face; he looked surprised. Then he slid down to the ground and I saw the other guy was holding a knife. I'm sure Nico hadn't seen it.'

'What did you do?'

'I screamed. And then I ran. I headed back around the rim. The guy was following me. I go running a lot, I'm pretty fit and I was really scared, so although the guy was catching me I managed to keep ahead of him. The visibility was really bad by this stage.

'I saw Dieter and ran toward him. I tried to tell him what was going on. Then the guy who had stabbed Nico appeared through the snow. He saw us and came toward us holding out the knife.'

Erika swallowed. 'I could see Nico's blood on it. Anyway, Dieter picked up a rock and squared up to him. I could tell Dieter was scared, but he's big. Then Dúddi showed up and the guy with the knife disappeared back into the snow. I guess he figured three was too many to take on, even with a knife.'

'Did you see where he went?'

'No, he ran down the slope by the volcano, but I couldn't see the cars at the bottom because of the poor visibility. So I don't know what he did when he was down there. And I couldn't hear either, with the noise of the volcano.'

'What can you tell me about the guy? Was he young or old? Tall, small, fat, dark?'

Erika hesitated. 'Tallish. Fit and strong. Not a kid, but not middle-aged either. He was wearing a bright red jacket and the hood was up, but he had dark hair.'

'Would you recognize him again?'

'Probably not, no.'

'Did he look like an Icelander?'

'He wasn't fair or red-headed, if that's what you mean. But quite a lot of Icelanders have dark hair, don't they? Come to think of it, his complexion was darker than most of them.'

'Mediterranean? Asian? Indian?'

'I don't know. I said I didn't see him clearly.'

'But he definitely wasn't one of your group?'

Erika's eyes flashed. 'That's a dumb question.'

'I like to ask dumb questions,' said Magnus calmly.

Erika raised her eyebrows. 'No, he definitely wasn't one of our group. Bigger than most of them except Dieter, and I don't think the others had red jackets. Of course he wasn't one of our group.'

'OK,' said Magnus. 'I understand. So what did you do then?'

'We went back down to check out Nico. He was bleeding badly from the stomach. He was still alive when we got to him, but then . . .' A tear ran down Erika's cheek. She sniffed. Tried to say something and couldn't. Fell silent.

Magnus waited.

'Then . . . then he wasn't alive any more.'

'I'm sorry,' said Magnus.

'I studied medicine for years. I should have been able to do something to save him. But there was so much blood.' She looked down at her hands, which were now washed clean, but there were brown stains on the cuffs of her sweater. And all over her coat, no doubt. 'I tried to stanch it. But . . .'

'Were you friends?' Magnus asked gently.

'Yes,' said Erika. 'Yes, we were. I've known him for a year or so. We've worked together on some projects.'

'Stories?'

'Yes.'

'Tell me a bit about him. He was a journalist?'

'Not exactly. In fact he used to be a banker of some kind. Worked for a hedge fund in London trading oil futures or something. He said he was originally a geologist.' Erika smiled. 'That's why he was so eager to see the volcano. Anyway, he gave up the hedge fund business a couple of years ago.'

'To do what?'

'I'm not sure, exactly. I know he had saved up some money. He was a bit of an idealist.'

'Were you and he having a relationship?' Magnus asked.

'Oh, no,' said Erika. 'He's married. Three small kids, I think. His family are in Milan now.' She closed her eyes. 'Someone's going to have to tell his wife.'

'Do you know her?'

'Not well,' said Erika. 'Her name is Teresa. I stayed with them once in Italy. I have their address and phone number.'

'If you give it to us, we can do it,' Magnus said. 'We'll call her right away.'

Erika smiled. 'Thanks.'

'Did he have any enemies as far as you know?'

'None that I know of. Nico didn't make enemies. He was just a great guy. Big smile; nothing was too much trouble for him. You know, one of those people everyone loves.'

'You'll miss him,' said Magnus softly.

'Yeah,' said Erika. 'I'll miss him.' She took out a tissue and blew her nose. 'I'm sorry. It's been a rough night.'

'Yes,' said Magnus. 'Yes, it has. Just a couple more questions. I don't understand why Nico was in Iceland. If he wasn't a journalist, I mean.'

Erika pulled herself together. Looked Magnus straight in the eye. Too straight. 'I told you. He knew about volcanoes.'

'Yes, but he wasn't an expert, was he?' Magnus said. 'I mean he's not a, what do you call them, vulcanologist? Or is he?'

'No. But he was a friend and he wanted to come.'

'To help you with your article?'

'Yes.'

Magnus examined Erika. This wasn't *quite* right. She was sitting up straight now, alert. She had been shattered a moment before. Something about his questions had caused her to raise her defences. To look him straight in the eye.

'You say you are a journalist. So who do you write for?'

'I'm freelance,' Erika said.

'What about the others out there?'

'They are freelance too.'

'I see. So who have you written for? Anyone I would have heard of?'

'The *Washington Post*. The *Chicago Tribune*. A lot of online stuff.'

'Online stuff?'

Erika nodded.

'So if I were to Google you, your name would come up?'

Erika shrugged. 'I guess.'

There was a computer screen on the desk by Magnus in the interview room, but it was blank. Magnus turned to his colleague.

'Árni, have you got that iPhone you're always talking about?'

'Right here.'

'Can you Google Erika Zinn?'

'Sure.' Árni pulled out his little gadget and tapped. Erika watched Árni. Magnus watched Erika. He knew he was on to something.

'Jesus,' said Árni. Magnus saw Erika close her eyes. Árni handed the gadget to Magnus.

Magnus tapped and scrolled, skimming the words on the tiny screen. 'Tell me about Freeflow, Erika.'

Erika didn't reply.

Magnus tapped on a link to Freeflow's website. 'That's weird. Doesn't seem to be the kind of site that would be interested in volcanoes. What's this? African arms deals? Bribing Italian judges? Ah, Icelandic banks. But no volcanoes.'

'You speak very good English.'

'Freeflow?'

'Are you sure you are not an American?'

'I was born here,' said Magnus. 'But I have lived most of my life in Boston.'

'And you?' Erika asked Árni.

'I went to college in the States,' said Árni. 'Indiana.' Although Árni's English was good, his Icelandic accent was obvious, even in those few words.

'OK,' said Erika. 'But what about you, Sergeant Jonson? What are you doing here?'

'I'm attached to the office of the National Police Commissioner,' said Magnus.

'I don't believe you.'

Magnus frowned. The Icelanders were much less prone to waving their badges around than American cops, but that was clearly what was required. He pulled out his ID and slid it across the table to Erika. He had been made to do a six-month programme at the National Police College, and since graduating from there he had full status as a member of the Icelandic police.

Erika picked it up, glanced at it and tossed it back on to the desk.

'I don't believe it.'

'What do you mean, you don't believe it?'

'I'm involved in a murder on a mountain in the middle of Iceland. I get taken to some hick small town and who shows up to interview me? An American. Just where the hell did they find you?'

Magnus fought to control his temper. 'You've seen my ID, now answer my questions.'

'You work for the CIA, don't you?'

'The CIA? You're nuts!'

'What happens next, you fly me out to Morocco or somewhere and interrogate me?'

'Erika, I work for the Icelandic police. I am an Icelandic policeman. Now answer my questions.'

'Or what? You'll waterboard me? I want a real Icelandic policeman in here now. Someone with a uniform. In fact I'd like to speak to the chief superintendent. He must be in the building somewhere.'

'Don't be ridiculous.'

'I'm not being ridiculous. My lawyer will be here soon.'

'Your lawyer?'

'Yes. I have an Icelandic lawyer in Reykjavík. I called from the station. He'll be here in a few minutes.'

'Stay here!' snapped Magnus. He left Árni with Erika and went to look for the chief superintendent. He was interviewing a small dark-haired woman with Vigdís.

'Got a minute?'

Kristján and Vigdís joined Magnus in the corridor. Magnus quickly explained about Erika, Freeflow, Erika's suspicions that he was in the CIA and the lawyer.

'Wait a moment,' said Vigdís. 'I remember seeing her on *Silfur Egils* last year. She was good.'

'Did you let them make calls?' Magnus asked Kristján.

'Of course I did,' said Kristján. 'She's a victim, not a suspect.'

'Yeah, of course, sorry. What does the woman say? Is she the priest?'

'Yes,' said Vigdís. 'Her name is Ásta. She hasn't mentioned Freeflow. She says the foreigners were all there to report on the volcano.'

'That's bullshit,' said Magnus. 'We need to move fast, before the lawyer gets here. Kristján, is there a way of keeping the witnesses separate? I don't want them talking to each other. Perhaps we can get one of the others to give us something.'

'I can organize that.'

'What is it?' Magnus noticed the look of doubt in the chief superintendent's eyes.

'You don't work for the CIA, do you?'

'What kind of question is that?' Magnus asked.

'A good one,' interrupted Vigdís. 'Kristján, I'm sure you must have heard of Magnús. He caused a bit of a stir in Reykjavík last year. I've worked closely with him since he arrived last April, and I can assure you that he would make a really bad spy. But perhaps you should call the Police Commissioner as soon as he gets in in the morning?'

Kristján hesitated, and then smiled. 'I'll do that. In the meantime, you are in charge of the investigation and I will help you as best I can. I'll split the witnesses up now and then have a word with Erika myself.'

'Thanks,' said Magnus. 'And I'm sorry. Vigdís is right, you needed to be sure. OK, Vigdís, let's talk to this priest. You never know, she might tell us the truth.'

Magnus sat opposite the young woman, examining her. She looked more like a student than a minister, with her jeans and her young fresh face. An honest face – that was good. The clerical collar merely made her look more innocent.

'So, Ásta, how long have you been a priest?' Magnus asked.

'Just over a year.'

'And do you have a parish?'

'Not at the moment, no. I did six months covering for a pastor on maternity leave in Mjódd last year, but since November, nothing.' The woman smiled thinly. 'It's quite difficult to get a job these days, even for ordained priests.'

Her voice was clear and authoritative.

'So what is your connection with Freeflow?'

Ásta paused. Her large blue eyes held Magnus's. 'It has nothing to do with the Church. I am just a volunteer.'

'I see. And when did you first meet Erika Zinn?'

'This afternoon. When I picked her up from the airport.'

'And took her . . . where?'

'To a house in Thórsgata that Freeflow are renting,' Ásta replied carefully.

'Tell me about Freeflow,' Magnus said.

'I don't really know that much about them. I've never worked for them before. I believe they receive leaked information and make it available to the world. Information about corruption, human rights abuses, that kind of thing.'

'And Erika Zinn is their leader?'

'Effectively. I'm not sure that she calls herself that, but the others all look up to her.'

'By the others, do you mean the people who went up the volcano with you? Are they all working for Freeflow?'

Ásta hesitated, and then nodded.

Magnus turned to Vigdís. 'Did she tell you any of this about Freeflow?'

'No,' said Vigdís, staring at the priest. 'No, she didn't.'

'Why not?' Magnus asked Ásta.

'She didn't ask.'

Magnus slammed his hand on the table. Ásta jumped. 'Oh, come on. You're not some schoolgirl caught smoking weed in the girls' bathroom; this is a murder inquiry. Why did you lie?'

'I didn't actually lie.'

'That's semantics. You knew it was important and you didn't tell us. Why not?'

Ásta said nothing.

'What is Freeflow working on at the moment? Why did they come to Iceland?'

'I'm sorry,' Ásta said. 'I'm afraid I can't tell you.'

'Aren't you supposed to tell the truth? You know, as a priest?'

Ásta nodded. 'But I am also supposed to respect confidences.'

Magnus fought hard to contain his frustration. 'Even when it protects a murderer? Someone killed Niccolò Andreose this evening. We don't know why, but one line of inquiry has to be that it had something to do with whatever Freeflow is working on at the moment. We can find out. We'll search this house on Thórsgata.'

'Well, that's what you will have to do,' said Ásta calmly.

Magnus had hoped that Ásta would prove to be a soft touch. But he could tell she was going to be stubborn when confronted directly. Increasing the pressure would just make her dig her heels in more deeply; a new tack was required. He glanced at Vigdís.

'Are you willing to help us to find the killer?' she asked.

Ásta nodded.

'OK. Then let's go through what you did today from when you picked up Erika from the airport, but this time don't leave anything out.'

Ásta's description of events was detailed and thorough, with the exception of what it was that Freeflow was actually planning to do in the house in Thórsgata; she deftly dodged Vigdís's indirect questions around the subject.

'Tell me some more about the snowmobilers,' Magnus asked.

'There were two of them. I saw their snowmobiles at the bottom about twenty metres from where we parked, and when we arrived they were up at the volcano. I think I saw them up at the rim when we got up there. Then they were gone.'

'Did you see where they went? Did they follow Nico and Erika?'

'No, I didn't see. And they were on the other side of us – I mean Nico and Erika went off to the left and they were on the right.'

'What about Franz? You say you lost track of him?'

'Yes – I don't remember seeing him at all when we went up the volcano. Dúddi was a little worried about him, until we got back to the car and found him there waiting for us.'

'You didn't see him talk to the snowmobilers?'

'No. But he could have done. I mean the visibility was only clear for part of the time we were up there, and we were concentrating on the volcano.'

'Do you know anything about Franz?'

'No – I had never met him before today. He speaks good English, but he's not a native speaker. Perhaps German?'

Magnus smiled. 'We'll speak to him next. And the two people on the snowmobiles? Can you describe them?'

Ásta thought hard. 'I got a look at them when we were waiting in the car for the others and they were mounting their snowmobiles. They were wearing hats and ski jackets, so it was hard to see. Both men, for sure, one of them big with a bit of a belly. But I wouldn't recognize them again.'

'What about their ski jackets?' asked Magnus. 'What colour were they?'

Ásta closed her eyes. 'One of them I remember. Bright red. It was the bigger man. The other man I don't remember.'

Magnus smiled. 'Thank you, that's very helpful. Now tell me what happened after Dúddi told you about Nico.'

Ásta was just about to answer when she was interrupted by a commotion outside in the corridor. Magnus opened the door to take a look. A tall silver-haired man with a pointed chin was in a heated discussion with Kristján. He was wearing jeans and a smart black jacket and sported a nice tan, unusual in Icelanders in April.

'I want to see my client,' the man was saying.

'I'm sorry, we are interviewing her at the moment.'

'Is she a suspect?' the man asked.

The door opened behind Kristján and Erika appeared. 'Viktor!' she said in English. 'Boy, am I glad to see you.'

'What's going on here?' Viktor asked.

'Nico has been killed, up on the volcano. I was with him – it was horrible. I told the police what happened, and then they suddenly started asking me a lot of questions about Freeflow. Especially that one.' She nodded towards Magnus. 'He's American. CIA would be my guess.'

The lawyer frowned. He turned to the chief superintendent. 'What is an American doing here?' he asked in Icelandic.

'Sergeant Magnús is attached to the National Police Commissioner's Office,' Kristján said. 'Show Viktor your ID, Magnús.'

Magnus handed his identity card to the lawyer, who examined it carefully.

'The guy may have Icelandic ID,' said Erika, who was watching closely. 'But he's American. His accent is perfect. And I want to know what he is doing here.'

'I'm trying to catch the man who killed your friend,' said Magnus. 'And I would appreciate some more cooperation from all of you. In particular we need to know what Freeflow is working on.'

'So you can tell the US government?' said Erika.

'No, so we can ascertain who had a motive to kill Mr Andreose.'

Viktor looked at Erika and then at the chief superintendent. 'My clients are leaving now.'

'I can't allow that,' said Kristján. 'We haven't finished questioning them.'

'I ask you again, are they suspects?'

'No, but they are witnesses. Witnesses in a murder investigation.'

Viktor took a step towards him. He was taller than the chief superintendent and pointed his chin down towards the police officer.

'In addition to being a lawyer, you know that I am a Member of Parliament and one of the sponsors of the Icelandic Modern Media Initiative, which has been endorsed by the government. The initiative was developed in conjunction with Freeflow. Our country should be a haven for organizations like them. Freeflow's activities are of no interest to the police, and certainly the Icelandic authorities should not be cooperating with foreign governments to force Freeflow to reveal what they are working on.'

'I do not work for a foreign government!' Magnus growled. 'I don't care what Freeflow is working on, beyond the obvious point that whatever it is, it's probably pissing off someone, and that someone might be trying to stop them. I'm just trying to solve a crime. And I don't appreciate you obstructing the police in doing that.'

Viktor switched his attention to Magnus.

'Are you threatening me?'

Magnus was very tempted to arrest the man for obstruction of justice, but he knew that would lead to more trouble than it was worth. 'I suggest you wait until we have finished with the witnesses.'

'Where are they?' the lawyer asked.

'Through there,' said Erika, pointing to the door of the common room at the other end of the corridor.

'Out of my way,' said Viktor as he pushed past Magnus. Vigdís stepped in front of him, with Árni next to her.

'Who the hell are you?' he asked her.

Tall and black, wearing jeans and a sweatshirt, it was true that Vigdís did not look like your typical Icelandic detective.

'Detective Vigdís Audardóttir,' she replied in Icelandic.

'Give me a break,' said Viktor in English. 'You're another Yank. A nigger CIA spy.' He barged past Vigdís and down the corridor. Vigdís lost her balance and almost fell.

Árni grabbed the politician by the collar and pushed him up against the wall. 'Don't talk to a police officer like that,' he shouted.

Viktor was bigger than Árni, and stronger. He pushed Árni backwards and took a swing at him, catching him on the cheek.

In a moment Magnus was on the politician, grabbing him from behind and pinning his arms to his sides, while the chief superintendent grabbed Árni. Viktor struggled for a few seconds, but Magnus was stronger.

'He assaulted me!' the politician said. 'You're all witnesses, you saw him.'

'You took a slug at him,' said Magnus. 'And you racially abused my colleague.'

'Árni! Back off,' said Kristján. He jabbed a finger at Viktor. 'You, in my office! Everyone else wait.'

Kristján led the MP into his office, turfing out the open-mouthed Ásta, and shut the door behind him.

CHAPTER FIVE

Tuesday 13 April 2010

THE FREEFLOW TEAM drove back to Reykjavík in two vehicles: Dúddi's father's superjeep and Viktor's Mercedes four-by-four. They had left Ásta behind to show the police the crime scene in daylight. Erika sat next to Viktor in the front of his car, with Dieter in the back. After an initial flurry of conversation about what had happened, they lapsed into silence, each of them absorbing the horror of the previous evening.

As soon as they arrived at the house, Erika called everyone into the living room for a meeting. They stared at her, anxious, tired, uncertain.

'What happened to Nico on the mountain was horrible,' she began. 'I wasn't lying to the police when I told them I had no idea who killed him. As you all know, Nico was a vital part of Freeflow and a good friend, a great friend to many of us.

'I have been thinking hard about this. It is tempting to abandon the project because of what's happened. In fact it is going to be very difficult to carry on without Nico.' She paused. Took a deep breath, controlling the emotion in her voice, channelling it. 'But carry on we must. If there was one thing Nico believed in it was Freeflow and what it stands for. In addition to doing this for Tamara Wilton and the other victims we saw in that video, we are doing it for him. In memory of him.'

She glanced around the room. 'Are you with me?'

There was silence for a moment, and then murmurs and nods of assent.

'What if Nico was murdered by the Israeli government?' asked Zivah. 'To shut us up?'

'Then we don't let them,' said Erika. 'For Nico's sake, we don't let them. If that was indeed why he died, then we cannot allow his death to be in vain.'

'What do we say to the police about the Gaza video?' It was Franz, looking tired and a little scared.

'Nothing. For as long as we can, we continue to say nothing. Sorry, Viktor, but I don't trust the Icelandic police, and especially not that American – what was his name – Magnus?'

'Nor the black woman,' said Viktor.

'Can you keep them off our backs?'

'I can try,' said Viktor. 'That is what the Icelandic Modern Media Initiative is all about. You gave us the idea after all, so you deserve to be protected by it. I'll start off by putting in a complaint to the National Police Commissioner. And I'll go to the District Court when it opens this morning. The police are sure to apply for a warrant to search this property and I'll see what I can do to contest it.'

'Thank you,' said Erika.

'With Nico gone, there are all kinds of questions,' said Dieter. 'Not the least of which is money. Nico was the only one of us who knew where all of it is. And there were some Icelandic volunteers we were planning to draft in to help with the editing. What shall we do about them?'

Erika sighed. 'Yes, I am sure there are lots of good questions to be answered, lots of difficulties to be overcome. Anything from Apex on when the video will be ready?'

'I just checked,' Dieter said. 'Eleven a.m. at the earliest.'

'OK,' Erika said. 'We are all exhausted, and we have a lot of work ahead of us. It's now five-thirty. I suggest we sleep until ten-thirty, then get some breakfast and start work. Ask me all your questions then.'

Relieved to have permission to collapse, the team melted away to the various crowded bedrooms.

Erika was sharing a room with Zivah, who had taken the floor, leaving Erika with a single bed. But rather than collapsing into it, she pulled on running clothes.

She *had* to get out of there.

She ran hard uphill along Thórsgata towards the massive spire of the church, a smooth sweeping silhouette against the lightening sky in the east. From the church she pounded down the empty narrow streets towards the bay. In a few minutes she was speeding along the bike path by the shore, the air cold and fresh in her straining lungs. She upped the pace until she was sprinting, the wind tearing through her hair, the blood pumping in her ears, the muscles in her legs screaming in pain and anger.

Finally she could go no faster and stopped, bending down for a few moments. She stood up, her chest heaving, her heart thumping. In front of her, just across the narrow fjord at the edge of the bay, was a broad ridge of rock, topped by snow, glimmering pink. Mount Esja, Ásta had called it. She was right, it looked completely different than it had the previous afternoon.

With Nico gone, Erika felt alone, and vulnerable, here in this tiny northern capital, with its clear light and cold air, a thousand miles from the nearest civilization.

The others were all relying on her to do the right thing. And she *would* do the right thing. She knew what her duty was. She knew that from somewhere deep inside her she would find the strength to see this through.

But it was going to be difficult. Very, very difficult.

She took a deep breath, and screamed into the wind.

It was a spectacular dawn up on the glacier. The clouds had rolled away to the south, nudged by the red ball slowly emerging over the eastern horizon. Pinks, oranges, golds and purples streaked sky and ice. The beauty was breathtaking, like no other crime scene Magnus had visited.

Magnus had been up all night in Hvolsvöllur police station. Chief Superintendent Kristján had managed to persuade Viktor not to press charges against Árni, but had not allayed the MP's suspicions about Magnus's CIA connections. The forensic team had driven out from Reykjavík to meet Magnus at the police station before five a.m. and, together with one of Kristján's officers, they had set off up to the volcano through driving snow. But suddenly, as they mounted Mýrdalsjökull, the snow had ceased and clear sky had appeared.

The surface of the glacier was pristine, covered with new snow, brushed pink in the dawn light. The multitude of vehicle tracks that the local cop explained usually criss-crossed the route towards the volcano had completely disappeared. The two police jeeps proceeded cautiously westwards towards a plume of smoke.

The volcano.

They crested a ridge and a clear view of a broken landscape of ice, steam, cooling lava and rock spread out before them. A dome of rock thrust out from the saddle between the two glaciers, Eyjafjallajökull and Mýrdalsjökull, and nestling in the broken crown of this dome was a glowing pool of orange.

'That's odd,' said the policeman. 'It's gone quiet.'

'Yeah. I was expecting sparks and plumes of lava,' said Magnus, who had seen the eruption several times on TV over the previous couple of weeks. The glow fascinated him, signifying as it did the subterranean power of the earth to create and destroy, but it fell short of the pyrotechnics he had been expecting.

They pulled up next to the only vehicle in front of the volcano, another police jeep with the two poor bastards who had spent the night up there guarding the scene. The night watchmen accepted the thermos of coffee proffered to them by their colleague gratefully.

'God, are we glad to see you,' said one of them. 'It was a vile night.'

'No sign of anyone?' Magnus asked.

'No,' said the policeman. 'Good luck finding anything after all that snow. Here, you'd better sign the log.'

Magnus felt faintly ridiculous signing a crime scene logbook a couple of thousand feet up in the middle of nowhere, but he appreciated the insistence on correct procedure. He looked around. There would be no tracks. And it would be extremely hard to find something that had been dropped under the new snow. He glanced at the leader of the forensic team, a tall long-legged woman with short blond hair named Edda, whom Magnus had never met before. She was stunningly beautiful in a classically Nordic way, and Magnus had tried hard not to stare at her on the journey up to the glacier. He was sure that policemen stared at her stupidly all the time, and he didn't want to be that obvious.

At that moment, she looked grim. She could see her team had a long, cold, pointless day ahead of them.

The wind was still brisk and bit through Magnus's coat, although he could feel heat emanating from the volcano ahead of him. Apart from the odd rumble, it was silent. Asleep? Or just taking a nap?

They all put on extra-large forensic overalls which covered their snow jackets, and Ásta led Edda and Magnus up the lava bank towards the volcano, each one following carefully in the other's footsteps so as to keep disturbance to a minimum. Ásta pointed out where the Freeflow team had parked the evening before, where the other jeep and the two snowmobiles were located, where the team had paused on the rim to watch the volcano and where Erika and Nico had wandered off.

And there was Nico's body, lying on its back, covered by a layer of snow.

As she caught sight of it, Ásta uttered a small cry and stopped in her tracks.

You cannot be cruel to the dead, but it seemed cruel to have left that body up there, cold and alone, abandoned to the volcano and the blizzard.

The volcano grumbled, a seismic belch, and spat a single gobbet of orange magma up into the air.

'Stay here,' Magnus said to Ásta.

Edda approached the body, with Magnus following. Edda motioned for Magnus to wait a few yards back while she crouched down beside Nico. Magnus watched as she gently brushed snow from his face and then his front. 'Single stab wound to the abdomen,' she called back to Magnus. 'The blade was removed. There's a lot of blood. Do you want to take a look?'

'Yes, please,' said Magnus.

'OK, but don't touch him.'

Magnus waited until Edda had made her way back to him and then he took up her former position, crouching by the body.

Nico had been a good-looking man, late thirties probably, fine features, a shaven skull under his hat, tiny snowflakes clinging to the couple of days' of stubble on his cheeks. His lips were bluish. Silent. A diamond stud glinted on one earlobe. His jacket was stained with blood. Magnus prodded where Edda had zipped it open to reveal the wound. One stab was all it had taken.

Magnus felt the familiar urge coursing through his veins. He would find the person who did this. He owed it to Nico, to the people who loved Nico. Magnus had seen dozens – no, hundreds – of dead bodies in his time as a homicide detective in Boston. But however many there were, he never forgot that each one had been an individual, who loved and was loved, who would be mourned, who had things to do that would never be done.

He stood up. Looked at the ground around the body. Already the snow that had fallen overnight was beginning to melt from the warmth of the lava.

'I suppose one of these stones was the one the killer tried to crack over the victim's head,' said Magnus. 'I don't know how the hell you tell which one. There won't be fingerprints, of course, the guy must have been wearing gloves up here.'

Edda surveyed the ground sceptically. 'We might get some fibre, you never know.' She frowned. 'Perhaps it'll be possible to figure out which stone he dropped. The witnesses said it had just started to snow, didn't they? Obviously most of the snow would have fallen later, but there just might be a thin layer of new snow underneath the rock we are looking for.'

'Worth a try,' Magnus said, impressed.

Edda stood up straight. 'It all looks pristine now, but the trouble is there have been hundreds of people up here over the last few weeks, thousands. And they will all have been dropping stuff. There's no way of telling what came from the killer and what came from a tourist a few days ago.'

'I see what you mean,' said Magnus. He was still finding it hard not to stare. Even wrapped up in forensic overalls over a heavy snow jacket she looked gorgeous. Ridiculous. If you worked in Iceland you just had to get used to working with women like Edda.

Or like Ingileif. Funny how he kept on thinking about her in the strangest places.

'OK, I'll leave you to it,' he said. 'Let me know if you turn up anything.'

He retraced his steps to the police jeeps where Ásta was waiting for him together with the local Hvolsvöllur cops.

'You got a call on the radio,' one of them said. 'Inspector Baldur from Reykjavík. He wants to talk to you. Channel seventeen.'

Baldur was head of the Violent Crimes Unit and kind of Magnus's boss. 'Kind of' because actually Magnus reported directly to the National Police Commissioner and was 'attached' to Baldur's department. Baldur was a cop of the old school, suspicious of new foreign methods. Although he was ten years older than Magnus and held a higher rank, he had significantly less experience of homicide investigations. He knew that, as did Magnus and the Police Commissioner.

A recipe for trouble. Which, Magnus suspected, was on its way. Especially since Baldur wanted to avoid the Hvolsvöllur police channel and switch to a more private frequency.

'Good morning, Baldur.'

'What the hell happened last night, Magnús? I've had the Commissioner on the phone. Apparently Árni assaulted an MP.'

'Viktor isn't pressing charges, is he?' Magnus said.

'No. Not this time. But he's very angry. And he has lots of powerful friends.'

'Did he say why he isn't pressing charges?'

'No.'

'Because he slugged Árni himself. And accused me of being a CIA spy. And called Vigdís a "nigger". And I tell you if he does that again, I'll slug him myself.'

'But she is a "nigger", isn't she?'

Magnus took a deep breath. They were speaking Icelandic and Magnus had used the English word, as of course had Viktor. Baldur's English was poor and his cultural sensitivity even worse. Even so, it seemed to Magnus that Baldur should stand up for his officers.

'I want Árni off the case,' Baldur said.

'I'm telling you, it wasn't his fault,' said Magnus. Not entirely true, but someone had to stand up for Árni, and it clearly wasn't going to be Baldur. Árni had a reputation for incompetence, but he was keen and he was loyal and he had once saved Magnus's life, and that was good enough for Magnus. 'If he's off the case, I'm off the case.'

There was a pause on the radio. 'We'll discuss it later. Anything at the crime scene?'

'Forensics will give it a thorough going over, but I doubt they will find anything. The victim died of a stab wound to the stomach. Has the press release gone out, do you know? It would be good to find the snowmobilers and the couple in the other jeep.'

'It has. And Chief Superintendent Kristján is doing a press conference at nine o'clock.'

'We need a warrant to search the Freeflow house in Thórsgata. And their computers. Especially their computers.'

'Vigdís is going to talk to Rannveig as soon as she gets in.' Rannveig was the assistant prosecutor in Reykjavík. She would need to take a warrant to the judge at the District Court on Laekjargata. It shouldn't be a problem: from Magnus's limited experience, judges in Iceland were quite cooperative about that sort of thing.

'OK,' said Magnus. 'I'm on my way back to Reykjavík.'

He hung up. The two policemen who had stayed on the glacier overnight were ready to go back to Hvolsvöllur, and so Magnus asked them to give Ásta and him a lift. He would pick up his own vehicle from outside the police station.

The priest's face was pale, her expression thoughtful.

'I hope none of the information you refused to give us would help us find Nico's killer,' said Magnus. 'Because otherwise you are going to feel very guilty for a very long time.'

Ásta glanced at Magnus quickly and climbed into the jeep.

CHAPTER SIX

'"EARL HÁKON STAYED at Hladir that winter. He became great friends with Vermundur and treated him well, since he knew he came from a distinguished family out in Iceland.

'With the earl were two Swedish brothers, one called Halli and the other Leiknir. They were big strong men, bigger and stronger than any other men in Norway or elsewhere. They used to go berserk, and when they got themselves into that state they were not like other men, but like mad dogs who feared neither fire nor steel."'

Jóhannes Benediktsson glanced up at his class of thirteen-year-olds as he turned the page. He had them transfixed, every one of them. He read *The Saga of the People of Eyri* to his Icelandic class of this age every year. And every time he remembered how his own father had read the saga to him so many times when he was young, especially this passage. For Jóhannes's father Benedikt had been brought up on a farm in the Snaefells Peninsula where the saga had taken place, indeed the very farm where Vermundur's brother had taken charge of the two berserkers back in Iceland a thousand years before.

The lava field between the two brothers' farms was called the Berserkjahraun, and Benedikt had had all sorts of stories to tell about it.

Jóhannes might just be a middle-aged man in a nondescript classroom in modern grey Reykjavík, but he could bring some of the magic of that ancient time into the lives of his mobile-phone-toting, PlayStation-and-Facebook-obsessed city kids.

The bell rang for break. They didn't move. Jóhannes was tempted to continue, but it was best to keep up the suspense. He snapped the book shut with his customary flourish. The class groaned.

As he followed his students out of the classroom, Jóhannes was surprised to see Snaer, the head of the Icelandic Department, waiting for him in the corridor.

'Reading *The Saga of the People of Eyri* again?' he said.

Snaer was fifteen years younger than Johannes and fifteen centimetres shorter. 'Were you spying on me?' Jóhannes answered, his brows knitting in disapproval.

'I thought we had discussed this,' said Snaer.

'Oh, we have, we have,' said Jóhannes. 'On numerous occasions.'

'Well, it looks as if we need to discuss it again,' said Snaer, leading Jóhannes back into his classroom and shutting the door behind him. He took up a position in front of the teacher's desk and turned towards the older man. The break-time chatter of adolescents interspersed with the regular thud of a football seeped in through the window.

'You know that the syllabus requires you to teach *Njáll's Saga* and *Laxdaela Saga* to this age group. Those are possibly the two greatest sagas in the Icelandic language. So why can't you teach them?'

'Because they are in baby talk,' said Jóhannes.

'They are simplified, perhaps, but they convey the essence of the originals. Much more than the essence.'

'Baby talk,' said Jóhannes.

'But thirteen-year-olds can't understand the originals. I have been teaching them for nearly twenty years, and I know they can't.'

'And I've been teaching them for over thirty years, and I know they can,' said Jóhannes. 'You spied on me just now. You saw my class. They love that saga. There's something for everyone: love, honour, fighting, murder, treachery, ghosts, witchcraft; everything a teenage child could possibly want. Sure, at first they might find it hard to follow, but they learn. They learn quickly, and that's the point.'

'I admit you have a good reading voice. But why don't you read them *Njáll's Saga*?'

'I won't read them anything in baby talk.'

'Even though it is laid down in the National Curriculum?'

'Even then.'

Snaer glared at him. 'I also understand that you have been teaching Form Ten that Halldór Laxness is a lightweight.'

'I have been teaching them to think critically. Just because he won a Nobel Prize it doesn't mean everything he wrote is perfect. And the arrogance of the man! He took it upon himself to make up his own rules for how Icelandic should be spelled, he thought our Viking ancestors were all vulgar brutes, and' – here Jóhannes pulled himself up to his full height – 'he thought we should wash more. Why should I be told how often to have a bath by that communist?'

Snaer closed his eyes. Jóhannes waited. It was true that they had had this conversation before, three months before, shortly after Snaer was promoted to head of department. And indeed Jóhannes had had the same discussion with all three of Snaer's predecessors over the years.

The fact was that Jóhannes was a brilliant teacher of Icelandic literature. And language for that matter. Three of his former pupils held positions in the Faculty of Icelandic at the University of Iceland; another one had won the Icelandic Literature Prize the year before. He inspired people to love their country's language. And when push came to shove, all heads of department respected that.

Except, perhaps, Snaer.

The younger man cleared his throat. 'You have probably heard the rumours that with the government spending cuts the school is going to have to reduce its teaching staff by ten per cent?'

'No. I don't listen to staffroom tattle,' Jóhannes said, lying. Of course he listened to staffroom tattle.

'The Principal has told me that we need to lose one member

of staff from this department. He and I have discussed it, and we feel that as the teacher who is the least willing to embrace what the school is trying to do, indeed what the government is trying to do to raise educational standards—'

Jóhannes couldn't contain himself. 'Raise standards? Lower them more like.'

Snaer ignored him. '—that you should be the one to leave.'

Suddenly Jóhannes realized what Snaer was saying. No one had ever called his bluff before. 'You can't be serious?'

'I am serious. The Principal is waiting to talk to you in his office now. Unless you want to change your mind? If you could be persuaded to teach what you are supposed to teach, you could be a very good educator.'

'Educator! What kind of a word is that?' Jóhannes demanded.

'Just because your father was a novelist—'

'A great novelist!'

'A novelist. It doesn't mean that your position is untouchable.'

'What about the younger members of staff? Why get rid of your most experienced person?'

'You mean someone like Elísabet? She's young, she's hard-working, she's enthusiastic, she teaches what she's supposed to teach and does it well.'

Jóhannes's indignation subsided a touch. 'I know. I taught her when she was a pupil here.' Elísabet had been teaching at the school a year and a half, and she was popular with staff and pupils. She had a genuine love of Icelandic.

'And she will no doubt go on to teach many fine educators herself. Unless I fire her today, of course.'

'It's all the illiterate bankers' fault,' Jóhannes grumbled. 'If they hadn't got the country into this mess there wouldn't be these cuts.'

'You mean if someone had just taught them about a couple of berserkers raging around a lava field a thousand years ago, everything would be different?'

'It may have been,' said Jóhannes defensively.

'Well, it's a bit late now. You and I have an appointment with the Principal.'

Jóhannes left the Principal's office and headed straight for the car park. The Principal had been more polite than Snaer, more respectful, but his message was clear.

Jóhannes's career as a teacher at that school was over.

He had offered to give Jóhannes the rest of the day off, and Jóhannes had accepted. He needed to get out of the school right away.

As he drove the couple of kilometres from the school to his home in Vesturbaer, Jóhannes's brain was in turmoil. His bluff had been called as he should always have known one day it would be. Why should he be the only teacher in Iceland who got away with ignoring the National Curriculum? Sure, there were famous people in the Icelandic literary world whom he had taught as schoolchildren, but would they really care about what happened to him? 'I thought old Jóhannes had already retired,' would be their response.

Jóhannes was only fifty-five, but people thought he was older. He was physically fit, big, lean and erect with a shock of thick white hair and a craggy face, but he behaved like someone ten years older. He wore tweed jackets and a tie, he smoked a pipe; he was from another era.

He pulled up in front of his house in Bárugata. It was a big house for a teacher, on a street that had been popular in the old days with sea captains, since from the upper storeys of its buildings you could look down the hill to the Old Harbour. He had grown up there; his parents had lived and died there, and after his father's death he had inherited it. The house was built for families and for a few years Jóhannes had brought his own family to live there, until his wife had left him, taking their children with her. Why, Jóhannes had never quite understood.

A big house for a lone teacher. A very big house for a lone unemployed teacher.

It had been worth a fortune before the crash. He could probably still sell it for a reasonable price even in the current depressed market. Maybe one day he would have to, but not yet.

He pulled out his pipe and sat in his favourite armchair. It felt strange to be at home during the day in school term-time. Very strange.

He felt a wave of depression sweep over him. If Jóhannes wasn't a teacher, what was he?

His father, who was indeed a great novelist, superior to Halldór Laxness in Jóhannes's opinion, was at the height of his powers at Jóhannes's age. He did a quick calculation. At fifty-five, Benedikt had had four more years to live, four years until Jóhannes found him right there in the hallway, stabbed.

What a strange, inexplicable way for such a good and talented man to die.

Jóhannes had dropped in unannounced early one evening to return a book. The front door was unlocked, as it sometimes was. He had shouted a greeting, walked in and found his father lying in a pool of his own blood out there in the hallway.

The case had never been solved, but not for want of trying. Jóhannes had himself been interviewed a number of times, as had all Benedikt's friends. Suspicion had flitted from one to the other of them, even resting briefly on Jóhannes's shoulders, but no one had been arrested. A burglar was perhaps the most likely candidate, but no one really knew.

The irony was that the autopsy had revealed a tumour in Benedikt's brain that would have killed him in a few months anyway. Benedikt's doctor confirmed that Benedikt had known about it for almost a year, a knowledge that he had decided not to pass on to his children.

Jóhannes had tried, but he found it difficult to forgive his father for that.

Benedikt had taught Jóhannes everything he knew: his love of language; his love of literature; his respect for other people, especially the young. Teaching, in Benedikt's eyes, was a noble profession and one that Jóhannes had been proud to follow all these years. And he was good at it, really good. It was one of Jóhannes's greatest regrets that his father had never been inside one of Jóhannes's classrooms, never seen how enraptured those thirteen-year-olds could be with Vermundur and Styr and Arnkell and Snorri and all those other colourful characters who beckoned from the tenth century.

Of course Jóhannes's teaching career wasn't necessarily over. He could fight to keep his position. Or he could look for another: times were very tough and teachers were being laid off all over Iceland, but there might be a job for him somewhere else. It would be a long struggle, a very long struggle and it might end in failure.

Or . . .

Or perhaps this was one of those opportunities dressed up as disaster. For years Jóhannes had been collecting all the information he could on his father. His books and manuscripts, of course, letters both to and from him, articles written by him and about him, and in recent years the dissertations on his life and works that various literature students had produced. They were lying in a series of untidy piles next to his desk. One day, Jóhannes had promised himself long ago, one day he would write a biography of his father.

Perhaps that day was now.

CHAPTER SEVEN

MAGNUS STOPPED OFF at Hvolsvöllur police station where he reported back to Chief Superintendent Kristján. He decided not to wait for the press conference at nine, but to head straight back to Reykjavík. He wanted to get at that house on Thórsgata.

He switched to his own car and offered to give Ásta a lift back with him. He could hardly leave her stranded in Hvolsvöllur.

It was an hour-and-a-half's drive to Reykjavík, but Ásta swiftly fell asleep in the seat beside Magnus. He considered trying to grill her, but he doubted that there was much more he could get out of her. The countryside of south Iceland sped past: clumps of sodden yellow grass with the odd horse looking cold, wet and hungry. The area was renowned in Iceland for its rich soil, and the horses for their cheerful hardiness, but it all looked a bit miserable to Magnus.

As they reached the steep bank just beyond Hveragerdi and climbed the switchbacks on to the snow-covered heath above, Ásta woke up.

This was an active geothermal area, with steam leaking out of fissures in the rock, and indeed there was a power station to the right fed by the heat bubbling up from the centre of the earth. Pylons marched across the bleak landscape a short distance from the road, channelling all that energy towards the light and heat of Reykjavík. Lava, congealed after an eruption thousands of years ago, rippled under the snow.

'Sorry about that,' said Ásta, yawning. 'It's been a long night. And a strange one.'

'How did you say you got caught up with these people?' Magnus asked.

'Through my uncle. Viktor – the man you made friends with last night.'

'Nice guy,' said Magnus. 'Did you hear what he called my colleague?'

Ásta winced. 'That was bad. But he is a good guy really. He's an idealist, and our country needs more of those.'

'I should know who he is, but I've only been back in Iceland a year,' Magnus said. 'Which party is he?'

'The Movement. He was elected in 2009. He's ambitious: I'm sure he'd like to be a minister.'

'Well connected?'

'I think so. Well, he's good friends with the Prime Minister.'

'So, I'll take that as a yes.' Magnus sighed. A bad enemy to make. He had hoped that there would be less politics in Reykjavík than Boston. Silly idea. The politics were just different.

'What's this Icelandic Modern Media Initiative?' he asked.

'It all started when Freeflow came here last year. Erika was on TV saying that Iceland should become a kind of offshore centre for free speech and a haven for investigative journalists worldwide. Viktor was watching and got very excited. He and some other MPs believe that Iceland's troubles during the credit crunch of 2008 are the result of secrecy among the establishment of bankers and politicians. So he got in touch with Erika and Nico the next day.'

'So it's all Freeflow's idea?'

'That's where it started,' said Ásta. 'But my uncle is the driving force behind it here in Iceland. The initiative itself is a resolution before Parliament to amend Iceland's laws to make all this happen. It's a good idea, actually.'

'So has he kept in touch with Freeflow?'

'Oh, yes. I wouldn't be surprised if he was involved in the Ódinsbanki leaks. Oh!' Ásta paused. 'I shouldn't have said that to a policeman.'

'I think there's a lot more you should be saying.'

'I have to keep a confidence.' Her voice was firm.

'Look, Ásta. When I get to Reykjavík I will go to the District Court and get a warrant to search the house those people are staying in, and their computers. By lunchtime I will know what they are working on. It would help me a lot if you could tell me now. In a murder investigation every hour counts.'

Ásta turned away from him and looked out across the snow-covered moor.

'Suit yourself,' said Magnus.

Magnus was expecting silence for the rest of the trip, but after a minute, Ásta spoke. 'Are you really in the CIA?'

'Of course not,' Magnus said. 'Erika Zinn is paranoid. That's an absurd idea.' He glanced across at the priest in the seat next to him, whose big blue eyes were watching him closely. 'Don't you believe me?'

'I believe you,' she said. 'But even I could tell that your English accent was very good. Or rather American accent. And you said just now that you came back to Iceland a year ago?'

'I was born here. My dad was an academic – he taught mathematics at the University of Iceland, and then he got a job at the Massachusetts Institute of Technology in Cambridge. My mother died when I was twelve and so I went over there to live with him. Went to the local high school, went to college. Then, after he was . . . after he died, I decided to become a cop. I ended up as a homicide detective in Boston. But no, I never joined the CIA.'

'Are you glad to be back? In Iceland?'

Magnus hesitated before replying. 'It's hard to say.'

'Do you think of yourself as an Icelander?'

Magnus smiled ruefully. 'That's probably why it's hard to say.'

'What do you mean?'

'I mean in the States I definitely saw myself as an Icelander. I read and reread all the sagas, I kept up with the language, I loved coming back here with my father on vacation: this was my homeland. My younger brother was completely different, he became an American through and through and was happy to do that, but I felt I was *different* from the other kids, and I liked that.'

'So what was the problem?'

'When I came back I felt like a foreigner here as well. I spoke Icelandic with a bit of an American accent when I arrived – I don't know if you can still tell?'

'Barely.'

'Good. But it was more than that. Everyone here knows each other. They have family, friends from school and university. People are friendly enough, but it's impossible not to feel like an outsider. So I don't know who the hell I am. And, yes, sometimes that bugs me.'

'But don't you have family here?'

'Not on my father's side – he was an only child. There are loads on my mother's side, but they don't seem to like me very much. It's a family feud in the best saga tradition.'

'Oh.'

Magnus laughed. 'How come you can get me to tell you everything when I can't get you to tell me anything? We should give you a job in the police department.'

'I think I'll stick to the Church, thank you,' said Ásta.

'The side of the angels?'

'Sometimes I wonder,' she muttered so quietly that Magnus barely heard.

Half an hour later, Magnus pulled up outside the address at Thórsgata. The lights were off and the curtains drawn.

'Looks like they are asleep,' he said.

Ásta thanked him for the lift and got out of his car. Magnus left her dithering whether to ring the bell or not, and drove back to the Reykjavík Metropolitan Police Headquarters on Hverfisgata. He summoned Árni and Vigdís into the conference room, and gave the assistant prosecutor, Rannveig, a quick call to join them.

'So what was the volcano like?' asked Vigdís.

'Haven't you seen it yet?' asked Árni. 'I went up there just after it erupted. It's pretty cool.'

'It had gone quiet this morning,' said Magnus.

'Really?' said Árni. 'That's a bad sign. It means Katla is about to blow.'

Magnus paused a moment. He had heard of Katla and the mayhem it had caused when it last erupted in 1918. In fact he had noticed the posters all over the Hvolsvöllur police station detailing evacuation plans should the volcano erupt again and a *jökulhlaup* flood the local area. 'Are you sure about that, Árni?'

'He's guessing,' said Vigdís.

'I saw this guy on TV—' began Árni.

Magnus held up his hand. 'The main point is that the overnight snow did a pretty good job of obliterating any signs of what happened last night. Certainly no tyre tracks. If anything was dropped, we can't see it.'

'Hey, was Edda leading the forensics team?' asked Árni. 'I heard she's back from Quantico.'

'Er, yes,' said Magnus. Quantico was the FBI's academy in Virginia; presumably Edda had just returned from a course there.

'Impressive, eh? She'd keep you warm in a blizzard up a mountain.'

'Oh, please, Árni,' said Vigdís, rolling her eyes. Whatever those eye muscles were called, Magnus thought, Vigdís got to exercise them a lot working with Árni.

'I think she has a pretty cold day ahead of her. OK, Vigdís, what did you find out about Freeflow?'

'They have been very active in the last three years. They started in 2007 publishing leaked United Nations documents which suggested that the United States, Britain and France were holding back from taking action in Darfur because of fears of getting involved in another war. That was followed up with about twenty or so other leaks, some of them big news, some of them less so.'

'Wait a minute. Was all this information in Icelandic?' Magnus asked. He was sceptical about Vigdís's professed lack of English.

'I've got a dictionary,' said Vigdís. 'And Darfur is the same word in either language.'

'OK, OK,' said Magnus. For Vigdís, life was a battle to prove that she could be black and an Icelander. Not speaking English was the way she had chosen years ago to prove the point, although Magnus was sure she actually understood the language pretty well. But it was a sore point, so he decided to shut up and pretend not to notice. 'Sorry. What about these other leaks?'

'Well, there was the publication of Ódinsbanki's loan book here in Iceland – you probably remember that. Some of the Chinese government's measures to silence dissidents and a list of the websites they block – the Chinese got *very* unhappy about that. An investigation into Sabine Dumont, the Belgian Finance Minister, and her dodgy past. An Italian corruption scandal—'

'Is that news?' asked Magnus.

'Hey, we Icelanders are hardly in a position to complain, are we?'

'True,' said Magnus. Before the *kreppa*, as Icelanders called the financial crisis of 2008, Iceland had prided itself on being rated the least corrupt country in the world. Since the *kreppa*, they knew they were not.

'There was a big scandal about arms exports to Zimbabwe breaking sanctions,' Vigdís went on. 'The Luxembourg subsidiary of a German bank laundering money . . .'

'Anything against the United States?' Magnus asked. 'Anything that might interest the CIA?'

'Not really, apart from the Darfur leak right at the beginning. And there are the handbooks of a bunch of secret student clubs at colleges in America. They sound very strange.'

'Fraternities?' said Magnus with a smile. 'They *are* very strange. But not really something the CIA would bother themselves with. Nor the FBI for that matter.'

'OK, but I suppose the other stuff would interest them. They are interested in pretty much everything, right?'

'I guess so,' said Magnus. 'I imagine someone like Erika Zinn is bound to be paranoid about them.'

'Perhaps with good cause,' said Vigdís.

'Do you want me to get in touch with them?' asked Árni.

'With the CIA?' Magnus couldn't hide his surprise.

'Sure. I could call the US Embassy in Reykjavík. Ask to speak to someone.'

'No, Árni, I do not want you to indulge your espionage fantasies. I think it would be a thoroughly bad idea to get in touch with the CIA; it would just make things more political. But if we do, we will do it through official channels.' Magnus turned to Vigdís. 'What about Erika Zinn herself? Anything from Interpol?'

'Yes. I mentioned the Italian corruption case. In 2007 there was a judicial investigation in Rome into the takeover of a company called Gruppo Cavour. The investigation was dropped, but then Freeflow published details of discussions between government ministers about bribing judges. The Italians didn't like that. Erika spent a week in jail there three months ago: it looks like she has pissed off some pretty important people in Rome. She was released, but she is still officially under investigation.'

'No outstanding warrant for her arrest?'

'No,' said Vigdís.

'Pity.'

'But Dieter Schroff has a couple of convictions for hacking into computers. Been to jail twice, once in 1991 and once in 2000. Let out in 2003 and nothing since then.'

The door opened and Rannveig, the assistant prosecutor, came in. She was a red-haired woman in her late twenties, hard-working and effective.

'Did you get the warrant?' Magnus asked.

'No,' said Rannveig. 'At least not yet. The judge is thinking about it.'

'*Thinking* about it?' Magnus was surprised. Icelanders didn't like to think about things. They took quick decisions. Sometimes with good results, sometimes with bad, but as a rule they didn't like to dither. 'What's the problem?'

'Viktor Símonarson got to the District Court the same time I did,' said Rannveig. 'He objected to the search warrant, in particular to the warrant to search Freeflow's computers. It's the Icelandic Modern Media Initiative.'

'But from what I understand that's just a resolution before Parliament. It hasn't changed the laws yet, has it?'

Rannveig shrugged.

'I hope the judge told him to piss off?'

'He didn't, I'm afraid. He needs to consult. But we should hear soon.'

'We need to know what Freeflow is working on!' cried Magnus in frustration. 'Why they are in Iceland. Doesn't he get that?'

'Oh, he gets that all right, Magnús,' said Rannveig reprovingly. 'It's just that he also gets the rights of journalists to protect their sources.'

'OK, Rannveig, I'm sorry,' said Magnus. 'What about arresting them?'

'On what charge? We don't have any evidence to suggest that any of them committed the murder, do we?'

Magnus paused, thinking. 'Not yet,' he said. 'What about obstruction of justice? Article one hundred and twelve.' The Icelandic Penal Code was still fresh in his mind after the six months he had spent learning it.

'Difficult,' said Rannveig.

'But can't we just bring them in and hold them for twenty-four hours before we go to a judge?' That was the way that Icelandic law worked as far as Magnus understood it. He had seen it in action many times before over the last year. For all their relative leniency with convicted criminals, suspects had fewer rights than in the US.

'In this case you would have to be very careful before you do that,' said Rannveig.

'You're probably right,' Magnus conceded. 'We need to see Baldur.'

'Here he is,' said Vigdís.

Inspector Baldur Jakobsson strode into the conference room. A tall, bald man, with a bit of a stoop and a long lugubrious face, he did not seem happy to see Magnus. He took a seat at the conference table.

'I wanted to talk to you,' said Magnus.

'Good. Because I wanted to talk to you,' said Baldur. 'That was a right mess of things you made last night. It never makes sense to assault politicians.'

'Árni was provoked,' said Magnus.

'You shouldn't have let the situation get out of hand,' said Baldur. 'None of you should. Tell me about the crime scene.'

Magnus told the inspector about the lack of likely clues, given the fresh snow.

When he had finished, Baldur nodded. 'Well, let's hope the forensics people find something. Now, I'm sorry, I know you have been driving around all night, but I want you back in Hvolsvöllur. We need someone there to liaise with the local police on the ground.'

'Hey, hold on right there,' said Magnus. 'The key information we need is in Reykjavík in that house on Thórsgata. I'm waiting for Rannveig to come up with the warrant. And I want to interview them again. Especially Erika and Franz, the kid who was by himself on the volcano for a while.'

'I can do that with Vigdís and Árni,' said Baldur.

'But I'm in charge of this investigation!' said Magnus.

'No you're not,' said Baldur, one corner of his thin lips twitching upwards. 'I am.'

'But you don't speak English!' protested Magnus. 'The witnesses are foreigners, or at least most of them are. I need to talk to them.'

'I speak reasonable English,' said Baldur. 'And Árni can help me. Look, if you get bored in the police station you can go back to the crime scene, see what you can do to help there.'

'I'm sure Edda could use the help,' Árni said with a wink. Everyone around the table ignored him.

Róbert, one of the other detectives in the unit, put his head around the door. 'The Big Salmon has been on the phone. He wants to see you in his office, Magnús. Now.'

The twitch on Baldur's lips spread to both sides. Magnus sighed and stood up. He wanted to focus on who had killed Nico and why, not on defending himself and his detectives. He was tired and he was getting grumpy.

The National Police Commissioner's office was close to police headquarters, on the other side of a busy junction. It was in a modern building with a great view over the bay. Magnus could see Mount Esja basking in the sunshine and, way over to the north-west, the white cap of the Snaefells Glacier floating above the sea.

The Commissioner, Snorri Gudmundsson, was an energetic man in his late fifties, short with thick grey hair brushed back in a Soviet-style bouffant. Magnus had a lot of time for him. It was he, after all, who had requested Magnus's presence in Iceland. Although Magnus had had some successes over the last twelve months, they had not been trouble-free, and Snorri had stood by him. He was perhaps too concerned with politics for Magnus's tastes, but that's what you expected from a police commissioner.

As he entered the Commissioner's office, Magnus prepared himself for the inevitable bawling out.

The Commissioner looked stern. 'I've had Viktor Símonarson on the phone,' he began.

'I guessed as much,' said Magnus.

'He says Detective Árni assaulted him.'

'Is he pressing charges?'

'No. Is it true?'

'Partly.'

'Tell me what happened.'

And so Magnus did. The Commissioner listened closely, wincing at the word 'nigger'.

'Magnús, you let things get out of hand. Viktor is a troublemaker, but an extremely well-connected troublemaker. He has many friends in the government.'

'Yeah, I figured that,' said Magnus.

'We are going to have to launch a disciplinary inquiry into Árni's actions.'

'I don't think you should do that, Snorri.'

Magnus would much rather call the Big Salmon 'Commissioner' or, at the very least, 'sir': the Icelandic custom of using first names, however important the person, was hard to get used to.

'We can't just stand by while our officers assault parliamentarians.'

'No. And I will speak to Árni. What he did was unacceptable. But he was standing up for a fellow officer. That kind of racism cannot be left unchallenged, in my opinion. If you discipline him you will be condoning it.'

'That's absurd. Árni broke the rules. He should get punished.'

Magnus realized he had gone a bit too far. 'OK, frankly sometimes he's an idiot. But Árni took a bullet for me a year ago. He stood up for Vigdís last night against someone much more powerful than him. I admire the guy.'

The Commissioner shook his head.

Magnus didn't give up. 'If Viktor was pressing charges I agree you would have to do something. But he's not. And there's a reason for that. He knows he's in the wrong.'

The Commissioner smiled. 'OK, OK. But have a word with Árni. And as for you, Magnús . . .'

'Yes?' Here it came. Magnus wondered if he would get by with a ticking off, or whether he was in for something worse. He had already got a result with Árni, though.

'I want you to lead this investigation. Reporting to Chief Superintendent Kristján.'

'What?'

'You look surprised, Magnús?' The Commissioner was smiling.

'Actually, I am,' said Magnus. 'What about Baldur?'

'The crime was not committed in the Metropolitan area, it's in Hvolsvöllur's jurisdiction. Chief Superintendent Kristján is a very capable man – I think you and he will work well together. And this is exactly the kind of case for which we have you here. Baldur will support you with any inquiries you make in the Reykjavík area. My understanding is that this Freeflow group are staying in town?'

'Yes. On Thórsgata.'

'I have every confidence in you as an investigating officer, Magnús,' the Commissioner went on. 'But so far I haven't been impressed by your political sensitivity.' The Commissioner's blue eyes twinkled. 'I'm sure you know what I mean. You do need to tread carefully here. Viktor could make life very difficult for you. For all of us.'

'I understand,' said Magnus. His instinct was to burst into the house on Thórsgata, preferably with the 'Viking Squad' SWAT team breaking down the doors, and cart everyone off to the cells until they broke down and told him everything. But even he realized that that was not exactly what the Commissioner had in mind. 'Given that, can I ask your advice?'

'By all means.' Snorri looked pleased. Like many senior officers he missed the excitement of a live case.

'I don't understand what the problem is with this Icelandic Modern Media Initiative. Parliament hasn't actually changed any of the laws yet, has it?'

'That's true. But Parliament will pass the resolution in a couple of months and then the laws will be changed. The problem is that the sponsors of the initiative, and it's not just Viktor, there are lots of others, would love a cause to rally around, and if we are not careful we could give them just that. So the judge is being very careful.'

'OK,' said Magnus. 'But I would like to talk to Rannveig about taking the Freeflow team in for questioning. If not on suspicion of murder, at least then for obstruction of justice. What do you think?'

'Why?'

'I need to find out what they are working on. Who their enemies are.'

'I don't think bringing them in is a good idea. With Viktor Símonarson acting as their lawyer, I think it is highly unlikely they will tell you anything, don't you?' said Snorri. 'They'll just sit tight.'

'You're probably right.'

'I'm not saying you're not on the right track. But go gently. If you can't find out by direct means, go indirectly. I have every confidence in you. Now, you had better get cracking.'

Jóhannes had spent a couple of hours at his desk, going through his father's documents, trying to get them into some sort of order. There were some parts of Benedikt's life that Jóhannes knew very well. Others would require a little more research, such as his childhood at the farm of Hraun. And then there were the mysteries. Like the one that had erupted the year before Benedikt's death.

Benedikt's last novel, his best in some people's estimation – including Jóhannes's – was entitled *Moor and the Man*, published a few months before his death in 1985. A powerful scene in the book described how two boys, friends from neighbouring farms, had come across the father of one of them having sex with the mother of the other one in a barn. A month later the boys were playing by a lake, when they saw the woman's husband dumping a heavy weight in a sack into the water. That evening, her lover never returned home. He had been murdered.

What interested Jóhannes particularly was the rumour that had sprung up in the Snaefells Peninsula that there were parallels with the disappearance of Benedikt's own father, Jóhannes's grandfather, from his farm at Hraun in 1934. That mystery had never been solved: some people thought he had run away to America, some that he had fallen into the fjord by Hraun. And then, after reading the book, some felt he had been murdered by a neighbouring farmer.

Benedikt didn't live long enough to deny the rumour and as far as Jóhannes was aware it had never been substantiated. Jóhannes's own provisional opinion was that Benedikt had simply invented a solution to a problem that had haunted him from his childhood, but there was no doubt that more research was needed.

As Jóhannes sorted the documents, one particular piece of paper forced itself to the top of the pile.

It was a letter Jóhannes had received two months earlier from a former pupil whose late grandfather had been a friend of Halldór Laxness. The pupil had been going through his grandfather's papers and made an interesting discovery. In 1985, when Halldór himself was a very old man, he had written to the pupil's grandfather from Búdir, a hotel on the south coast of the Snaefells Peninsula, over the mountains from Hraun. The pupil had enclosed a photocopy of Halldór's letter with the relevant passage highlighted. It was dated 14 November 1985, only a month before Benedikt was murdered.

Jóhannes read it through, although the paragraph was so familiar he had probably memorized it by now.

I saw an extraordinary thing yesterday while riding through the lava field with the stable boy. Benedikt Jóhannesson was involved in an altercation with a man with a shotgun. For a moment I thought that the man would actually shoot Benedikt. The stable boy – Hermann was his name – was quite brave, he rode down and somehow calmed things down.

I had no idea that Benedikt was staying at the hotel. I looked out for him at dinner that evening, but he must have left.

Odd.

Odd indeed. And something Jóhannes had been meaning to clear up. He had got as far as checking with the Hotel Búdir. There had indeed been a stable boy named Hermann employed by the hotel in the 1980s. What was more he was still there: now he was in charge of the stables attached to the hotel.

Jóhannes could sit in his chair and mope about his lost teaching career all day.

Or he could get off his backside and *do* something.

CHAPTER EIGHT

'YOU KNOW WHO'S behind this, don't you?'

Erika and Dieter were sitting on the bed in her room with her laptop open in front of them. Erika was sipping a can of Red Bull, Dieter Coke Zero. They were on encrypted Skype to Apex. Although Apex could see Erika and Dieter, they couldn't see Apex: he had his video camera turned off. Erika still had no idea what he looked like. Dieter liked Skype: because it had been developed in Sweden, his theory was that the CIA had never had the chance to build a backdoor into the software through which they could eavesdrop. Apex had his doubts about that, but then Apex always had doubts.

The door was shut. Zivah and the others were having breakfast downstairs in the living room.

'Who?' Erika asked.

'Mossad, of course,' said the Australian.

'We don't know that,' said Erika.

'No – we never know who is watching us, do we? But it's not the Chinese, is it? And Mossad are mean.'

'How would they know we've got the video?'

'Good question,' said Apex. 'But I suggest you all get out of Reykjavík right away before anyone else gets killed.'

'No, Apex. We are publishing this. And we are doing it in the next week. For Nico's sake.'

'Hey, Erika, you don't want to mess with Mossad.'

'Apex, we will mess with anyone. No one can intimidate Freeflow into not publishing. No one.'

'I don't think that's a good idea.'

'What do you care?' said Erika. 'You're safe in some pit in Melbourne or Sydney or wherever you are. We're the ones who are taking the risk and we have decided we're running with this.'

Erika was aware of Dieter's bulk beside her. She knew she could railroad Apex as long as Dieter didn't back him up.

'We could publish it right now,' the German said. 'Just put it up on the web for everyone to see. Get it out there. Then there's nothing they can do to us. It will be too late.'

'No,' said Erika. 'That's a non-starter. We used to do that, remember, and no one ever took any notice. Journalists are pathetic, they need to be told what's exciting and why.'

Dieter nodded. Their original Darfur leak had been met with total indifference until Erika had stirred things up, telling people where to look.

'Plus, we don't know it's genuine yet,' Erika continued. 'We have to make sure it's authentic or they'll crucify us. We need to get people double-checking the facts on the ground in Gaza. We need to get the websites up and secure, with back-ups if the Israelis launch cyber attacks on them. We need editing, commentary, a coordinated release. Samantha Wilton in tears at a press conference. We need to make maximum impact with this video. Otherwise it will just be flitting around on the edge of the Internet: the Israelis will dismiss it as some daft conspiracy.'

'She's right,' said Apex. 'If we are going to publish it, we need to do it properly.'

'Oh, by the way, I think the CIA is on to us,' said Erika.

'Are they following you again?' Apex asked.

'Worse than that. After the police took us to some police station in the middle of nowhere an American showed up. He had a police badge and he spoke Icelandic, but he also spoke English perfectly. With an American accent. He claimed he was some kind of cop on secondment, but he sounded like a well-educated kind of cop to me.'

'Jesus,' said Apex.

'Are you sure our computers are safe?' Erika said. 'Viktor's holding out against a warrant to search them, but he might fail.'

'Quite sure,' said Apex. 'Or at least ours are. Military-grade encryption. Even the CIA won't be able to read them. But you'd better check that the volunteers don't have anything on theirs. And of course the police can always read notes written on paper.'

Erika trusted Apex. She had her whole life on her laptop, but everything was encrypted and backed up on a cloud of servers in Germany, Sweden and Australia. The passwords were in her head.

'I made sure that none of the volunteers has brought their own laptops into the house,' said Dieter.

'Once you are all working on the video, shut everything down as soon as the police appear,' Apex said. 'Once when I was a kid I got raided in Australia by a SWAT team trying to catch me red-handed logged into a network.' Apex chuckled. 'Scared the wits out of my mum, but I heard them coming.'

'We'll be careful,' said Dieter.

'What about finances?' said Erika. 'We're going to need some cash here. Can you send us some over, Apex?'

'Ah.'

Erika glanced at Dieter. She didn't like the sound of that. 'What do you mean, "Ah"?'

'With Nico gone, there isn't any money.'

'Hold on. That can't be right! I thought we had back-up procedures so if something happened to him, you and I would still have access to Freeflow's accounts.'

'Oh, yes, those procedures are in place. We can access the accounts. The trouble is . . .'

Erika didn't like the sound of this at all. 'The trouble is what?'

'The trouble is there is nothing in them.'

'Even in the reserve account in Guernsey?'

'Even in that.'

'But Nico didn't tell me we had run out of cash?'

'For the last couple of weeks he had been using his own money to run Freeflow. Out of his personal bank account. Which will now be frozen.'

'Jesus,' said Erika. 'That's a problem. Shit! Shit, shit, shit, shit!'

Money. Money was always Freeflow's problem, always had been, always would be.

Dieter and Apex were silent. 'OK,' Erika sighed. 'Let's think this through. The rent on this place is paid in advance, right, Dieter?'

'Yes. And in fact there will be a deposit returned when we leave.'

'Good. I'll need some cash for my air fare out of here to the press conference in London. I guess everyone else has return tickets. We've got all the computer equipment we need here from volunteers. Do you need to buy anything else?'

Dieter shook his head. 'Nothing major.'

'OK, so it's just groceries and the air fare,' said Erika. 'We can get by for a few days, at least until we publish the video. That should crank up the donations.'

'Not quite,' said Dieter.

'What's the problem?'

'The Swedish ISP who are hosting our site. They know there is going to be a surge of traffic, and possibly denial-of-service attacks when we go live and they want payment before then. They are sending through an invoice to me today. Nico was going to do a bank transfer as soon as we received it.'

'How much?'

'Fifteen thousand euros.'

'Can't they wait a week? Don't they trust us?'

'They trust our ideals,' Apex said. 'I'm not sure they trust our finances.'

'Damn!' Erika put her head in her hands. She knew none of the three of them had fifteen thousand euros. Dieter was maxed out on his credit cards. It was years since any card company had allowed her credit, and Apex didn't cough up money however hard one pleaded.

But . . . She had an idea.

'Apex. Can you hack into Nico's account? Transfer the money across?'

'No.' Apex's voice was firm.

'You mean no, you can't do it, or no, you won't do it?'

'Of course I can do it. But I'm not going to. It's stealing and you know I don't do that. I've never done it. And I know what you're thinking, Erika, but don't you dare ask Dieter to do it either.'

Dieter flinched next to her. Dieter and Apex were old friends, and old enemies. As teenagers in the late eighties on different continents they had met up on a West German chat channel called Altos, where they discussed their hacking exploits. Apex had hacked into NASA, the US Air Force Strategic Command and British Aerospace; Dieter into the US Department of Defense's Network Information Computer, Deutsche Telekom and the French Commissariat of Atomic Energy. But they all played by some straightforward rules: leave a system the way you found it, don't change it, don't damage it and don't steal from it.

Nevertheless, Dieter had been prosecuted in 1991 and spent two years in a German prison, where he met some people who persuaded him to use his skills to download credit card details, which he did by the thousand once he was released. He was caught again, and spent some more time in jail. Apex had felt personally betrayed by Dieter's time on the dark side, as he saw it, and when Dieter was released for the second time, Apex persuaded him to go straight. Since then, the two of them had developed freelance jobs as computer security consultants, testing supposedly secure websites for vulnerabilities.

For both of them, Apex especially, their integrity as defined by their own code was everything. Erika knew that.

So she gave up.

'OK. Well, I'm just going to have to find fifteen thousand euros. Dieter, you had better get to work on everyone's laptop before the police get here. Apex, are you happy our system is secure now?'

'Yes, but I'd better work on backing everything up with Dieter before we download the video.'

'OK, guys,' said Erika. 'Let's get to it.'

Outside, in the dining area, the others were waiting for Erika with cups of coffee and bowls of Cheerios, which seemed to be Iceland's cereal of choice.

Erika noticed the priest, her clerical collar firmly attached. Viktor was there as well. 'Are you back already?' she asked Ásta.

'Yes, I got here about an hour ago.'

'Did you go up the mountain?'

'I did. With the snow last night, it's going to be difficult for the police to find anything. I saw Nico.'

'Hadn't they taken him away?' Erika couldn't bear to think of her friend left lying up there on the glacier all night, in the cold and the dark, all alone. She shuddered.

'No,' said Ásta. 'Forensics people are crawling over everything. What is happening about Nico's family? Do you know them?'

Erika sighed. 'I've met his wife once when I stayed with him in Milan, but I don't know her really well.'

'Who is going to tell her?'

Erika felt a pang of guilt. 'The police said they would, but I never got around to giving them her number last night.'

'Do you want me to handle that?'

'Yes please,' said Erika. 'Did you tell that American anything about the Gaza video, the CIA guy?'

'No, I didn't.'

Erika noticed that Viktor was smiling, proud of his niece. And so he should be. Ásta had been involved with Freeflow for less than a day and already her loyalty was impressive.

'And by the way, Magnús doesn't work for the CIA,' Ásta said.

'How do you know?' Erika asked.

'Because he told me.'

'I see,' said Erika, not bothering to contradict her. So priests were gullible, what else was new? She was just pleased Ásta had taken the problem of Nico's family off her hands. 'Can we expect the police soon, Viktor?'

'They are trying,' said Viktor. 'I've just come from the District Court. They wanted a search warrant, but I put up a good case against it.'

'The Icelandic Modern Media Initiative?'

'That's correct – the right of you guys to protect your sources. The judge is thinking about it: I can't guarantee that he won't grant the search warrant, but I might be able to protect your computers.'

'The computers are safe. Encrypted. Unbreakable.'

'Hmm.' Viktor looked thoughtful. 'We might let them have that then – a good bargaining chip. But you should make sure the house is clean in case they do get a warrant.'

'OK. You hear that, everyone? If you have made any notes or printed out anything you shouldn't have done, I want it burned in the next thirty minutes.'

'And the ashes flushed down the toilet,' said Dieter.

'I've got some notes,' said Zivah. 'Translations of the audio.'

'That definitely needs to be destroyed,' said Erika.

'If you need to keep anything, I can scan it in first and we'll back it up remotely,' Dieter said.

Erika looked around her new team: Viktor, Zivah, Dúddi, Franz, Ásta. Which, if any, of them had fifteen thousand euros? Viktor was the obvious candidate. The best way to play him was to make an appeal to all of them and hope he might approach her later. She hated taking advantage of volunteers like this, but there was no choice.

She explained Freeflow's financial situation and their requirements for the next few days. Ásta immediately agreed to provide groceries, as did Dúddi, who also said he would come up with any necessary computer equipment. The idea of either of them coughing up fifteen thousand euros was clearly absurd.

'I can cover your air fare to London,' said Viktor.

'Thank you,' said Erika coolly. She held his gaze.

He wasn't going to offer more, she could see that. A few hundred dollars, but not thousands. He would twist arms and call in favours with his well-placed friends, but he wouldn't give Freeflow real money.

Was that because he didn't have any? Erika had heard of Iceland's *kreppa*. She imagined that there were many middle-class lawyers and businessmen who were overwhelmed by debt. Was Viktor one of them? Or did he have tens of thousands stashed away somewhere?

She could see in his eyes that he wasn't going to tell her.

'I've only got a few thousand shekels in my savings account,' said Zivah. 'About a thousand dollars, maybe a bit more. You can have that if you really need it.'

'That's great, Zivah,' said Erika with a smile. 'Thank you. It's a start. We have to begin somewhere.'

She glanced at Franz, the Swiss guy. Maybe he would be good for another couple of thousand? She had never met him before; he was a contact of Dieter's from somewhere on the Internet. He was in his early twenties, short, with curly black hair and a chubby face. If he wasn't still a student, he couldn't have been out of college for more than a year or two.

'I don't even have that much,' said Franz. 'I could give you maybe five hundred euros.'

Erika smiled weakly. She knew even that amount could be a lot of money for a young guy.

She glanced at Viktor again. He looked down at his tanned hands.

Silence.

He wasn't going to be shamed into giving money he didn't want to. Tight bastard!

'OK, everyone,' Erika said eventually. 'Get rid of the written evidence first. Then give your laptops to Dieter. And then we'll get to work on the video.'

The group broke up.

'Oh, by the way,' Erika said. 'Just before he died, Nico came up with a code name for the video.' She paused. 'Project Meltwater.'

CHAPTER NINE

MAGNUS'S PHONE RANG. He grabbed it. He had been waiting for Rannveig's call since he had returned from the Commissioner's office.

'OK, I've done a deal,' said Rannveig. 'I have a warrant to search the house *and* their computers.'

'Well done!'

'The agreement is that we can question the Freeflow team for a few hours today on the premises. They are not obliged to answer any questions about the project they are currently working on. We are not allowed to examine any documents or computer files relating to this project. After today we have to leave them alone unless there is a compelling reason to interview them again. And if we do that, we do it at the house, we don't take them to the station. Unless they are under arrest, of course.'

'Once we have mirrored their hard disks, I don't see how they can stop us from figuring out what they are working on,' said Magnus. 'Just from file titles or e-mail subject lines. And that's all we need. We don't need the details.'

'That's what I thought,' said Rannveig.

'So, what are we waiting for?' said Magnus. 'We're on our way.'

'I'll meet you there,' said Rannveig. 'Viktor is at the house and I'm sure he's going to be hovering over you. I want to make sure he sticks to his side of the deal.'

Magnus, Árni and Vigdís all went in one car, with Magnus driving. Árni was still sulking from the harsh words Magnus had had with him over his behaviour the night before. Magnus had promised the Commissioner he would talk to Árni, and talk to him he had. But Magnus knew Árni's sulk wouldn't last long: he got into trouble too frequently to let it bother him overmuch.

'I wonder about that guy Franz,' Magnus said. 'I'm curious about where he was when the others were up on the volcano. Maybe he knows more about the snowmobilers.'

'Now we've had the press conference we should hear from them soon,' Vigdís said.

'If they are innocent,' said Magnus. 'It will be more interesting if we *don't* hear from them.'

He turned up the hill towards the Hallgrímskirkja and braked as a woman on a bicycle shot out of a side road right in front of him at high speed. It wasn't just the drivers in Reykjavík who were dangerous nutters.

'I should get a transfer to the Traffic Department,' Magnus said. 'Sort some of these guys out.'

'They'd pedal rings round you, Magnús,' said Vigdís with a laugh. 'You'd never catch them.'

'So, is it this week you're going to Paris, Vigdís?' Árni asked.

'Yeah. Tomorrow. Boy, am I looking forward to it.'

'You meeting the guy from New York?' Magnus said. 'Daníel?'

'Yes. And his name's Davíd.'

'Oh, yeah. Sorry.' Davíd was some kind of television executive in New York, originally from Vigdís's home town of Keflavík, although according to Vigdís they had only met for the first time the year before. 'How's that going?'

'Transatlantic relationships are tough,' said Vigdís.

'Especially when you cancel on the guy all the time,' Árni said. Davíd had come back to Iceland at Christmas, ostensibly to see his parents, but really to see Vigdís. Which he had failed to do. She had been caught up in a rape investigation that took a week of intense work to solve. She had got her man: the rapist had been found guilty in March, but it was clear Davíd hadn't been impressed.

'He understands,' Vigdís said. 'And I'll make it up to him in Paris.'

'Lucky guy,' said Árni.

Magnus agreed, but decided it was best not to say so. 'Look, Vigdís. On the off chance we don't have this case wrapped up by dinnertime, don't cancel your trip. We'll manage without you.'

'Great to be missed,' said Vigdís. But she couldn't help a smile spreading across her face.

'Here we are.' Magnus pulled into a space a few yards from the house on Thórsgata. He saw Rannveig striding purposefully up the street from the other direction in her lawyer's trouser suit. He rapped loudly on the door.

It was opened by Viktor. Magnus suppressed the urge to barge past him and waited for Rannveig, who handed Viktor the warrant. He took his time reading it. Magnus slowed right down, controlled his impatience. He was not going to let this asshole wind him up.

Viktor glanced at him. 'All right, you may come in.'

The living space was full of computer equipment. Magnus recognized everyone from the night before; he noted there were no new additions.

'Right!' he said. 'Can I have your attention? In a few minutes a team will be here to search your house and any computers we find. We won't take the computers away, but we will mirror the hard drives, which means taking a copy of everything on them. The sooner you cooperate with us, the sooner we can leave you alone. And, more importantly, the sooner we can find whoever it was who killed your friend.'

Magnus turned to Viktor. 'OK, everyone should wait in the kitchen area. Is there a bedroom where we can conduct the interviews? I'd like to start with Erika again.'

'Sure,' said Viktor.

Magnus's phone rang. He answered. 'Magnús.'

'It's Edda.'

Magnus picked up the hint of excitement in the forensics team leader's voice. 'What have you found?'

'Much as we thought. There is a lot of junk under the snow, and we have no way of telling who dropped it. But we did isolate the rock the assailant tried to strike Erika with. And there is a fibre of some kind on it.'

'Any chance you can get any DNA?' Magnus asked.

'Impossible to say with the naked eye. But you should take DNA samples from all the witnesses and bring in the clothes they were wearing yesterday, especially gloves.'

'I'm with them now,' said Magnus. 'We'll do that. Let me know if you find anything else.'

There was another knock on the door: it was a team of uniformed police officers plus another member of the forensics unit. Magnus gave them instructions, and a couple of minutes later he was crammed into a small bedroom with Rannveig, Viktor and Erika. It looked out over a scrappy garden at the back. Some personal touches from the owners of the property remained: bright yellow curtains and some artistic photographs of Icelandic horses galloping along beaches. A sleeping bag was rolled up in a corner.

Erika and Viktor sat on the bed, at different ends, and Rannveig and Magnus took the two chairs.

Erika looked very cool and composed, as if she was just about to begin a difficult business meeting or negotiation.

Magnus didn't like that.

'You were very nearly killed yesterday, Erika,' he began.

Erika nodded.

'And your friend *was* killed.'

'That's right.' *And I couldn't give a damn*, her expression seemed to say.

Well, Magnus gave a damn.

'So I'd like you to do everything you can to help us find who killed him.'

'Sure, I'll do that.'

'Provided you don't ask her about what Freeflow are working on now,' said Viktor.

Magnus ignored him. 'OK. I would guess that Freeflow has some enemies. Can we go through them?'

'All right,' said Erika. 'I've been thinking about that. You're correct; we have a lot of enemies. The Chinese, the Zimbabweans, the Sudanese, some people in Belgium, lots of powerful Italians, a big German bank, a whole bunch of American frat boys, and probably some other people we've pissed off along the way. But the guy I saw on the mountain wasn't Asian and he wasn't African, so that narrows it down a bit.'

'Maybe,' said Magnus. 'But there's nothing to stop these people paying a white guy to do their dirty work.'

'I really can't imagine the Sudanese doing that.'

'Well, let's go through them one by one. We'll figure out the likely candidates once we've done that.'

Magnus spent the next twenty minutes writing down details of the various entities Freeflow had exposed. It was an impressive list, and most of them deserved to have their dirty washing aired. There was no doubt that the Italians were top of the list of suspects. Stirring up corrupt politicians and organized crime in the land which gave the world the word 'Mafia' was clearly a dangerous activity.

'Was Nico involved in the Italian leak at all?' Magnus asked. 'He was Italian, after all.'

'No. It was before his time: he wasn't part of the team then.'

'OK. What about the Chinese?' Magnus asked.

'That's an interesting one,' said Erika. 'The main reason they hate us is that we eavesdropped on *their* eavesdropping. They have been harvesting information from the Internet for years using weaknesses in the Tor nodes. We saw what they were getting and helped ourselves to it. Since then they have been trying to break into our own computer systems. You could say we are at war with them. But it's a war in cyberspace, not the real world.'

'I see. And the CIA? Nothing you have said so far seems to affect the CIA directly.'

'No. But we know that it has also been trying to hack into our network. And I have been followed many times.'

'Were you followed when you arrived here yesterday?'

'No, I don't think so. I did look. But of course, if people like the CIA really don't want you to see them, you won't.'

The ideal adversary for the paranoid. An enemy so clever you could never detect them. A little bit like Iceland's hidden people; you didn't want to get on the wrong side of them.

'Why are you smiling?' asked Erika. 'I *know* I have been followed in the past. And, as you say, someone died yesterday.'

'Sorry,' said Magnus. She had a point. 'There's one more possibility we should add to this list of enemies.'

'Who?'

'Whoever will be upset by what you are working on right now,' Magnus said.

'We've agreed not to discuss this,' Viktor said. 'Rannveig?'

Erika held up her hand. 'The attack on Nico and me has nothing to do with that,' she said.

'How do you know?'

'Because the people we are about to expose don't know we are about to expose them. That's why we are not telling you who they are.'

'Are you sure they don't know?'

'Absolutely sure.'

Magnus looked at her doubtfully. 'How can you be?'

'We're good with secrets,' Erika said.

Magnus wasn't convinced, but he changed tack. 'OK, what about people within Freeflow? Do you have any enemies? Did Nico?'

Erika raised her eyebrows. Magnus could tell the idea had genuinely never occurred to her. 'No. We've had disagreements about policy, plenty of disagreements. And I tend to get my way on those. We've had a couple of volunteers drop out last year. But no one who would have a reason to kill.'

'What about the people here? Are any of them your enemies?'

Erika laughed. 'No. Dieter and I have worked closely together since Freeflow started. I came here to Iceland last November and that's when I met Dúddi and Viktor. We're very much on the same side.'

'And Nico?'

Erika allowed herself a small smile. 'Everyone liked Nico. And we all needed him. He was the guy who drummed up the cash.'

Magnus nodded. 'Tell me about Franz. What do you know about him?'

'Very little,' said Erika. 'He comes from Zurich. I think he's a friend of Dieter's. He's just a typical volunteer. This is the first time I've met him.'

'And Zivah Malach? Why do you have an Israeli on the team?'

'Our volunteers come from all over the world,' said Erika. 'It's the same story with her. And the Icelandic priest. Never met either of them before.'

Magnus studied Erika. That left him looking for a couple of Italian heavies, probably called Luigi and Salvatore, wandering around a glacier in raincoats with their hats pulled over their eyes, making offers that Freeflow couldn't refuse.

Well, they would follow that line of inquiry, but Magnus was sure it wasn't the only one.

'OK, Erika. Thanks for your help.'

Erika stood up from the bed. As she was leaving the room, Magnus stopped her.

'One more thing. I strongly suggest that you and your team spend as much time as possible indoors,' he said. 'We'll have people watching the house. Whoever tried to kill you before may try again. No need to make it easy for them.'

Magnus noticed the fear flash in Erika's eyes, but then it was gone. One brave woman, he thought.

'Of course,' she said. 'And that will give you the perfect opportunity to keep an eye on us.'

'So it will,' said Magnus with a grin. But he was glad she wasn't dumb enough to turn down the offer of protection.

Magnus checked downstairs. The searchers hadn't found anything apart from some ash in the bathroom. Burned paper, they said. Magnus was not amused.

Computers were propped up next to other computers, whirring away. A guy of about thirty in jeans and a T-shirt was crouching down beside them. It took Magnus a moment to realize that he was with the police rather than Freeflow.

'Hi,' he said when he saw Magnus. 'My name is Ossi. Computer Forensics.'

Magnus shook his hand. 'Magnús.' He lowered his voice so the Freeflow team couldn't overhear him. 'Do you think you'll recover anything?'

'I don't know,' said Ossi. 'It's all password protected, of course. Ordinarily that wouldn't necessarily be a problem, but I suspect that simply typing in "1, 2, 3, 4" won't open sesame with this lot.'

Magnus glanced over to the Freeflow group sitting at the dining table drinking coffee. The big German guy, Dieter, shook his head, smiled and winked at them.

'No, I have a feeling it is not going to be easy to get into these machines,' Ossi said. 'Keep your eyes open for passwords when you search the house.'

Magnus left him to it, and instructed Vigdís and Árni to interview Zivah and then Dúddi in one of the other rooms.

'Franz Freitag?' Magnus addressed the Swiss student. 'Come with me, please.' He led the student and Rannveig back upstairs. Viktor began to follow them.

'Sorry,' Magnus said. 'You can't join us.'

'But I'm his lawyer.'

'No, you are Erika Zinn's lawyer. Perhaps Freeflow's lawyer. But you are not Mr Freitag's lawyer.'

'Come on! There can't possibly be a conflict.'

Franz had stopped on the stairs and was watching the discussion with interest. They were speaking in English.

'There certainly can,' said Magnus. 'Your client was nearly killed yesterday. This man spent some time unaccompanied on the volcano at the time she was attacked.'

'Are you saying he's a suspect?'

'Not yet. But he might become one. In which case he shouldn't have you acting for him. Right, Rannveig?'

Rannveig nodded. 'Don't worry, I'll ensure we keep to our agreement. But there could be a clear conflict between your client's interests and the witness's.'

Viktor looked nonplussed. 'Then he should have his own representation.'

'If he wishes,' said Magnus. 'That will, of course, take a while to set up.'

Viktor's frown deepened. Magnus knew Viktor and Erika wanted the police out of the house as soon as possible so that they could get on with whatever they were there to do.

'I tell you what, let's ask him,' Magnus said. 'Do you want us to find you a lawyer, Franz?'

Franz glanced at Viktor and then turned back to Magnus. 'You said I might be a suspect. I'm not a suspect, right?'

'It all depends what you tell us,' Magnus said.

Franz took a deep breath. 'I don't need a lawyer, actually. Once I tell you what happened I'm sure you'll realize I'm not involved.'

'Let's go then,' said Magnus.

The bedroom felt less cramped with only three people rather than four. Magnus examined Franz's red Swiss passport with its little white cross in the top right-hand corner. François André Freitag, born Genève, 23 October 1985. The photograph must have been taken when Franz was eighteen, but he didn't seem to have aged much in the last six years, except perhaps put on some weight. His round pale face was more that of a kid than a young man.

'Tell me how you got to know Freeflow?' Magnus began.

'When I was at high school I had gotten interested in Darfur,' Franz said. 'It was a cause I got really fired up about. I still am, actually. Like I can't believe that the world can watch while hundreds of thousands of people sit in camps in the desert waiting to die of hunger or cholera or be raped by gangsters.'

'I can see that,' said Magnus.

'So, when Freeflow came out with the leak about the British, French and Americans agreeing not to intervene, I was really angry. And I took some notice where the leak came from. I began to follow what Freeflow were doing; I thought it was pretty cool. Eventually I got in touch with them to see if I could help. I've done a few things for Dieter over the last year or so: cleaning up some of the links on the site, making sure the formats are consistent, proofing the content.'

'Do you know him well?'

'Reasonably well – but only online. This is the first time I've met him offline. I think he trusts me now, which is why I am here. A couple of days ago, he asked me to come to Iceland. It was short notice, but I thought it was a great opportunity for me.'

'What about the others? Erika? Nico?'

'I've read about Erika, of course, but never met her until yesterday. Same with Nico.'

'What about work?'

'There's not much of that around,' Franz said. 'I graduated from university last summer. Since then I've been waiting tables and doing some work for a video-production company in Zurich. Music videos, mostly. Cheap ones.'

'You speak pretty good English,' Magnus said. 'Where did you learn it?'

'University. I spent a year at Ohio State in Columbus. I had a blast.'

'Glad to hear it,' said Magnus. 'And what do you do for Freeflow?'

'I'm what you might call a general-purpose hacker,' Franz said. 'I'm no genius like Dieter, but I know my way around computers and I can pull all-nighters if necessary.'

'And have you had any disputes with Freeflow over anything?'

'No,' said Franz, puzzled. 'What kind of disputes?'

Magnus let it drop. 'OK, can you tell me exactly what you did up by the volcano yesterday?'

Franz went through the drive up the glacier to Fimmvörduháls, and how he followed the others up towards the rim. He said that he dawdled at the foot of the bank of cooling lava because he was fascinated by it. When he got up to the rim, he was a bit of a distance away from the others. As soon as it started to snow he went right back down to the jeep. On the way he bumped into the two snowmobilers.

'Did you talk to them?'

'Yeah,' said Franz. 'Didn't say much, just how cool the volcano was.'

'Can you describe them?'

'Sure. They were both in their thirties, I would say. One was an Icelander, the other was French. The Icelander was, like, medium height, round glasses. The French guy was older, a bit taller, with a bit of a gut, you know? Dark hair, I think, but he was wearing a hat. Wore a bright red ski jacket.'

'Did you see where they had come from, where they were going to?'

Franz shook his head. 'They were kind of going around the volcano, I think. I don't really remember.'

'Would you recognize them again?'

'I think so. Probably the French guy. Not sure about the Icelander. It was hard to see much of his face in those conditions.'

'How do you know he was French?' Magnus asked.

'We spoke in French. I mean I started off in English, but he wasn't very good at it and I could tell he had a French accent. The Icelander spoke French too.'

'And you?' Magnus was aware that French and German were spoken in Switzerland, but he wasn't sure whether everyone spoke both.

'My father is Swiss German, but my mother was a French speaker. François is a French name, of course, but I call myself Franz.'

'I see.' The French weren't on the list of Freeflow's victims. 'Is there any chance that this man could have been an Italian speaking French?'

'No, his accent was perfect. And he looked French, if you see what I mean.'

Magnus had no sense of what a Frenchman on a volcano would look like as opposed to an Italian, but he believed Franz did, or at least thought he did. In fact, Franz was turning into quite a credible and helpful witness.

He had an idea.

'Rannveig, I wonder if you could see how the search is getting on?'

The assistant prosecutor didn't miss a beat. 'Of course,' she said. 'You seem to be doing fine here.'

After she had left, Magnus stared hard at Franz. 'We only have your word about where you were on the mountain. Until we locate the snowmobilers we can't corroborate your story.'

Franz frowned. 'You don't really think I killed Nico? I mean, Erika saw the guy who did it, didn't she? And it wasn't me.'

'That's right. But you could have spoken to the people who did. Like your so-called Frenchman, for example.'

Franz thought for a moment. 'All I can do is tell you the truth. I have to rely on you to figure out that it is the truth.'

Dead right, thought Magnus. But he needed to up the pressure a bit. 'Until we've confirmed your story we might have to take you into custody.'

'Is that why you got rid of the lawyer?' Franz said. 'To threaten me?'

'Not exactly,' said Magnus. 'We need to know what Freeflow is working on right now.'

'I won't tell you that,' said Franz. 'It would be betraying the others.'

'They wouldn't know it came from you,' said Magnus. 'I can guarantee that.'

'And why should I trust your guarantee?' said Franz.

'Let me tell you how things work in Iceland,' Magnus said. 'People who are arrested on a murder charge don't get bail here. If I were to arrest you in the next couple of minutes, you'd go to the prison at Litla Hraun where they would throw you into solitary confinement. We'd keep you there for three weeks, and then, if a judge says so, we'd keep you for another three weeks, and another.'

'But I know I'm innocent,' said Franz.

'In which case you'll be let out eventually. Although sometimes I wonder about Iceland's record with foreigners. It's just so much easier to blame them for crimes.'

'So you are threatening me.'

'You got it.'

Franz's expression was unchanged. But Magnus could see he was thinking it over.

'Is it something to do with the US?' Magnus asked.

Franz didn't respond. But his eyes locked on to Magnus's. Encouraging him perhaps?

'France?'

No movement.

'Switzerland?' After all, Franz *was* Swiss. After Icelandic banks and German banks, the Swiss made sense next.

Nothing. But Franz's eyes were steady.

Magnus ran through the other volunteers in his mind. Then it came to him. The Israeli student Zivah Malach did not seem like your average computer hacker. What the hell was she doing with these people?

'Israel?'

Franz's eyes dipped downwards in a kind of ocular nod. 'Actually, I can't help you any more,' he said.

'That's no problem.' Magnus smiled. 'You have been very cooperative.'

CHAPTER TEN

JÓHANNES PULLED UP outside the Hotel Búdir and switched off his engine. It was mid-afternoon; it had taken him two hours to drive up here from Reykjavík. The hotel was situated on the south side of the Snaefells Peninsula, a long, slightly crooked finger that stretched eighty kilometres out into the Atlantic from the west coast of Iceland. It was named after Snaefellsjökull, a smooth round glacier, fifteen hundred metres high at the western tip.

The glacier was free of clouds, its ice cap gleaming in the low afternoon sun. Beneath it slept a volcano that hadn't erupted for eighteen hundred years, but the glacier retained an aura that had inspired Icelanders and others for generations. Jules Verne had chosen Snaefellsjökull as his entrance to the centre of the earth. There were tales about a half-man, half-troll named Bárdur, who had been one of the first settlers in the area and given the glacier its name, 'Snow Fell', before disappearing into the glacier himself. More recently, New Age types had designated it one of the seven energy centres in the world and a frequent landing site for aliens.

Jóhannes preferred his tales medieval, but he couldn't deny the power of the glacier on the imagination. He had been transfixed by it when he had stayed at the Hotel Búdir on family holidays as a boy, as, of course, had his father, who had frequently taken two-week trips up here alone to write.

The hotel was all that was left of what once had been a thriving trading post, apart from the isolated black church a couple of hundred metres away. The hotel was perched at the mouth of a small river, with the glacier on one side and a broad sweeping beach on the other. A group of half a dozen horses and their riders were gliding across the sands in a *tölt*: the rapid smooth trot known only to the Icelandic horse. To the north, stretching eastwards from the glacier, was a ridge of forbidding mountains, and on the other side of those was Hraun, Jóhannes's father's childhood home.

The air was fresh and crisp and the sea sparkled blue, tossing gentle waves on to the sand. There were clouds dashing about the sky, but for the moment they were not obscuring sun or mountain.

Jóhannes entered the quiet hotel lobby and asked for the manager, to whom he had spoken after he had received the letter from his former pupil. Hermann, the head groom, was out with some guests on the sands, but would be back soon.

Jóhannes strolled outside to wait for the horses. After ten minutes they were back at the stables and Jóhannes waited another ten minutes until the guests were dismounted and the horses returned to their stalls.

A broad-shouldered man in his forties with a thick dark beard seemed to be in charge. Jóhannes approached him.

'Hermann?'

'Yes?' The voice was gruff, but the blue eyes were friendly.

'My name is Jóhannes Benediktsson. My father Benedikt Jóhannesson used to be a regular visitor here.'

'Yes, yes, I remember him,' said the groom. 'Although that was a long time ago.'

'And you remember Halldór Laxness, no doubt?'

'Yes.' Hermann lifted up a saddle and took it into a tack room. Jóhannes followed him. He avoided Jóhannes's glance.

'A letter has just come to my attention from Halldór to a friend of his. Apparently Halldór was staying here in 1985 when he saw my father and a man with a shotgun having an argument. He says you broke it up. He mentions you by name.'

'Does he now?' said Hermann. He dumped the saddle and turned towards Jóhannes, his eyes wary.

'I wonder if you could tell me a bit more about it.'

Hermann hesitated. Then he nodded. 'All right,' he said. 'Although there is not much to tell. I was sixteen, something like that. Halldór was very old at that stage. Like your father he had been a regular visitor to the hotel in the past; he used to write some of his books here. I read one of them: *Under the Glacier*. Couldn't make head nor tail of it.'

'I'm not surprised,' said Jóhannes dryly.

'Anyway, he got it in his head he wanted to get on a horse again. He must have been in his eighties at least, and he hadn't ridden for years.'

'Eighty-three,' said Jóhannes: Halldór Laxness's date of birth was part of his professional armoury.

'Sounds about right. It was a real struggle, but I got him up into the saddle in the end, and we rode up to the church and on into the lava field. Just at a walk, you know. We hadn't gone far when he pointed to a couple of figures in a hollow by the shore. One of them had a shotgun. Their voices were raised, I could hear, although the old man couldn't. He did a good job to notice them before me.

'So, I left Halldór there and rode down to see what was going on. One of the men was your father, Benedikt – he had been staying at the hotel for a couple of weeks, writing. The other was a poacher. When the poacher saw me he backed off.'

'Can you show me where this was?' asked Benedikt.

'Sure,' said Hermann. 'Follow me.'

They left the stables and walked around the hotel up to the little church. All around them stretched the lava field. This was a broad extent of stone criss-crossed with folds and crevices, in the middle of which, about two kilometres away, rose a large crater. Jóhannes remembered the scene well. There were no berserkers in this lava field, unlike the one near the farm at Hraun, but there were hidden people, that parallel race of invisible beings that Icelanders believed shared their country with them, living in rocks or, in this case, tunnels. A concealed lava tunnel lined with gold and precious jewels was supposed to lead from this spot a hundred kilometres to the mountains to the east. Jóhannes smiled as he remembered clambering around the rocks with his father looking for it.

'Do you know what the argument was about?'

'No. Your father didn't tell me. I was only a boy, remember. I assume that your father had confronted the poacher and asked him what he was doing.'

'So what happened then?'

'Your father looked shaken. He went straight back to the hotel and checked out. I went back up to where I had left Halldór.' Hermann paused. 'Look, it was down there.' He pointed down to a grassy hollow in the stone, not far from the shore. It was exposed, but out of sight of the hotel or the road. 'And in fact Halldór and I were right here when we saw them.'

'I see,' said Jóhannes. 'And the poacher?'

'Must have gone straight back up to the road, I suppose. I don't really remember.'

'You know that my father was murdered a few weeks later?' Jóhannes said.

'Yes, I do,' said Hermann.

'I wonder if there was any connection. Did the police talk to you about this?'

'As a matter of fact they did. A tall miserable bastard from Reykjavík. They said that Halldór had contacted them. I told them then what I am telling you now.'

'And did you recognize the man?'

'No. Never seen him before. That's what I told the police.' Hermann's voice was firm and strong, but his eyes flicked quickly to one side. Jóhannes raised his eyebrows. Hermann held his gaze but touched his left ear bricfly.

There was no ill discipline in any of Jóhannes's classes. Ever. He had numerous tricks up his sleeve, but one of them was an unerring ability to tell when a child was lying to him. Keeping silent and raising the eyebrows was the clincher. The liars always cracked then.

Hermann might be a grown man in his forties, but Jóhannes knew he was lying.

'Look, Hermann,' Jóhannes said. 'It was a long time ago, and you were only a kid. You didn't like the policeman who was asking you questions. So you lied then – I understand that. But this is my father we are talking about now and I need to find out what happened to him. It's all a long time ago. Halldór Laxness is dead. My father is dead. Maybe the man with the shotgun is dead. But please tell me who he was.'

'Are you suggesting I was lying?'

Jóhannes raised his eyebrows again.

Hermann sighed and pursed his lips. Jóhannes waited.

'You're right,' the groom said. 'It was a long time ago. I wondered how I got away with it. This is hardly the most crowded part of the country: of course I knew who it was. I knew who everyone was. And why shouldn't I tell you now?'

Jóhannes returned his smile. 'So who was it?'

'My cousin from Bjarnarhöfn. Hallgrímur Gunnarsson.'

'Really?' said Jóhannes. 'And was he poaching?'

'No chance. There's no reason for Hallgrímur to come here to poach. He had his own perfectly good farm.'

'Bjarnarhöfn, eh? He and my father must have been neighbours when my father was a boy.'

'At Hraun, wasn't it?' said Hermann.

'Yes. My grandmother moved away to Stykkishólmur in the 1940s some time and my father went on to high school in Reykjavík. So why didn't you tell the police who he was?'

'He was family and at that time my family were all pretty angry with your father. And I was scared of Hallgrímur. He came to see me the next day and warned me not to talk to anyone about it.'

'You were scared of him then, but not now?'

'I was sixteen then and he was in his fifties. He was a mean bastard, still is, I suspect, but now he's got to be in his eighties.

I haven't seen him for several years, not since my uncle's funeral. He is my father's cousin, that's the exact relationship.'

'So this Hallgrímur is still alive?'

'Oh, yes. I would have heard if he'd died.'

'You said that your family were angry with Dad?'

'Yes. He'd written something in a book which seemed to suggest that his father had had an affair with Hallgrímur's mother, and then Hallgrímur's father had killed him and dumped him in the lake. I think that's right.'

'*Moor and the Man*?' said Jóhannes.

'I don't know. I didn't read the book. But it got my father very upset, and Hallgrímur, of course.'

'So that's why this man Hallgrímur was threatening my father with a shotgun?'

'Yes. I think he was telling him not to make up any more tales about our family. Wait a moment.' Hermann paused, running his fingers through his beard.

'Yes?'

'I remember now. He said something about some other story Benedikt had written. About how someone had killed someone else.'

'Really? Can you remember the name of the story?'

Hermann shook his head. 'No chance. And I can't remember who had killed who. Maybe Hallgrímur's father was supposed to have murdered somebody else as well? I don't know.'

'Did your family talk about this other story?'

'No. Just Hallgrímur that once.'

Jóhannes looked down towards the hollow, wondering what that story could be. Benedikt had published a collection just before he died, it might be one of those.

'Didn't it occur to you that Hallgrímur might have killed my father?' Jóhannes said.

'No, not at the time. I mean, that happened in Reykjavík, didn't it? And Hallgrímur was family. But you know, he is mean. He always has been. He could have done it, I suppose.' Hermann grimaced. 'Killed him.'

'Would you speak to the police now?'

Hermann scratched his head. 'Would I get into trouble for lying to them all those years ago?'

Jóhannes shrugged. 'I don't know. But if you did do something wrong then, this would be a way of putting it right.'

Hermann sucked through his teeth, and looked up towards the shimmering glacier. 'I might,' he said. 'I'm not saying I would, but I might.'

'Thanks.' Jóhannes held out his hand. 'Thank you very much.'

As Hermann made his way back to the stables, Jóhannes stood outside the lonely little church, his brain racing.

He was getting somewhere! He was genuinely getting somewhere. Halldór Laxness's letter was dated 14 November 1985, about six weeks before his father had been murdered. What if Hallgrímur had not been merely threatening Benedikt, what if he had been about to shoot him when Hermann had interrupted them?

But would a man in the 1980s kill another man over something that had happened fifty years before? It was 1934 when Jóhannes's grandfather and namesake had disappeared from Hraun. And the revenge motive was the wrong way around. Hallgrímur's father had been slandered, perhaps, but it was Benedikt's father who had actually been killed.

Unless this other story held a clue.

Jóhannes looked up at the small black church, with the figures 1847 etched in iron under the cross on its roof, its churchyard surrounded by a turf-covered wall with a white wooden gate. All around was a breathtaking view: the fjord to the south, the lava field to the west, mountains to the east and north, and to the north-west, only a few kilometres away, floated the mystical glacier. The clouds had lifted to reveal the volcano, an almost perfect cone, snow covering the permanent ice at its summit. At the very peak was a hooked pinnacle of rock, a stone thorn piercing the ice cap.

He looked at the rows of gravestones and for a moment wished that he had buried his father here. The old man would have loved to spend eternity in this spot. As would he, for that matter.

He ran through Benedikt's short story collection in his mind. They were much less well known than the novels, especially *Moor and the Man*, but Jóhannes had read them all many times.

'The Slip'! That must be it. It was only a few pages long, but it described how a boy took revenge over the rape of his sister by pushing the rapist off a cliff. If that was the case, then who had been raped? And who had been pushed?

Jóhannes remembered the words from *The Saga of Grettir the Strong*: 'A tale is half told when one man tells it.' He had his own relatives he could speak to: his aunt Hildur was still alive and living in Stykkishólmur, the nearest town to Hraun. And there were cousins there as well. If there was a family feud buried somewhere, they might be able to give him a clue as to where or what it was. He liked his aunt and hadn't seen her for a couple of years. Time to pay her a visit.

He checked his watch. It was not yet four. It would take less than an hour to get to Stykkishólmur, plenty of time to get back to Reykjavík that evening so that he could go in to school the following morning.

School! How he had loved that place. But not any more.

He surveyed the glacier, the lava field, the sea and the beach beyond the hotel. It was wonderful to be outside Reykjavík in the fresh air on a school day. It was at least five years since he had taken a day off sick. He remembered again how he had spent long days with his father and his brother and sister here, looking for the hidden people's tunnel of jewels. There was the crater and ruined houses and holes in the cliffs where the waves rushed in and leaped up against rock walls. And further to the west was the farm where Gudrídur the Wanderer had been brought up: the extraordinary woman who had been born in Iceland, married in Greenland, had a child in America, returned to Iceland and then gone on a pilgrimage to Rome.

All kinds of wonders.

He struck out across the rock and moss towards the crater in the centre of the lava field. He would treat himself to a night at the Hotel Búdir and see his relatives in Stykkishólmur tomorrow. And sod school.

CHAPTER ELEVEN

THE MAN HAD been sitting in the car for hours, but he wasn't tired.

His vehicle was parked in the car park to the side of the great church, facing west. Ahead of him was a statue of a Viking staring off towards the Atlantic, behind which was a hotel, the Leifur Eiríksson. Just to the left of the hotel a small road ran downhill. Thórsgata.

He had followed the tortuous one-way system through the warren of streets that tangled themselves around the slope of the hill down towards the Parliament Square and the lake in the centre of the city. It was odd: these must be some of the most expensive properties in town, but they had corrugated metal roofs. And where there wasn't metal there was concrete. No wood. No brick.

The trouble was Thórsgata was just a little too quiet. He couldn't park in the street itself in sight of the house that Freeflow had taken over without attracting attention. There was a marked police car opposite the building, and the officer inside was looking around.

Which posed a problem. Someone leaving the house could either turn left uphill, in which case they would pass in sight of him parked outside the big church, or else they could turn right, downhill, in which case he would never spot them.

He couldn't see a way around this. He would just have to take the fifty-fifty chance of missing them. He glanced at his phone resting on the passenger's seat next to him. That would help.

Many cars had passed up Thórsgata that afternoon: police, marked and unmarked; press; TV; and no doubt some legitimate inhabitants of the street, wondering what the hell was going on.

The man had brought a magazine, but he was too wired to read it. He kept his eyes on the entrance to Thórsgata and waited.

The moment the last policemen was out of the door, Freeflow got down to work, which for most of the team meant powering up their computers. It was pretty clear that the police had not found anything of value, although they had taken the clothes everyone was wearing the night before for analysis. After some discussion, Erika and Viktor had agreed to allow the team to give DNA swabs, and the others had complied. The police had been considerate: they had left the place in more or less the same mess it had been in when they arrived.

'Hold on, hold on,' Dieter said, interrupting the activity. 'Everyone turn off their computers. Now.'

'Why?' Erika asked, but as soon as she uttered the question she knew the answer.

'We don't know what little bugs they've planted in them.'

'They're not allowed to do that,' said Viktor.

'Governments do a lot of things they are not allowed to,' said Erika. 'That's why Freeflow exists. Can't you check them out?'

'It would take far too long,' said Dieter. 'And even then, I might miss something. We are going to need brand-new machines.'

'Oh, Christ,' said Erika. 'That's going to delay us some more.'

'And cost money,' said Dieter.

'How much?' asked Viktor.

'I don't know. A few thousand dollars. We can get by mostly with netbooks,' said Dieter. 'I'll need a more powerful laptop. All the software we need is stored remotely.'

'Probably a good idea to get some prepaid cell phones as well,' said Erika. 'I've got a couple, but they could be compromised.'

'OK,' said Viktor. 'Give me a list, and I'll go with Dúddi to buy whatever you need right away.'

'We should discuss nothing related to Project Meltwater aloud,' Dieter said. 'Only by chat. They could have planted listening devices in the house.'

'No. Dieter, that's ridiculous,' Erika said. 'It will be impossible to get any meaningful work done that way. The whole reason we came to this godforsaken country in the first place was so we could talk face to face.'

'My country might be godforsaken,' Viktor said, 'but it isn't a police state. I know the judge who granted the search warrants. Bugs like that would need a warrant from him, and if he had granted one I would know about it. And the Police Commissioner is a smart guy: he wouldn't want to risk getting caught planting unauthorized listening devices. In fact, I doubt very much they have bugged the computers.'

'No way are we using those computers now that the police have been all over them,' Dieter said.

'OK,' Erika said. 'We get new computers. But we have to assume the house itself isn't bugged. And, Viktor, thank you so much for buying the new machines. This is an important thing you are doing here. It *will* make a difference.'

Erika wondered why Viktor had dug into his pocket this time. Perhaps it was the urgency of the situation, or maybe just the smaller amount that was required. Either way she was grateful. She smiled at him, giving it the full force of her conviction. Viktor was clearly touched. They always were, in the end. He was a handsome man, much smoother than her normal type. He probably had a beautiful blonde wife at home, but then he might like a change. Many men did.

But Freeflow still needed fifteen thousand euros for the Swedish ISP. Perhaps she'd leave it for a bit and try him again the next day. Never give up, that was the rule she lived by.

Something would turn up; it always did; if it didn't come from Viktor it would from someone else.

Dúddi and Viktor were quick. In less than an hour and a half they had returned with the computers and four prepaid phones and a handful of SIM cards. While Dieter supervised setting the machines up and downloading the backed-up software, Erika dialled Washington on one of the new phones.

'Alan? It's Erika.'

'Hey, what's up? Where are you? I don't recognize the country code on your phone number, not that that means anything.'

'Iceland,' Erika said. In the past she had used elaborate means to disguise which country she was in, but at that moment there was no point. 'What are you doing this week?'

Alan Traub was a freelance journalist in his fifties. He had been a staff reporter for the *Washington Post* for twenty years, but had parted company after one blazing row too many with the editor. He was a passionate believer in freedom of information and a great supporter of most of what Freeflow did. But he kept his distance, firmly maintaining his journalistic integrity. Which was fine with Erika. She trusted him and, by and large, he trusted her. And no, she had never slept with him.

'Something on US military aid to Pakistan.'

'Dull. How about a trip to London? Tonight.'

'And why would I want to go to London?'

'To speak with Samantha Wilton.'

'The sister of that woman who was killed in Gaza?' Alan said without hesitation. News seemed to go into Alan's brain and never come out.

'The very same.'

'What have you got? Something on her sister's death?'

'Yeah. Something she's gonna want to see.'

'Can you give me the details?'

'Not yet.' Erika waited for Alan's decision. But they both knew he wasn't going to say no.

'OK,' he said. 'But I get first crack at the story?'

‘Yeah. If your old buddies at the *Post* will still talk to you. Don’t worry, Alan, this one is going to be big.’ Despite his past disagreements with the paper, Alan Traub was a good entrée into the *Washington Post*. And this way the *Post* would pick up his expenses eventually. ‘We’re aiming for a press conference on Monday in London. I’ll be there, and your job is to get Samantha Wilton there as well. The *Post* will get the story first that morning with the *Guardian* in London. Probably *Der Spiegel* in Germany. I’d like you to fix up the press conference.’

‘I can do that.’

‘We also need someone to check out the Gaza angle. On the ground.’

‘On the ground? That’s going to be difficult, I’d say impossible in the time. I went there a couple of years ago. You need a permit from the Israeli government and that takes weeks.’

‘What about the other side? The Egyptian border?’

‘Rafah? I’m pretty sure that crossing is still closed. You’re going to have to use someone already there. And that means either a local journalist or someone at the UN. What exactly is it you need to check?’

‘I can’t be specific,’ Erika said. ‘Yet. But we have photographs of the incident. We need witnesses to corroborate them.’

‘I’ve got a buddy at Reuters who has been there plenty of times. I know he has good local sources. But then you’d have to cut Reuters in.’

Erika took a deep breath, thinking it over. The *Washington Post* wouldn’t like Reuters’ involvement. Nor would the *Guardian*.

Tough.

‘OK – give him a call. But from now on we do everything on Jabber. You remember the password you used last time?’

‘Got it.’

‘So can you get on a plane tonight?’

‘Sorry, Erika, not even for you. There’s some stuff I need to do here. But I can go tomorrow. I’ll be in touch as soon as I get to London.’

Erika hung up. She was pleased: she trusted Alan to get things done.

Things were moving.

'Here you are.' Dieter handed Erika a brand-new netbook computer. 'I've downloaded the software. You'll need to restore your files yourself using your own passwords.'

'That was quick.'

'There's a lot to do,' said Dieter.

Erika sat down and tapped in her password: 'janjaweedare_murd_eringBASTARDs'. She had found that mangling up a memorable line in this manner was the easiest way to create complex passwords. Dieter and Apex insisted on them being changed regularly. Soon her machine was chugging away, and within a couple of minutes her familiar screen settings were up.

There was a message already from Dieter: *what about zivah? could she be a mole from mossad? maybe she alerted them? i'm worried about her. should we send her back?*

Erika glanced up at Dieter, who was tapping furiously on his own laptop, headphones firmly clamped to his head, streaming music directly into his brain. Dieter always used chat when he could, rather than speaking face to face. It frustrated her, but she could hardly change his habits now.

'Zivah!' she called across to the Israeli student, who was typing on her own new netbook. 'Can I have a minute?'

Erika led her into their bedroom and shut the door. She sat on the bed, and Zivah took one of the chairs. Zivah managed to project a mixture of earnestness and innocence that Erika found appealing. She had short light brown hair and a thin, intelligent face. She looked nervous.

'Sorry to be so direct, Zivah, but I need to know. Can you think of any way that the Israeli government could have found out what we are up to?'

Zivah shook her head. 'Not from me, if that is what you are asking. I have no idea about the rest of the team, I don't know them at all.'

'Didn't you do military service?'

'Yes, everyone does it, but I had nothing to do with the security services,' Zivah said. 'Do you think it was Mossad who killed Nico?'

'I don't know,' said Erika. 'But it could be. We are messing with the Israeli government and that's always a dangerous thing to do.'

Zivah nodded and swallowed. 'I was thinking that.'

'Nico brought you on board here, right?'

'That's right,' said Zivah. 'I've been following Freeflow almost since you started – putting posts up on your message boards. Six months ago, Nico asked me to translate some stuff he'd been sent in Hebrew by an Israeli civil servant. It was about Israeli plans to attack Iranian nuclear facilities, but it wasn't really concrete enough to be interesting. And then he contacted me on Friday night about the video.'

'So you'd never met him before Sunday?'

'No,' said Zivah. 'Not in person. But I've been commenting online for years.'

'Yes, I recognize your name,' Erika frowned. Volunteers were managed by Dieter or Nico, depending on their role. Usually they were set unimportant tasks over a period of months, and then if they performed these well they were given more sensitive duties. In Zivah's case Nico had hardly done a thorough background check, but then he hadn't had time. If she was a plant the Israeli government would have had to have been very forward thinking to have tried to infiltrate Freeflow that early on.

'Are you studying?'

'I'm doing my masters in International Relations at Tel Aviv University.'

'Did you tell any of your friends where you were going?' Erika asked.

'No. I said I was doing something for Amnesty International in London and I would be out of contact for a few days. I said it was secret and I couldn't talk about it. Everyone knows I am heavily involved with Amnesty, so I think they believed me. And I did fly to Reykjavík via London.'

'You know that this video will seriously undermine your country's standing in the world?' Erika asked.

'I know that,' said Zivah.

'Yet you are happy to be a part of promoting it?' Erika allowed a hint of contempt in her voice to change the question into an accusation.

'I am,' Zivah said, her voice gaining in strength. 'I believe in my country passionately. I believe that Israel has a future, but only if we can live in peace with the Palestinians. And I believe that we of all people should recognize basic human rights. By and large I think we do. My brother is in the army; lots of my friends are. They are decent people who have shown great restraint in really difficult situations. They have told me about the fighting in Gaza, about how they didn't shoot back when they were attacked from schools or hospitals, about how they warned civilians before bombing buildings. A lot of these guys are now members of Combatants for Peace.'

'That's not what we saw in the video,' said Erika.

'Precisely!' said Zivah. Her cheeks were flushed now. 'And that's what the Israeli government needs to understand. We should be rooting out that kind of behaviour ourselves. And if the government won't do it, then I will. What about you?'

'Me?'

'Aren't you Jewish?'

'Yes, I am,' said Erika. 'And my family are passionate supporters of the state of Israel. I guess I agree with them: Israel should exist as a homeland for the Jews. I think that there are a lot of unscrupulous Arab terrorists who would like to destroy it. Releasing this video might help those terrorists.'

'So why didn't you bury it?' Zivah asked.

Erika took a deep breath. 'I believe that transparency of information is more important than my views or your views or the views of anyone out there. If governments are transparent, the bad stuff will come to light and a lot less of it will happen in the first place. And this video is bad stuff.'

'Very bad stuff.'

Erika stared hard at Zivah. She saw a lot of herself in the Israeli student; she didn't believe she was a Mossad agent. Erika's instinct was to trust her. And in Rwanda, in Darfur, during the frequent crises that beset Freeflow, Erika had learned to trust her own instincts. She was just smarter than other people; her intuition was more reliable.

Besides, she didn't have the time to do otherwise. They needed a Hebrew speaker, if not Zivah then someone else, and anyone else they found at short notice would be no less likely to be a spy.

'All right,' Erika said. 'One last question: if it turns out the Israelis are on to us, are you willing to stick it out?'

Zivah swallowed. Looked Erika straight in the eye. 'Yes,' she said. 'I believe in this. I'll stay.'

Erika smiled. 'Good. Now, back to work.'

She returned to her computer on a makeshift table and typed a simple message to Dieter: *zivah stays.*

She stared at her screen. Why had she brought up her own family? Her father she didn't care about. A cosmetic surgeon at a prestigious Manhattan clinic, he had disapproved of almost all of Erika's choices in life. Going to Rwanda as a student, returning with a husband, quitting med school to go to Darfur, divorcing the husband and finally publishing rumours and gossip on the Internet. He had given her all the opportunities she could possibly want and she had thrown them back in his face.

Erika's grandmother was of course very proud of her son, the doctor. But she was also proud of her granddaughter for standing up to him. She understood what Erika was doing and why she was doing it and Erika loved her for it.

A widow, nearly ninety now, she had left Poland for the United States as a girl in the 1930s and had met Erika's grandfather, a young émigré from Berlin, in Queens during the war. Her husband had worked hard and prospered; a passionate supporter of the state of Israel, he had been a regular giver to Zionist causes all his life.

Since his death twenty years before, his widow would occasionally criticize the more extremist right-wing factions in Israel, but never the state itself. Her husband and her ancestors had given up too much, fought too hard for her to betray their dream.

She would be dismayed at what Erika was doing. She might never forgive her. That would be difficult for Erika to bear.

The doorbell rang. The house froze.

'That's not the police, is it?' said Erika.

'If it is, I'll tell them to go away,' said Viktor. 'The agreement was they would leave us alone.'

'I'll answer it,' said Ásta.

She went to the door and opened it. Erika heard insistent questions asked in Icelandic and English. She recognized her own name.

Ásta came back inside and closed the door. 'It's RÚV. Icelandic TV. They want to speak to you, Erika.'

'Tell them to go away,' said Viktor. 'We have no comment.'

'No,' said Erika. She took a deep breath. Nico's murder was a big deal in the Icelandic news. Of course the press would want to speak to her. It wasn't surprising that they would find out where she was eventually. 'No, I'll talk to them. Otherwise they'll never go away.'

She took a moment to compose herself and then went to the door. A reporter was waiting for her – a young blonde woman who looked as if she was just out of high school – and a cameraman in a woolly hat. Behind them she could see a police car parked on the other side of the street, its occupant watching them with interest.

'Good afternoon,' Erika said. 'I am Erika Zinn. Can I help you?'

'How are you feeling after the attack?' the reporter asked.

Erika answered as blandly as she could, and dealt similarly with a couple of follow-ups. The questions were hesitant; it was like talking to the cub reporter on the *Chappaqua Journal*. Erika was preparing an emotional appeal for people to come forward for information that might help the police when she was surprised by a new tack.

'Do you think that the attack had anything to do with Freeflow?'

'I don't know what you mean,' Erika said, stalling.

'You are the leader of Freeflow, aren't you? The website that channels leaks? The organization that leaked details of Ódinsbanki's loan book? We saw you here in Iceland last fall.'

'That's right,' Erika admitted.

'So do you believe that the murder of your colleague was related?'

Erika's instinctive response was to blame the CIA; that was usually a useful diversionary tactic. But she was afraid that would raise questions she didn't want raised.

'Freeflow has made a number of enemies over the years, so we cannot rule that out,' she said.

'Why have you come back to Iceland?' The reporter was beginning to irritate Erika. She had suddenly developed an aggressive, blunt manner.

'It has nothing to do with any Icelandic issues,' Erika said.

'Then what issues does it have to do with?' the reporter asked.

'As you may know, Freeflow has no headquarters,' Erika replied with a smile. 'But every now and then we need to get together. We admire Iceland's Modern Media Initiative, so Reykjavík seemed a good place to choose. But we are not working on anything in particular.'

'We have information that the leak you are working on is related to Israel.'

Erika felt a spark of anger flash inside her. 'What part of "we are not working on anything in particular" do you not understand?' she said. 'That's all I have time for. Goodbye.'

With that she turned on her heel and strode back into the house, ignoring the shouted questions following her.

She clapped her hands. 'OK, people, let's get to it! Quit messing about. Let's get this video downloaded.'

CHAPTER TWELVE

'IDIOT MACHINE!' ÁSTA swore. That wasn't really good enough, so she switched to English. 'Fucking thing!'

It still didn't fix her all-in-one printer and scanner. A blinking light demanded that the red cartridge be changed even though she was only scanning something in black and white. Why did the stupid machine care?

She sat back at her desk in her tiny studio apartment and took a couple of breaths. She had scurried home after the Freeflow team had got down to work on the video. She had her own affairs to attend to. If her damned scanner would let her.

She looked over towards the familiar church opposite. It was new, Iceland's newest. It was named after Gudrídur the Wanderer, who not only had travelled to Iceland, Greenland, America and Rome in the eleventh century, but was also one of the earliest female Icelandic scholars. It was a rectangular block of concrete, and instead of a tower or spire at the eastern end, it had a walled garden with a reflective pond, visible through a glass wall behind the altar. Ásta loved it. Her ambition was one day to be its vicar.

No chance of that in the foreseeable future. Like just about every other institution in Iceland, the Church was short of money, and finding a job if you didn't already have one was hard. Very hard.

It had been a long day, a mix of horror and excitement. She couldn't get Nico's cold pale face out of her mind, his eyes staring meaninglessly into the snow under frosted lashes. The image would never leave her, she knew. But she was impressed by the Freeflow team and their dedication to what they were doing. She was particularly impressed by Erika. Clearly Nico's murder had hit her badly, but she was brave enough and strong enough to continue with Project Meltwater.

Or was she just so driven by her own obsessions that she wouldn't let anything knock her off her chosen path, even the death of a colleague?

Perhaps both were true. Ásta was convinced that publishing the Gaza video was right, as Nico had been, she was sure. Did his death make it more or less right that Freeflow should go ahead?

Her instinct was that Erika was doing the right thing. And she couldn't deny that the danger and the secrecy made the whole experience exhilarating.

Unlike the document she was scanning.

It was a journal. She had read and reread it at least three times, and each time it made her sad and it made her angry. The handwriting was small and spiky. Ásta remembered the girl who had written it. Soffía was the daughter of a neighbour, several years older than Ásta, who used to babysit her sometimes. Ásta remembered her as a pious girl; Ásta herself had had little interest in religion when she was a child. But it was Soffía's mother, Berglind, who was a good friend of Ásta's own mother, who had given Ásta the journal.

Berglind had discovered it among Soffía's things after Soffía had died. She thought its contents should be made public.

Ásta agreed.

She had probably scanned in about forty pages of the 120. Fortunately Soffía's handwriting was in thick black ink and the pages scanned legibly. When it was all in her computer Ásta would figure out the best way to send it to Freeflow. An anonymous CD in the post as Erika had advised wasn't strictly necessary. Once she read what the journal said, Erika would know it came from Ásta. Maybe the best thing was just to e-mail it to the Freeflow website.

Ásta knew she could trust Erika to treat her own leak carefully. It would make a big impact, in Iceland certainly, if not globally, and in Ásta's own world. And once the scanned pages from Soffía's journal were up there on the Freeflow website, no one could take them down.

Eighty more pages to scan. Ásta sighed and began looking for a spare red cartridge.

Magnus got into the rhythm as he powered up and down the open-air swimming pool at Laugardalur. He had twenty minutes before closing time at nine o'clock but it was still light. A thin layer of mist hovered over the geothermally heated pool. Even though he had barely slept the night before, he needed to swim to unwind.

The interview with Franz had been helpful. Vigdís had called a journalist contact of hers at RÚV and given her the tip about Israel. Erika's reactions on the evening news had more or less confirmed that Franz had been right. Of course it didn't mean that the Israelis were definitely behind the attack, but the police were trying to track down every Israeli in the country. There couldn't be that many of them.

There were more Italians. That angle couldn't be ignored.

However, what they really needed was to find the snowmobilers. The couple in the other jeep by the volcano had come forward, but they hadn't seen anything. They lived in Reykjavík, the husband was retired and the wife had recently lost her job at a store in the Kringlan Mall. They had never heard of Freeflow. As for the snowmobilers, the Hvolsvöllur police were out asking about them, but no one had seen anything. The murder was all over the news, but no sign of them.

The snowmobilers were definitely at the top of the list of suspects for Nico's murder.

Refreshed, Magnus jumped out of the pool – no time for a hot tub – showered, changed and drove home. He parked on Njálsgata outside the small cream-coloured house with its lime-green corrugated metal roof where he lived, and pulled out his key. It was getting dark: the lights illuminating the spire of the Hallgrímskirkja at the top of the hill had just been switched on.

He heard light footsteps just behind him. Felt a hand on his ass. A squeeze.

He turned in surprise.

Before he could say anything, familiar lips met his. A familiar kiss.

'Ingileif!'

'Hi.' She smiled. Her blond bangs hung over her eyes; he searched out and found the little nick above her left eyebrow. 'Are you pleased to see me?'

'Yes, of course I am.'

'Good, in that case let me in.'

Magnus unlocked the door. 'So what are you doing here? Why didn't you call? I didn't know you were coming back to Iceland.'

Ingileif put a finger on his lips. 'Too many questions, Mr Detective.' She laughed, taking his hand and leading him up the stairs to his room. 'We've got some catching up to do.'

They lay naked on the bed, Ingileif snuggled into Magnus's chest where she felt most comfortable. Where he felt most comfortable. Where she ought to be.

'So how's Hamburg?' Magnus asked.

'It's great. I really like it. There's a lot going on there. And the gallery is doing really well.'

'But what about the credit crunch?'

'Doesn't seem to apply in Germany. Or rather it did, but they seem to be getting out of it already. They still love Scandinavian design. And the Icelandic stuff gives them something more exotic to put with their blond wood and white walls.'

'That's good,' said Magnus. Of course he didn't mean it. What he had really wanted her to say was that Germany was a disaster and she wanted to leave at the first opportunity.

She hauled herself up on to an elbow and kissed him quickly. 'Sorry,' she said.

Magnus was about to ask her what she was sorry about, but of course she knew what he was thinking, how disappointed he was.

'What *is* all that stuff on your wall?'

She was staring at the yellow Post-its, the photographs and the notes.

'That's my father's murder,' Magnus said sheepishly.

'Magnús, that is seriously weird. I shouldn't have left you alone like that.'

'It helps, I think.'

'Does it help? Or does it just feed your obsession?'

'Hey, you were the one who kept on telling me to face up to my past.'

'Weirdo, weirdo, weirdo,' she giggled.

Magnus untangled himself from Ingileif and sat up, looking at the wall. 'Ollie's coming over from the States tomorrow,' he said. 'I want to talk about all this with him. Get him to let me investigate it more.'

'Will I get to meet him finally?'

'I guess so. Don't worry, he'll like you.'

'How do you know?'

'Because Ollie likes gorgeous women. Even if they are totally insensitive.'

'Sounds like my kind of guy.' Ingileif leaned over and kissed Magnus on the cheek. 'Sorry about the weirdo comment. I always knew you were a little strange. But why do you let your brother dictate what you do?'

'I went over to Boston a few months ago. Began asking around in Duxbury where my father was killed. But Ollie was unhappy about it, very unhappy. He asked me to lay off.'

'And you did? Why?'

'I've told you what a tough time we had as kids at Bjarnarhöfn. What my grandfather used to do to him. Since then I feel like I have to look after him, watch out for him.

Especially after Dad was killed. If he says he can't handle me digging into the past, I believe him.'

'So it's his weird obsession against yours?'

'I guess so.'

'Sounds like you should talk to him tomorrow. Where's he staying?'

'Where are you staying?'

'My bag's at María's house. You remember her?'

'Yeah.' Ingileif had loads of friends in Reykjavík, none of whom Magnus had got to know. They were beautiful people, beautifully dressed, with beautiful taste, who had all gone to school together. Magnus wasn't beautiful. They were nice to him, but he didn't fit in, and he didn't try. Ingileif didn't seem to mind. 'Your bag? What about you?'

'Well ... I thought I could sleep here. If that's OK with you.' She stroked his thigh.

'That's fine with me. How long are you here for?'

'Just three days. I've got to see a load of people tomorrow, but can we meet for lunch?'

'It's going to be difficult,' said Magnus. 'There's a big homicide investigation on at the moment.'

'How exciting! Then we should definitely meet for lunch. You can give me your clues and I can solve it for you just like I solved your last case.'

'Getting the chief suspect drunk and making him brag about what he's done is not a recommended technique for the modern detective.'

'Why not? It should be.'

'Besides, we are lacking even a chief suspect at the moment.'

'Well, you can find one in the morning and we can discuss him at lunch. Or her.'

'I'll call you if I can make it,' said Magnus.

'What about Ollie?' She kissed him. 'Where is he going to sleep tomorrow night?'

'Katrín has a spare room downstairs. He can sleep there.'

'Good.'

She kissed him again. And moved her hand a bit higher up his thigh.

The man wasn't used to it getting dark this late in April – after nine o'clock. Spotlights sprang to life, illuminating the church next to him and its phallic spire thrusting up into the night sky. He had the hunting knife he had bought the day he had arrived in Iceland. He had his torch. He would wait.

The traffic died away. Peace settled on the church and the statue. The odd tourist wobbled into the hotel. All seemed to be quiet down in Thórsgata.

At eleven, he pulled on his red jacket and strolled down the street running parallel to Thórsgata, Lokastígur. Back to the car and another couple of hours' wait.

At a few minutes past one, he put on his gloves, pulled the knife out from under his seat and shoved it into the pocket of his jacket. He walked the long way round, along Baldursgata and then up Lokastígur. The street was dead. It was reasonably well lit by the streetlamps, but there was barely a light on in any of the houses. He paused outside the property he had calculated earlier backed on to the Freeflow house – cream concrete walls, red-painted corrugated metal roof – and slipped into a shadow.

He crept around the side of the house, stepping over a kid's bike. It was much darker here, and he paused to let his eyes adjust. The rustle of his clothes and the rasp of his breathing were uncomfortably loud in his ears.

The back garden was small, less than ten metres across. There was a fence at the back, about one-sixty high. He crossed the garden and hauled himself over, landing with a gentle thump in the back garden of the yellow Freeflow house.

He looked up. The lights were on in just about every room.

Damn.

The curtains were all drawn. The ground floor was slightly raised, so the window sills were at eye level. His fingers closed around the handle of the knife in his pocket. He crouched down and approached the widest window. There was a tiny gap in the curtains.

Through it he could see the staff of Freeflow hard at work, laptops open, a couple of them wearing headphones. And in the middle of them all was Erika Zinn, staring intently at the black-and-white images on her own computer.

Damn!

He pulled back. His grip loosened on the knife handle. So much for that idea. This was a house that never slept. He would need another plan.

CHAPTER THIRTEEN

Wednesday 14 April 2010

DESPITE THE LACK of sleep, Magnus felt invigorated as he bounded up the steps of police headquarters at just after seven. He had left Ingileif asleep in his bed. He doubted he would have time to see her at lunch, and didn't know how or when he would see her that evening, but it would happen and he was looking forward to it.

Shame about Ollie arriving that day. He reminded himself to send Ollie an SMS telling him he couldn't meet him at the airport. There was work to be done.

Magnus was surprised and gratified to see Árni at his desk already. The young detective's eyes were shining with excitement. 'Did you hear about the eruption?'

'Not Katla?' Magnus said.

'No. Eyjafjallajökull. But they think it's bigger than the Fimmvörduháls volcano.'

'When did this happen?'

'The middle of the night some time. They've evacuated several hundred people.'

'Has there been a *jökulhlaup*?'

'Not yet, but they're expecting it.'

Southern Iceland bore the scars of frequent flooding over the millennia as the various volcanoes had erupted, melting vast quantities of glacier ice and sending the resultant walls of meltwater rushing to the sea by the fastest route.

'Damn!' Magnus swore.

'What is it?'

'This is going to really screw up the investigation.'

'True,' said Árni. 'I don't think we can expect much help from the Hvolsvöllur police in the next few days.'

Magnus called the chief superintendent.

'Kristján,' he answered.

'It's Magnús. I guess you've been busy?'

'Very busy. We've got almost everyone evacuated, all the farmers anyway. But there are still some tourists we need to track down, including a bunch of English schoolgirls. And the Norwegian ambassador is out there somewhere apparently, in a tent.'

'Any sign of flooding yet?'

'Not yet. But they say it's coming.'

'Can you see the eruption?'

'Too cloudy. Look, Magnús, I've got to go. You're on your own with the investigation for the next few days.'

'I understand. One question, though. Any leads on the snowmobilers?'

'Nothing. No one saw anything. And if anyone saw snowmobiles that day, we have no way of knowing whether they were *those* snowmobiles.'

Damn, again. 'OK. Is there any way you can join in the conference at eight?'

There was a conference planned first thing that morning to discuss the case, and Kristján and some of his officers had intended to patch themselves in on a speakerphone.

'No way, Magnús. As I said, you're on your own.'

'Of course. Good luck.'

'Thanks.'

The conference room was full. Magnus, Árni, Vigdís and the other detectives from the Violent Crimes Unit were there, as were Edda from forensics, the computer guy Ossi, Baldur, and a uniformed inspector who was supposed to provide resources to do some of the legwork of the investigation.

Although the Icelanders were less in awe of rank than the American cops Magnus was used to, he felt uncomfortable leading the proceedings in front of Baldur. It would have been better to have the Hvolsvöllur chief superintendent nominally in charge on the other end of the speakerphone.

But Baldur was silent, his fingers steepled, tapping against his chin as he listened. He looked unhappy. The Commissioner's decision to give the investigation to Magnus rather than him had obviously not gone down well.

There was some excited chatter about the latest eruption, and then Magnus outlined the case as he saw it so far. The most likely motive for the attack was either revenge for something Freeflow had done in the past, or an attempt to prevent whatever they were working on in the present from seeing the light of day. If that was the case, the assailants might be Israelis or Italians. Or the murderer could well be the French snowmobiler in the red snow jacket that Franz had spoken to by the volcano. But it was far too early in the investigation to rule out other possibilities. The only thing that did seem certain was that none of the Freeflow group on the mountain had attacked Nico and Erika.

Edda reported on the forensics results so far. All the men in the room stared as she spoke, and despite his night with Ingileif, Magnus had to struggle to focus on what she was saying.

Which was nothing new. The blood on Erika's clothes was Nico's blood type – big surprise. They had analysed the fibre on the rock that the assailant had handled and were searching for a match with commercially available gloves. There was no match yet with any of the clothes from the Freeflow group. The autopsy had been carried out and although the report wasn't quite ready yet, the conclusion was that Nico had died following a single stab wound to the abdomen with a knife whose blade was at least eight centimetres long. Once again, no surprise.

Ossi and his computer forensics team had been unable to

recover anything at all from the mirrored laptop hard drives. The encryption was impregnable. If they were to get anywhere they would need help from a major intelligence agency, and even then it might prove impossible.

Magnus divided up tasks. Tracking down and interviewing all Italian and Israeli tourists in the country. More research through Interpol into the Freeflow leaks in Belgium, Luxembourg and anything from the United States and Britain. And greater efforts to track down the snowmobilers.

'I'm sorry, Magnús, I can only spare you three men,' said Gudjón, the uniformed inspector.

'What?'

'They need help over in Hvolsvöllur.'

'But this is a murder investigation!'

'I know. But we are talking about one man who is already dead, compared to dozens who might be.'

Magnus took a deep breath. 'I understand.'

'Good. I'm sorry. As soon as I can free up resources I will. Now, I have to go.'

As the inspector left, Magnus reflected on how well the Icelanders dealt with the kind of natural disaster that would have paralysed an American police department, whereas a complex murder investigation failed to excite them. Not surprising, really. And that was, after all, why he was there.

'Can I make an observation?' It was Baldur, who had been silent throughout.

Magnus nodded.

'In my humble experience, assault or murder is usually committed by someone close to the victim. If a woman is attacked, it's the husband or the boyfriend who did it. I know that there are all these exciting international secrets involved in this case, but are we not forgetting the basics?'

'What do you mean?'

'I mean, was the killer someone Erika knew? A rival? A boyfriend? Or perhaps Nico was the real target after all, in which case was it a jealous husband? Or someone he knew?'

Magnus took a deep breath. It was important to encourage participants in an investigation to question assumptions at every stage, but he hated to be questioned by Baldur, especially when he had a good point.

'We've found no sign of any jealous lovers or husbands,' Magnus said. 'Or of any internal antagonism among the people at Freeflow.'

'Perhaps you haven't looked hard enough,' said Baldur.

'It's a point worth bearing in mind,' said Magnus. 'OK, let's go to it.'

He went straight from the meeting into a press conference. With the new eruption, there were fewer journalists present than there might have been, but nonetheless Magnus was nervous. Although he had spoken to the press many times in Boston, it was not something he was used to in Iceland.

There were plenty of questions about Freeflow, none about Israel, and he focused once again on the snowmobilers who had been on the volcano at the same time as the Freeflow team.

He wound things up as soon as he could. Ossi was waiting for him.

'What's up?' Magnus asked.

Ossi led Magnus out of the room, where some journalists were still packing up their stuff. 'I was working on our system at three o'clock this morning when I spotted an intrusion.'

'Someone broke into the station?'

'No. Someone broke into the computer system. More particularly, they broke into your account. I don't know what they were doing there. As soon as they realized I was logged on and had spotted them, they left.'

'Have you any idea who it is?'

'Whoever they were, they were accomplished hackers. There is an obvious suspect, of course.'

'Freeflow?'

'Precisely.'

'Can they get in again?'

'I've closed the backdoor they used. In theory our system is secure, but in practice there might be another backdoor we don't know about. I suspect they can break in again if they want to. I'll keep an eye out for them. But you should all be careful what you put on the computer.'

'How can you run a police investigation these days without using a computer?' Magnus said.

'Yeah. Perhaps if there's anything important insist that it's written down with pen and paper? You can enter it on to the system once the investigation is concluded.'

'That's a good idea,' said Magnus. He was glad that he hadn't made any formal notes of his conversation with Franz, or at least the bit relating to Israel. A near miss.

As he got back to his desk, he looked at his terminal. He wondered which of the Freeflow team had broken in. Dieter the German probably, although it could have been Franz or even the Icelander, Dúddi. Or some other member of the organization thousands of miles away.

Or it could have been someone outside Freeflow entirely. The people who had killed Nico and tried to kill Erika. The Israelis. Or the Italians. The Chinese. Anyone.

Whoever it was, Magnus wanted to talk to them.

He sat down at his keyboard and set up a file named *Freeflow Secret Leaks*. That should attract the attention of any future intruders.

Then he composed a message. In English.

```
Hi,

I really don't care what Freeflow is working on, what the details of its secret leaks are. If you have looked through my files you will see that I am not working for the CIA or anyone else.

But I do care who killed Niccolò Andreose. And I am going to find that person.

I don't know who you are. Perhaps you are behind Nico's death yourself. But if you
```

```
aren't, and you knew him, and perhaps worked
with him, you owe it to him to help me. So if
you have any information that might be of use,
please share it with me.

Magnus
```

As Magnus read through the message, he doubted that it would provoke a response. But it might. And it couldn't do any harm.

'Hey, Magnús!'

Magnus looked up. It was Vigdís, and she was holding the telephone.

'I've got a call here from someone I know you are going to want to talk to.'

'Who is it?'

'A guy who claims he was on a snowmobile at Fimmvörduháls on Monday evening.'

Magnus grabbed the phone. 'This is Sergeant Magnús speaking. I understand you were up on Fimmvörduháls when Niccolò Andreose was murdered?'

'I think so,' said a man's voice. 'I didn't see the murder, but I was up there at about dusk that evening. And the man I was with was wearing a red jacket.'

'What's your name?' asked Magnus.

'Mikael Már Sigthórsson. I live in Selfoss.'

'And the guy you were with?'

'Pierre Joubert. He's French, a potential client of mine. He was visiting me for a couple of days and wanted me to take him up to the volcano. So I did.'

'And where is this Monsieur Joubert now?'

'Back in Lyons. He flew back yesterday.'

'Look, Mikael Már, I have a lot of questions for you. Can I see you in an hour?'

'Sure.'

'Give me your address.'

*

It was less than an hour's drive to Selfoss, a medium-sized town by Icelandic standards, on the plain between Reykjavík and the two volcanoes. The address Mikael Már had given Magnus was a small one-storey house just off the main road that ran through the centre of town.

Mikael Már was a lean dark-haired man of about Magnus's age, wearing small round glasses. He led Magnus through into a room which functioned as an office and offered him some coffee.

'I'm sorry I didn't get in touch earlier,' he said. 'I just didn't see any of the news yesterday. It was only late last night that my wife mentioned you were looking for two snowmobilers. So I listened to the news this morning and gave you a call.'

'Thanks for doing that,' said Magnus. 'Can you take me through what you did up on the glacier?'

'Sure. Pierre had spent the day with me. He works for a big dealership in France, and I was hoping to join up with him to sell vans and light trucks here in Selfoss. I lost my job in a bank in Reykjavík a few months ago, as did my wife, but she found something at the hospital here. So I've been trying to figure out what I could do and this seemed like a good idea.'

Magnus nodded. Iceland was full of people who had lost their jobs in the previous year and were trying something new.

'I thought he was interested, so when he said he wanted to see the volcano, I agreed to take him, even though the weather forecast was bad. I have a snowmobile and a trailer, and I borrowed another machine from my brother-in-law, and we headed up there. I've been several times over the last few weeks.

'Anyway, the visibility was poor until we actually got to the volcano, when fortunately it cleared for a bit. We spent about half an hour up there, and then came down.'

'OK,' said Magnus. 'And who did you see on the volcano?'

'We met several jeeps coming down as we were going up, and snowmobiles. There was a middle-aged couple sitting in a jeep up there. And a group of five or six others. And also a single guy in another jeep, a smaller one.'

Magnus's pulse quickened. 'OK, we'll come back to the last guy. Tell me about the group.'

'They arrived just after us, I think. They all went up to the rim. We spoke to one of them who was kind of off by himself.'

'What did you say?'

'Just how amazing the volcano was, that kind of thing. Pierre did most of the talking. He spoke French.'

'Did you see where he went?'

'No, except that he returned to the jeep early, I saw that.'

'What about the others? Did you see a man and a woman go off to the side?'

'No.'

Magnus examined Mikael Már. There was no obvious link between him and Freeflow. He didn't look like a hired hit man or an Italian Mafioso. His Icelandic was perfect.

'Have you ever heard of Freeflow?' Magnus asked.

Mikael Már shrugged. 'Not until I listened to the news this morning.'

'Or Erika Zinn.'

He shook his head. 'Never.'

'OK, what about Pierre Joubert? Did he seem interested in the Freeflow group?'

'Not at all,' said Mikael Már. 'He just wanted to see the volcano. Although he kind of liked talking to the guy in French.'

'Do you know him well?'

'No. This is the first time I have actually met him. We've been e-mailing back and forth for a month or so.'

'And did you contact him or did he contact you initially?' Magnus realized that was the key question. If Mikael Már had approached the Frenchman first, then it meant that Joubert's visit to Iceland was not a result of Freeflow's decision to meet there. Whereas if Joubert had got in touch with Mikael Már out of the blue, that would have been more interesting.

'I contacted him. Or rather his boss in Lyons. Here, I've got some of their sales literature.'

Mikael Már leafed through some papers on his messy desk and pulled out a glossy brochure of French vans. On a middle page was a tiny picture of a tall, slightly overweight man in his late thirties. The caption read 'Pierre Joubert, Directeur Régional'.

Realistically, it would be impossible to fake all this at short notice. The mysterious Frenchman in the red ski jacket was off the list of suspects. But there was the other visitor to the crater.

'Tell me about the other jeep. The one with the single guy.'

Mikael Már winced, concentrating. 'I didn't really see much of him. The jeep came up after us and after the Freeflow group. It was parked a couple of hundred metres away from our snowmobiles and the other two jeeps. Out of sight of them. We only saw it when we walked around a bit. And he left before we did. But we overtook him on the way back down.'

'And the guy? Did you see him?'

'Not then. I'd seen him before on the way up, just by Skógafoss. He was wearing a red jacket and staring at his mobile phone.' Mikael Már raised his eyebrows. 'Just like Pierre. The red jacket, I mean.'

'How do you know it was the same guy?'

'Same jeep. A black Suzuki Vitara. I remember thinking it was a bit small to take up a glacier, especially when the weather was bad. I suppose it is possible that there were two vehicles of the same type.'

'Possible, but unlikely,' said Magnus. 'Can you describe him?'

Mikael Már screwed up his eyes, thinking. 'No. I think he was young. But no, not really. I certainly wouldn't be able to identify him. I could show you the spot where he was waiting.'

'Could you do that now?' asked Magnus.

'Yes, if you like,' said Mikael Már. 'But what about the new eruption?'

'Oh, don't worry about that,' said Magnus. 'Let's go.'

*

They went in Magnus's Range Rover. The cloud was low as they drove over the plain to the east of Selfoss. It was impossible to see Hekla or the Westman Islands. They followed Route 1, the national highway known as 'the Ring Road' that circled Iceland. The road was good and straight and Magnus drove fast.

Eyjafjallajökull was the nearer of the two glaciers that lay on either side of Fimmvörduháls, the site of the first volcano. On a clear day they would have had a perfect view of the glacier and the eruption, but that morning all they could see was grey moisture. They sped through Hvolsvöllur and in a few more minutes they approached the Markarfljót, the broad river that flowed down behind the northern slope of Eyjafjallajökull and curved around its western edge down towards the sea. Only the bottom couple of hundred feet of the ridge of mountains that supported the glacier and its volcano were visible beneath the cloud on the other side of the river. A narrow stream of water slipped down a cliff out of the clouds.

The river itself looked normal. It was broad and powerful but not in full spate. Magnus had a soft spot for the Markarfljót. It featured in one of his favourite sagas, *Njáll's Saga*. There was a wonderful scene where Njáll's son Skarphédinn slid across the ice from one side of the river to the other, swinging his axe and decapitating one of his father's enemies as he did so. All that had happened only a few kilometres to the north.

A white jeep with the word *Lögreglan* emblazoned on its side was parked across the road in front of the modern bridge. Magnus stopped beside it and got out of his own car. Although there was no visible sign of the volcano, he could hear a distant rumbling. He recognized the patrolman as one of the officers from Hvolsvöllur police station.

'Any sign of a flood yet?' he asked the policeman.

'Not yet. But we're expecting it.'

'Can you let me across?'

'Sorry, Magnús. The road is closed.'

'But the bridge looks fine.'

'The bridge might be fine but see that guy in the Caterpillar over there?' The policeman nodded over the bridge towards a lone yellow backhoe perched on the raised dyke which carried the road, waving its bucket in the air. 'He's making some holes in the road so that when the flood does come it doesn't take out the bridge.'

'Is there no way across?'

'There's a little bridge a few kilometres up from here. We are not letting the public across, but I guess it's OK for you, as long as you don't try to cross if there is a flood.'

'Thanks.' Magnus climbed back into his Range Rover and headed up a dirt track along the western edge of the river.

'Shame we can't see anything,' said Mikael Már, nodding towards the clouds under which Eyjafjallajökull was apparently erupting.

'They say it's bigger than Fimmvörduháls,' said Magnus.

They reached the bridge, a narrow stone construction of one vehicle's width, and crossed the river, turning south. In a few more minutes they had reached the main bridge and the Caterpillar, and headed eastwards again on the national road.

'Are we going to be OK if there is a flood?' Mikael Már asked.

'Sure we are,' said Magnus. He wouldn't mind seeing one of those famous *jökulhlaup*. But what he really wanted to see was where the man Mikael Már had spotted was standing.

'Have you noticed there aren't any cars?' Mikael Már asked.

'Yes,' said Magnus. 'There are probably police roadblocks ahead.'

'And the farms look very quiet.'

'Probably evacuated.'

'Oh.'

Magnus could tell his passenger was nervous. He could also tell he didn't want to admit to it.

The best way to reach the Fimmvörduháls volcano, and the way that the Freeflow team had used two days before, was to drive eastwards along Route 1 to the south of Eyjafjallajökull, and then turn north on to Mýrdalsjökull and double back to the saddle between the two glaciers. Skógafoss was to the south-east of Eyjafjallajökull, just a little way off the Ring Road.

They reached it in a few minutes. Skógafoss was one of Iceland's many spectacular waterfalls, a broad sheet of water pouring over the edge of a cliff two hundred feet into a pool below, transporting glacial water down to the sea. Partly because of its proximity to Route 1, there were a number of tourist facilities nearby: a car park, some toilets, a hotel.

All quiet.

Magnus pulled off the main highway and on to a little paved road that led to the falls. 'OK, where was this guy?'

'We stopped just outside those toilets there.' Mikael Már pointed to a sizeable wooden hut. 'I waited for Pierre. The man was parked just up here on the left.' Mikael Már indicated a strip of grass on the edge of the access road with a good view of the highway.

Magnus pulled over. 'Show me.'

They walked on about thirty yards. 'I'm not sure where it was precisely. About here, perhaps? He was leaning against the bonnet of his jeep.'

Mikael Már hesitated.

'Yes?' said Magnus. 'Take your time.' Memories couldn't always be rushed.

'He was checking his phone. And then checking the road. Concentrating, you know?'

'I know. OK, if you don't mind waiting here, I'll take a look.'

Magnus put on gloves, took out tweezers and some small plastic evidence bags, and bent down. It was a long shot, it was always a long shot, but you never knew. Fortunately this part of the access road was a fair distance from the waterfall and the car park. Not the kind of place most tourists would park. Which meant if Magnus did find something, there was a good chance that it might be connected to the mysterious man in the red jacket.

He had covered about twenty yards. Nothing. He stood up and turned towards Mikael Már to ask him if it was worth going on further, when he saw a police jeep cruising towards them, its blue light flashing.

He stood up and trotted over to the vehicle.

An officer got out of the car – Magnus didn't recognize him.

He pulled out his badge. 'Magnús. Reykjavík CID,' he said. 'I'm investigating the Fimmvörduháls murder.'

'Might be an idea to do that some other time,' said the policeman. 'We're evacuating the area.'

'Any sign of a *jökulhlaup*?'

'One has been reported on the north side of the glacier,' said the policeman. 'It's flowing down into the Markarfljót right now. But there might be another one on this side of the glacier any time.'

Mikael Már looked up at the waterfall. 'Could it come down there?'

The policeman shrugged. 'Maybe. I'd say this isn't an intelligent place to be right now. And we are expecting ash fall tonight.'

'Ash?'

'Yeah. Apparently this thing is throwing ash kilometres up into the sky. Lots of it. And it's going to come down soon.'

'And cover up any evidence,' said Magnus.

Overhead, thick moisture pressed down upon them. Magnus glanced over towards the north-west, where Eyjafjallajökull lurked beneath its grey cloak of clouds. He had been considering trying to persuade Mikael Már to go back up the glacier and show him exactly where he had seen the Suzuki Vitara parked on Fimmvörduháls. But now it didn't really seem like such a smart idea.

There was a deep boom and the ground shook.

'Hear that?' said Mikael Már.

'So, I suggest you leave,' said the policeman. Forceful but polite. 'And head east, not west.'

'But how will I get back to Reykjavík?' said Magnus. There was no other route to the west, unless you followed the Ring

Road anti-clockwise around the whole island. A couple of days' drive. Or took an airplane from somewhere in the east.

'I know. I live in Hvolsvöllur,' said the cop. 'Somehow I don't think I'm going to be home for supper tonight.'

'OK. I'll pack up here and be right along,' said Magnus.

The policeman drove off. Magnus returned to the patch of ground he had been examining.

'Come on, Magnús, let's go!' said Mikael Már.

'Is there any way your guy might have been parked a bit further along?'

'No. Let's go!'

Magnus didn't believe him. He had spotted some scraps of litter on the grass verge forty yards away, and, abandoning his methodical search, went over to take a closer look. A piece of chewing-gum wrapping and a cigarette butt. And another piece of paper ground into the dirt.

Magnus picked it up with tweezers and examined it. It was a receipt. Part of it had faded. But he could read the words *Caffè Nero* and *Heathrow Terminal One*. Dated *11 April 2010.* Timed *12:17. Server's name Rosa. 1 latte £2.10.*

With a grin, Magnus slipped the receipt into his evidence bag. He collected the chewing-gum wrapper and the cigarette butt for good measure. He spent a further couple of minutes checking the immediate vicinity of the spot where he found the receipt, but then gave up.

Perhaps it was a good idea to leave the scene.

Mikael Már was looking distinctly anxious as Magnus joined him in the Range Rover. He started the engine, pulled out of the Skógafoss tourist area on to the main road. And turned right.

'Hey, didn't the cop say go east?'

'I need to get back to Reykjavík,' Magnus said. 'And I'm not driving all the way around this island to do it.'

'OK, but put your foot down,' said Mikael Már. 'The sooner we're out of here, the better.'

Magnus did as his passenger suggested. They had been

driving for five minutes when the mountain on the right rumbled and then roared.

'Oh, my God! Look at that!'

Magnus looked. They were only half a mile from the base of the escarpment of the mountains. A small green valley bit a mile into the ridge, and at its head a massive wall of grey and brown water surged out of the clouds, flinging mud and rocks into the air as it went, and tumbled down the valley towards the highway ahead of them.

For a second, Magnus just stared. It was as if the volcano had thrust a mighty fist of violent meltwater down the glacier towards the sea, knocking all before it in a churning, grinding tumult of destruction. He had never witnessed such raw power before in his life. It was magnificent.

It was also very frightening.

He put his foot right down. He estimated the *jökulhlaup* would take a couple of minutes to reach the road. The Range Rover should make it in sixty seconds.

The churning mass of meltwater and debris gouged its way into a field just by the side of the road, tossing ten-foot circular bales of hay into the air.

Magnus's estimate was wrong: they would have a lot less than sixty seconds' leeway. Either the water was accelerating or Magnus had just misjudged it. He was committed now – if he braked they would be swept away for sure. He glanced at his speedometer as it edged above 120 kilometres per hour.

The foremost tongue of the *jökulhlaup* ripped through the fence by the side of the road just as Magnus sped past, and leaped over the highway and across the flat farmland on the other side towards the sea.

'Jesus, that was close!' said Mikael Már.

'Yeah,' said Magnus. He glanced in his mirror at the long stretch of submerged road behind them, and then fought to control his vehicle speeding at 150 kilometres an hour round a gentle bend, only just managing to keep the Range Rover on the road.

'You know if there is another one of those ahead of us, we're screwed,' said Mikael Már.

Magnus didn't have an answer for that.

A few minutes later, they were at the Markarfljót. The Caterpillar was working furiously at building a makeshift dam over the road. On the far side of the bridge he could see the police car parked across the road. Road closed.

Magnus pulled up next to the machine and jumped out.

'Any sign of the *jökulhlaup*?' Magnus asked the operator. 'We just missed one back there.'

'It's on its way,' said the Caterpillar driver, not pausing at his controls.

'Do you know if it's reached the little bridge up river?'

'No. You shouldn't hang around here, you know.'

'Should you?'

'Almost done,' the guy said. 'I've punched a few holes in the dyke to ease the pressure on the bridge. Once I've done this stretch it should hold the flood.'

'Good work,' Magnus said. He jumped back in the Range Rover and drove north along the track along the bank.

The river looked calm.

'God, there it is!'

Ahead of them a broad ridge of brown water about six feet high surged down the river. From what Magnus could see, the *jökulhlaup* was contained within the river's banks, and the road on which they were driving was sufficiently high to keep above the flood. He hoped.

They could see the narrow concrete bridge ahead when the flood hit it. Remarkably, the bridge held. The water came thundering down towards them and then swept by towards the sea and the lone Caterpillar. Magnus hoped the guy had done his calculations right.

Behind the initial surge the river had set up a strange undulation of what seemed to be a spine of static waves in the middle of the flow.

Magnus reached the little bridge and slowed down. On the

other side was another patrol car. A policeman jumped out and waved, both arms crossing above his head.

The message was clear. Stay back.

'What are you going to do?' Mikael Már asked. 'The flood will have weakened the bridge.'

'I'm going across. Coming? You can get out if you want.'

Mikael Már shook his head. 'What the hell. Go for it.' He grimaced and put his hands over his eyes, fingers splayed open so he could see through them.

Magnus put his foot hard down on the accelerator and the Range Rover surged forward. Magnus had a hunch the faster he went the more likely he would be to avoid falling in if the bridge collapse. They hit the bridge and in less than ten seconds were over the other side. Mikael Már let out a whoop.

The policeman's hands had stopped waving and were now raised in a stop sign. Magnus slowed. 'Sorry about that,' he said to the face red with anger. 'Got to get back to Reykjavík. Give my regards to the chief superintendent.'

CHAPTER FOURTEEN

JÓHANNES WAS PLAYING hooky and he was loving it. He got up at what for him was a late hour, eight-thirty, and ate a leisurely breakfast in the hotel dining room, with its wonderful view over Faxaflói Bay. It had been cloudy all night, but a northerly wind seemed to be ushering the bad weather off to the south. He decided not to call the school. After all, what could they do? Fire him?

There was a flurry of conversation in the dining room about a new eruption on Eyjafjallajökull, 250 kilometres to the south-east, evacuations and possible flooding, but there was nothing in the morning paper, or at least the edition that had made it to Búdir. He went for a brisk walk along the beach, letting the rhythmic sounds of the waves wash over him, and then got into his car for the drive to Stykkishólmur. He had rung his old aunt Hildur and agreed to meet her later that morning.

It was a glorious morning. He sang to himself as he drove up over the Kerlingin Pass, crossing the mountain ridge that formed the spine of the Snaefells Peninsula. He was a member of a choir, a baritone, and a year before they had given a concert of seventeenth-century hymns. They were quite catchy, and Jóhannes had taken to singing them when alone and out of earshot of other people. 'Lánid Drottins lítum maeta', a song about drinking too much wine at the wedding at Cana, was one of his favourites.

That was the glory of the Icelandic countryside. It was very easy to be alone and out of earshot of other people.

He crested the summit of the pass and in a few moments a broad view stretched out before him. He paused, and drove into a lay-by. He walked a few metres away from the car and sat on a stone to look.

It was a view he remembered well. He had sat close to this very spot with his father when he was about ten. They were driving to see his grandmother in Stykkishólmur, just his father and him, when they had pulled over. He and his father had already read *The Saga of the People of Eyri* together at least twice, in the original version of course, and Benedikt wanted to show his son where it had all happened.

In the foreground was Swine Lake, walled in by the several kilometres of congealed lava which was the Berserkjahraun. Beyond that was Breidafjördur, a long, broad fjord between the Snaefells Peninsula and the West Fjords, sixty kilometres to the north. Along the coast were two farms. One, nestling under its own fell, with a little black church in the home meadow just beneath it, was Bjarnarhöfn. This was where Björn the Easterner, the son of Ketill Flat Nose and one of the first settlers of Iceland from Norway, had landed eleven hundred years before. It was where Vermundur the Lean had brought the two berserkers back from Sweden.

It was also where Hallgrímur had lived. Still lived from what Hermann was saying.

A couple of kilometres to the east was Hraun, now, as it was a millennium ago, a prosperous farm. This was where Vermundur's brother Styr had lived, whose daughter one of the berserkers had demanded to marry. Styr had promised the Swede that he could do this as long as the berserkers hacked a path across the lava field to Vermundur's farm at Bjarnarhöfn. This they did, collapsing in exhaustion in their master's brand new stone bath-house afterwards. They were steamed out by Styr, who ran them both through as they emerged. The path was still there, winding its way through the rearing waves of lava, as was the cairn where the berserkers were buried.

Jóhannes remembered the verse Styr spoke at the cairn:

I dread not my enemy
nor his tyranny.
My bold brave sword
has marked out a place for the berserks.

Hraun was where Benedikt had been brought up.

In fact, throughout the whole plain before Jóhannes, signs of the saga persisted, one thousand years later. To the north-east was Helgafell, the holy mountain, although it was little more than a knoll, less than a hundred metres high. Here Snorri Godi and later Gudrún had lived, two of the leading figures of the sagas. And most of the farms that were so familiar to Jóhannes were still inhabited, as they had been in the days of Arnkell, Thórólfur Lame Foot and the other characters of the sagas.

He remembered his father pointing out all these locations to him from this very vantage point.

'Do any of the farmers still fight each other, Daddy?' Jóhannes had asked.

'No, I don't think so,' his father had answered.

'Why not?'

'Because people don't do that any more. They would go to jail.'

'But what about honour?' the ten-year-old Jóhannes had asked. 'And revenge. In the sagas they always have to take revenge. Why not today?'

Then his father had said something that had stuck with Jóhannes all his life. It was his father's sudden expression of seriousness tinged with sadness that emblazoned the words in Jóhannes's memory. 'Sometimes they do. Sometimes they do.'

What had he meant? Jóhannes had asked himself that question many times over the years. What had he meant?

Jóhannes drove down past the Berserkjahraun and on through the ancient farmland to the fishing village of Stykkishólmur, on a spit of land a few kilometres north of Helgafell.

He remembered his aunt Hildur's house. It was a few metres back from the harbour. It was tiny, and it was about a hundred years old, ancient by Icelandic standards. It had a red corrugated iron roof and a red-painted picket fence surrounded it. The walls, also of corrugated metal, were painted green. Various elves peeked out behind net curtains.

Jóhannes had loved visiting his aunt Hildur when he was a kid. There was a particular kind of toffee that she always seemed to possess in large quantities with which she was very generous. She was already a widow – her husband, a fisherman, had gone the way of many local men to the bottom of the North Atlantic.

Jóhannes was looking forward to seeing her.

He rang the doorbell. In a moment a tiny woman with a crooked back and bright blue eyes appeared. She had shrunk considerably since the last time Jóhannes had seen her.

'Jóhannes! Come in, my dear, come in.'

He bent down to kiss his aunt and followed her into a cosy sitting room, stuffed with knick-knacks of all descriptions, among which were a fair few little Icelandic flags. A grey-haired woman of about his own age stood to greet him. He recognized Unnur, who was Hildur's husband's niece, if he remembered correctly.

'I asked Unnur to be here when you visited,' Hildur said. 'I knew she would want to see you. She has a couple of free periods this morning, so she said she could come along.'

This surprised Jóhannes. He had a number of cousins scattered around Stykkishólmur and the Snaefells Peninsula, but he wasn't close to any of them. He remembered being impressed by Unnur. Like him, she was a teacher. And she had been quite beautiful when she was younger; in fact she was still attractive, with her smooth skin, her fine cheekbones and her air of composed gracefulness.

Hildur fussed over coffee. She must be closer to ninety than eighty, Jóhannes thought, but she was still sprightly. He wondered whether she still had the toffee: he was tempted to ask for some.

'I've forgotten what you teach,' he said to Unnur.

'English and Danish,' she said. 'You teach Icelandic, don't you?'

'I do,' said Jóhannes. 'Or indeed I did until yesterday.'

Unnur's eyebrows rose. 'How do you mean?'

'You could say I lost my job.'

'Oh, I am sorry,' said Hildur. 'How dreadful.'

'What happened?' asked Unnur. 'Or shouldn't I ask?'

Jóhannes explained his strong views on how Icelandic literature should be taught and how these did not fit in well with the syllabus. He was gratified with Unnur's response – she agreed with him forcefully. She was angry that Shakespeare had almost disappeared from the English syllabus at high school – in her day they'd had to study it in the original.

Jóhannes remembered why he liked her.

'So what brings you up here?' Unnur asked. 'Aunt Hildur said you are researching Benedikt's death?'

'Yes,' said Jóhannes. He recounted his impulsive trip to Búdir and his conversation with Hermann, the head groom.

'I remember Hallgrimur,' said Hildur. 'An unpleasant boy. He was our neighbour when we were at Hraun. He and your father were the best of friends when they were little, they used to play together all the time, but then they grew apart. Which pleased me. Your father was a good boy, and Hallgrímur wasn't. He was stupid and he used to try to bully Benni.'

She sighed. 'After your grandfather died, it was hard work on the farm. In the end we sold up and moved here. You remember the shop that your grandmother ran?'

'Oh, yes,' said Jóhannes. The shop itself hadn't interested him much, his grandmother sold and mended women's clothes, but he had enjoyed the warm atmosphere that his grandmother and her friends who staffed the shop gave the place. 'And what was Hallgrímur like as an adult?'

'He didn't really grow up well. He was notorious for his bad temper. His wife and children were scared of him. I tried to avoid him; in fact I haven't seen him for many years. But he is a good farmer, I'll give him that, and they say that his son is just as good. Bjarnarhöfn has always been a prosperous place.'

'I've read *Moor and the Man* and I've heard the rumours that the novel implied Hallgrímur's father killed my grandfather because he slept with Hallgrímur's mother.'

'Oh, those,' said Hildur. 'There's no stopping gossip.'

'Do you think they were true?'

'Oh, I don't know, dear. People had all sorts of strange ideas about Father's disappearance. That he went to America. Most people think he must have fallen into the fjord and been swept out to sea. The truth is no one knows.'

Jóhannes persevered. 'Is that really the truth?'

Unnur glanced at their aunt. Jóhannes knew she wasn't telling him something.

'Did my father ever talk to you about it?' Jóhannes asked.

'No,' said the old woman. 'Not in so many words. But when I read that book, it explained a lot.' Hildur smiled at her nephew. 'Benedikt was always an honest boy. I think that was his way of telling the truth.'

'I see,' said Jóhannes. 'The groom at Búdir mentioned another story that my father wrote just before he died. He suggested that that might be why Hallgrímur was so upset with him. I think that story might have been "The Slip". It's about a boy who kills the man he accused of raping his sister by pushing him off a cliff.'

'I think I remember that one,' said Hildur.

'Is there any chance that Benedikt might have pushed Hallgrímur's father off a cliff?'

'No!' said Hildur. 'Absolutely no chance at all. I think you are on quite the wrong track. I was Benedikt's sister. I think I would have noticed if someone had raped me.'

'Yes, of course, sorry,' said Jóhannes. 'I meant it was revenge for the murder of your father, not rape.'

'I think you are getting yourself confused, dear.'

'Well, perhaps you could you put me back on the right track?'

'I don't know, dear. It's all a long time ago. Won't you have some more coffee?' The old lady refilled Jóhannes's cup. 'Unnur, would you like some more? And tell me, Jóhannes, how is your sister? It's years since I have seen her either, and of course I never go to Akureyri. And your little brother?'

Jóhannes got the message. After half an hour of family chat, he got up to leave. Unnur saw him out of the door and walked him to his car.

'I'm not confused,' Jóhannes said. 'She knows perfectly well what I was getting at.'

'I think she's torn, you know,' Unnur said. 'On the one hand she feels she must keep her brother's secrets; on the other, she really does believe that he was trying to tell the truth.'

'And you?' Jóhannes asked. 'Do you know anything about "The Slip"?'

'I have read the story,' Unnur said. 'And I can tell you how Hallgrímur's father Gunnar died.'

'Please do.'

'It was in 1940. Gunnar was riding out to Ólafsvík around Búland's Head. I don't know if you remember but the cliff path used to be very narrow there.'

'I know Búland's Head.' It was a dramatic headland that reared out of the sea near the fishing village of Ólafsvík further along the coast to the west.

'Well, Gunnar's horse slipped and he fell into the sea.'

'Really?'

'Yes. Really. And your father Benedikt was coming back from Ólafsvík that same day. Around Búland's Head. He told everyone he hadn't seen Gunnar, and of course they all believed him because your father was known for his honesty.'

Jóhannes felt a shiver of horror run through him as he realized what Unnur's words meant.

His father was a murderer. He had killed a man, and a horse, in cold blood when he was only, what, fourteen years old.

'Which is why he chose to write about it forty years later?' Jóhannes said. An honest murderer, but still a murderer.

Unnur shrugged. 'Maybe. Remember, Benedikt knew he was going to die, even if he thought it was from a brain tumour and not a knife in the back. If Aunt Hildur doesn't want to tell you, then I really shouldn't. But there was a man who came round here last year and spoke to me – to both of us. He has figured a lot of this out for himself. He's in Reykjavík. You could talk to him.'

'What's his name?'

'He's a policeman. Magnús Ragnarsson. He's Hallgrímur's grandson.'

CHAPTER FIFTEEN

THE HOUSE WAS a mess and that was exactly the way Erika liked it. Empty cups of coffee and cans of Red Bull littered every free surface. It was also beginning to smell, of food, of sweat, of too many people locked inside together for too many days.

To Erika this was the smell of action, of work, of results.

She had slept very little for the previous few days, but her brain was firing on all cylinders. Finally things were slotting into place. The video had been downloaded and she and Dúddi were analysing it frame by frame, deciding what to cut and what to keep, and also trying to figure out exactly what all the grey smudges were. Franz was augmenting the resolution as best he could, but this was when they really needed Gareth and his experience of interpreting aerial photography. Ásta was just about to leave for the airport to meet him. Once they had figured out what was going on, then they could work on an edited three-minute version of the attack for maximum impact.

Zivah had finished a transcript and translation of the radio traffic. It made chilling reading. Although she had seen it so many times and in so many places before, Erika was still shocked by how callous men could be when exposed to violence that should horrify any normal human being. She knew that it was a soldier's job to kill, and a certain amount of humour and detachment helped deal with that, but she felt utter contempt for the voices on the radio.

They deserved to be exposed, as did all those in high places trying to protect them.

Dieter and Apex were establishing the network of websites around the world that would host the video once they published. They could expect distributed denial-of-service attacks from angry supporters of Israel. This was a form of electronic assault: tens of thousands of computers all over the world were directed without their owners' knowledge to send millions of messages to a certain website, with the aim of overwhelming it. Dieter was setting up a chain of sites which would pop up whenever one of their brethren was taken down by an attack.

But of course that all relied on them finding the fifteen thousand euros to pay the Swedish ISP. Where the hell was Erika going to find the money? If only Nico was still alive.

Erika had delayed getting in touch with the *Guardian* in the UK until Alan had got to Samantha Wilton. But Alan had warmed up his contacts on the *Washington Post*, who were eager to be involved provided their bosses were happy with the verification of the video. If they were going to publish something that would damage Israel's reputation they had to be absolutely sure of the source. Fair enough.

Alan's contact at Reuters had also come up with the goods: two local journalists in Gaza were on standby to talk to witnesses of the attack the year before. They already knew whom to go to; they were just waiting for the photographs to show to the witnesses. Erika had begun a negotiation with Reuters about how the material was handled, all on Jabber. She had also warmed up *Der Spiegel*, the German weekly magazine with a publication date on Mondays. This fitted Erika's timetable perfectly, but meant she needed to give them a few days' warning to leave space for an article.

'*Scheisse!*' The expletive from Dieter was particularly loud, causing Erika to lift her head from her computer.

'What's up?'

'Gareth's missed his flight.'

'What?'

'He says he has to stay in England today to finish up his current project. He'll fly in tomorrow morning.'

'Let me see.' Erika leaned over Dieter's shoulder to look at the chat. 'Here, let me in.'

She shoved Dieter out of the way, took his seat and began typing: *gareth, you asshole, how can you do this? we have a whole team here waiting for you. we need you to analyse the images and for verification.*

Gareth: *i know, i know. i'm sorry erika. but this is my most important client and i need to finish the job for them. the deadline is this evening. i'll definitely be on the flight tomorrow morning. i promise.'*

Erika: *you'd better be.*

She turned away from Dieter's computer in disgust.

'It's never easy,' said Dieter.

Erika smiled at him. He was always there, Dieter. Always reliable. He would never miss a flight. He knew Freeflow was the number-one priority. Always.

She touched his arm. He gave her a shy smile in response.

'Ásta!' she called out. 'Hold your horses. Gareth's not coming. No need to go to the airport today.'

'Actually, I still need to go in a couple of hours,' Ásta said. 'To meet Nico's wife.'

'Oh, yes,' said Erika. She had forgotten about Teresa Andreose. 'What are you going to do with her?'

'I'll look after her,' Ásta said. 'I'll bring her to the house for a little bit to meet you. I know you are busy, but I think it's important. Then I'll get her a hotel and take her in to see the police.'

'Thanks for your help, Ásta. I really appreciate it.'

The last thing Freeflow needed was a hysterical Italian woman under their feet. It turned out there was some point in having a priest on the payroll after all.

Now, Apex. *have you heard?* Erika began typing. *gareth can't make it until tomorrow.*

Apex: *yeah. dieter told me. that's bad news. especially since i'm a little doubtful about the video.*

Erika: *really? what's the problem?*

Apex: *the helicopter background noise. i don't think it's an ah-64 apache. i think it's something else, but i'm not sure what.*

Erika: *and the actual attack was by an apache, wasn't it? we know that for sure?*

Apex: *that's right.*

Erika: *that doesn't sound good. so are you saying the video's a fake? are you certain about the noise?*

Apex: *no, i'm not certain. there may be reasons why the noise might sound different to other recordings of apache helicopters i've listened to. that's why we need gareth.*

Erika was worried, but only a little. Apex was always cautious. He was bound to find some problem with the video, even if it was genuine. But all doubts needed to be checked out thoroughly before it was released.

Apex: *how are the police getting on with their investigation?*

Erika: *it's okay. they are out of our hair now, viktor saw to that. but there was a question from the press about israel last night.*

Apex: *shouldn't we be helping them some more? i mean* Nico *is dead. perhaps we should hand everything we have over to them and get them to investigate properly.*

Erika: *no! no. nico wouldn't have wanted that. it sounds like a cliche but i know it's true. besides, if mossad killed him the icelandic cops are hardly going to be able do anything about it. and if it was a random killing, then there's not much more we can do to help them.*

Apex: *and if it was the italians?*

Erika: *i've told them all about italy. i am sure they are raiding every pizza joint in the country as we speak.*

The screen was still. Erika let Apex think.

Apex: *ok. we'll do it your way.*

Erika: *good. see if you can work with franz on identifying the objects in the videos. we should get as much done without gareth as we can.*

She sat back from the screen and rubbed her eyes. Dieter was right, things were never easy. But they weren't usually this hard either.

But if she could hold herself together, hold the rest of the team together, they *would* do this. It would be Freeflow's greatest moment.

Nico would be proud of them. Of her.

Magnus dropped Mikael Már off at his house in Selfoss and drove on to Reykjavík. He had made progress of some kind: he was pretty sure he could rule out the snowmobilers after all. And Franz's story of what he had been doing on the mountain seemed to stack up.

Which left what? A mysterious man in a red ski jacket who was driving a black Suzuki Vitara up on the glacier. Possibly someone who was upset with what Freeflow had done to them. An Italian, an Israeli, or maybe someone who worked for those people. Or someone else entirely.

They still had a long way to go.

His phone rang. 'Magnús,' he snapped.

'Where the hell are you?' It was Ollie, his brother. 'I've been at the airport for an hour waiting for you. What's the story?'

'Hell, Ollie, I'm sorry,' said Magnus. 'I've been caught up in a case. I meant to send you an SMS and I forgot.'

'Some things never change.'

'Yeah. Look, I really am sorry. I can't meet up with you until this evening. Get a cab into town and come to my apartment.'

'A cab? How much will that cost?'

'Yeah, you're right. You can get a bus right outside the terminal. You've got my address, right?'

'Nigelsgate?'

'Something like that. When you get there, Katrín will let you in.'

'Katrín?'

'Yes. She's my landlady. You'll like her.'

'Does she speak English?'

'Don't you remember *any* Icelandic?'

'No. You know that.' Ollie had worked hard over the years to blank out his Icelandic past: he was all American now.

'Yes, she does speak English. See you later. And I am sorry.'

Magnus hung up with the feeling of guilt so familiar after any conversation with his brother. He quickly called Katrín, Árni's sister, from whom he rented his room. Fortunately she was at home, and even more fortunately she was happy to stay home to let Ollie in.

Then he rang Ingileif.

'Hi,' she said. 'How's the case going?'

'Just went up to Eyjafjallajökull,' Magnus said.

'Wow. Did you see the eruption?'

'Too cloudy. But I caught a couple of *jökulhlaup*.'

'A couple?'

'I'll tell you later.'

'At lunch, I hope?'

'Sorry. I can't make that – too much to do on the case.'

'That's a shame, but never mind.'

'Ollie has arrived in Iceland. Do you want to meet us for dinner tonight?'

'I'm having dinner at Rakel's house. Anna Kristín is coming.' Magnus recognized the names but couldn't remember who they were. 'It's kind of business – I need some of Anna Kristín's chairs for the gallery in Hamburg. I'll see you later on tonight.'

'I'm looking forward to it.'

'So am I.'

Magnus smiled as he hung up. He knew that Ingileif meant it, and he was really looking forward to seeing her later on.

But it was all so matter-of-fact. He remembered Colby, his former girlfriend of several years in the States. She would have gone apeshit if he had stood her up for lunch after being apart for a few months. Ingileif was a definite step forward from that.

But then he had thought that his relationship with Ingileif was finished in November when she had gone off to Hamburg. It obviously wasn't.

Which was nice.

Magnus drove straight to police headquarters to drop off the cigarette butt at the Forensics Unit. Edda promised to get a DNA analysis done as soon as possible, but Magnus knew it would take days, possibly even a couple of weeks. The sample had to be sent to a lab in Sweden. Magnus didn't understand why this was the case when Iceland had the most comprehensive genetic database of its citizens in the world. The whole population's DNA had been analysed and stored by a private company, who hoped to sell the results for research into genetic diseases. So the labs were there, the database was there, the police just couldn't access them.

He had asked whether the analysis could pick up any Jewish or Italian matches in the DNA. Edda said she would ask for a detailed haplogroup breakdown, which should be a good guide to the origin of the subject's ancestors. Magnus took her word for it. Waiting for DNA results was a feeling familiar from his days at the Boston PD.

Back at the station, Árni, Vigdís and the other detectives were ploughing through Israeli and Italian citizens in Iceland. There were only a handful of Israelis, mostly tourists, so that wasn't too difficult, although Vigdís pointed out that when Mossad agents had assassinated someone in Dubai the previous January, they had used passports from Britain, Ireland, Germany and France. Italians were a different problem. According to the Italian consulate, there were 158 permanent residents with Italian citizenship in Iceland, including the father of the famous Icelandic singer Emilíana Torrini; he ran a restaurant in Laugavegur. Then there were temporary workers including engineers and other technical staff, plus all the tourists. Although April was not a big month for tourism in Iceland, the volcano had attracted a higher number than usual.

And of course once they had been identified, the Israelis and Italians needed to be interviewed. Priorities needed to be set: tourists rather than permanent citizens; males under fifty; Israelis first, then Italians. If the Israelis were travelling under false passports, the police were stuffed: they couldn't interview every foreigner in the country.

Magnus gave Árni a break from calling hotels and asked him to investigate the Heathrow café receipt, and to contact car-hire companies to check who had rented a black Suzuki Vitara on or in the week before the day of the murder.

'Hey, Vigdís,' Magnus said. 'I thought you were supposed to be in Paris? I hope you haven't cancelled.'

'Just postponed it for a day.'

'I told you not to.'

'Davíd's got some kind of business meeting in Paris tomorrow, that's why we're meeting there. It'll be OK if I don't see him till the evening. And we'll have Friday and the whole weekend together.'

'All right, but you get on that flight tomorrow, do you hear?'

'Yes sir!' But Vigdís grinned.

Árni was hovering. 'Magnús?'

'Yes, Árni?'

'I've had a thought. It might be a bit far-fetched . . .'

'Yes?' Magnus had a theory that far-fetched ideas were always to be encouraged – difficult cases were sometimes solved by fresh thinking – but he hesitated to encourage Árni.

'What about these fraternities?' Árni said in a whisper.

'What about them?'

'Well, there's a secret society I read about at Harvard or somewhere that George Bush is a member of. The Crossed Skulls, I think it's called.'

'The Skull and Bones,' said Magnus. 'And it's Yale.'

'Yeah. Well, maybe Freeflow posted their secret initiation ceremony or something and they are angry about it.'

'They might be angry. But angry enough to go to Iceland to kill someone?'

'Maybe the CIA *are* involved. Maybe the head of the CIA is in this crossbones club as well. Maybe there's something secret about George Bush. We don't know.'

'No, Árni, we don't know. Tell you what. Take five minutes to look at the Freeflow website and check out whether it has busted the Skull and Bones society. If it has we'll talk some more. If not, forget it and get on to the Heathrow café.'

'You're not a member of it, are you, Magnus?'

'No, Árni, I'm not. I went to Brown not Yale. And I wasn't a member of any fraternity; they wouldn't have had me.'

Back in the real world, Magnus picked up the phone and called Rannveig, asking her to meet him at the house on Thórsgata.

'That wasn't part of the deal,' she said.

'We're making a new deal,' said Magnus.

Magnus arrived first and approached the cop sitting in his car watching the yellow house. 'Seen anything?'

'A bunch of journalists were here earlier this morning. They seem to have given up now.'

'Anyone else?'

'There's a guy over there reading a newspaper. On that bench.'

About fifty yards down the road there was indeed a man sitting on a bench facing the house reading what looked like the *International Herald Tribune*.

'Bit cold to be sitting outside reading a newspaper, wouldn't you say?' said Magnus.

'I would say,' said the cop. 'He's been there about an hour. I wasn't sure whether to speak to him: I thought I'd wait for you.'

'OK – I'll have a word with him later. Keep your eyes peeled.'

Rannveig's car pulled up and Magnus greeted her before ringing the doorbell. The door was answered by the Israeli student, Zivah.

'Hi,' said Magnus. 'Can I speak to Erika?'

'I'll see.' They were left waiting for a couple of minutes before Erika arrived at the door.

'We had a deal. We're busy working. If you tramp around the house we will be seriously disrupted. So will you leave, or shall I call Viktor?'

'I understand that. I just want to speak to you. But we had better do it inside the house. You shouldn't take risks outside.'

'What about?'

'Israel.'

She hesitated. 'All right, come in. But make it quick. Just wait a moment.'

Erika turned and yelled into the living area. 'OK, everyone. Turn your monitors off. There's a cop coming in – I don't want him to see what you're working on.'

Magnus and Rannveig followed Erika to the kitchen table. Magnus pushed aside a plate dusted with toast crumbs.

'How do you know about Israel?' Erika said.

'The press,' Magnus replied. 'They asked you about Israel and you evaded the question.'

'So?'

'So it means that we have had to check on every Israeli that was in Iceland the day Nico was killed.'

'And what if I were to tell you that what we are working on has nothing to do with Israel?'

'Then I wouldn't believe you,' said Magnus.

Erika shrugged. 'OK – that's your problem. But we have a deal: leave us alone.'

'I'm suggesting another deal. Or shall we call it an appendix to the original deal?'

'No new deals,' said Erika. 'I *am* going to call Viktor.'

'Sure, you can do that if you want. But look at it from my point of view. A murder has been committed and a possible line of inquiry is Israel. I have to investigate that now, whatever you say, even if you say nothing. Now, I can do this noisily – talk to the consulate, call the Israeli police, their secret service, make an appeal on TV. Or I can do this quietly. Which I am prepared to do, if you tell me what you are working on and who it might piss off.'

Erika picked up a table knife and fiddled with it. Magnus and Rannveig waited.

Her eyes flicked up towards him. Magnus was struck again by their intensity. 'You promise me you have no connection to the CIA?'

'None whatsoever.'

'And you won't discuss what you see with the Israeli authorities?'

Magnus hesitated.

'Well?'

'I don't want to make a promise I can't keep,' Magnus said. 'I certainly won't contact them now. If we find a genuine suspect, we may need to talk to the Israelis. It would be impossible to arrest an Israeli citizen without that.'

Erika blew air through her cheeks. 'OK. OK. Let me get my computer.'

She grabbed a small netbook computer and opened it up on the kitchen table. Magnus and Rannveig watched as a grey image flickered into life. As the death of Tamara Wilton and her colleagues unfolded, Erika gave a rough translation of the radio traffic.

It took sixteen minutes. When the video footage eventually froze at its end, both Magnus and Rannveig were still staring at the screen.

'So what do you think?' Erika asked.

'I think it's appalling,' said Magnus. 'Especially when you hear the radio commentary.'

'So do we. That's why we want to publish it.'

'Is it genuine?' Rannveig asked.

'We *think* so. But we're not one-hundred-per-cent sure yet. That's part of what we are doing here. Verifying it.'

'Who did it come from?' Magnus asked.

'We don't know,' said Erika. 'That's the whole point of Freeflow. Our sources' identities are protected: even we don't know who they are.'

'Does the Israeli government know about this?'

'We don't think so. But of course the press seemed to know. How they got it is a mystery. It worries me.'

It didn't worry Magnus, of course, but despite Erika's candour he had his own sources to protect.

'OK. Well, thank you, Erika. As I promised, we will leave you alone. And we will investigate as quietly as we can.'

'Are you making progress?'

'Some. We can rule the snowmobilers out. But there does seem to have been another jeep up on the mountain, a black Suzuki Vitara, driven by a guy in a red ski jacket. Do you remember seeing him, or his vehicle?'

'No,' said Erika. 'Unless of course he was the man who attacked us. You think he might be, don't you?'

'That's the most likely theory at the moment.'

'Wait. I think I do remember noticing headlights behind us on the way up the glacier. The other jeep with the couple in were ahead of us, weren't they? So if there was someone following us, it could be your guy. You should ask Dúddi – he was driving our jeep.'

'I'll do that.'

Just then the door opened and Ásta walked in, followed by a tall woman dressed in an expensive cream leather jacket, designer jeans and high black leather boots. She had long brown hair; her face was lined, her eyes dark under her make-up.

Erika got up from the kitchen table and moved over to her, holding out her arms. 'Teresa! I am so sorry.'

The room was silent. The woman stopped a few paces away from Erika. Her face was ravaged with emotion; she was shaking with the tension.

Erika took a step forward, her arms still outstretched.

'Keep away from me, you whore!' the Italian woman roared. Erika took a step back.

'I know all about you and Nico. I know you were fucking my husband!'

Erika let her hands fall to her sides. She stood up straight, facing her adversary. Calm.

'It's your fault he's dead. You know that, don't you?' Teresa's voice had dropped, making it if anything more menacing. 'You are the reason he came here. The man who killed him was trying to kill you, when Nico stopped him. Why he did that, I do not know. I wish he hadn't. I wish it was you who had been killed on the volcano.'

'I know,' said Erika quietly.

'You know! How can you stand there and say you know! I am his wife, for God's sake! The mother of his children.' She took a deep breath. 'You took their father away from them. Not only did you fuck him, but you snared him with all this Freeflow crap. You tempted him to the North Pole and yes, you caused his death. May you rot in hell! I flew to Iceland to tell you this. I'm going now and I never want to see you again. Don't you dare come to his funeral!'

'I won't,' said Erika.

'*Puttana!*' spat Teresa. She turned on her heel and left the house, banging the front door.

Ásta followed her.

Erika's face was motionless, cold. She turned to the assembled team, who were staring back at her, their expressions frozen in shock. 'Don't look at me like that, Dieter,' she said. 'Back to work, everyone.'

She walked past Magnus and sat down in front of her computer.

'Erika?' Magnus said.

Erika paused, closed her eyes. 'Yes?'

'You didn't tell me anything about your relationship with Nico. I specifically asked you about it.'

'I didn't think it was relevant to your investigation,' Erika said. 'And I didn't want to cause his widow distress. Although it looks like I needn't have worried about that.'

'Can you tell me about it now?'

'What do you want to know?' Erika said. 'Yes, we had an affair. Yes, I slept with him. Yes, I am upset that he is dead. What do you want? The dates? Let me see . . .' She tapped on some keys. 'Yes, just checking my calendar. The last time I slept with him was two months ago. February fourteenth. Valentine's Day. Stockholm. Got that?'

There were tears in her eyes. Finally, there were tears in her eyes.

CHAPTER SIXTEEN

'WOW,' SAID RANNVEIG, once they were outside. She took a deep breath of fresh air.

'Yeah. Wow.'

'Lucky we've got someone watching the house. I wouldn't want to be unprotected if I was Erika with that woman on the loose.'

'No,' said Magnus. He was glad Ásta had informed Teresa: it was something that he should really have done himself. But just then Baldur's words came back to him. The first place to look was always the husband or the wife or the boyfriend. It was true in Boston. It was true in Reykjavík.

Something to think about.

'See you later, Rannveig,' Magnus said, and he trotted over to Ásta's small Peugeot. She had just started the engine.

He stooped down on the passenger's side. Teresa was weeping. Ásta pressed a switch to wind down the electric window. 'Signora Andreose,' Magnus said. 'I know you are upset now, but I would really like to speak to you at the police station.'

The woman nodded. Magnus glanced across to Ásta, who nodded also, mouthing in Icelandic, 'I'll bring her when she is ready.'

Ásta drove off and Magnus looked down the hill to where the guy was still reading his paper on the bench. Magnus nodded at the cop in the police car and strolled down towards him. The bench was in front of a tiny grass playground, with swings and a multicoloured little elf house.

The man lowered his paper. It *was* the *International Herald Tribune*.

'Hi, Magnus, how are you?' he said in English. 'My name's Tom. Tom Bryant. I've got my car here. Do you want a ride?'

'Can't we just talk here?'

'It's a bit cold. It might be better to be in the car.'

Magnus shrugged and followed Bryant to a bland saloon crammed into a space between a van and a BMW four-by-four.

Bryant started the car. He was about forty, neatly dressed in a bland kind of a way: jeans with a belt, decent shoes, plain zip-up jacket. Not really a businessman, but not a tourist either.

'I take it you work for the CIA?' Magnus said.

Bryant smiled. 'I'm temporarily attached to the US Embassy here in Reykjavík.'

'I'll take that as a yes. Are you following Erika Zinn?'

'No.'

'She says the CIA is following her.'

'Well, she's wrong,' said Bryant.

'Really?'

Bryant smiled. Good American teeth. 'Yeah, really. It's not the CIA. Different department. It's actually the Diplomatic Security Team.'

'Oh, right. That's OK, then.'

'Yeah.'

'Where are we going?'

'We are just driving around. I thought we should have a little chat.'

'I'm not sure there's any point in that,' said Magnus in Icelandic.

'What?'

'Don't you speak Icelandic? What's the CIA doing sending a spy to Iceland who doesn't speak Icelandic? I saw through your disguise, by the way.'

'I know you're a good detective, Magnus. And no, I don't speak the language. I am more of a Freeflow specialist than an Iceland specialist. We have other people who work for the government who speak Icelandic.'

'Ah.'

'Yes. People like you.'

Magnus turned to the driver. They had passed the Hallgrímskirkja on top of the hill and were driving down the other side towards Snorrabraut. 'What do you mean?'

'You work for the government, don't you?'

'Not the American government. I'm attached to the National Police Commissioner's Office in Iceland.'

'Yeah, but you're still on the BPD payroll. And you're getting your pension contributions; I know, I checked. Come on, you're a cop, you know it's all about the pension rights.'

'Hey, I'm thirty-four, what do I care about pensions?' But Magnus knew that while that was true for him personally, a lot of his colleagues in the BPD became fixated on their earliest retirement date years in advance.

'I'm just saying,' said Bryant.

'Saying what?'

'That you are a US citizen.'

Magnus sighed. 'So what do you want?'

'I want to know what Freeflow is working on right now.'

'No,' said Magnus.

Bryant drove on. They were down to the bay now, and he turned eastwards on Saebraut. Mount Esja was free of clouds, its rocky ramparts gleaming full of sprightly spring promise. 'Nice town, Reykjavík,' Bryant said. 'Very pretty. This reminds me a bit of Maine, you know. I used to go there on vacations when I was a kid.'

'More trees in Maine,' Magnus said.

'True,' Bryant said. 'I know it has something to do with Israel.'

'You watch TV in Icelandic, then?'

'I have people to do it for me. Have you been following the peace negotiations between the Israelis and the Palestinians?'

'Not really,' said Magnus.

'Well, even if you had you wouldn't know that they are at a crucial stage. The Palestinians have indicated that they might show some flexibility if the Israelis do. There's a chance that we could get an agreement in the next month or so. A real agreement. The State Department is cautiously optimistic.'

'That's good.'

'It's very good, Magnus. This is *the* most intractable problem in the world today. But the main difficulty that both sides have isn't with each other, it's with their own people – the right wing in Israel that believes in the God-given right of Jews to settle the occupied territories, and the Palestinian terrorists who want to see an end to the state of Israel.'

'What are you saying?'

'I am saying that if a leak came out that harmed the reputation and good faith of either Israel or the Palestinians, it could disrupt the negotiations at a delicate stage.'

'How do you know that what Freeflow is working on would do this?'

'I don't, for sure. It's just a guess. But the balance of probability is that a big leak would screw things up. What do you think?'

Magnus thought of the images of those bullets from the Israeli helicopter thudding into Tamara Wilton's body. He thought of the chuckles, the jokes. 'I'd say it might.'

Bryant indicated and pulled over to the side of the road. The car behind hooted; he ignored it.

He turned to Magnus and looked him straight in the eye. 'If you could disrupt or delay this leak, whatever it is, it might save the peace process.'

Magnus hesitated. 'No,' he said.

'Why not?' said Bryant. 'Tell me why not. It's your duty to your country, the United States. Plus it will help stop one of the worst conflicts of the last fifty years.'

'It's true I am an American,' Magnus said. 'But I am an Icelander as well. And the job I am doing at the moment is for the Republic of Iceland. If you want the leak disrupted, then you should speak to the Icelandic authorities. It's up to them to decide what to do. I will simply do what they tell me. Have you spoken to them?'

Bryant didn't answer.

'You have, and they said no, didn't they? The Modern Media Initiative, I'll bet. My job is to solve a murder. And that I will do. But no more. Now I'm going.' He reached for the latch of the car door and opened it. 'Nice talking to you.'

'Think about it, Sergeant Detective Jonson.'

Magnus slammed the door and crossed the busy road looking for the nearest bus stop.

The man drummed his fingers as he pressed his mobile phone to his ear. He was on hold, and had been for two minutes. His eyes flicked to the statue of Leifur Eiríksson, over to the church spire and then across to the entrance of Thórsgata. He saw a small white car emerge, driven by the guy he had seen hanging around the street for the past hour or so, and the big detective.

Interesting.

He considered whether to follow them, but decided not to. Curiosity was one thing, but it was the Freeflow people he was really interested in. Besides which, he couldn't afford to break off the call.

'Hello? . . . Yes, that's right, fifteen thousand euros . . . And are you quite sure they won't know where the funds come from? I want this to be an anonymous donation, you see . . . Thank you. Thank you very much. Goodbye.'

The man cut the connection and tossed the phone on to the passenger seat beside him. He turned back to the entrance to Thórsgata and waited.

It was a couple of hours from Stykkishólmur back to Reykjavík. It was a beautiful drive, scarcely another car on the road, lava fields and farmland stretching down to the sea. The capital lurked beneath the horizon, but the hazy grey shape of Mount Esja floated like a distant island in the burnished bay.

Normally, Jóhannes would have felt a sense of euphoria

driving through this isolated beauty, especially on a school day. But he couldn't help turning over in his mind the importance of what he had learned.

If indeed his father had pushed Gunnar into the sea off Búland's Head seventy years before, he was a murderer.

His father, the man he admired most in the world, was a murderer.

The words that Benedikt had spoken to him while they were both surveying the Berserkjahraun made sense now. *Sometimes they do.* Sometimes people do take revenge for family honour, just as they had done in *The Saga of the People of Eyri.* And *Njáll's Saga* and *Gisli's Saga* and all the other sagas.

It was an admission. More than that, it was a justification. Benedikt was justifying to his son what he had done, even if it would take nearly fifty years for that son to appreciate it.

But Jóhannes was surprised to find that the discovery that his father was a murderer didn't fill him with revulsion. It filled him with a kind of pride. Benedikt knew right from wrong: that was why he was such a good writer. Like some of the sagas, his novels dealt with terrible moral dilemmas. He put his characters in positions where doing the right thing forced them to break the law, to alienate the people they loved, sometimes to destroy their own lives. That was why novels like *Moor and the Man* were so popular.

So if Benedikt had pushed his neighbour Gunnar over the cliff all those years ago, it had been the right thing to do.

And, like the characters in his books, it had eventually destroyed him.

Because although Jóhannes did not know for sure who had killed his father, he now knew why.

Revenge.

If Benedikt could kill Gunnar for murdering his own father, then Gunnar's family could kill Benedikt for the same crime.

A surge of anger rushed through Jóhannes's veins. The road was long and straight, and without realizing it, Jóhannes put his foot down. He nearly came off at a corner.

He slammed on the brakes, pulled off the road and jumped out of the car, flinging the door shut behind him.

He was in the middle of a flat plain near the Eldborg crater, an oval-shaped stone circle bursting up from the congealed lava surrounding it.

He kicked the wheel of the car. That was satisfying, but he wanted to kick the car itself.

Stupid. There was a boulder a few metres away. He ran over to it and booted it hard, swearing as he did so. He kicked it again and again and again. Words tumbled out of his mouth. His eyes stung. His face was hot; his whole body was on fire. He gave the stone one last kick and then hunched his shoulders and stomped off across the lava field towards the crater. He tripped and fell over some of the heather, stumbled on some more, fell again, and then a third time; he lay, panting on the grey stone.

The heat left him. His toe hurt like hell. A golden plover fluttered over the mossy lava next to him, peeping its displeasure at the disturbance he had caused.

He sat up, took off his shoe and rubbed his toe, still breathing heavily.

He felt a little scared. He hadn't done that for years, not since he was a child. He used to lose his temper sometimes then, when he was bullied or when things didn't go well at school. His father had comforted him, called him his little berserker.

Jóhannes the adolescent had controlled his temper with difficulty at first, but then with more and more ease. In fact one of his main qualities as a teacher was his patience. It was strange how out of nowhere that temper tantrum had hit him.

But of course it wasn't out of nowhere. He had lost his job. He had discovered that his father was a murderer. And that raised all kinds of questions about why his own father had in turn been killed.

Life would never be the same again for Jóhannes Benediktsson.

*

Ásta picked up a new cartridge on her way home from Thórsgata and installed it on her scanner. It was happy again now – no more whining.

Eighty pages to go. It was a slow bottom-of-the range machine that liked to grind, slide and wink before each page. It was trying Ásta's patience.

It had been a tough day. Ásta was good at dealing with the bereaved, but Teresa Andreose's distress was of an intensity she had rarely seen before. She had booked her into a hotel, and then taken her to the police station and left her there. Teresa had eventually warmed to her a little bit, but understandably she was suspicious of Ásta's connection with Freeflow.

Ásta wasn't sure now what to think about Erika. Like everyone else in the room she had been shocked at Teresa's accusation. There was no doubt that Erika had slept with another woman's husband, and that was clearly wrong. Erika had a lot to answer for. Yet Ásta couldn't help admiring the way that Erika had stood and accepted Teresa's tirade, not arguing with it, not making excuses.

It also put Erika's insistence that they continue to work on Project Meltwater in a different light. Ásta had been suspicious that Erika was using the claim that 'Nico would have wanted it' to justify her own ambition to promote Freeflow. Now it was clear that Erika really did care about Nico. Perhaps in her mind there was no conflict: she wanted to go ahead with the project for her own sake and for Nico's.

Thirty-eight pages to go. Ásta was tempted to multi-task.

Her eyes were drawn to a sheaf of paper she had printed out the previous weekend when she had heard Freeflow were coming to Iceland – press reports on their past leaks. She had skimmed them on Saturday, but there was something she had heard later in the house in Thórsgata that she wanted to check out.

She leafed through the printouts. After eight more pages of the journal had been scanned, she found what she was looking for.

She called up Wikipedia on her machine, and typed in a name.

She stared at the result. And stared, as the consequences of what she was reading sank in.

It could be a coincidence, of course. It must be a coincidence. But the more she thought about it, the more unlikely that seemed.

She needed to know.

CHAPTER SEVENTEEN

MAGNUS DIDN'T TELL his colleagues about his conversation with the CIA. They were doing well on the list of Israelis in Iceland: most of the tourists had been accounted for; there were still half a dozen to be followed up. The Italians were harder: half of Reykjavík's hotels seemed to be harbouring at least one Italian tourist, and five had been booked into the Hotel Rangá the night of the murder, the nearest big hotel to Fimmvörduháls. Of course none of them was still there. Vigdís had driven out there to talk to the manager and the staff. That would probably be her last task before going to Paris.

Árni had tracked down a black Suzuki Vitara rented from Keflavík Airport by two Canadian men, both dark haired and in their twenties. He had their names, but no idea where they were staying. They could be anywhere in the country.

Chief Superintendent Kristján called. 'What were you doing driving across the Markarfljót in the middle of a *jökulhlaup*?' he demanded.

'I wanted to get to the other side,' Magnus said.

'This is no joke, Magnús.' And indeed the chief superintendent didn't sound amused. 'So far we have managed to avoid any fatalities. We found the British schoolgirls and the Norwegian ambassador. But how stupid would we have looked if the only casualty had been one of our own men? In this country you have to treat nature with respect. Icelandic policemen know this.'

Magnus winced at the slur on his American background. He hated it when Icelanders made the point that he wasn't really one of them. He almost mentioned that they had natural disasters in the United States too, hadn't Kristján heard of Hurricane Katrina? But he thought better of it; that event had hardly covered the American authorities in glory.

'I had to look for the evidence,' said Magnus. 'Especially since they say there is going to be ash falling later on.'

'Did you find any?'

'Yes.' Magnus filled Kristján in on the state of the investigation.

'It sounds like you are making some progress,' said Kristján. 'Keep me informed. But I won't be able to spare any of my officers for the next couple of days. And don't take any more stupid risks around the volcano.'

'I won't. How's the guy in the Cat?'

'The Caterpillar? He's a hero. The highway isn't too badly damaged, and the bridge is still standing. I think he's gone home now for supper.'

Ásta brought Teresa Andreose into the station and Magnus interviewed her. Teresa was much calmer until Erika Zinn's name was mentioned. She had been jealous of Erika for months. Even though she suspected her husband of having an affair with Erika, she had had no evidence. But two weeks earlier, she had confronted her husband about his relationship with his Freeflow colleague. Nico had admitted that they had slept together a couple of times, but promised he wouldn't do it again. However, when he had said that he was going to Reykjavík with the Freeflow team, including Erika, Teresa had exploded.

Nico had gone regardless, and now he was dead.

'Did Nico speak to you much about Freeflow?' Magnus asked.

'Only in the most general terms. He kept on telling me what a wonderful organization it was, but he didn't talk about the details.'

'What about the Gruppo Cavour scandal?'

'That happened before Nico got involved. And we live in Milan: fortunately we have nothing to do with those Roman scandals.'

Magnus studied the Italian woman. She looked exhausted after her earlier eruption. Although she had reapplied her make-up, she could not hide the despair in her eyes.

'When can I have them send his body back to Italy?' she asked.

'I'm sorry,' Magnus said. 'We need to keep it here for a while. With the murder investigation.'

'You can't do that! I won't let him stay in this horrible country a moment longer!' For a moment it looked as if the fight would flare up in her again. But when Magnus shrugged, her shoulders slumped. 'Can I at least see him?'

'Of course,' said Magnus. 'I'll get one of my colleagues to take you to the morgue.'

'Thank you.' Teresa smiled quickly. 'And when I have seen him, I will go home. There is nothing more I can do here.'

Magnus hesitated. Could Teresa have paid someone to follow her husband to Iceland and kill him? Magnus doubted it, but it had to be an outside possibility. Erika's testimony suggested she was the real target on the mountain, but then Teresa could have wanted both of them dead. So now there were two reasons to look for an Italian.

Magnus considered insisting that Teresa stayed in Iceland, but decided to let her go. He had her address in Milan; the next step if he was serious about investigating her would be to get in touch with the police there. So he finished the interview and got hold of Róbert to take her to Barónsstígur to see the body of her husband.

At about seven, Magnús packed up to leave the station. Ordinarily he would have stayed later at this early stage of the investigation, but he hadn't had much sleep in the previous couple of days, and he knew he should see Ollie.

Before shutting down his computer, he checked the file he had added that morning. Sure enough there were some words added to the bottom:

we at ff have no idea who killed nico. like you we suppose it was someone with a grudge against us.

i am worried. whoever killed nico was trying to kill erika. he might try again. i want you to catch him. so if you have any questions about freeflow, ask me. maybe i can answer them maybe i can't.

Magnus smiled. That was interesting. Clearly someone at Freeflow wanted to help him. He wondered which of the group had written the message. Not Erika, obviously. Probably not Ásta. Perhaps Franz? Or someone with a longer period of involvement: Dúddi or Dieter?

What to ask?

He remembered Baldur's words. If there were any tensions within the Freeflow group, they hadn't come out in any of the interviews so far. But Teresa's dramatic outburst had demonstrated that there were things going on between members of the group that Erika and the rest of them had kept from the police.

Magnus began to type:

No one told us about Nico and Erika's relationship. Is there anything else going on between the people at Freeflow that we should know about?

Also who are you? I appreciate that you might not want the others to know that you have been in touch with me, but it would help me to know what to ask you.

Thanks for your help.

Magnus

Erika needed to get out of the house. The big cop, Magnus, might have warned her against it, but she just had to get away from the tense silence of the crowded room. She would explode otherwise. She pulled on her running kit and without saying anything to anyone, stepped out into the road.

The air was wonderfully fresh after the foetid house. Patches of blue came and went behind fast-moving clouds, and there was a brisk, salt-laden breeze blowing.

She hadn't looked at a map since she had arrived, but uphill to the big church and then down to the left would take her to the bay. She set off at speed.

It wasn't far to the top of the hill, but the wind was stronger there. She eased off as she loped down a small street, crossed a larger road lined with stores, dodging a couple of meandering tourists on the sidewalk, and headed down towards the water.

She crossed the busy road and hit the bike path right along the shoreline. At last she could get into a rhythm.

As a rule, Erika didn't do guilt. She saw guilt as one of those negative impulses injected into her psyche when she was young by her parents, with the intention of holding her back. Others were a desire for status, a duty to have children and a need for a monthly pay cheque.

She had fought them all and won. Provided you knew what you stood for, were open and honest at all times, and believed in your fellow humans, then Erika knew that you had nothing to feel guilty about. And she was all of those things: OK, sometimes she wasn't exactly honest, but you couldn't get anywhere unless you were willing to bend the truth for a good cause.

Yet it was hard to avoid the sense of guilt. Teresa's pain was real. Her hatred of Erika was real. Her love of Nico was real.

Was Teresa right? Had Erika not only taken her husband away from her, but also caused his death?

For a moment, Erika's steps faltered. She slowed down, became aware of how tired she was. The wind blew down cold from the big block of Mount Esja to the north. Perhaps she should just pack her suitcase and move out of the house as soon as she got home.

And then what would she do?

No, Erika was committed to her life, to her cause. Teresa was wrong. Teresa *must* be wrong.

Erika thought it all through, sensibly this time. Although she was quite capable of seducing married men, it was Nico who had seduced her. Right here in Reykjavík the previous November. Erika had been planning to stay at a cheap guest-house when Nico had changed the reservations to the 101 hotel, the smartest hotel in town, paying the bill himself. He had booked two rooms, but they ended up only using one of them.

He wouldn't have done that if he had loved Teresa.

He might have loved her once, but he loved Erika more. And Erika knew why. She and Freeflow had given Nico a sense of purpose. He had had a bad couple of years at his hedge fund in London, but he had thrown himself into helping her build up Freeflow. He had loved it.

He had loved her.

It was all his choice. All of it. She needn't point that out to Teresa, but she herself shouldn't forget it.

She had gone quite a distance – past the white mansion with the flags, and almost to the end of the road of plush new office buildings.

She turned around. She was tired, but the blood was flowing. Things were rearranging themselves in her head, as she knew they would.

She wasn't sure precisely where she had emerged on to the wide green strip next to the bay on the way down, but she could see the spire on the hill above her. She jogged past a skeletal bronze sculpture of some kind of Viking ship which she hadn't passed on the way out, and decided to cut up through some narrow roads, past half-finished blocks rising unnaturally high above the low city skyline.

Her earlier speed had tired her, especially as she was going uphill. She glanced behind her, back towards the bay.

And saw a man running up the hill, only fifty yards behind.

The way his eyes were focused on her, she knew he hadn't just happened on the same route as her.

He was chasing her.

*

The man saw Erika pound across the square in front of the Hallgrímskirkja in sweatpants and a hoodie with the faded name of some American college on her chest.

Car or foot?

Foot. The man was fit; he knew he could keep up. And all it would take would be for her to cut down a one-way street and he would lose her in a car.

He was wearing trainers and his own sweatshirt, which was good, but also jeans, which would make him look less like a runner and more like someone chasing someone else.

Nothing he could do about that. He grabbed his hunting knife, hidden in a plastic supermarket bag, and jumped out of the car.

She was running fast, this Erika woman. Soon he was panting. He kept well back from her, but nonetheless he attracted some strange looks from passers-by. The knife was swinging in the plastic bag – he hoped it wasn't too obvious what it was. He fell back. Tried to run with less purpose.

He was fairly sure that Erika was heading down towards the line of the bay, in which case he could allow a hundred metres or more between them, perhaps try to catch her on her way back.

His blood flowed faster, and not just from the running. He was going to get his chance. This time he wouldn't blow it.

This time he would kill the bitch.

He followed well behind her along the shoreline, until she suddenly turned and retraced her steps. Realizing she was going to pass right by him, he slowed down, began panting more heavily and rolling his head from side to side like a runner in pain. There were a couple of other runners along the shore path, together with the odd walker and half a dozen cyclists.

Erika didn't even register him as she jogged past. Her mind was miles away.

He left it a minute and then turned, keeping his eye on her. Suddenly she cut across one of the two carriageways of the busy road. He lengthened his stride and made up some of the distance between them as she waited at the next carriageway.

He knew he had to act fast. Within ten minutes she would be back in the house in Thórsgata, and who knew when she would next emerge?

He ran across both carriageways, dodging traffic, and pounded up the hill. He was nearly on her when she turned and saw him.

He lengthened his stride to close to a sprint.

She turned left down a narrow side street and he lost sight of her for a second. As he sped around the corner the street ahead was empty. It was only a short road with a recently constructed block of flats on one side and some derelict houses on the other. At the end of the street a slightly bigger road ran uphill.

He was really moving now as he headed for the next corner. But his eye caught a narrow path to the left.

He stopped.

Erika hadn't been going quite fast enough to reach the far end of the road before he would have seen her.

Which meant that she was still in the street somewhere.

He scanned the road. There were no people. Good.

There were only a few doorways, and all the doors seemed firmly shut. Good.

And there was the one little path.

He jogged up to the gap between two derelict buildings. The path led to a small courtyard surrounded by buildings on all sides. It was empty apart from a half-filled skip.

He pulled the knife out of the plastic bag and jogged towards it. He was only a metre or so away when Erika leaped out of the skip.

She ran away from him into the corner of the courtyard. He held his arms wide. There was nothing she could do now but try to rush past him. He was ready.

He'd got her.

Magnus felt bad about leaving the station before Vigdís and Árni, but he felt worse about keeping Ollie waiting too long.

As he walked across the compound behind police headquarters to his Range Rover, he thought about what Tom Bryant had said. Magnus's instinct was to avoid the CIA. In his experience, whenever government intelligence agencies got involved, things got complicated. That was true of the FBI, and it had to be even more true of the CIA. Magnus had promised Erika that he had nothing to do with the CIA, and he wanted to keep things that way.

And yet he understood Bryant's point. The video Magnus had watched that afternoon would horrify the international community. It would incense the Palestinians, reigniting the sense of injustice on both sides caused by the Gaza war. If the two sides were really that close to peace, perhaps it would be better if the release of the video was delayed?

Perhaps. But it wasn't up to him to make that decision. While he was in Iceland his loyalties lay with the government of Iceland. It was that simple.

As he turned on the Range Rover's engine, his phone rang. 'Magnús.'

'It's Gudmundur. I'm watching the house in Thórsgata. A woman has just left the property in running gear. I think it's Erika Zinn. Do you want me to follow her?'

Magnus paused. Idiot! He'd told her to remain inside. Once she was out on the streets of Reykjavík she was vulnerable.

'No. You'd better stay outside the house. I'm in my car at headquarters, I'll see if I can find her. Which way did she go?'

'Up the hill to the Hallgrímskirkja and then turned left.'

'OK – I'll check for her along the bay. That's the most likely place to go for a run in that direction. What's she wearing?'

'Black sweatpants. Grey hoodie with "Princeton" on the front. White baseball cap.'

'Got it.'

Police headquarters was only a few yards from Saebraut, the dual carriageway that ran along the shore of the bay. Presumably Erika didn't know Reykjavík very well. She could have gone anywhere, of course, but the long green strip with its bike path would be the natural place for a runner to head for.

He drove slowly west along Saebraut. There were a small number of joggers on the bike path. He soon saw one with black pants and a grey top running away from him. No cap, but he accelerated to catch her up. She crossed the road and ran up a side street.

Magnus turned to follow her. He lost her in the cluster of streets around government buildings, including the big black block of the hated Central Bank. It took him several minutes before he caught up with the woman on Hverfisgata.

Not Erika.

Back to the Saebraut.

And then he saw her. Crossing the road a hundred yards ahead of him, her dark hair bobbing up and down under her white baseball cap. She disappeared up a side road.

Behind her was another runner, a man wearing jeans, moving fast.

Magnus accelerated, and followed them up the little street, only to be met by two cars heading downhill towards him, one behind the other. There was no room to pass. Three horns blared. Rather than argue with the other drivers, Magnus leaped out of his car and ran up the hill, just in time to see the man turn a corner to the left.

Magnus followed.

The road was empty.

OK. This was where Magnus needed a gun. In any halfway sensible country he could pull out his firearm. But not in Iceland. In Iceland he had to go in with just his fists.

Oh, well. Magnus knew how to use his fists.

He jogged along the road, slowing when he came to an opening. And there, at the end of a narrow path, was the man, holding his arms out wide, a hunting knife in his right hand. Erika was literally cornered.

'Hey, you!' Magnus shouted, in English. 'Police! Drop the knife!'

The man turned and Erika saw her chance. She darted along one wall, but the man was too quick for her. Too quick and too strong.

In one movement he grabbed her, twisted her around and,

holding her with one arm around the neck, held the knife to her face.

'Stop!' he shouted.

Magnus had lunged forward himself, but froze at the man's words. If only I had a goddamned gun, he thought.

Magnus was about ten yards from the man. He studied his face. Youngish, late twenties, maybe, at six feet a couple of inches shorter than Magnus. Narrower shoulders, but strong and wiry. A long thin face, unshaven; a narrow pointed nose; longish dark hair, brushed back, receding slightly at the temples; brown eyes. Magnus would remember that face.

The eyes worried him. They were bright, shining, excited, manic. But they were also angry. And full of hate. Lots of hate.

Magnus held up his hands. 'OK. Let's talk about this. Let the woman go and we can talk about it.'

'Why should I let her go? I want to kill her. I *will* kill her.'

Magnus glanced at Erika. Her eyes were wide, desperate. She was several inches shorter than the man. Slowly she began to slide down his chest. Just as slowly she drew her own right arm upwards.

Magnus knew what she was planning. If this was a genuine hostage situation Magnus might have told her to stop. But he had a feeling that she only had seconds to live. In which case her idea was her best chance.

'So why do you want to kill her?' Magnus said, more to distract the man than because he expected an answer. 'Surely Freeflow is harmless, isn't it?'

The man stared at Magnus, his eyes wild. 'I have my reasons,' he said. 'There's nothing you can say—'

Then Erika made her move. She slipped down another couple of inches, thrust her arm downwards and jammed her elbow into the man's groin.

He cried out in pain, and Erika twisted as he tried to slash her neck. He caught something, and she too yelled.

Magnus dived at the man's knife hand. The two of them tumbled on to the ground. Magnus focused on the man's hand, bending back the thumb until the man let go of the knife. Magnus felt a fist slam into his neck and then his ear, before he was flung sideways.

Both men lunged at the knife, Magnus sending it spinning into the corner just before the man's fingers could grasp it.

Magnus scrabbled across the ground to grab the weapon. He pulled himself to his feet and saw the man take off, planting a kick on Erika's head as he went.

Magnus sprinted after him, gripping the knife. Magnus was fast, and he was pretty sure he could catch the other man, but Erika was lying motionless in the dirt and Magnus knew it was more important to make sure she was OK. So he stopped after a few yards and turned back to where she was sprawled unconscious in a small pool of blood.

He knelt beside her. She was breathing. There was a fair bit of blood, but it was dribbling from a cut in her cheek rather than spurting out of her jugular.

He pulled out his phone and called in help.

CHAPTER EIGHTEEN

MAGNUS UNLOCKED THE door to his house and opened it. A faint smell of marijuana tickled his nostrils.

So Ollie had found the place then.

Magnus was very late. Erika had been taken to the National Hospital nearby, where her cheek had been discreetly patched up. Magnus had given a detailed description of her attacker, and the police were looking for him in Reykjavík. He would be hard to find. Although Magnus was sure he would recognize him again, there were hundreds, possibly thousands of men in Reykjavík who fitted his general description.

'Hi!' Magnus called out and walked into the kitchen. The house was small. His room was upstairs with his own little bathroom. Downstairs was larger: it was where Katrín lived. The kitchen, which Magnus had the use of, was just off the entrance hallway.

Katrín and Ollie were sitting at the table, smoking cigarettes, a couple of Magnus's cans of Viking beer open in front of them.

'Hey, bro!' said Ollie as he pulled himself laboriously to his feet and gave Magnus a hug.

'Sorry I didn't meet you at the airport,' Magnus said. 'And I was supposed to be here a couple of hours ago but something came up.'

'I've been OK,' Ollie said.

'It looks like you've made yourself at home.'

'Yeah, you didn't tell me what a great landlady you had,' Ollie said.

Magnus smiled at Katrín. She was very tall with a pallid complexion and short dark hair cut in a bob. She was wearing black jeans and T-shirt. She was going easy on the facial metal these days – the rings and studs were confined to her ears. She gave him a small triumphant smile. Magnus and Katrín had lived together for a year and he knew her pretty well by now. It was an I've-slept with-your-brother type smile.

Ollie's eyes were shining. He looked happy to be in Iceland. Although you could tell from his features that they were related, Ollie was skinnier than Magnus and his hair was light brown and curly, compared to Magnus's red. He was wearing a Sam Adams T-shirt and jeans. Both he and Katrín were in bare feet.

'Yes, she is nice, isn't she? What have you been up to all day?'

'Just hanging here,' Ollie said. 'I didn't sleep well on the plane, you know?'

'Any sign of Ingileif?' Magnus asked.

'Haven't seen her,' Katrín said. 'I wondered who you had with you last night. I didn't know she was back in Iceland.' She smiled. Magnus could see she was genuinely pleased for him. Although they had never spoken about it, Katrín knew he missed her. She stubbed out her cigarette. 'I'll leave you two alone.'

'See you later,' said Ollie.

'Oh, Katrín,' said Magnus. 'Can Ollie use your spare bedroom tonight? I thought he could sleep on my floor, but with Ingileif in town . . .'

'I'm sure I can find room for your cute little brother,' she said with a quick glance at Ollie, and left the kitchen.

'Come upstairs, Ollie,' said Magnus.

'Katrín and I became quite well acquainted,' Ollie said, following Magnus up the stairs. 'She's very friendly, you know?'

'Yeah. I knew you'd get along, I just didn't think you'd get along that well.'

Ollie did well with women, always had. He had a mixture of cockiness and vulnerability that seemed to appeal to some of them; why, Magnus wasn't quite sure.

'Nice view,' said Ollie, looking out of the window and up the hill at the swooping spire.

'Yeah, it's not a bad place,' said Magnus. 'Katrín doesn't charge me too much.'

'And Ingileif is back? I remember you talking about her. Will I get to meet her?'

'Probably later. She's out with clients this evening. And she's not staying in Iceland very long. She's still working in Hamburg.'

'What is all that?' Ollie exclaimed looking at Magnus's wall. 'Is that all about Dad's death?'

'Yes,' said Magnus. 'And the death of Benedikt Jóhannesson the author. I told you about that.'

'You're seriously strange, you know that?' said Ollie staring at the wall. 'Hey, that's a photo of me! What am I doing there? Where do I fit in?'

'You don't, really,' said Magnus.

'Too right, I don't. Hey, can we go out to a bar or something?'

The words *I don't want to stay in a room with that on the wall* were unsaid, but Magnus understood them.

'Sure,' he said.

Magnus's regular hangout, the Grand Rokk, had closed a couple of months before, much to his sorrow – yet another victim of the credit crunch. So they went to a bar down the hill, Kaffibarinn. It was just a small black-painted building with a London Underground sign above the door. It was empty on a Wednesday evening, cosy and civilized. It was difficult to imagine the seething crowd of drink- and drug-fuelled bodies heaving to the music that crammed into the place on a Friday or Saturday night.

Magnus bought his brother another beer.

'How are things going?' Magnus asked.

'Not good,' said Ollie. 'I keep on thinking that the market's coming back, but then it goes dead on me. And the rent isn't quite enough to cover the mortgage payments.'

'The students are still coming though?'

'Yeah. But as you know the plan was always to make capital gains.'

Ollie had purchased half a dozen houses in Medford, a suburb of Boston near Tufts University. They were the kind that students liked to rent. He had borrowed heavily to do it, hoping to flip them as prices rose. It was something he had been doing for several years, and he had made some good money, all of which he had ploughed back into more properties. He had urged Magnus to join him, but Magnus had resisted. Then the crash came, house prices fell, but the debt Ollie owed to the banks only got bigger.

Perhaps Ollie was more of an Icelander than he realized.

'Maybe things will get better in the summer,' Magnus said.

'Yeah, maybe. Maybe. Hey, any chance I can get to see this volcano? That sounds cool.'

'The pretty one has stopped erupting,' Magnus said. 'There's a big ugly one going at it now.'

He described his morning drive out to Skógafoss and the *jökulhlaup*. And then his evening entertainment with the guy with the knife.

'And you told me life here is dull,' Ollie said.

'It is most of the time. And then something happens, and an interesting case crops up. I guess I should just be more patient. I'm used to a couple of murders a week.'

'Yeah, but those are on the streets of Southie, not on the edge of a friggin' volcano.'

'That's true,' said Magnus.

'Another beer?' said Ollie. He went up to the bar and bought them from a girl with green hair and a ring through her nose. Magnus couldn't hear what Ollie said to her, but he did hear her laugh. Turned out she was from New Hampshire, Ollie announced when he returned with the drinks.

'Speaking of murders in Boston . . .' Magnus said.

'Here we go,' said Ollie, eyeing his brother as he took a gulp of his beer.

'I did what you wanted,' Magnus said. 'I haven't asked anyone any more questions here about Dad.'

'Thanks, bro, I appreciate it.'

'But I want to.' Magnus leaned forward. 'You've seen the wall in my room. It's true I want to know what happened to him. I *need* to know. It was why I joined Boston PD in the first place. It's like I feel every murder I investigate is his murder, except I never get to solve it. Or *re*solve it. So I go on to the next and the next.'

'I can't help you with that shit, Magnus,' Ollie said.

'But you can, that's just it. I think finally I might be getting there. When we go back to the house I'll show you the wall. There is this writer called Benedikt Jóhannesson who was killed in 1985 in Reykjavík with exactly the same MO as Dad.'

'MO?'

'*Modus operandi*. Method. A stab wound in the back and two in the chest. Just like Dad.'

'Except Dad was killed five thousand miles away and ten years later.'

'Two thousand miles.'

'Whatever. You get my point.'

'Yes, but Benedikt was brought up at Hraun, over the lava field from Bjarnarhöfn. You remember the place?'

'I remember as little as possible of all that.'

'Well, he was. And they've got some kind of family feud going. Grandpa's father Gunnar killed Benedikt's father, and then Benedikt killed Gunnar.'

'So you think Grandpa killed them both?'

'Not necessarily. He's left-handed for a start and the killer was right-handed. Also there is no record of Grandpa ever going to America, let alone him being there when Dad was murdered in 1996.'

'Sounds to me like you've got the wrong guy then,' Ollie said.

'Perhaps. But I know I can find the right guy.'

'So what are you saying?'

'That I'm going to start asking more questions about our family. About Benedikt. About Dad.'

'But you promised not to!' Anger flared in Ollie's eyes.

'I know, and now I've changed my mind.'

Ollie put his head in his hands. 'Look, I'm just about getting my shit together again, Magnus. This is the last thing I need now. What happened at Bjarnarhöfn was really bad for me. I get nightmares about that potato cellar that Grandpa shoved me into. The dark. The cold. The smell. The slime of those rotten potatoes. It might not sound like much but I was a little kid, my mother was drunk all the time, my father had abandoned me and this horrible man made my life hell.'

'I was there.'

Ollie smiled. 'Yeah, you were there for me. You're always there for me. Which is why I'm begging you to leave all this alone, man.'

'But what if I don't tell you what I discover? What difference would that make to you?'

'Oh, come on. You will tell me. You'll drag me back to that hellhole one way or another. Come on, man!' Anger was rising in Ollie's voice. 'You know I've been to different shrinks over the years. They all say the same thing, and frankly it's a pretty easy diagnosis. My problems come from those four years at Bjarnarhöfn.'

'And mine come from the year Dad died.'

'You can handle it better than me,' Ollie said, jabbing his finger at his brother. 'You've always been able to handle things better than me.'

'Perhaps,' said Magnus. 'But I am going to do some more investigation. I won't tell you what I discover, if you like, but I'm going to ask those questions.'

Ollie's lips were pursed and his head was shaking in anger and frustration. 'You're gonna push me over the edge here, Magnus. I'm not kidding you, man.'

Magnus didn't reply.

Ollie finished his beer. 'Let's go back. I'm tired.'

They walked back to Njálsgata in silence. Back at the house, Ollie was just about to go through to Katrín's room when Magnus touched his arm.

'Ollie?'

Ollie glared at his brother.

'Why did you come to Iceland?' Magnus asked. 'If you wanted to leave all this behind you?'

'See the sights. Catch some rays. Spend some quality time with my brother. What do you think?'

His voice was dripping with sarcasm, and before Magnus could reply he had gone through to Katrín's room.

Magnus had no idea what to think. He stomped up the stairs to his own room.

He stared at the wall. At the photograph of his father. At the picture of Benedikt Jóhannesson.

He knew Ollie's fear of what had happened to him at Bjarnarhöfn when he was a kid was real, but he didn't understand why that meant Magnus couldn't pursue his own investigations. He had a perfect right to, whatever Ollie said.

Magnus felt the anger rise within him. Once again he was being manipulated by his brother, who was taking on his habitual role of injured victim. Magnus was always being manipulated by his brother. Well, this time Magnus wasn't going to let him get away with it. He picked up the photograph of Ollie with his cocky smirk, and stuck it dead centre in the middle of the wall.

Ollie was involved, and no amount of whining on his part would change that.

His doorbell rang. He went downstairs to see Ingileif, smiling broadly on the doorstep. She kissed him.

'Hi,' she said. 'I finally get to see you.'

They went up to his room. 'Is Ollie here?'

'He's downstairs. He said he was going to sleep.'

'So I won't get to meet him?'

'Perhaps not tonight. Although he seems to have made good friends with Katrín.'

'Really? Last time I saw her, she liked girls.'

'A passing phase, I think. Ollie and I had a fight.'

'Already?'

'Yeah. Over that.' Magnus nodded to the wall.

'You want to find out more and he doesn't?'

'That's right.'

Magnus slumped on to the bed. Ingileif flopped next to him, and snuggled into his chest. He put his arm around her and squeezed.

'At some point you need to do what you need to do,' Ingileif said. 'I know you worry about him, but this is important for you too. And maybe once you have figured out what's going on, you can take all that down.'

'Maybe,' said Magnus. 'Maybe a lot of things would be better.'

'I hope so,' said Ingileif. But Magnus could hear the note of doubt in her voice. Perhaps he would never be able to live in peace with the death of his father. But he had to try.

'How's the other investigation going?' Ingileif asked. 'The guy who died on the volcano?'

'Not brilliantly.'

'Tell me about it.'

So Magnus told her about Freeflow and Erika and Teresa. As he talked he unwound, relaxed.

And then they made love.

As Magnus lay in bed staring at the ceiling, his thigh lightly touching Ingileif's naked, slumbering body, he thought how good it was to have her back.

He smiled.

CHAPTER NINETEEN

Thursday 15 April 2010

'THE ASH IS falling,' said Árni. 'Did you see it on TV?'

His eyes were shining. It was eight o'clock and all the members of the Violent Crimes Unit were huddled together in a meeting room to discuss the case. The uniformed inspector was there, as were Rannveig and Chief Superintendent Thorkell Holm, the head of CID and everybody's boss. And Baldur, of course.

'Some of us have better things to do in the morning than watch TV,' said Baldur.

'Like sleep,' said Róbert.

'There was a shot of a farm in Mýrdalur,' Árni continued. 'The whole place is covered in this horrible grey stuff, including the sheep. The farmer said he was screwed. The ash will poison his crops and his animals. Fluorine.'

'Is the eruption getting worse?' someone asked.

'It's still going strong. And there is a *lot* of ash. They have closed some airspace as far away as Scotland. Apparently the ash can ruin aircraft engines.'

'It looks OK here,' said Róbert. And indeed it did. In Reykjavík it was a bit cloudy, a bit cold, but no sign of ash.

'The wind is blowing it all to the east,' said Árni. 'Although they say it's going to blow south today.'

Thorkell cleared his throat. He was a bluff grey-haired man with a shiny good-natured face. Not quite as sharp as Snorri, the

Commissioner, but no dummy. And he was Árni's uncle. 'Let's start. We have a lot to get through this morning. Magnús?'

Magnus ran through the attack on Erika the evening before and the attempts to find the attacker. Several witnesses had seen him run across Laugavegur up the hill towards the Hallgrímskirkja, but no one had seen him get into a car. Erika had confirmed that she was pretty sure that he was the same man who had attacked her and Nico on the volcano. She herself had spent a couple of hours in hospital – her cheek had been badly cut – but now she was back at the house on Thórsgata.

Magnus repeated his description and said he was due to spend some time with a police artist that morning.

'You heard him speak, did you, Magnús?' Baldur asked.

'Yes.'

'In English?'

'Yes.'

'What kind of accent did he have?'

'I don't know,' said Magnus. It was a good question. 'He only said a few words.' Magnus closed his eyes trying to remember. 'It was foreign – I mean he wasn't a native English speaker. And definitely not Icelandic or Germanic. Could have been Italian . . . French . . . Spanish, something like that.'

'Israeli?'

'I guess. I'm not really sure what an Israeli accent sounds like.'

'Did he look like a professional killer?' Vigdís asked.

Magnus remembered the manic eyes. The failure to cut Erika's throat when he had her in his grasp.

'No. No, I don't think so, but we shouldn't rule it out. He could be an idealist. And we know he's capable of killing. Whatever he is, he's still out there. We ought to increase the police presence at the house on Thórsgata.'

The uniformed inspector nodded. 'I'll do that.'

'Now. Let's go through all the possible suspects again.'

They spent an hour going through Israelis, Italians, Canadians driving Suzuki Vitara rental cars, US college fraternities, Mikael

Már and his French business client, Teresa, the inhabitants of the house. There were leads to follow up: an Israeli tourist unaccounted for, last seen in the east of Iceland. And leads to drop: the group of Italians who had stayed at the Hotel Rangá were having dinner there the moment Nico was attacked. There was plenty to do and not enough people to do it. Vigdís wasn't there – her flight to Paris was that afternoon. Magnus could have used her.

'Did you check out the café receipt at Heathrow, Árni?'

'The receipt was timed at 12:17 and there was an Icelandair flight departing from that terminal at 13:00.'

'Anyone interesting on the flight?'

'Nico Andreose was the only member of the Freeflow team. It was Sunday; presumably he flew over earlier than the others.'

'I wonder if he recognized the killer?' Magnus said.

Árni pondered Magnus's question. 'I suppose he might have done. He might even have chatted to him – since there was no one else from Freeflow on the plane we wouldn't know.'

'Yes. It's worth checking whether he mentioned anything to the rest of the team later. You know: "Guess who I saw on the plane yesterday?" What about Israelis? Italians?'

'No Israelis. Apart from Nico there was one Italian couple, but they were in their sixties.' Árni checked his notes. 'Mostly Icelanders, quite a few British, three US citizens, then a couple of Canadians, French, Belgian, Japanese, Thai, Irish. No real lead that I could see.'

Magnus was disappointed, especially given the risks he had taken to find the damn receipt.

'I checked the Skull and Bones society on the Freeflow website,' Árni said.

'And?'

'Nothing. Nothing from Yale at all.'

'Check Ohio State,' said Magnus, thinking of Franz, who had said he'd spent a year there. Although he doubted very much that a year in Columbus, Ohio would inspire enough loyalty in the young Swiss to kill.

'What about the CIA?' Árni asked.

The whole room looked at Magnus. He hadn't told any of them about his meeting with Bryant, and he didn't intend to. The CIA had an agenda and Magnus had no idea what it really was. He had had few dealings with the agency in the States. The FBI, all the time. Homeland Security occasionally; there was no predicting what *they* might get up to once they had an idea in their heads. But not the CIA.

'I'll think about that one,' said Magnus.

'Do you want me to make inquiries with the American Embassy?' said Thorkell.

'Yes,' said Magnus. 'I'm not sure they'll tell you anything, but they might.' Bryant had suggested that the CIA had been in touch with the Icelandic government for its help in impeding Freeflow's activities. Clearly Thorkell knew nothing of that. But it would be useful if he could unearth the Icelanders' side of the story.

'What about Teresa?' Baldur asked.

Magnus suppressed a flash or irritation. 'I interviewed her briefly yesterday.'

'And?'

'She's angry about her husband. Angry *with* her husband, that's for sure. And with Erika. Understandably.'

'Very understandably,' said Baldur. 'Did she pay someone to kill them?'

Magnus swallowed. 'I didn't ask her.'

'Shouldn't you have?'

'Yes,' Magnus said. 'Yes, of course.' Baldur was absolutely right. Teresa needed a grilling, however unpleasant that would be for all concerned, and Magnus really should have done it the day before. His instinct then was that her anger at her husband's death was genuine, but Baldur's suggestion was theoretically possible, and should be followed up, if only to rule it out. 'I'll bring her in this morning.'

'Can I join you?'

'By all means,' said Magnus.

Magnus spent ten minutes dividing up tasks, and then the meeting broke up just in time for a press conference, which he attended with Thorkell. Lots of questions, lots of answers. Plenty of excitement that there was a foreign killer on the loose in Reykjavík. Magnus gave a description, but didn't mention the Vitara. If the suspect was still using that vehicle, Magnus didn't want him to ditch it – which he would certainly do if he heard about it on TV.

'We need to find this man soon, Magnús,' said Thorkell. 'They're excited today – they'll be angry tomorrow.'

'I know,' said Magnus.

Erika was afraid. She had worked almost all night on the video, hoping to push the fear out of her mind, but the more tired she got, the more it crept back.

She had been in danger before, in the hellhole that was Rwanda, when she was much younger. Twice she had had the barrel of a Kalashnikov shoved into her face. Once a bunch of heavily armed Hutus had threatened to rape her. Somehow, Guillaume, the Rwandan doctor who later briefly became her husband, had talked them out of it. She had been scared, but at the age of twenty she had somehow always known she would come through alive.

She was kidding herself then, of course – it was the illusion of invulnerability of youth – but she had believed it, and she had stayed in Rwanda for nine more months, returning to the States with a husband.

She was older now and she knew she wasn't invulnerable. If Nico could die, so could she.

Of the many things she felt guilty about, at least she no longer felt guilty about betraying Israel. If the Israelis had killed Nico and were trying to kill her, they deserved all they got. If anything, it was the Israeli state who were betraying people like her grandmother, loyal Jews who believed in the Promised Land. It was up to Erika and Freeflow to expose that betrayal.

It was always the same: the closer you looked at the secrets of a government, any government, the more filth you found.

She wondered about protection. They could use a couple of guns. She glanced around the room. She would never trust Dieter with a firearm, but she knew how to operate a handgun. Franz seemed capable and she had read somewhere that the Swiss did military service. As did Israeli women. That was three of them.

She would ask Magnus when she next saw him, which would no doubt be some time that morning.

She swigged from a can of Red Bull and touched her cheek. The doctor had said there would be a small scar, but it would fade. Erika wasn't too bothered. She had never been a classic beauty, and somehow she felt her allure to men would only be enhanced with a war wound.

She was exhausted. She could work long hours without sleep. Her brain was a battleground, the forces of fatigue fighting the caffeine, adrenaline and pure determination. She knew she should rest, or her judgement would begin to go. And a misjudgement could blow the whole project.

The corner of her screen flickered. A message. From Gareth.

Gareth: *bad news.*

Erika: *please don't tell me you're not at heathrow.*

Gareth: *i'm at heathrow. and so is my plane. but it's not going anywhere, at least today. all flights are cancelled. uk airspace is closed.*

Erika: *why?*

Gareth: *because of your volcano. there is an ash cloud over the atlantic and all over britain.*

'Damn liar!' Erika growled to herself. She stood up and went to the living-room window, flicking back the curtain. Grey clouds. Clear air. She stalked back to the computer.

Erika: *there's no ash. get your ass over here!*

Gareth: *hey, it's not up to me. if they won't let the planes fly there's nothing i can do.*

Dieter: *i just checked. he's right. there's a big cloud of ash blowing south from Iceland stopping flights into the uk.*

Erika glanced across at Dieter only a few feet away from her, cocooned in his headphones. He, of course, had drawn his observation from his computer screen and not the real world outside. He shrugged and shook his head.

Erika: *have they said when you can fly?*

Gareth: *they say they will make another announcement at 3pm. it all depends on the wind apparently.*

Erika: *okay, don't leave the airport. get your ass on the first plane to reykjavik.*

Gareth: *ok. i'll let you know as soon as they tell me my flight's leaving.*

Erika stared at the screen. The video editing was going well. Dieter and Apex had set up a complicated series of websites to host it. The big weakness was verification.

Erika: *apex, did you get that?*

Apex: *yeah.*

Of course he did. It might be the middle of the night around the other side of the world, but Apex would be faithfully staring at his screen.

Erika: *are you still worried about the engine noise of the helicopter?'*

Apex: *frankly, yes. gareth says it's probably just the wind conditions at the time of the incident, or the pitch of the rotor blades, but i need him to check it out properly, which he hasn't been able to do yet.*

Erika: *maybe he'll get out tonight. or tomorrow.*

Apex: *he had better. but i do have some good news.*

Erika: *what?*

Apex: *15,000 euros just hit our account.*

'Yes!' Erika punched the air. 'See that, Dieter?' she shouted across the room to her colleague, but he was still staring at his screen, earphones on, waiting for her to type something.

Erika: *yay!!! where did it come from?*

Apex: *no idea. all donations are anonymized. you know that.*

Erika: *yes, but can't you get into the system and find out?*

Apex: *i set it up so I couldn't. we agreed it was better all round if we didn't know where the money came from.*

Typical Apex, Erika thought. What a warped sense of integrity he had; she didn't understand it. She wondered who the donor was. Viktor, perhaps? But why would he make it anonymously?

Still, fifteen thousand euros was fifteen thousand euros. She wasn't going to quibble.

Erika: *can you send it on to Sweden?*

Apex: *it's on its way. i contacted them and they confirmed as long as their bank gets the funds by friday, they'll host our sites over the weekend.*

Erika: *so we are all set. as long as gareth gets here tomorrow.*

Apex: *what about alan? wasn't he flying to london this morning?*

'Shit!' exclaimed Erika.

Erika: *i'll check.*

She picked out one of the phones Viktor and Dúddi had bought, and dialled a US cell-phone number.

'Alan Traub.'

'Hey, Alan, it's Erika. Where are you?'

'At the Hertz desk at Heathrow.'

'Thank God. I thought your flight might have been cancelled. There's an ash cloud from the volcano here heading for Britain.'

'They didn't tell us anything about that. But I'm definitely in England now.'

'Are you going to see Samantha Wilton?'

'Called her yesterday. She lives in Beaconsfield: it's not far from the airport. I'll probably be there in an hour or so. When can I say she can see the video?'

'We're aiming to have it finished noon Sunday. I'll fly to London that afternoon and I'll bring it with me. She can see it that evening. We'll do the press conference on Monday and put it up on our website then. I warn you, she's not going to like it.'

'I'll tell her that. But I know she'll want to see it.'

'And she's happy with attending the press conference?'

'I'll talk to her about it this morning.'

'OK, I won't keep you. Give me a call when you've spoken to her.'

Erika hung up. Things were coming together. She called across to Franz. 'How are you doing with the end credits?'

Ásta checked the bathroom door upstairs. It was still locked. Someone had been in there for at least ten minutes.

She heard a sound from inside. She put her ear to the door. A sob. It was definitely a sob.

'Zivah?' It sounded like a woman and she knew Erika was downstairs. 'Zivah? It's Ásta. Do you want to talk?'

Ásta heard sniffing, and then a voice, Zivah's voice. 'Do you need the bathroom?'

'No, I'm OK. But are you?'

The door opened. Zivah's eyes were red, and her cheeks were stained with tears.

'What's wrong?' Ásta asked.

'Oh, Ásta, I'm scared. I'm so scared.'

Ásta opened her arms and enveloped Zivah. 'Hey. Let's go into your room and we'll talk about it, eh?'

Ásta led Zivah into the room she shared with Erika. Zivah avoided the bed, which was Erika's, and flopped on to her sleeping bag neatly folded on the floor. Ásta sat herself down next to her. They both leaned back against the wall, shoulder to shoulder.

'They're going to kill Erika. They've tried twice and failed, but they'll get her next time. And then they'll kill me.'

'No, they won't,' said Ásta. 'You'll be safe here. The police are outside.'

'We're talking about Mossad here!' said Zivah. 'If they want me dead, I'm dead. Believe me.'

'But why would they want to kill you?'

'Because I've betrayed my country. At least in their eyes.'

'No, you haven't. All you have done is translate the words that Israeli soldiers actually used. Erika's right: you are helping Freeflow reveal the truth. If that looks bad for Israel, that's Israel's fault, not yours.'

'You know my brother is in the army?' Zivah said. 'He actually fought in Gaza last year. He had no choice, of course, but he wanted to go. We had massive rows about it; I told him I hated him. But the whole time I was scared sick that he would die.'

'Did he come out of it OK?'

'Yes,' said Zivah. 'We don't talk any more, but he was OK. But now it's me who's going to die, not him. And I'm going to be killed by an Israeli, not a Palestinian. I think I should just leave now. Go right to the airport. I've translated everything for them downstairs; they don't need me any more.'

'You can't, I'm afraid,' said Ásta. 'All flights are cancelled. The volcano.'

'No!' Zivah brought her fist up to her mouth and bit it. 'So I'm trapped here, with those killers. They're going to get me. They *will* get me.'

She leaned into Ásta and burst into tears. Ásta stroked her hair.

'It's not necessarily the Israelis who tried to kill Erika,' Ásta said quietly.

'Of course it is,' said Zivah. 'Who else could it be? I know it must be them.'

'And I know it isn't.'

Zivah sat up and looked at Ásta in puzzlement. 'You know? How can you know?'

'Trust me,' said Ásta. 'I know.' She looked Zivah straight in the eye. 'Do you trust me?'

Zivah's eyes were wide. She nodded. 'I trust you.'

'Good,' said Ásta. 'Now, do you believe in God?'

Zivah hesitated and then nodded again.

'Perhaps we should pray?' Ásta said. 'Together.'

'That won't do any good,' said Zivah.

'I find it generally does,' said Ásta.

Ten minutes later they came down the stairs together. Zivah was still sniffing, but she seemed less desperate. Everyone was tapping away on their computers, apart from Franz, who had his head in the fridge. 'Hey, Ásta, have we got any milk?'

'No, we need some,' said Ásta. 'In fact, I've got a list of lots of stuff we need. Do you want to come to the shop with me, Franz? You can help carry.'

'Sure,' said Franz.

Ásta checked her list, and added a couple of items. Zivah was sitting in front of her computer. Ásta gave her a smile of encouragement, which Zivah returned. She was going to be OK. Ásta couldn't blame her for being scared. *She* was scared.

She grabbed the list and she and Franz left the house and walked up the hill. Krambúd, the nearest convenience store, wasn't far, just opposite the statue of Leifur Eiríksson at the top of the hill.

Franz was chatting excitedly about the editing he was doing for the end credits, but Ásta wasn't listening. She had too much on her mind.

She glanced up at the spire of the Hallgrímskirkja, bold, clean and strong. She took a deep breath. She needed some of that strength.

As she turned back towards Franz, she caught a glimpse of a man staring at her out of a parked car, a Suzuki four-wheel drive. As soon as he saw that she had noticed him, the man looked away and started up his engine.

Ásta realized that she was still wearing her clerical collar, which always attracted attention. Perhaps that was what he was staring at. In any case, the Suzuki pulled out of its space and drove away.

They went into the shop.

'This is ridiculous! I spoke to you yesterday. Why you want to speak to me again?'

Teresa Andreose was angry at being dragged from her hotel to the interview room in the heart of police headquarters. Somehow, Magnus had expected that. A swirl of expensive perfume had surrounded her as she swept into the room, as out of place there as its wearer.

'This is a murder inquiry, Signora Andreose. We need to ask you some questions.'

'Well, you had better not take long. I have a flight booked this afternoon. I cannot stand another day in this horrible little country. Do you know what temperature it was in Milan when I left yesterday? Eh?'

Magnus didn't reply.

'Twenty-two! Twenty-two degrees. And you know what temperature it is here? Two!'

Magnus thought it was more like five or six, but he wasn't going to argue. There were four of them in the room: Magnus, Teresa, Baldur and an interpreter.

'Signora Andreose, the rules of interviewing in a foreign language in Iceland are a little cumbersome. I will ask the questions in Icelandic, you can answer in English and Helena here will translate.'

'That's stupid. I demand to answer in Italian.'

'We'd have to find an Italian interpreter,' Magnus said.

'*Parlo italiano*,' said Helena. The other people in the room looked at the young interpreter in surprise. Magnus knew she was doing a PhD in languages at the University of Iceland and that she spoke English and Danish. Italian was a good addition.

'No,' said Teresa. 'I can speak English.'

'Good,' said Magnus. He leaned over and pressed a couple of keys on a computer. The interview rooms had video, not just audio tape. Switching to Icelandic he said: 'Interview with Teresa Andreose, 9:24, 15 April, 2010. Present: Teresa Andreose, Sergeant Magnús Ragnarsson, Inspector Baldur Jakobsson and Helena Gudrúnsdóttir interpreting.' Helena translated.

He looked up at Teresa. 'Can you confirm your name for me please?'

'Teresa Andreose.'

'Date of birth?'

'None of your business.'

'Can you give me your passport then?' Magnus asked.

Teresa dug it out of her bag and tossed it to him. He read out the details for the record.

'Now, Teresa, would you say you were angry with your husband?'

'Yes.'

'Why?'

'Because he cheated on me. He slept with a slut.'

'How angry would you say you were?'

'Very angry.' Then she frowned. 'You're not going to say that I killed him, are you?'

'It's possible,' Magnus said.

'Hah! I thought so. That's ridiculous.'

'Is it?'

'Of course it is! I was in Milan when he was killed.'

'You could have paid someone else to do it.'

'That's absurd!'

'No, it's not,' Magnus said calmly. 'It's perfectly possible. Milan is a big city. There are bound to be killers for hire there. You could have found one, paid him to fly to Iceland to kill your husband and his lover. Couldn't you?'

Teresa shrugged. 'Yeah, I guess I could have done. But I didn't.'

'Who else might have killed him?' Magnus asked. 'Apart from you.'

Teresa shrugged again. 'Erika. I wouldn't put it past her.'

'That doesn't make sense,' Magnus said. 'Who else?'

Teresa was silent. Magnus waited. She shrugged again. 'I don't know. Perhaps some people Freeflow had exposed.'

'Like who?'

'I don't know! That's your job to find out. You are the policeman.'

Then Baldur spoke for the first time. Softly. 'What is it you are not telling us, Teresa?'

It took a moment for the interpreter to translate the question, during which Teresa focused on Baldur for the first time. Magnus noticed hesitation as she heard the question.

'Why do *you* think he was killed?' she asked Baldur.

'If you can't give us a good suggestion, then we will have to assume that you paid people to murder your husband,' said Baldur. 'It's always the wife. Or the husband. That's the rule.'

'And if I don't tell you, what are you going to do? Put me in an igloo and throw away the key?'

'Iceland doesn't have igloos,' said Magnus.

'And igloos don't have keys,' Baldur said. And then Magnus saw Baldur do something extraordinary. He smiled.

So did Teresa, briefly. She took a deep breath. 'OK. I tell you. But I need a cigarette.'

'Sure,' said Baldur, and he passed a plastic cup to her to use as an ashtray. No one took any notice of the large *No Smoking* sign.

She reached into her bag and pulled one out. Lit it. Took time to gather her thoughts.

'I met Nico at graduate school in Rome. We were studying geology. We both went on to join oil companies and then he went to work for a big commodity trader based in London, trading oil derivatives. He was a good geologist, but a lousy trader. I realized it, but he never did. And he was such a charmer that it took a while for the people he worked for to realize it too.

'He was paid well; we got married; I stopped working and started having children; we all lived in London. He lost money, quit his job before he was fired and joined a hedge fund, still in London. Then the crash came in 2008 and he lost money again. He was out of there. I insisted we go back to Milan – I knew he would never cut it in London. And he spent a year looking for a job.'

She took a drag of her cigarette. 'Then one day he said he was going to see an old friend of his from college, Giovanni Panunzi. Now, Giovanni works for Roberto Tretto, the minister involved in the Gruppo Cavour scandal. Right after that meeting Nico took a sudden interest in Freeflow. He claimed he had suddenly discovered a passion for freedom of information. I went along with this for a little bit, but when he began to spend more and more time on Freeflow I called him on it. Said he was doing stuff for Tretto. He denied it. I just let it drop.'

She glared at Magnus. 'That was before I knew about Erika.'

'When did you discover about Nico and Erika?' Magnus asked.

'When she came to stay with us in Milan. It was only for a couple of days: she had just spent a week in jail in Rome. They were very distant with each other, very formal. Nico is never distant with anyone, and I knew he was enthusiastic about Erika and what she was doing, or at least he claimed to be. There was only one conclusion. They were having an affair.'

'And did you confront him on this?'

'Only after he said he was coming to Reykjavík this week. I told him that I would tell Erika he was a plant. He denied there was anything going on between them, and then begged me not to tell her. He said it might put his life at risk.'

'Did you tell her?' Baldur asked.

'No,' said Teresa. She swallowed. 'No, I believed him. And although I was angry with him, I love him. Love him. I will always love him.' She stared at Magnus defiantly.

'Why didn't you tell us this when you heard he had been killed?' Magnus asked.

'He wouldn't have wanted me to,' Teresa said. 'He had grown fond of the image of being an idealistic champion of the truth. You know, I think once he got involved he genuinely did believe in what Freeflow are doing. He would hate people to think of him as someone who sold out to corrupt politicians.'

'But he did,' said Baldur.

Teresa nodded. 'He did.'

'Do you have proof of this?'

'No concrete proof,' said Teresa. 'But it's all on his computer at home, I bet.'

'Will you give us or the Italian authorities permission to analyse your husband's computer?' Magnus asked. He wasn't sure whether they needed it, but in a multiple jurisdiction situation the more boxes that could be ticked the better.

Teresa nodded.

'Please say "yes" if you agree,' said Magnus. 'For the record.'

'Yes.'

'Thank you. If it was someone connected with Tretto who killed Nico, do you have any idea why?' Magnus asked.

'No,' Teresa said. 'Perhaps they are afraid of more revelations.'

'But why kill Nico?' Magnus asked. 'If he was on their side?'

'I don't know!' Teresa shouted. 'I've told you all I know. Now you have to figure out the rest. That is your job.'

She had a point.

Magnus took a deep breath and glanced at Baldur, who nodded. 'That's all for now, Teresa. Thank you.'

'Can I have my passport back?' she asked.

'We'll keep it for a bit,' said Baldur.

'But I'm not still a suspect,' said Teresa. 'After what I've told you.'

'You are an important witness at the very least,' said Baldur. 'A very important witness.'

CHAPTER TWENTY

'NICE,' SAID MAGNUS. Baldur and he were returning to their desks. 'Did you know she was hiding something, or was it just a guess?'

'An educated guess,' said Baldur. 'There was too much noise. She was hiding something.'

'So, Nico was a plant,' said Magnus. 'I never considered that. But it makes sense as a way to disrupt Freeflow from the inside.'

'But if Nico was working for this man Tretto, why kill him?' said Baldur.

'That's the question. Perhaps they never meant to kill Nico, just Erika. Or Nico might have gone native and decided to tell Freeflow what he was up to. We still have a lot to find out.'

'And don't forget the wife,' said Baldur. 'She couldn't prove that she wasn't involved.'

'No, you are right,' said Magnus. 'And we can't be sure that it wasn't the Israelis either.' What had seemed a breakthrough was actually widening out the possibilities, not narrowing them down. 'I'll talk to Matthías. We are going to need serious co-operation from the Italians on this.'

He called Matthías, an inspector at the International Liaison Bureau in the Police Commissioner's Office, which acted as the Interpol National Central Bureau for Iceland. Communications within Interpol had to go from National Central Bureau to National Central Bureau: a clumsy system at the best of times. Matthías was a mild-mannered man with a wispy blond beard and glasses and a facility for languages, who prided himself on his speed. Foreign police forces were amazed at how quickly the Icelanders could respond to requests for information. The same could not usually be said for the Italians, although they had been cooperative so far.

Magnus explained that he needed the police in Milan to seize Nico's home computer right away, with no delays over paperwork that would give someone more time to tamper with the machine before they got to it. If it hadn't been tampered with already. He also wanted a list of known contract killers in Milan to cross-reference with the manifests of flights into Iceland the previous week. If Baldur was right and Teresa had hired someone to off her husband, it would probably be a local guy.

Matthías promised to get right on to it, and was optimistic that he could get the Italian police to move that day. Magnus passed on the information about Nico to his team, or those of them who weren't already out interviewing Italian tourists.

Should he break the news to Freeflow, or hold it back? Magnus could imagine that Erika would be devastated, especially given what he knew about her affair with Nico. Perhaps she would finally talk to him straight. But somehow he knew she wouldn't. And the other members of the team would follow their leader.

Except for one, perhaps.

He turned to his computer and called up the file named *Freeflow Secret Leaks.* Nothing new had been left there by his mysterious correspondent. He began to type.

```
I have some news for you. It turns out that Nico
was a plant. He was an old friend of a man
named Giovanni Panunzi who worked for Roberto
Tretto. Nico's wife is pretty sure that Nico was
encouraged by Panunzi to infiltrate Freeflow.

Did you or anyone else at Freeflow suspect
that?

If the people who killed Nico were related to
Tretto or Gruppo Cavour in some way, do you
```

have any idea why they might want to kill him? Had he spoken to anyone at Freeflow about his real agenda?

Any help you can give us is much appreciated. We are on the same side in this.

Magnus

PS What's your name?

Magnus was frustrated that he would have to wait several hours or perhaps days until whoever had broken into the police system checked it again. He was just about to close the file when he saw text appearing in front of him: i don't believe it! are you sure? and you can call me apex.

Magnus began typing: Not one hundred percent sure, but pretty close. And thanks for your help, Apex.

He waited, staring at the screen.

After two or three minutes, letters began to appear: i had no idea, and i am quite sure no one else at ff did either. there are things i can check though. i will be back. apex.

Magnus switched off his computer and prepared to leave for Thórsgata. Just as he was putting on his jacket, his cell phone rang.

'Magnús.'

'Is that Sergeant Magnús Ragnarsson?' The voice was deep and mellow.

'It is. Who's speaking?'

'My name is Jóhannes. Jóhannes Benediktsson. My father grew up at Hraun, in Helgafellssveit.'

Magnus went still. It was almost as though a voice from the dead was calling him. He sat back down in his chair.

'Oh, yes?'

'My father became an author. He was murdered in 1985.'

'I know,' said Magnus.

'I am planning to write a book about his life. I have just been up to Stykkishólmur to see my aunt Hildur. And a woman named Unnur, whom I think you know.'

'Yes,' said Magnus. 'Yes, I do know her.'

'Well, she said that you had been asking about my father, and your grandfather. I have some information you might find interesting. And some questions to ask you. Would you like to meet?'

'Yes,' said Magnus. 'Yes, I would.'

'Lunch today?'

'Um. I'd like to, but I'm in the middle of a case.'

'I'd really like to see you as soon as possible,' the man said.

Magnus hesitated. There was no question where his priorities should lie. But. But . . .

'OK. I'll meet you at lunchtime, but we'll have to be quick. And somewhere on Hverfisgata.'

'The café in the Culture House. Twelve-thirty?'

The Culture House was actually down the other end of Hverfisgata from the police station, but it seemed an appropriate place. It was where the best of Iceland's national saga treasures were exhibited, including *Gaukur's Saga*, which had turned up in a case Magnus had been involved in when he had first arrived in Iceland a year before.

'Yes. See you there, twelve-thirty.'

As he walked out of the station to his car he thought about Ollie. His brother would be really upset if he knew Magnus was asking questions about their father's death. But, as Magnus had made clear, his need to know was just as great as Ollie's desire not to know.

Yet he felt guilty about going behind his brother's back. Perhaps he should invite him along? After all, there was precious little chance he would actually come.

He took out his phone.

'Hey, Magnus. What's up?'

'Where are you?' Magnus asked.

'In bed,' Ollie said. 'I'm on vacation.'

'I take it you are not alone?'

'Hey, I'm having fun.'

'That's good to know, Ollie. Listen, I've just had a call from a guy named Jóhannes. He's Benedikt's son and he says he has some interesting information about his father's death.'

'Benedikt?'

'You know. The author who died the same way as Dad. I told you about him.'

'Oh, yeah.'

'Anyway, I'm meeting him for lunch at the Culture House on Hverfisgata at twelve-thirty. Do you want to come?'

'Jesus Christ, Magnus, I thought you promised me you wouldn't ask any more questions?'

'No, Ollie, I told you I would. I'm just giving you the option of being there as well, that's all.'

'Well, I think I'll pass.'

The line went dead as Ollie hung up.

The house on Thórsgata was beginning to smell, Magnus noticed as he walked in. All the occupants were up and awake and working at their terminals, apart from Ásta who had answered the door. She looked agitated when she saw him, but she offered him some coffee. Magnus accepted, and took his cup to where Erika was sitting at one end of a dining table, laptop open. Her face was pale and she had a dressing across her cheek.

She glanced up at him. 'Hi,' she said.

'You look exhausted,' Magnus said.

'I am,' said Erika. 'But we're nearly there.'

'When are you planning to go live?'

Rather than answer she just raised an eyebrow.

'State secret?' said Magnus.

'You could say that.'

'Well, I need to know the answer,' Magnus said, suppressing his irritation. 'Because until you go live you are particularly at risk from anyone trying to stop you.'

Erika sighed and gave him a weak smile. 'Yes, of course. Sorry. The current plan is to finish up by midday Sunday, and launch the video at a press conference on Monday.'

'Volcano permitting.'

'The ash won't last that long, will it?' Erika asked. 'Doesn't it get blown away?'

'I've no idea,' said Magnus. He sipped his coffee.

'Thanks for yesterday, by the way. I should never have left the house.'

'No, you shouldn't,' Magnus agreed. 'We've doubled the police presence outside.'

'Two guys sitting in a car eating doughnuts instead of one?'

'That kind of thing,' said Magnus with a grin. 'Just stay indoors. No more runs, OK?'

'I was meaning to ask you, how can we get hold of a handgun or two? For our own protection.

'Hah!' said Magnus. 'No chance of that. I don't even have one.'

'I wondered why you didn't pull out your gun yesterday.'

'I've got to admit I haven't figured out this country,' said Magnus. 'The rural police seem armed to the teeth, ready to repel any amphibious invasion by polar bears. But in town, the idea that a cop should carry a gun gives them the heebie-jeebies. They think their streets will turn into war zones overnight.'

'What, like Baltimore or Detroit? They may have a point.'

'They don't have a point. If I'd had a firearm with me yesterday, the guy who attacked you would never have gotten away.'

'True. So we need to rely on the cops outside with their doughnuts?'

'*Kleinur*. They are like doughnuts but smaller.'

'Great.'

'Look,' said Magnus. 'We know that this guy doesn't have a firearm himself. I tell you what. You are all looking a bit pale. You need exercise.'

'What are you talking about?' said Erika.

'You should try softball. I can bring you over a couple of baseball bats. And a ball of course.'

'Do you really think that will make a difference?'

'I've worked the homicide beat in Boston, and I can tell you a baseball bat applied with maximum force to a skull makes a big difference.'

Erika smiled. 'Thanks.' She leaned back. 'Any luck with the guy who is after me?'

'No,' said Magnus. 'But we're looking hard. We think he might have been on the same plane as Nico coming into Iceland on Sunday. Nico didn't mention bumping into anyone he recognized, did he?'

Erika shook her head. 'No. I'm pretty sure he didn't.'

Magnus paused, sipping his coffee, letting the mood turn serious.

Erika picked it up. 'What is it?'

'I've got some bad news about Nico.'

'He's dead. How can there be worse news?'

'He's a plant. Or he was. He was working for Roberto Tretto. The politician in the Gruppo Cavour scandal.'

What little colour there was in Erika's face drained away. 'No,' she said, her face crumpling in anguish. She shook her head. 'No. That can't be true.'

'Teresa told us this morning. About a year ago he was approached by a friend from college who works for Tretto. Until then he had shown no interest in Freeflow. Afterward he became obsessed.'

'I can't believe it. Teresa's lying.'

'I don't think she is,' said Magnus. He had considered holding back the information about Nico from Erika, but she was a victim not a suspect, and he needed to provoke leads any way he could. 'There was no indication at all that he worked for Tretto?'

Erika shook her head. 'No, of course not.'

'Or that he was planning to tell you something? Something important?'

'No. None.'

'You see, we don't know why, if he was working for Tretto,

Tretto would want him killed. Or whichever crime boss in Italy is in this with Tretto – I assume the minister keeps his distance from those details.'

'I see that. But to be honest, Magnus, I can't think straight at the moment,' Erika said. 'It's a lot to take in.' Colour returned to her cheeks under the bandage. Anger. 'If it's true . . . the bastard! He deceived me. He totally deceived me.'

'Totally,' Magnus said. 'I'll talk to you this afternoon. When you have had a chance to digest this.'

He left Erika staring blankly at her computer screen, and the rest of the Freeflow team staring at her.

Magnus was just getting into his car on Thórsgata when his phone rang.

'Magnús.'

'Hi, it's me.'

Magnus smiled as he recognized Ingileif's voice. 'Oh, hi.'

'Where are you?'

'Just by the Hallgrímskirkja,' Magnus said. 'Thórsgata.'

'Well, I'm just outside the gallery in Skólavördustígur. Do you want a quick coffee?'

Magnus winced. 'I'd love to. But I'm not sure I've got time.'

'Oh, come on. We can't just meet in the middle of the night, like a pair of vampires.'

'Or trolls.'

'You be the troll, I'll be the vampire.'

'Romantic,' Magnus said. 'All right. I'll be there in five minutes. Mokka?'

'See you there.'

Mokka was just down the hill from the gallery Ingileif used to own with a group of five other artists. It was a cosy place with leather benches, wood-panelled walls and a smell of waffles. It was the first Italian-style coffee house in Reykjavík, notable for the paintings on the walls, which changed monthly. Many of the artists were friends of Ingileif.

She was waiting for him, reading an Icelandic style magazine. Her face lit up when she saw him: it made Magnus's day.

She kissed him quickly on the lips. 'You know if you'd only let me solve your cases for you, you'd have plenty of time for cups of coffee during the day,' she said. 'In fact, I was wondering . . . You've had a tiring morning, you look as if you need a lie-down.' Her eyes were twinkling.

'Do you mean what I think you mean?' Magnus said.

'Of course I do.'

Magnus grinned. 'I'd love to, but I've got an appointment at lunchtime.'

'It wouldn't take long,' Ingileif said. 'You never take long.'

'That's not true!'

Ingileif smiled. 'OK. So where are you having lunch?'

'At the Culture House.'

'Oh. Well, say hello to my favourite saga. Who with?'

'Jóhannes Benediktsson.'

'Not Benedikt Jóhannesson's son?'

'The very same. He called me out of the blue this morning. He wants to share information about his father's death.'

'Fascinating. Ollie won't like that, though, will he?'

'No, he won't.' Magnus sipped his coffee and eyed the pastries under the counter. 'Have you heard anything about your flight tomorrow?'

'Nothing,' Ingileif said. 'Why should I?'

'Loads of flights to Europe have been cancelled. The ash from the volcano.'

'Really? Then I would have to stay here a few days longer. That would be a shame.'

'Actually, I think it would be rather nice,' Magnus said.

Ingileif smiled. 'So do I.'

'You know, I wish you'd given me some warning you were coming to Iceland,' Magnus said.

'It was all over my Facebook page,' Ingileif said. 'Didn't you see?'

'No.'

'Why not, Magnús? I set you up your own page.'

'I just didn't get around to it.' Magnus had successfully avoided Facebook in America, but Ingileif's life revolved around it, so she had set a page up for him when she left for Hamburg. He had looked at her page a couple of times, but it just made him depressed. It was visual proof that she was having a frantic, fun-filled life without him.

'You know, I checked your page last week,' Ingileif said.

'Why did you do that?'

'Do you know you only have one friend? And that's me.'

'That's in Facebook world,' said Magnus. 'Not the real world.'

'Oh, yes, and how many friends do you have in the real world?'

Magnus winced but didn't answer. His phone vibrated in his pocket. He ignored it.

'Ninety-five per cent of Icelanders between twenty and thirty are on Facebook, Magnús. You have to use it. Otherwise you'll never meet anyone.'

Magnus glanced at Ingileif sharply. 'What do you mean, meet anyone?'

Ingileif's cheeks reddened slightly. 'Oh, I don't know. Friends.'

'You mean women?'

'Well. Do you see any women?'

'Do you see any men?' Magnus asked. 'In Hamburg?'

'What I do in Hamburg is my own business, Magnús, just as what you do here is yours.'

'Precisely,' said Magnus. As usual, the status of his relationship with Ingileif was confusing him, but this time he felt more uncomfortable than usual. Wait. Wasn't 'Status' something Facebook sorted out? They would probably need room for a paragraph for that section in Iceland, he thought. 'Look, I've got to go.'

Ingileif reached over and gripped his hand. 'Hey. Sorry. I can cancel my dinner this evening if you like. We could go out somewhere nice. No more vampires and trolls.'

Magnus grinned. 'That's a very nice idea. I would like that.'

CHAPTER TWENTY-ONE

IT WAS ONLY a few minutes from Mokka to the Culture House, and so Magnus walked, leaving his car by the café. He checked his phone: one missed call from a number he didn't recognize.

He called it back.

'Hello?' a female voice answered.

'This is Magnús. Who is this?'

'Oh, it's Ásta.'

'You called me?'

'Um, it's nothing,' Ásta said uncertainly.

Magnus stopped on the pavement. 'Are you in the house?'

'Yes,' said Ásta.

'Well, if you can't speak now I can call you back in a few minutes. Give you a chance to go back outside where no one can hear you.'

'No, it was nothing, really.'

'Are you sure?'

'Yes, yes, I'm quite sure.'

'OK, but if you do want to talk to me call me right back. I'll pick up this time.'

'All right.' Ásta hung up.

Magnus frowned. Next time he saw Ásta he would be sure to take her to one side. He was certain there was something she had wanted to tell him. It might turn out to be 'nothing really', or it might not.

The Culture House was a grand building at the western end of Hverfisgata near the town centre. It had formerly served as the National Library, but now displayed a selection of the best of the saga manuscripts. The bulk of the collection was housed in the Árni Magnússon Institute at the university.

The café was a small room reached through the gift shop. It was three-quarters full and there were two men sitting alone: one was a young guy with a beard, obviously an American tourist, flipping through a guidebook. The other was a big man with a shock of white hair, wearing a tweed jacket, and scanning the room expectantly.

Magnus approached him. 'Jóhannes?'

The man got to his feet. He was the same height as Magnus. 'Yes. You must be Sergeant Magnús?'

'That's right.' They shook hands and sat down. 'I'm very glad you called, Jóhannes, but I don't have much time. Shall we order now?' He waved down a waitress. He ordered a salad, Jóhannes a sausage.

'Good choice, this,' said Magnus.

'Yes, I think so,' said Jóhannes. 'I bring my classes here whenever I can.'

'You're a schoolteacher?'

'Yes. Icelandic. Have you been inside recently?'

Magnus smiled. 'It's one of my favourite places in this city.'

'Mine too. Have you seen *Gaukur's Saga*?'

Magnus nodded. 'Yes, I have seen it.'

'Remarkable, isn't it? I can't believe it's real.'

'Oh, it's real, all right,' Magnus said. A lot of people had gone to a lot of effort twelve months before establishing that. 'I used to read sagas over and over when I was a kid in America. It's wonderful to see the real things here.'

Jóhannes smiled. 'I'm glad to hear it. I suppose you could say it has been my life's work to bring the sagas to adolescent children.'

'A noble thing to do,' Magnus said.

Jóhannes nodded. 'I think so.'

'Hi, Magnus.'

Magnus looked up in surprise to see his brother approaching the table. Ollie's face was grim. 'Hi, Ollie, I'm glad you came.'

Ollie nodded curtly and looked at Jóhannes with an air of insolence. Magnus could feel the schoolteacher bridle.

'Let me introduce my brother, Óli,' Magnus said in Icelandic. 'This is Jóhannes Benediktsson. His father was a neighbour of Grandpa's at Bjarnarhöfn.'

'Hi,' said Ollie. Or was it '*Hae*', the Icelandic greeting?

'Oh, I'm sorry, Jóhannes,' said Magnus. 'Do you mind if we speak English? My brother doesn't speak Icelandic.'

'That will be acceptable,' said Jóhannes in a precise accent.

'What do you want, Ollie?' Magnus said, catching the waitress's eye. Ollie's surliness irritated him, but maybe it was a sign that his brother was finally accepting that Magnus was going to ask difficult questions, whatever Ollie thought.

'I'll take a Coke,' he said, and sat down, crossing his arms.

Jóhannes was watching Ollie with ill-disguised distaste.

'I've read a couple of your father's books,' Magnus said to him. 'But only recently.'

'Let me guess,' said Jóhannes. '*Moor and the Man* and "The Slip"?'

Magnus nodded. 'I enjoyed *Moor and the Man*. It reminded me a bit of—'

'Halldór Laxness?' Jóhannes interrupted. 'But not quite as good?' He eyed Magnus suspiciously.

'I was going to say Steinbeck.'

Jóhannes smiled. 'I'm sorry. I am a little sensitive about my father and his literary reputation. I have had a trying time recently. I lost my job two days ago, and I've discovered some disturbing facts.'

'Sorry about the job,' said Magnus.

'Thirty-one years I've been showing children the wonders of our literature. Thirty-one years.'

'That's tough.' Magnus paused while the waitress delivered their meals. 'So, what did you find out?'

Magnus ate while Jóhannes told him about his trip to Búdir and the confrontation that the groom there had witnessed between Hallgrímur and Benedikt a few weeks before

Benedikt's murder. Magnus listened closely. Ollie's arms were firmly folded and a scowl was fixed on his face, the Coke in front of him untouched. But he was listening too.

'So when I left Stykkishólmur, Unnur, who is my aunt's niece, told me that you had done some investigating yourself last year.'

'I have,' said Magnus. 'Like you, I spotted that *Moor and the Man* and "The Slip" both seemed to describe real events: the murder of Benedikt's father by Hallgrímur's father, and then the killing of Hallgrímur's father by Benedikt on Búland's Head.'

'I notice you don't say murder,' Jóhannes said.

'I suppose I should have done,' Magnus said. 'It was murder, wasn't it?'

'It was revenge,' said Jóhannes. 'We were just talking about the sagas. My father was a good man. I think he thought it was his duty to avenge the murder of his own father. You remember what Thorstein's father tells him in "The Tale of Thorstein the Staff-Struck" just before the duel? "I would rather lose you than have a coward son." I often think of that.'

'I'm a policeman,' said Magnus. 'That counts as a motive, not a duty. It was murder all right.'

'Hm,' Jóhannes grunted.

'There's something else you might find interesting,' Magnus said. 'Our own father was murdered eleven years after yours. In 1996.'

Magnus felt Ollie's shoulders tighten next to him. He knew his brother wouldn't like what he was about to say.

'I'm sorry about that,' said Jóhannes.

'It was in the States. We were at the beach in a place called Duxbury for the summer. Everyone was out. Somebody rang the doorbell, my father answered, he let the man in, and then he was stabbed once in the back and twice more in the chest.'

'But that's what happened to my father!' Jóhannes said.

'Exactly. Even down to the stab wounds.'

'Do you think there's a connection?' Jóhannes asked.

'I'm a cop. I have to think there's a connection.'

Jóhannes paused. 'Could it be Hallgrímur?' he asked. 'Was there any tension between him and your father?'

'There was plenty of tension,' said Magnus. 'Our mother drank. A lot. Our father had an affair with another woman – Unnur, in fact – and Mom found out about it. They split up. Dad went to America and Mom stayed in Iceland. Ollie and I stayed with Hallgrímur at the farm at Bjarnarhöfn. It was no fun.'

Beside Magnus, Ollie snorted. It was true – 'no fun' was an understatement.

'After four years of hell, Dad came to fetch us and take us over to America with him. Then, eight years later, he was murdered.'

'It sounds as if Hallgrímur had plenty of reason to hate your father.'

'Yes. Although according to Unnur, he was actually glad to see him leave Iceland and our mother.'

'The question remains, could Hallgrímur have murdered your father and my father?' Jóhannes asked.

'I don't *think* so,' said Magnus.

'Why not?'

'He has never left Iceland, never even been issued with a passport. He certainly never went to America in 1996. And he is left-handed.'

'And the stab wounds were inflicted by someone who was right-handed?'

'You got it.'

'Interesting,' said Jóhannes. 'Do you know anything about the police investigation into my father's murder? I've read press reports, of course.'

'Yes, I read the file last year. It was very thorough. The investigating officer was Inspector Snorri Gudmundsson who is now the National Police Commissioner. But they didn't find any real suspects.'

'Apart from me.'

'Yes, I remember reading about you,' said Magnus. 'You discovered the body, didn't you?'

'That's right.'

'You were never a real suspect. No one was ever a real suspect.'

'But what about the similarities with your own father's murder?' Jóhannes asked.

'That was something I spotted last year when I read the file.'

'And what did they say about that?'

Magnus lowered his eyes. 'Nothing. I didn't tell them.'

'You didn't tell them! Why not?'

'I . . .' Magnus glanced at Ollie. 'We. We didn't want to reopen the case.'

'What do you mean, you didn't want to reopen the case!' Jóhannes's voice was raised in anger, and a number of other diners were staring at him. 'This is an unsolved murder we are talking about. Two unsolved murders. You *have* to reopen the case. It's your duty as a police officer.'

'You're right,' said Magnus. And he was right. He was glad that Ollie was there to listen to this. 'You are absolutely right. And it's something I will do.'

'When? This afternoon, I hope.'

'Soon. There's another murder investigation going on at the moment. The Italian man killed on the Fimmvörduháls volcano. You have probably seen it on the news.'

Jóhannes jabbed a finger at Magnus. 'If you don't reopen this investigation immediately, I will talk to the Commissioner myself.'

Magnus glanced at Ollie, whose scowl had deepened. 'Fair enough,' he said. 'Now, I have to go. Can you give me your number so I can let you know what I find out? We should stay in touch.'

Jóhannes tore a page out of a notebook and ripped it in two. He scribbled an address and phone number on each half and pushed the pieces of paper across the table to Magnus and his brother. 'I look forward to hearing from you soon.'

*

'Where have you been, Magnús? Ragga's been waiting for you.' Árni looked frazzled.

'Ragga?'

'The police artist.'

'Damn.' Magnus had had an appointment to see her at eleven that morning. They needed to get a good impression of Erika's attacker out to the police throughout the country. 'I'll be with her in a moment. What's going on?'

'Some progress,' said Árni. 'We've found the Canadians who rented the Suzuki Vitara from Hertz. They are in Akureyri.'

'Good. Get the police there to find out where they were on Monday evening. If they have a firm alibi let them go, otherwise lock them up.'

'They are checking on that now.'

'What about Italian tourists?'

'The attack on you last night means we can rule out all those who have left the country in the last couple of days, which helps a bit. And the volcano means that the attacker is trapped in this country for a few days at least. He can't get out.'

'Good point.'

'We have two possibles waiting for you. They are both Italian tourists, they match your description and neither one of them has an alibi for Monday night.'

'Good work! I'll go see them right now. Anything from Interpol?'

'Not yet.'

'Well, keep on to them. How's the ash cloud?'

'Getting bigger. The volcano is still spewing. The wind is blowing it due south over Britain and the North Atlantic. Flights still cancelled. And it's falling hard on the farms around Eyjafjallajökull.'

'OK – take me to these Italians, and then I'll see Ragga. Oh, one last question, Árni. Where can I buy a baseball bat?'

*

The Italians were a bust. Although they both fitted Magnus's general description, he was quite sure that neither of them was the man he had seen holding a knife to Erika's throat. He let them off with an apology.

Then he went to see the police artist. He could see the value of some kind of image of the assailant: it would save the police a lot of time.

Ragga was an ample forty-five-year-old with long curly red hair and big green eyes. She was waiting for him in an interview room with a stack of cards and a sketchbook. She was reading a book.

'Sorry I kept you waiting,' Magnus said. 'How long will this take?'

'About an hour,' she said.

'An hour! I'd have thought they'd have E-Fit or one of those other computer systems.'

'They keep trialling them,' said Ragga. 'But they always end up with me. They say I'm better. The first three-quarters of an hour I do pretty much the same as a computer; I show you these cards and ask you which image each part of the face most resembles. It's the last quarter of an hour I make the image into a person. That's the bit the computer can't quite do.'

'OK, well, draw me,' said Magnus. 'Take just two minutes.'

'Why?' asked Ragga calmly.

'I want to make sure I'm not wasting my time.'

'OK.' Ragga worked fast, glancing with those big eyes at Magnus as she sketched. In a couple of minutes she showed him his portrait.

It looked a lot like the man he saw in the mirror every day. Except: 'Do I really look that suspicious?'

'You do right now,' said Ragga.

Magnus laughed. 'OK, let's get to it.'

An hour later they had a very good likeness of the attacker full face and profile and wearing a woolly hat. Ragga said that in Reykjavík it was good to know what people looked like wearing woolly hats. Magnus was impressed.

Back at the Violent Crimes Unit, Vigdís was at her desk, working on her computer.

'Flight cancelled?' Magnus asked.

'Yes,' she said. Her lips were pursed in frustration.

'Any chance of it going tomorrow?'

'They said I should show up at the airport. I'm doubtful though. The eruption is continuing and there's no change in the weather forecast.' Usually so cool, Vigdís seemed distinctly unhappy.

'Did you call your man? Is he in Paris yet?'

'He is.' Vigdís sighed. 'And he's not pleased.'

'It's hardly your fault.'

'I told him that. He said it's never my fault when I cancel on him. He has a point.'

'Make sure you're at the airport tomorrow. I don't want you missing a flight.'

Vigdís smiled quickly at him, and turned back to her screen.

'What are you doing?' Magnus asked.

'Trying to track down a loose Suzuki Vitara.'

'Any luck yet?'

'Nothing.'

'What about the Canadians, Árni?' Magnus asked.

'They claim they were in Húsavík that evening,' said Árni. 'The local police there are checking with their hotel now.'

Húsavík was on the north coast of Iceland. It looked as if the Canadians were ruling themselves out.

Magnus called Matthías. 'Any news from Interpol?'

'The Italians have asked for a Blue Notice.'

'Damn it. Is that really necessary?'

'I asked for an update and that's what they told me. You'd have thought they would have been happy with message traffic; after all, it was one of their own citizens who was murdered.'

Message traffic was the usual informal way that information was passed around Interpol without going through headquarters at Lyons. A Blue Notice was an official request for information on suspects and was a royal pain in the ass. 'Are they stalling or are they just being Italian?'

'Both, I guess. I've almost got the Blue Notice together, though. I'll send it in the next hour.'

'We need to get at that computer! Isn't there any way we can get around them? Go direct to the police in Milan?'

'In Italy, no way. The Blue Notice should work. I'll keep on top of them.'

'Thanks, Matthías.'

'Magnús?' It was Árni. 'Can I ask you something?'

'Yes?' Magnus was on his guard. Árni looked uncomfortable, as if he was about to own up to a screw-up.

But that wasn't it.

'Do your brother and my sister have something going on?'

'I don't know, Árni. Whenever I look for him, he seems to be in Katrín's bed. Maybe he just gets tired a lot?'

'Very funny. I'm not sure he's a good influence on her.'

Magnus laughed out loud. '*He's* not a good influence on *her*?'

'Yeah. You know. She is my sister.'

Magnus considered telling Árni about Katrín's recent flirtation with lesbianism, about the smell of weed that often hung about the house when he got up in the morning, about her homecomings on a Saturday or Sunday morning, out of her head on drink and probably other substances, in the company of God knows who.

But he didn't. He knew that one of the reasons Árni had suggested Magnus as a lodger was so that he could keep an eye on his sister, but although Magnus had seen a lot, he had never told Árni any of it. It didn't say much for Árni's detection skills that he thought his sister was just a nice girl who dressed a little weirdly.

But Magnus liked his housemate just the way she was.

'Yes, you're right to be concerned, Árni,' he said. 'I'll have a word with Ollie.'

*

He had switched cars. He felt vulnerable in the Vitara, which he had left in a residential street in a suburb a few kilometres from the middle of town, and got himself a silver Ford Focus. He was parked on the eastern side of the Hallgrímskirkja church, the other side from Thórsgata. He had stopped shaving and bought himself a black woolly hat with a little Icelandic flag on the front – not much of a disguise, but it might help.

He had the engine on, partly to keep him warm – it could be pretty cold in Iceland in April – and partly to ensure he could pull out quickly. He had positioned himself so that the car he was waiting for would drive straight past him.

And there it was: an old dirt-encrusted Peugeot. It was easy to keep in sight as it followed the highway to the east through Reykjavík's commercial suburbs, over the Ellidaá River, past the new port and then finally off on to a smaller road into a settlement of newly built apartment blocks perched on a hill.

The signs suggested the suburb was called Grafarholt.

The car drove on and parked outside a modern block of flats opposite a rectangular white building that seemed to be some kind of church – a large black cross adorned one wall. He found a spot in the car park of the neighbouring block which gave him a view. The young female priest climbed out of the car and rang a bell – not her own flat then. She waited a few moments before the door was opened by a tall man in his thirties wearing a sweater. The priest disappeared inside with him.

It was almost dark when she reappeared. She ignored her car, and walked rapidly towards the church, head bent, shoulders hunched. He watched as she pulled out some keys and let herself inside.

Ásta was distraught. Her conversation with Egill, the pastor of Gudrídur's church, hadn't really helped.

There was only one thing to do.

She let herself into the church and turned on the lights. She loved the place. It had a warmth and peace and spiritual tranquillity, which seemed extraordinary for a building so new. The room in which the congregation sat was a simple rectangular space, but it was dominated by the glass eastern wall.

The lights were on in the church's little white-walled garden behind the window, red being the dominant colour. Egill changed the colours according to the ecclesiastical calendar. The altar was very simple, but behind it loomed the silhouette of the cross in the garden.

She knelt to pray. She would stay there all night if need be.

Time passed; she was not sure how much time. A feeling of serenity slipped over her, like a gentle down blanket.

She knew what she had to do.

She heard a bang behind her. Someone was coming into the church. She hoped it was Egill and not one of the parishioners. She would like to pray with him.

But it was no one.

She stared up at the altar, the cross, admiring its simple beauty.

Then she heard rapid footsteps behind her.

Ingileif ran her fingers over Magnus's cheek. 'What are you thinking?'

They were in his bed. They had both been good to their word and had managed a late dinner at the Laekjarbrekka restaurant in Bankastraeti. Magnus had driven there via the Kringlan Mall, which stayed open late on a Thursday, where he had bought the promised baseball bats, and delivered them to Thórsgata. Plus a softball.

'I'm thinking I hope your plane is cancelled tomorrow.'

'That's not very nice.'

'Oh, yes it is.'

Ingileif kissed him. 'I don't suppose you'll be waiting with me in the terminal.'

'No, I don't suppose I will. I will drop you off at the airport if I can.'

'Fat chance.'

'You're right,' said Magnus. He did need to focus on the investigation: he had felt guilty leaving at seven that evening. And once that was done, he should have a conversation with Snorri about Benedikt's murder.

There was another thing he wanted to do when the investigation was over. 'Can I come and visit you in Hamburg?'

'Why would you want to do that?'

'To see you,' Magnus said. 'I'd like to see you again. Soon.'

'Oh, yes, of course,' said Ingileif. 'That would be nice. Yes.'

Magnus could tell she didn't mean it.

'When?' he asked, although he wanted to ask 'why not?'

'Oh, I don't know. The summer's quite busy.'

Magnus sat up in bed. 'Ingileif. What are you saying?'

She sat up next to him. 'Nothing,' she said. She leaned over to kiss him and moved her hand down his stomach.

He pushed her away. 'No, Ingileif. You don't want me to come and see you in Hamburg. Why not?'

She straightened up and put her hands in her lap. Not looking at him she said: 'It might not be a good idea.'

'Why not?'

She took a deep breath. 'Kerem wouldn't like it.'

'And who the hell is Kerem?'

'Kerem is a friend of mine. He's an artist.'

'I thought so,' Magnus said through gritted teeth. 'I thought so. So who is this Kerem guy? And what kind of a name is Kerem anyway?'

'It's Turkish. But he's German; he was born in Germany. We're just friends, that's all. I'm not hiding him: if you ever looked at my Facebook page you'd know all about him.'

'Like you and me are just friends?'

'Look, Magnús, we discussed this. I am not going to pry into your life if you don't pry into mine. When I went to Hamburg we didn't say we wouldn't see other people. Quite the opposite.'

'No, Ingileif, we didn't discuss this. And you pry into my life all the time. Which I quite like, by the way. Does this Kerem know where you are right now?'

'No,' said Ingileif. 'And he doesn't have a right to know.'

'Would he be happy if he did?'

'Why are you always so damn American? Everyone has to be in a relationship or out of a relationship. Can't you just enjoy life? Haven't you had fun the last few days?'

Magnus lost it. 'You're using me, Ingileif, and I don't like it!'

'You don't like it!' Ingileif said, throwing the covers off the bed. 'Fine! I'll stop using you. See how you like that.' She turned on the light and began to gather her clothes, putting each thing on as she found it.

'Yeah,' said Magnus. His voice had risen to a shout. 'I don't like it. And you know it's wrong! That's why you're giving me all this righteous indignation.'

'Go fuck yourself, Magnús,' Ingileif said. 'Because I sure as hell am not going to!'

The door slammed and she was gone.

Magnus flopped back on his bed and stared up at the ceiling.

'Shit.'

CHAPTER TWENTY-TWO

Friday 16 April 2010

MAGNUS WOKE UP early. Thoughts of Ingileif had been tumbling around his mind, and he felt as if he hadn't actually slept. He realized he had time to get to Laugardalur swimming pool before going into the station and the morning meeting scheduled for eight-thirty. He needed the energy boost.

He listened to the radio as he got dressed. Ash had been falling heavily on the countryside near Eyjafjallajökull, blotting out the sun and closing roads. Farms were ruined; livestock had been shut indoors. It sounded as if the countryside Magnus had been driving through two days before had been turned into a post-apocalyptic nightmare of darkness and ash.

A man on the radio was talking about the Great Haze of the eighteenth century when the whole island had been covered in an ash cloud from the eruption of the volcano Laki. Summer failed to come for two years; three-quarters of the nation's livestock died, as did a quarter of the human population, which was reduced to a mere 38,000. They had considered abandoning the island for Denmark. Europe and North America had been affected: subsequent poor harvests were said to have contributed to the French Revolution.

This eruption wasn't quite that bad. Yet. But flights were cancelled for another day.

A quick drive to the pool and then he was undressing again.

Was Ingileif right? Was Magnus just a conventional American hung up on high-school rules of dating?

Throughout their relationship, or whatever it was, Ingileif had maintained the initiative, keeping Magnus confused. She was always in control: she knew what was going on and he didn't. He felt like a mug.

The open-air pool was already filling up. As Magnus left the changing rooms, the cold air bit into his skin, causing him to take a sharp breath. Goose bumps sprouted all over his arms. The temperature wasn't that far above zero, probably three or four degrees.

He adjusted his goggles and plunged into the wonderfully warm water, and began to swim. In a minute he was in the rhythm.

Ingileif. Her anger the night before had been more than a little tantrum to keep him off balance. He knew her well enough to see that when she walked out, she meant it. She was seriously angry.

Another length.

A glimmer of understanding. She was angry with herself. She had perhaps intended to spend a couple of nights with Magnus for old times' sake, for a bit of fun. But it had meant more than that to him and she could see it. She knew she was betraying him, hurting him, and she knew that it was wrong. So she had pulled away. Blaming him because she couldn't blame herself.

So what was she going to do now? Go back to Kerem, whoever he was, the poor bastard.

Magnus swam faster. Understanding what Ingileif was doing didn't change the basic fact. She was dicking him around. And he didn't like it. He didn't like it one bit.

He got out of the pool, the cold air now wonderfully refreshing on his glowing skin. A quick shower and then dressed.

He checked his phone. A message. Árni.

He called back. 'Hi, Árni. What's up?'

'Where are you?'

'In the pool. What is it?'

'There's been a homicide. Grafarholt. You'd better get there now. I'm on my way.'

'Can't Baldur deal with it?' Magnus said. 'I need to focus on the Andreose case.'

'You'll want to be there,' Árni said. 'Gudrídur's church in Grafarholt.'

Magnus had a bad feeling. 'Who's the victim?' he asked, although as he uttered the words he realized he knew the answer.

Ásta was lying face down in front of the altar, her blue eyes open. The back of her skull was a gory mess and there was a significant amount of dried blood on the tiles beside her. Baldur had just arrived and he and Magnus bent over the body.

'Blow to the back of the head,' said Baldur. He scanned the church. It was full of heavy loose metal objects – crosses, candlesticks, lecterns –although they all appeared to be in their proper places. Both he and Magnus were wearing forensic overalls, but Baldur took his gloves off to touch Ásta's cheek.

'Cool,' he said. He tried to move the arm. Stiff. Rigor mortis had set in. Magnus was disconcerted at the potential contamination of the crime scene, but he didn't say anything. Baldur was the boss; and after all it was Baldur's DNA that would show up in the results.

'Assuming the heating was on all night, then I'd say she's been dead between eight and eighteen hours,' the inspector said. 'So that makes it between two-thirty yesterday afternoon and half past midnight? Obviously the pathologist will get a better idea once he checks her temperature.'

'Sounds right,' said Magnus. He could tell just by looking at her pale face that Ásta had been dead a few hours. The night before rather than that morning.

Magnus peered at Ásta's fingertips without touching them – no obvious blood or skin under the nails. Her hands, wrists and the parts of her face he could see seemed free of cuts or bruising.

'No sign of a struggle.' He stood up, surveying the scene. 'Someone crept up on her while she was in front of the altar, praying no doubt, and whacked her over the head. Probably kept the murder weapon.'

'Who found the body, Árni?' Baldur called. The detective was helping a uniformed constable fix tape across the entrance. He seemed to have got himself into a tangle.

'The church's pastor. He lives in a block of flats opposite. He saw lights on in the church this morning and came to investigate. He's waiting outside.'

Magnus glanced at Baldur. 'Let's talk to him.'

The pastor was a man of about Magnus's own age with wispy fair hair. His name was Egill and he was shaking.

Magnus and Baldur led him to a row of chairs at the entrance to the church, and sat him down. He repeated how he had found the body.

'When did you last see Ásta alive?' Magnus asked.

'Last night. She lives very close to here. She isn't formally attached to this parish, she doesn't work for me or anything, but she is a member of the congregation. She's lived around here for about six months, and I've got to know her quite well. She loves this church. It's a shame we don't have a paid place for her here, but you know how things are these days financially.'

Magnus nodded.

'Well, she came to see me last night. She wanted some advice.'

'About what?'

'It was confidential.'

'Of course it was confidential!' Magnus said. He was losing his patience with people not telling him things. 'It was also probably the reason why she died. Now what was it?'

The pastor swallowed. 'She was worried about her career, basically. It's become very difficult for priests to get parishes these days. She had been lucky to get six months covering for a woman on maternity leave. She was wondering whether she should try to go abroad to study for a couple of years in the hope that things would be better when she returned. She wanted my advice.'

'Did you give it?'

'I couldn't give her much help,' said the pastor.

'There is no way that any of that could be a reason for her death, is there?'

The pastor swallowed again. 'No,' he said, his voice cracking. 'No,' again, more clearly this time.

Magnus stared hard at him. The priest looked uncomfortable. Something was wrong. But how could worrying about getting a job in a church provide someone else with a motive to kill?

'Did she mention Freeflow at all?'

'No – at least not last night. I know she had been interested in the organization ever since they came to Iceland at the end of last year. But I did see the murder on Fimmvörduháls on the news. Did she have anything to do with that?'

'She was up there with them when it happened,' said Magnus. 'It's funny she didn't mention it.'

The pastor shrugged. 'I have just seen her this once since Sunday.'

'A couple more questions,' said Magnus. 'Did you see anyone hanging around here last night? A stranger? Or anyone speaking to Ásta?'

'No,' said the pastor. 'No. I didn't.'

'And what time was Ásta with you?'

'I don't know. Probably seven-thirty until about nine o'clock, something like that.'

'Was the heating on all night? At about this temperature?'

'Yes. Yes, it would have been.'

Important information for the pathologist, whose estimate of time of death would involve comparing the temperature of the body with that of the room in which it had been lying.

'All right,' said Magnus. 'I'm sure we'll have some more questions for you. But right now, can you please check the church? See if there is anything missing?'

'You think they stole something?'

'They might have done. More likely the murderer took away the murder weapon.'

The three of them went back into the church. It took the pastor a couple of minutes before he spotted it. 'A candlestick.' He pointed to one on a small table on one side of the entrance. It was made of brass and was about eighteen inches high. Its partner on the other side had gone, although the candle was lying in its place. The pastor reached out his hand to pick it up.

'Don't!' said Magnus sharply. 'This is a crime scene. Tidying up is not allowed.'

'Yes,' said the pastor. 'Yes, of course. I'm sorry.' He shook his head and took a deep breath. 'I liked Ásta. She was a good woman. A really good woman.' He glanced at the figure still lying there in front of the altar. A photographer was snapping away, and Edda and one of her colleagues were crouched down near the body in their white forensic overalls, tweezers at the ready. The pathologist hadn't arrived yet.

'Yes, she was,' said Magnus. 'We'll get the candlestick photographed. Thank you, Egill. We'll be back with more questions later.'

The pastor left with one last glance at Ásta's body.

'All right,' said Baldur. 'It looks as if she was murdered between shortly after nine and twelve-thirty last night. She probably came into the church to pray. Someone sneaked up behind her and whacked her over the head with a candlestick, taking it away with him. Why, we don't know yet, but I would not be at all surprised if it had something to do with Freeflow.'

'Did you think the pastor was telling us the whole truth?' asked Magnus. 'About what Ásta discussed with him?'

'No, I didn't,' said Baldur. 'It didn't quite feel right, did it? We should try him again, later on today. Maybe when we have some more information.'

'You know she called me yesterday?' Magnus said. 'On my cell phone. I missed it and when I called her back she said it was nothing.' He sighed. 'It clearly wasn't.'

'Shouldn't have missed it,' said Baldur.

It was a statement of fact. If Magnus had picked up the call and given Ásta the chance to say what she wanted to say when she wanted to say it, maybe she would still be alive. Maybe.

'How do you want to do this?' Magnus asked.

'I'll lead this investigation,' Baldur said. 'But we'll work jointly. I'm sure we'll find a link to Freeflow. Maybe you should get over there and see if you can find out what that is?'

'OK. Will you do the press conference at nine-thirty?'

'Yes, I'll handle that,' said Baldur. 'And I'll brief Thorkell. We could use some more officers here. Maybe I can borrow a couple of detectives from Narcotics.'

Magnus recognized Gudmundur, the officer inside the patrol car parked opposite the yellow house on Thórsgata. 'I thought you had a buddy out here with you?'

'He's gone for a stroll in Lokastígur round the back,' said the constable.

'Good idea. Seen anything?'

'Nothing this morning.'

'Did you hear about Ásta, the priest?'

'Yes, I did, over the radio. You just come from there?'

Magnus nodded. 'You were here yesterday, weren't you?'

'I was.' The constable pulled out a notebook. 'She arrived 9:12. Left the house with Franz at about 9:46. Returned with him with grocery bags at 10:32. Came outside on the street at 12:10. Walked a short distance from the house and made a quick phone call.'

That would be her call to Magnus.

'When did she leave?'

'Nineteen-twenty-six.'

'Anyone follow her?'

'No.'

'Are you sure?'

The constable thought about it. 'Not absolutely surc. If

another car had driven up the road half a minute after she left, I wouldn't have made the connection. But I didn't see anyone hanging around watching, and neither did my partner. We have been checking.'

Full marks for honesty.

'What about other people coming and going?'

The constable checked his notes. 'Dúddi arrived 10:14. Viktor arrived 20:06. Left 20:53. Pizza delivery 21:28. Dúddi left 23:37.'

'Nothing else? No one sneak out in the middle of the night?'

'Not that we saw.'

'Thanks.' Árni joined them. 'OK, I'll talk to Erika and Franz,' Magnus said to him. 'You take the others.'

Zivah answered the door. Magnus could tell from the expression on her face they hadn't heard.

There were five of them there: Erika, Dieter, Zivah, Franz and Dúddi. They seemed to be working hard. Computers on, coffee cups and cans of Red Bull strewn everywhere; the smell had grown stronger. It was a mixture of socks, sweat and electrical equipment.

Magnus stood in the centre of the room.

'I've got some news,' he said. They all turned to look at him; Franz and Dieter took off the headphones they were wearing. 'Bad news. Ásta was murdered this morning.'

There was a cry from Zivah. Erika looked shocked, Dúddi and Franz stunned, Dieter impassive.

'We found her this morning in the church near her home in Grafarholt. It's a suburb to the east of Reykjavík. She had been hit over the head, probably when she was praying some time last night, we think between nine and midnight. Now, as I'm sure you can understand, Árni and I will need to ask you yet more questions.'

There were a couple of grunts of assent.

'I'll start with Erika, and Árni with Dúddi,' Magnus said. 'Erika, let's sit at the kitchen table.'

They moved over there, Erika in a daze.

'I can't believe it,' she said. 'Did you see her?'

'I saw her dead body,' Magnus said. 'I've just come from there.'

'And you don't know who did it?'

Magnus shook his head. 'We don't even know if her death is connected to Freeflow, but that seems a good working assumption.'

'Yes,' said Erika. She looked very pale. 'I'm sorry, I can't quite take it in. I've seen death before, in Africa. That was worse in a way, much worse, but at least then you knew who the bad guys were.'

'And now we don't?'

'Now we don't,' said Erika. 'I didn't know her well, but I liked Ásta. She believed in things, you know? Not just God and Jesus. But truth. Honesty. Transparency.'

'The kind of things you believe in?'

'Yes,' said Erika. 'She was a good kid.' She took a deep breath. 'OK. What do you want to know?'

'First of all, where were you between, say, seven and one a.m. last night?'

Erika smiled feebly. 'A couple of days ago I would have been offended that you suspected me. Now, I'm getting used to it.'

Magnus shrugged and gave her a quick smile of encouragement.

'All right. I was here all evening, and I mean here, downstairs. I went to bed about one-thirty.'

'Working?'

'That's right.'

'What about the others?'

'The same. We ordered pizza in about nine-thirty, I'd say. Again. Actually, I just ate a salad out of the refrigerator. Dúddi left to go home about eleven. Zivah probably went to bed about then. Franz went to bed some time before me, Dieter was still working when I finished.'

'And no one left the house at any time during the evening?'

'Apart from Ásta. She left about seven, maybe? Viktor dropped in for half an hour at about eight.'

So, it didn't look as if anyone had sneaked out of the house past the patrol car.

'What can you tell me about the connections between Ásta and the other members of the Freeflow team?'

'I don't know,' said Erika. 'Everyone seemed to like her. I was doubtful about her usefulness at first, but she was good to have around. She added a layer of calm and sanity to the place. And she dealt with a lot of the domestic arrangements so the rest of us could concentrate on the video production.'

'Did anyone know her before she showed up here?'

'No. Apart from Viktor, of course. I think he's her uncle. She became interested in Freeflow when she saw me on TV here in November. She had talked to Viktor about us and I am pretty sure he was the one who got in touch with her when he knew we were coming to Iceland.'

'What about Nico?'

'Who knows about Nico?' Erika said bitterly.

Magnus raised his eyebrows.

'I don't think Nico had met her until he arrived here on Sunday to set things up. I know he had shown her the Gaza video before I arrived Monday.'

'Do you think there is any way she might have discovered his links to Tretto?'

Erika shrugged. 'Not that I know of. But she could have done, I suppose. I'm not sure how.'

'Did she have any arguments with any of the team at Freeflow?'

'No, not that I noticed.'

'Anyone she was particularly close to?'

'No. Apart from Viktor, of course. As I said, everyone here seemed to like her . . .'

Magnus could tell an idea had struck Erika. 'Yes?' He gave her an encouraging smile.

She frowned. 'It may be nothing, but the first time I met her, when she was driving me in from the airport, she said something about how *she* might have a leak for Freeflow.'

Magnus leaned forward. 'Did she say what it was?'

'I can't remember. I think I asked her whether it had anything to do with the Icelandic banks. We published Ódinsbanki's loan book last year. She said it didn't. Then we changed the subject.'

'Weren't you curious?'

Erika smiled. 'You would be amazed how many people tell me they have a secret they want Freeflow to publish. It's usually a waste of time. I had only just met Ásta. I think if she told me that now, I would take her more seriously.'

'And she hasn't given Freeflow anything?'

'No. Or at least not that I know of. We get stuff submitted all the time. To be honest, I haven't paid much attention to the new stuff over the last few days. I'll check.'

'Please do,' said Magnus. 'One other question I've been meaning to ask. Has Freeflow ever published or considered publishing anything to do with the Skull and Bones society?'

Erika's eyes widened 'At Yale?'

Magnus nodded.

'No,' said Erika. 'You think *it* might be responsible for all this?'

Magnus could almost see Erika latching on to Árni's conspiracy theory. 'No. Not unless you were about to publish something explosive. It's just you mentioned fraternities in US universities.'

Erika shook her head. 'Nothing on the Skull and Bones, more's the pity.'

'One last thing. We got an artist to do an impression of the guy who attacked you on Wednesday.' He took it out of his jacket pocket. 'What do you think?'

Erika. 'It's a good likeness. Very good. You know . . .'

'What?'

'He reminds me of someone.'

'Who?'

Erika stared at the picture and shook her head. 'No. No, I can't think. I'm imagining it.'

'Are you sure? If you do get some inspiration, let me know.'

'I will. But, as I say, I'm pretty sure I'm imagining it. Have you found him yet?'

'Not yet,' Magnus replied.

'Well, I wish you would hurry up,' said Erika. 'Before anyone else gets killed.'

Franz confirmed Erika's story about who was in the house at what times the previous evening.

'You went out with Ásta yesterday morning, didn't you?' Magnus said.

'Yeah. We went to the little store around the corner. What's it called, Krambud?'

'Krambúd,' Magnus said, giving it the correct Icelandic pronunciation.

'Yeah, Krambúd. Bought groceries for the house; there was too much for her to carry by herself.'

'How did she seem?'

'Thoughtful. Wrapped up in herself, you know?' Franz said. 'I mean, I wasn't really surprised. There's a lot of tension in the house and Nico did die four days ago.'

'What did she talk about?'

'I tried to make conversation. We spoke about the editing I was doing. The volcano. She had seen more of the news on that than I had.'

'Did you see anything strange? Anyone strange?'

Franz shook his head.

'And you've no idea why she was preoccupied?'

Franz hesitated. Magnus waited.

'Might have something to do with Zivah,' Franz said. 'They came down the stairs together just before we went shopping. I think Zivah had been crying.'

Zivah was crying still. In fact she was almost hysterical.

'Ásta was such a good woman,' Zivah sobbed. 'I can't believe they killed her. They'll kill all of us. I know they will.'

'We'll find them,' Magnus said. 'Just stay indoors here and you'll be safe.'

'Have you any idea who is doing this?' Zivah asked.

'We have a few ideas,' Magnus said. 'Do you?'

'I think it's the Israelis. Mossad. Ásta said I was wrong, but I'm pretty sure I'm right. I've got to get out of here.'

'Ásta said you were wrong?'

'Yes,' Zivah said. 'I told her how scared I was of them and she told me not to be. She said she knew it wasn't the Israelis.'

'She *knew*?' Magnus repeated.

'Yes,' said Zivah. 'She sounded positive. Like it wasn't just speculation.'

'Did she give you any idea who she thought was responsible?'

Zivah shook her head. Magnus questioned her for a few more minutes and then checked with Árni. Dúddi and Dieter had had nothing much more to add.

It was clear to Magnus that Ásta knew something, something that had suggested to her who was trying to stop Freeflow.

But what?

Magnus and Árni left the house and checked with Gudmundur in the police car outside.

'Your friend is here,' the constable said, nodding down the street.

Magnus turned and saw a figure sitting on the bench reading a newspaper.

Tom Bryant.

Magnus sent Árni back to the station and went down the road to meet him. Bryant lowered his *Tribune* and smiled at Magnus. 'Want a lift?'

CHAPTER TWENTY-THREE

BRYANT DROVE MAGNUS up to the Pearl, the globular exhibition building set atop geothermal hot-water tanks on a low hill overlooking the city. It was still early; there were few cars in the parking lot. They sat in the car, staring out over the scrappy trees that surrounded the hill towards the jumble of brightly coloured toy houses of Thingholt. In the foreground commuter aeroplanes manoeuvred around the taxiways of Reykjavík City Airport. It was a clear, breezy day – no sign of any ash.

'Do you have some questions for me?' Bryant asked.

'You've studied Freeflow?' Magnus asked.

'I have.'

'Who do *you* think hates it enough to kill?'

'The Zimbabwe government. The Italian mafia. Maybe some individuals who have been bruised along the way. And the Israelis. Perhaps.'

'Zimbabwe!' cried Magnus. 'Not another goddamned country. At least we don't have any black suspects.'

'They could pay white guys,' Bryant said.

'Don't,' said Magnus. 'What about the Gruppo Cavour scandal? Is that real?'

'That one will run and run,' said Bryant. 'It will keep the Italian courts busy for years. The key thing there is that powerful people in Italy believe there is more to come out from Freeflow. Implicating other politicians beyond Tretto.'

'So they might be trying to shut down Freeflow before it publishes?'

'Could be.'

'Did you know that Nico Andreose was a plant? He was working for Tretto all along.'

'Yes.'

'Why didn't you tell me?'

'You didn't want me to. You were very specific: no sharing of information.'

Magnus sighed. 'OK. Is there anything else you know?'

Bryant didn't answer at first. Over Reykjavík a little black cloud was gathering itself, ready to dump water on to the Hallgrímskirkja below.

'That depends,' the agent said at last.

'On what?'

'On what Freeflow is working on now.'

'I can't tell you that.'

'But you know?'

Magnus nodded. 'I know.'

'OK,' said Bryant. 'We have information that there is a videotape floating around. A video of the shooting of some UN workers in Gaza in January 2009.'

'Is there?'

'Yes there is. What we don't know is whether this video has found its way to Freeflow. And whether Freeflow is planning to publish it in the next few days. That would be very useful information to have.'

'I imagine it would.'

'Come on, Magnus, help me out here. I've helped you.'

'Not very much.'

Bryant was silent. The little black cloud a mile away opened up, dropping a grey curtain of rain on to the town below.

'OK,' Bryant said. 'We believe it's a fake.'

'What, so Tamara Wilton and the others weren't really killed?' Magnus knew that he was more or less admitting that Bryant was on the right track.

'Have you seen it?'

Magnus nodded. 'It didn't look fake to me.'

'It wouldn't,' Bryant said. 'But our information is that it's not the actual video which is fake. It's the audio.'

'Oh,' said Magnus.

'Would that make a difference?'

'Yes,' Magnus said. 'Yes, it would.' He thought about the images. Part of what had made them so disturbing, a big part, was the callousness of the crew. And that had only come across in the words they had spoken, or the translation Erika had given him of the Hebrew, and the laughter, the smug chuckles. What if the soldiers had actually been discussing how they were sure they were firing at an anti-tank crew? Or even if they had said nothing?

The video was still pretty disturbing, but the incident would be easier to dismiss as part of the confusion of war. Possibly a downgrade from 'war crime' to 'war accident'. That would be an important distinction.

'Who faked it? Not Freeflow?'

'No, definitely not Freeflow,' Bryant said.

'The Palestinians?' Magnus said.

'Could be. Obviously they want to make the Israelis look bad. Or it could be the Israelis themselves – or rather right-wing extremists in Israel.'

'Why?'

'There are a number of elements within Israel who don't like the peace process. You remember I told you that the Israeli government and the Palestinians are close to a peace accord?'

Magnus nodded.

'Well, there are some concessions in there from the Israelis about halting settlement on the West Bank. Some on the Israeli right wing think that those concessions go too far. If the video is released, the peace process is screwed, and Jews can continue to settle the West Bank.'

'You guys don't make things simple,' said Magnus.

Bryant smiled. 'Welcome to my world.'

'So is there any chance that Mossad is behind Nico Andreose's death?'

'You tell me. Mossad are pros. Was the guy who killed Andreose a pro?'

Magnus thought of the botched attack on the volcano. The failure to kill Erika again the day before. 'No,' he said. 'Not professionals. We're dealing with an amateur here. What about the Italians? You are saying it is more than just the minister Tretto involved?'

'Oh, yes. It's one of the Italian mafia organizations. Not as professional as Mossad, of course, but still professionals.'

That still didn't quite fit. 'Thank you, Tom,' said Magnus. 'Now, can you give me a lift back to my car?'

'Can you tell me when Freeflow is going to publish the video?'

'No,' said Magnus.

'Why not?' said Bryant, his voice edged with anger.

'They don't know themselves. Whenever the volcano lets them, I guess.'

'They are planning a press conference?'

Magnus shrugged. 'I think this conversation is over now. Thanks for your help.'

They drove back to Magnus's car in silence. Bryant paused at the bottom of Thórsgata to let Magnus out. 'Remember what I said. About the video. You may want to tell Freeflow.'

'I'll think about it,' said Magnus.

Erika, Dieter and Apex were online in the chat room. She was ten feet away from Dieter and many thousands of miles away from Apex.

Erika began to type: *did dieter tell you about asta?*

She found it very hard to type that last word. She stared at the line she had just written and was overwhelmed by a desire to burst into tears. She tried to press *Send* but she just couldn't.

She pushed her chair back from the desk and hurried over to the window. She stared out at the house's scrappy yard, her back to the others, and took some deep breaths.

She was finding it really difficult to hold it together. She was used to high-pressure situations, to high stakes; she thrived on them. Freeflow had received all sorts of threats over the years and she had never backed down. Never.

But this time . . .

She had been able to handle the murder of her lover. It had been hard, but she had dealt with it. But then there was the attack on herself. And the discovery that Nico had betrayed her all along. And finally the death of Ásta.

Ásta was innocent. She reminded Erika of a more innocent version of herself. Ásta hadn't deserved to die.

Erika's credo was that however much pressure Freeflow came under, they would always publish.

Now she wasn't so sure.

She felt a touch on her shoulder. She wanted to shrug it off, but she took one last deep breath and turned.

It was Dieter. 'Are you OK, Erika?'

His face was full of concern. Of tenderness. Dieter was always there for her, for Freeflow. He would do anything for the cause, *her* cause.

She couldn't let him down. Not now. Couldn't show weakness.

She took another breath. Somehow, miraculously, she had been able to hold back the tears. 'Yes. Yes, Dieter, of course I am.'

She pushed past him and back to her desk, sending her last message on its way as she sat down. She only waited a few seconds for a response.

Apex: *yes. presumably the police haven't found who killed her.*

Erika: *the police are useless. they asked whether she might have submitted her own leak in the last couple of days. anyone seen anything?*

Apex: *i checked the new stuff last night. yet another fraternity handbook. cornell. and something about waste dumping in the amazon in peru.*

Erika: *none of that sounds like asta.*

Apex: *what are we going to do?*

Erika: *what do you think we should do?*

Apex: *i think you should get the hell out of iceland.*

Dieter: *we can't. the volcano.*

Apex: *you could fly west. to america. get the hell out of there.*

Erika: *if we leave now, these people will have died for nothing.*

Apex: *if you don't leave you will die for nothing.*

Erika stared at her screen. Apex had a point. But so had she. She wished she could get out of the damn house, go for a run or something, get some perspective.

Erika: *let's leave tomorrow. the websites are ready, the video is edited. we can publish on sunday.*

Apex: *we haven't verified it properly yet. presumably gareth hasn't got to iceland?*

Dieter: *no flights. no it hasn't been properly verified.*

Erika: *and we could use gareth's help to identify some of the objects in the stills. but he isn't here. we have to do the best we can.*

Apex: *if it isn't verified, we shouldn't publish.*

Erika: *have you checked out the helicopter noise?*

Apex: *i've tried: i can't find any proof that there's anything wrong. it just doesn't sound right to me.*

Erika: *we've come this far. we have to publish. it really would be abandoning nico and asta just to drop everything and run away. i couldn't do that. could you?*

Dieter: *erika's right, apex. this is the biggest leak freeflow has ever had. we have been working for something like this for four years. we have to take the risk.*

The screen was still for a minute.

Apex: *ok. we do it. what about the press conference?*

Erika: *we'll do something in london with samantha wilton if I can get there. otherwise let's fly west as apex suggested. do a press conference in washington.*

Apex: *they think there's a chance airspace might be opened up over the north of britain and norway.*

Erika: *it will be tough to get tickets though.*

Apex: *i can help with that.*

Erika: *thanks apex.*

Erika knew what Apex meant: he would hack into the airline reservation systems to get them seats.

Erika: *okay. it's decided. i'll get hold of alan in london to see what he can do about a press conference either there or in washington, depending on the volcano. and we will have the video ready tomorrow, ready for publication sunday. agreed?*

Dieter: *agreed.*

Apex: *agreed.*

Erika: *thanks guys.*

Erika picked up the phone to call Alan in London. She felt better. Her breathing was steady, her eyes still dry. Only one more day holed up here in Iceland.

She could manage that.

Ollie staggered out of the house on to Njálsgata. He and Katrín had been out late the night before, had had a good time, and he had missed his brother entirely. He thought he had heard a door banging shortly after he had gone to sleep, Katrín beside him, but he wasn't sure. She had abandoned him earlier that morning, claiming she had to go to work somewhere. Ollie had had trouble believing that she could actually have something as mundane as a day job, but everyone had to earn money and she seemed pretty determined to leave the house by nine.

A stiff breeze was blowing and the sky was divided into complicated layers of clouds, underneath which a tight ball of grey was rolling towards him. Ollie climbed the hill to where the great penis-shaped church stood and scurried inside when the cloud burst. The shower only lasted a few minutes, and once it had gone, he escaped the church and headed down the other side of the hill.

Ollie had dreaded coming to Iceland, but he had to admit it wasn't so bad. All those brightly coloured little tin houses were cute, and the people were cool. He had met a load of random strangers in the bar the night before, many of them female, all of them friendly. Katrín had woman-handled him away from a couple of promising situations, but that was fair enough, he supposed.

The country wasn't the cold, bleak, cruel place he had remembered. Or rather that he had chosen to forget.

Ollie loved America. From the moment he had arrived at the age of ten he had had one aim: to become a normal American kid. And he had achieved it within a year. Strangely, his father, for all his talk of Iceland and endless readings of the sagas and reciting of poetry, had understood. There was no doubt that Magnus was his father's favourite, with his insatiable desire for all things Icelandic, but Ragnar had helped Ollie become an American kid. They had gone to Fenway Park together countless times, with Ollie explaining each time what was going on on the baseball field. If Magnus was the expert on long-dead Vikings, Ollie was the expert on the Sox. Ragnar always seemed to listen attentively, but Ollie could never figure out why such an intelligent man, a math professor no less, could never quite understand the intricacies of the game no matter how many times he was told.

Ragnar was easier on Ollie too, perhaps because he realized that Ollie's pain in Iceland had been greater. Magnus was expected to get into an Ivy League College, Ollie could go where he liked. Magnus was also expected to carry the torch of his father's Icelandic heritage, to read and learn the sagas and the poems, even to travel to Iceland with his father, whereas Ollie could watch TV and fool around at school. Ragnar had taken him to see a nice lady in Brookline every week, who Ollie had subsequently realized was a shrink. With the help of subsequent shrinks, Ollie had figured out what his father was doing. Ragnar thought Ollie was screwed up and he felt guilty that he was responsible for it.

So Ollie knew he was screwed up. Which explained the drugs, the failed relationships, the drinking. Maybe even his lack of ability to pull off the big real estate coup that always seemed just around the corner. And he knew it was his father's fault, along with his evil grandfather. But he had found his own way of dealing with things. Live for the present, enjoy yourself, and leave the bad stuff well behind you.

He reached the bottom of the hill, crossed a busy road and came to the pond in the middle of town. Fancy houses lined its shores, and a dozen different kinds of bird squealed and squabbled on its water. The base of a rainbow rested on the metal roofs on the hill behind him, chopped off at the beginning of its curve.

He sat down on a bench, ignoring the damp, to watch the birds.

All had been hunky-dory until his father had been murdered that summer afternoon in Duxbury. Ollie had been at the beach with a girl, and they had been the ones who discovered his father's body when they returned to the house. The following days and weeks had been hell for Ollie, for Magnus and for their stepmother, Kathleen, who had even been suspected of the crime for a while. The girl had lost no time in dropping Ollie.

Ollie knew how to deal with it. Forget it. Deny it. Obliterate it. Why couldn't Magnus do the same thing?

But Magnus couldn't. He had to stir and stir. Which was why Ollie was in Iceland.

At first Ollie had regretted his decision to come to the lunch in the Culture Institute the day before. But he had listened closely to what the old schoolteacher Jóhannes had said, especially those words from the saga of Thor the Tub-Thumper or whoever he was: 'I would rather lose you than have a coward son.'

He pulled out the scrap of paper on which the schoolteacher had written his address and phone number and stared at it.

CHAPTER TWENTY-FOUR

MAGNUS HAD INTENDED to see Viktor at his office after leaving Thórsgata, but it turned out that the lawyer was at police headquarters, offering himself for interview.

All the bluster was gone. It was clear that Viktor had been very fond of his niece and blamed himself for her murder.

'Have you seen much of Ásta over the last few days?' Magnus asked him.

'Not really. Not since we were both in the house in Thórsgata on Sunday afternoon, getting it ready. I probably haven't spoken to her alone at all since then.'

'And how do you think she got on with the members of the Freeflow team?' Magnus asked.

'Very well. They seemed to like her. She's good with people. She would have made a very good pastor.'

'She would have,' said Magnus, remembering his own conversation with her on the drive back from the volcano. 'Why was she so interested in Freeflow?'

'She bought into the ideal. You know, freedom of information, transparency. She was a political idealist as well as a religious one. I remember talking to her about it at my brother's house just after Erika and Nico had visited Iceland last year. She said then that she would like to help in any way she could. So I called her last week when I heard Freeflow were on their way. She had time on her hands, she was willing, and I knew she would be useful. Which she was. A bunch of geeks like that need someone normal to look after them.'

'It seems strange to me that she was the one who was killed,' Magnus said. 'I mean she was on the periphery of Freeflow, wasn't she? Did she give any indication why anyone would want to kill her? Did she have any specific information?'

Viktor frowned and shook his head. 'You are right. She had seen the Gaza video – I take it you know about that now?'

Magnus nodded. 'I've seen it.'

'OK,' Viktor continued. 'But then so had everyone else.'

'Do you think she might have had a leak of her own for Freeflow?' Magnus asked, remembering what Erika had told him.

Viktor glanced at Magnus quickly. 'I don't know. Maybe. A couple of weeks ago, before I even knew Freeflow were coming to Iceland, Ásta asked me how a potential leaker might get in touch with them.'

'What did you tell her?'

'I said the details were on the Freeflow website, but the best thing was probably to post a CD to one of their PO Boxes.'

'Did you ask her about it? Whether she had anything specific in mind?'

'No. That didn't occur to me. Until now.'

Once Viktor had gone, Magnus called Baldur to tell him what the MP had said, and how that corroborated Erika's impression. He also mentioned Zivah's feeling that Ásta knew who might be behind the attacks on Erika, or at least knew that the Israelis weren't. Baldur was just about to search Ásta's room, and he said he would keep a look out for possible leaked material.

There was a message from Matthías for Magnus to call him.

'What have you got for me?' Magnus asked the inspector.

'A stone wall.'

'What do you mean?'

'They said they've referred it to legal to see whether the Blue Notice complies with Article Three of the constitution.'

'What the hell does that mean?'

'It means the guy in Rome is trying to tell us something. It's politics. Article Three prohibits Interpol from taking action on political matters. Once it goes to legal it will be weeks before it comes out again. But at least they've told us why.'

'They are scared of upsetting Tretto?'

'Or his friends.'

'Can't you push them?'

'Sorry, Magnús. There really is no point. That's what the guy in Rome was telling me.'

'All right. Thanks for trying.' Magnus slammed the phone down in frustration. If it wasn't for the ash cloud, he'd fly to Milan himself and break into Nico's house to get a hold of that computer.

He turned to his own machine. It was nearly lunchtime and it was the first chance he had got to look at it all day.

There was a message from Apex.

i checked on nico. you are right that he was a plant. but it looks like he was just observing. the guys he was working for thought that ff had more information about gruppo cavour than we actually do. his job was just to stay in place and let them know if we picked up any further leaks. he definitely was not supposed to kill erika or help anyone else do it. apex

Magnus typed a response: `How do you know?`

He had to wait less than a minute for a reply. Apex had obviously set some kind of alert to tell him whenever Magnus typed anything into his machine.

`i took a look at his stored e-mails.`

Magnus couldn't resist a laugh. Of course he had. He didn't have to go through Interpol. `Thanks, Apex. You heard about Ásta?`

Apex replied: `yes. it has us all rattled. any ideas who did it?`

Magnus typed: `Not yet. You?`

There was no immediate response. Magnus sat back in his chair staring at his screen. He hadn't told anyone else about his contact with Apex, and of course Apex's hacking into Nico's computer could not be used as formal evidence.

Nico and his Italian friends could not be ruled out as suspects completely, but they were looking less likely.

Then a message appeared: `i hate to say this, but maybe dieter. he had a kind of crush on erika, always has had. he may have been jealous of nico.`

Magnus typed a response: `Did he ever sleep with her?`

The reply came quickly. `i don't know.`

Magnus typed again: `Do you think Dieter is capable of murder?`

`no, i don't. he went over to the dark side about fifteen years ago. stole a load of credit card numbers. after jail he sorted himself out. i really don't believe he would kill anyone. and none of that explains asta's death. but, you asked.`

Thanks, Apex, Magnus typed.

He rubbed his eyes. Another suspect! Magnus considered Dieter, the quiet, lumbering idealist. From what he understood of the way Freeflow worked, Dieter was Erika's right-hand man; he had been with her from the beginning. It was perfectly easy to imagine that he admired her commitment to the cause, her energy and her charisma. And although she was by no stretch of the imagination beautiful, she had a sexiness about her that Dieter would have had plenty of time to appreciate. Magnus thought it highly unlikely that they were sleeping together in the house on Thórsgata. Someone would have noticed; someone would have told him; he would have seen the signs. But in some other house in some other country in the past?

Possibly.

In which case if Dieter found out about Erika and Nico he could have been jealous. Jealous enough to kill? Magnus had no idea. Dieter was obsessive about Freeflow, he could be obsessive about its founder as well.

But if Dieter had killed Nico, it would mean that Erika's story of what happened on the volcano was pure fabrication. And it certainly wasn't Dieter who had chased Erika two days before.

Magnus's phone rang.

'Magnús? It's Vigdís.'

'I thought I told you to be at the airport?'

'Well, I'm not. I'm at a small garage in Kópavogur. They rent out cars occasionally, usually to Icelanders, but sometimes to foreigners who find them on the Internet. They are unlicensed, which is why it's taken us a while to find them.'

Magnus's pulse quickened. 'And?'

'And they rented a black Suzuki Vitara out on Monday morning.'

'To whom?'

'To a Dutchman.'

'A Dutchman!' Magnus's heart sank. Holland was about the only country in the world that hadn't emerged in the investigation so far. 'What's his name?'

'Jaap Peeters. Or at least that's what he said his name was.'

'Didn't the guy check his driver's licence? Or his passport? What about credit card?'

'No.'

'Why the hell not?'

'A big cash deposit. In euros.'

'E-mail address?'

'Hotmail. It will have been set up anonymously. But I showed him the picture of our assailant. The garage owner confirmed it was the same guy.'

Magnus shook his head. 'And has the car been returned yet?'

'No. It's due back on Monday. A one-week rental.'

'So the guy might not even *be* Dutch?'

'No. Except the garage owner says he was reading a Dutch magazine, he remembers.'

Magnus hung up and put his head in his hands. 'Árni!'

Árni looked up. 'Yes?'

'Get on to hotels in Reykjavík, and check the flight manifests again. We are looking for a Dutchman this time. Jaap Peeters.'

It didn't take Baldur long to find the journal. It was open, face down, next to Ásta's printer. For a moment, when he started reading, he thought she was the author. But the more he read, the more obvious it was that this was someone else's diary, someone else's life.

He skimmed it and his pulse quickened. This was going to be the beginning of something big, something nasty.

This was what Ásta had wanted to leak through Freeflow.

The journal belonged to a girl called Soffía. It was clearly one of several volumes, and had been written in 1993 and 1994. From what Baldur could make out, Soffía had been working in the office of the Bishop of Iceland at the time. A devout Christian, she had had a number of intense private conversations with him, which at first had left her inspired.

Baldur knew where this was heading. Sure enough, the Bishop had seduced her, or forced himself on her, Baldur wasn't sure which, and neither was the girl. He flicked forward through the pages. Much of the rest of the journal was taken up with the details of sex sessions with the Bishop and what they all meant. The girl's confusion was all too clear: Soffía was becoming more and more desperate. Baldur turned to the end of the journal.

The last page was as he suspected. On 13 November 1994 she decided she could carry on no longer.

There were a lot of people Baldur should call. He decided to call Magnus.

It took Magnus less than fifteen minutes to get to Grafarholt.

Baldur was standing outside the entrance of Ásta's apartment block.

'Thanks for waiting for me,' said Magnus.

Baldur shrugged. 'I thought you should be here.' He held up the journal in his gloved hand. 'This is going to make a lot of people unhappy.'

Magnus was desperate to read the journal for himself, but he knew that would have to wait. 'The Bishop of Iceland? That's the Big Salmon of the whole Church, right? There's only one bishop?' Iceland had an established national Church, which was Lutheran. Almost all Icelanders were nominally members, although few attended services every Sunday.

'That's right. This one died a couple of years ago. There was a big scandal in 1996 when two women went public with their complaints that he had sexually harassed them. He went after them, claimed they were delusional, pressed charges for defamation against them.'

'*He* accused *them*?'

'Fortunately, the prosecutor dropped the charges. But the Church crushed the girls. One of them had to leave the country.'

'And had he harassed them?'

'What are you saying?' said Baldur. 'A bishop in the Church of Iceland? You should be ashamed of yourself for even asking the question.'

Baldur's expression was deadpan, but Magnus was pretty sure he was being ironic. 'Anyone else come forward?'

'There were rumours. But after what had happened to the first two women, if there were any others, they were reluctant to speak out.'

'So no hard evidence?'

'Until now,' said Baldur, tapping the journal with his gloved finger. 'And if this girl really did kill herself like she said she was going to . . .'

'All hell will break loose. Árni's checking the records now. Shall we go and see our friend Egill?'

The pastor was standing anxiously outside the church, talking to curious neighbours, and watching the forensics people at work.

Baldur led him into his office in the church, a small room with a computer, a filing cabinet and a shelf full of religious texts. Wonky, highly coloured images of Jesus at work looked down at them, produced by someone who fancied himself as a twenty-first-century Icelandic El Greco, no doubt.

Egill sat behind his desk, picked up a pencil and began to fiddle with it. Magnus and Baldur took two chairs opposite.

'What did you say Ásta wanted to talk to you about?' Baldur asked.

'Her career,' the pastor said uncertainly. 'Her next job.'

'You're lying.'

'No, I'm not,' squeaked the pastor. He was clearly an honest man, Magnus thought. He was such a bad liar.

'Have you seen this before?' Baldur said, opening up the diary and showing it to Egill.

The pastor reached out to take it.

'Don't touch it!' Baldur snapped. 'It's evidence.' Baldur was still wearing his blue gloves.

The pastor whipped back his hand as if it had been burned. 'No, I've never seen it before.'

'Ásta didn't show it to you? Last night?'

'No,' said Egill. He looked afraid now. 'No, she didn't. Is it hers? Am I in it?'

Baldur frowned. 'No, it isn't hers, as you know very well.'

'I don't know,' said Egill, a bit bolder now. 'Then whose is it?'

'A girl called Soffía. She would be a woman now. If she were still alive.'

Egill looked confused. 'Was she a friend of Ásta's?'

'Probably,' said Baldur. 'Are you sure you have never heard of her?'

'Quite sure,' said Egill.

Magnus believed him. 'Did Ásta ever talk about a friend of hers who worked for the Bishop? Not the current one, the old one.'

'No,' said Egill. 'No, she didn't.'

'Or someone who had been sexually harassed by the Bishop?'

Egill's mouth opened. He slumped back in his chair. 'Is that what that journal says?'

'It certainly does,' said Baldur. 'It looks like the old pervert is going to be nailed after all. Just a pity he isn't around to see it.'

'He wasn't a pervert,' said Egill without conviction.

'Wasn't he?'

Egill didn't answer. 'What are you going to do with it?' he said.

'Read it. Transcribe it. It's evidence in a murder inquiry.'

Egill sat forward. 'You don't think Ásta's death had something to do with that, do you?'

'Don't you?'

'But that would mean . . . That would mean that someone in the Church had her killed to shut her up. That's not possible!'

'Isn't it?' said Baldur. Magnus was beginning to suspect that the inspector wasn't a regular on Sundays at his local church.

'No, it isn't!' said Egill, finally summoning some conviction. 'It certainly isn't possible.'

'We can't leap to conclusions quite yet about who killed Ásta,' Magnus said. 'But the fact we found this in Ásta's room suggests that there might be a link to her death. Doesn't it?'

'I don't believe so,' said Egill.

'Well, we do,' said Magnus. 'So Ásta didn't mention this at all in her conversation with you last night?'

'No,' said Egill.

'Even indirectly?'

Egill thought a moment. 'No. No, she didn't.'

'Or at any time in the past few weeks?'

Egill shook his head. 'No.'

'Do you believe that information given to a priest in confidence should remain confidential?' Magnus asked.

'Yes,' said Egill slowly. 'Yes, I do.'

'Even when that information relates to a crime?'

Egill took a deep breath. 'Um. Yes, I do.'

'Is that what you are doing in this case?' Baldur asked. 'Respecting confidential information?'

Something in Egill hardened. He leaned forward and looked both Magnus and Baldur in the eye, each in turn. 'Ásta never mentioned anything about this woman and the Bishop to me. Is that clear? That's all I have to say.'

'I believe him,' said Magnus as he and Baldur stood outside the church.

'You what?' Baldur exclaimed. 'That guy's lying. He's lying through his teeth. It was a good move to press him on the confidentiality question. He's lying because he thinks he has to, but he's still lying. And I'm going to bust him and any other damned priest who tries to cover this up.'

Magnus didn't argue. He agreed with Baldur that the pastor was hiding something; he just didn't think it was to do with Soffía's journal.

'You know, he could even have done it himself,' Baldur said. 'Ásta comes to talk to him about how shocked she is to read that their Bishop was a pervert. He realizes she is going to spill the beans and so he decides to shut her up right away.'

'You're not serious?' said Magnus.

'Maybe,' said Baldur. 'I'm certainly going to bear the possibility in mind.'

A uniformed constable approached them. 'Got something from one of the neighbours.'

'Tell me,' said Baldur.

'She lives in Ásta's building on the ground floor. She saw a man sitting in a car outside one of the other blocks when she came home last night. He was just staring at the pastor's block. She went to take the dog out half an hour later, and he was still staring. She thought it was slightly odd.'

'What time was this?'

'About eight-fifteen when she first spotted him, eight-forty-five when she took the dog out.'

'How long was she out with the dog?' Magnus asked.

'Just ten minutes. She didn't notice him get out of the car, or the car drive off.'

'Did she see Ásta go into the church?'

'No.'

'Did you get a description?' Baldur asked.

'Very vague. She couldn't really see him. He was wearing a woolly hat. I showed her the artist's impression of the man who attacked you, but she couldn't say one way or the other.'

'What about the vehicle?'

'Silver. A car. She has no clue about cars.'

'But not a black Suzuki Vitara?'

'Definitely not.'

'Thanks, Villi,' said Baldur. He turned to Magnus. 'Perhaps it's not the same guy who has been after Erika?'

'Or perhaps he has a new car,' Magnus said. Baldur's pastor theory was looking less likely too, he thought.

Baldur's phone rang. It was Árni, Magnus could tell. Baldur wrote down an address.

'Soffía?' he asked after Baldur had hung up.

'No record of any female named Soffía committing suicide in 1994. But they did get a call from a woman named Berglind in Kópavogur who saw the news about Ásta. She says she gave Ásta something before she died. She wouldn't say what it was over the phone.'

'That's the address?'

'Yes. And it was clear from her journal that Soffía lived in Kópavogur.'

'Let's go, then.'

CHAPTER TWENTY-FIVE

KÓPAVOGUR WAS A suburb to the south of central Reykjavík. Berglind lived on a quiet road in a single-storey detached house with a small garden. It almost looked American: it reminded Magnus of a 1960s ranch house in a middle-class suburb like Medford, where Ollie lived. Berglind herself was a blonde woman of about sixty. The house was tidy and very clean. It had once held a family, but it now seemed empty.

She had coffee ready and poured Magnus and Baldur a cup.

'Thank you for coming,' she said, the words tumbling out. 'I was stunned to hear about Ásta. She was a wonderful girl. Her mother will be devastated. She's a good friend of mine and she just lives down the road, but I haven't had the courage to go and see her yet. You see . . .'

'Yes?' said Magnus.

Berglind sighed. 'I didn't really want to make it public, but I feel I should now, given what's happened to Ásta.'

'Are you talking about this?' said Baldur. He showed her the journal in a clear evidence bag.

Berglind nodded. 'Yes. Yes, I am.'

'Was Soffía your daughter?' Baldur asked. His voice was low, and although Baldur didn't really do sympathy, he was pretty close.

'Yes, she was. She died in 2002. She was only twenty-six. It wasn't until just before last Christmas that I found this. She had hidden it in a closet in her bedroom. I found it under some of her old school notes in a box. I should have thrown them out years ago, but I couldn't bear to.'

'Two thousand and two?' said Baldur. 'I thought she died in 1994?'

'Oh, no. You read the last page of her journal, then?'

Baldur nodded.

'She did try to kill herself. Sleeping pills. But I discovered her before it was too late and took her to hospital where they pumped her stomach. She was eighteen at the time, working for the Bishop in the school holidays.'

Berglind shook her head. 'I had no idea why she did what she did until I read the diary. She just suddenly changed. Dropped out of school. Went travelling to America. Got a job in Los Angeles. She never told me what it was, but I found out after she died.'

A tear ran down the woman's face.

'How did she die?' Magnus asked, but he knew the answer.

'Drug overdose. I flew over there. Saw where she had been living. What she had been doing.'

'Is that her?' Magnus asked. There was a photograph of a shy girl of about seventeen with glasses. But she was pretty. Magnus was sure that in a porn movie or on Hollywood Boulevard she could be made to look sexy. He decided not to ask her mom any more about her job. 'And you think her experiences with the Bishop prompted all this?'

'I know it did,' said Berglind, her voice cold.

'Why did you give the journal to Ásta?'

'I wasn't sure what to do with it,' Berglind said. 'I wanted to publicize it, but because of what eventually became of Soffía I was wary of going to the press, or the Church, or the police. I didn't want the authorities to drag Soffía's name through the dirt. I saw what had happened to those two poor girls who did speak out.'

Baldur nodded. 'I understand.'

'So I talked to Ásta's mother, who is one of my best friends. She told me about Freeflow and said that Ásta and Viktor knew a lot about it. I trusted Ásta; I wasn't sure about Viktor. So I went to her with it. She thought if we put it up on Freeflow's website no one in Iceland could ever take it down.'

'What was her reaction to the diary?'

'She was shocked. Badly shocked. Ásta was only about eleven when Soffía left home, but she knew her; Soffía used to babysit her. Ásta was really determined that the journal should be made public.'

'Didn't she think it would harm the Church's reputation?'

'She knew it would,' said Berglind. 'But she said it was the Christian thing to do. She was adamant.'

Good for her, thought Magnus. 'When did you last see her?'

'I spoke to her on Monday on the phone. She said that Freeflow were in Iceland in secret, and that she liked what she saw of them. But she thought it would still be best to give them the journal anonymously – apparently they prefer not to know who the source is. So she was scanning it all into her computer and was going to send it by e-mail or CD or something.'

She paused. Shook her head sadly. 'And then she was murdered. Do you think there is a connection? I would feel awful if there was. I would never be able to face Ásta's mother again.'

'There may well be a connection,' Baldur said. 'This is very important information you have given us, Berglind.'

'But don't blame yourself,' said Magnus. 'It wasn't you who murdered Ásta.'

'Or who assaulted your daughter,' said Baldur.

Outside Berglind's house, Baldur took a deep breath. 'Time to tell Thorkell. And the Commissioner.

'That will be fun. Can you really believe that the Church is trying to cover this up?'

'It's a possibility,' said Baldur. 'I say it's a strong possibility. Don't you?'

'What are you planning to do? Bust the current Bishop?'

'I might ask him some questions.'

Magnus blew air through his cheeks. 'I think I'll leave that to you,' he said.

*

Back at Thórsgata, Project Meltwater was making good progress. The video was finished, both in its three-minute edited and its sixteen-minute unedited versions. The websites and their back-ups were ready. The ISP in Sweden had confirmed that they had received the fifteen thousand euros and were willing to host Freeflow's sites. Alan had been in touch with Samantha Wilton and she had agreed to appear at a press conference at a club in London on Sunday at nine o'clock. Invitations were ready to go out, once it was confirmed that Erika was actually in the air on her way to the UK. The *Guardian* wasn't happy about a press conference on Sunday, because it screwed up their exclusive on Monday morning, but the *Post* could publish on Sunday, given the time difference.

Erika: *any luck with flights tomorrow, apex?*

Apex: *no problems. with all the cancellations, icelandair's reservation system is a mess, no one noticed that i was messing it up more. i got you booked on 2 flights from reykjavik to glasgow. one at 1410, one at 1750. if you get on the first one, i'll cancel the second.*

Erika: *apparently one flight from iceland landed at glasgow airport this afternoon. there has to be a good chance for tomorrow.*

Apex: *a chance but not a certainty. don't forget cash to buy a train ticket from glasgow to london.*

Erika: *thanks apex.*

She would ask Viktor for the cash for the train fare. Of course she would have no money at all when she finally arrived in London. But she would be OK. She always was.

Once she got out of Iceland.

With the end in sight, she stretched her stiff shoulders. 'Hey, Dúddi!' she called. 'Is there any chance of stopping at the Blue Lagoon on the way to the airport tomorrow?'

Ollie checked his map. He was down by the Old Harbour in the centre of town. Bárugata seemed to be up the hill somewhere.

The houses in this part of town were nice, more solid-looking than the tin-roofed shacks around where Magnus lived. He checked the painted numbers for the address Jóhannes had given him. He found the house and stood outside it, hesitating.

He took a deep breath and rang the doorbell.

Jóhannes answered. He was wearing a tweed jacket and tie. It took him a moment to recognize Ollie. 'Ah, it's you,' he said eventually. 'The policeman's brother. How interesting that you've come. Would you like a cup of coffee?'

Jóhannes led Ollie into a darkened living room. It was full of books, photographs and papers. It smelled of pipe smoke. It was years since Ollie had seen anyone smoking a pipe.

'Do you mind?' Jóhannes brandished the instrument in question.

'No. Go right ahead,' said Ollie.

'Your brother isn't with you?'

'No,' said Ollie. 'In fact he doesn't know I'm here.'

The white eyebrows rose. 'Really?' It made Ollie feel like a schoolkid who had almost broken a school rule but not quite.

'Yeah. He's out somewhere solving crimes, I guess.'

'There was another murder this morning,' Jóhannes said. 'A young woman priest.'

'Well, I'm sure Magnus is in on that,' Ollie said. 'You see, he and I view things differently.'

'Things?' said Jóhannes puffing at his pipe.

It was odd. Jóhannes had slipped into his role of schoolteacher, with Ollie as his student. What was odd was that Ollie quite liked the feeling. This guy seemed to be listening to him, to be on his side.

'Yes,' Ollie said. 'Our father's death had a big effect on the both of us. As did the time we spent with my grandfather at Bjarnarhöfn.' Despite his years away from the Icelandic language, Ollie pronounced the name of his grandfather's farm perfectly, getting the *hurp* sound at the end just right. 'We both had a miserable time there, and I guess we both hate him.'

'So far, so similar,' Jóhannes said.

'Right,' said Ollie. 'But Magnus being a cop, what he wants to do is get to the bottom of everything. Find out what happened. Pick over it. It's as though he thinks if he can solve the crime of my father's murder then everything will be OK. Of course, it won't. Things won't be any different.'

'I know how he feels,' said Jóhannes. 'I'm the same. Except I want to write it down, put my father's life in a book. Explain his death. Understand it. And I think it *will* help. But what about you?'

'What about me?' Ollie smiled and sipped his coffee. 'I have spent my whole life wanting to blank it out, forget it, deny it, bury it. That's where me and my brother clash.'

'I can see that.'

'But, well, now I'm not so sure. Maybe I need to resolve things. But in my own way, not my brother's way. Maybe your way too.'

'I don't follow.'

Ollie hesitated. 'You know this talk of a family feud. Your family against my family, Bjarnarhöfn against Hraun?'

'Yes.'

'Well, I figure you and me are on the same side.'

'What do you mean?'

'I was listening to you closely yesterday. You said something like: "My father was a good man. I think he thought it was his duty to avenge the murder of his own father."'

Jóhannes smiled. 'I did. It's a common theme of the sagas, as I am sure you know. Many people think those concepts are from a bygone age. My father didn't.'

'Yeah. Magnus didn't get it, of course. It can be a pain in the ass having a brother who is a cop. But I got it.' Ollie looked straight at Jóhannes.

'Did you?' Jóhannes said, quietly.

'Yes,' said Ollie. 'Yes, I did.'

CHAPTER TWENTY-SIX

POLICE HEADQUARTERS WAS hopping all afternoon. The Commissioner, Thorkell Holm, the Prosecutor and the Minister of Justice were all trying to decide how best to approach the Church. Baldur was sent off to interview the current Bishop with Thorkell. Amazingly, the Bishop didn't confess to masterminding an operation of mass murder to hush up his predecessor's sexual misdemeanours. Fortunately that was a line of inquiry the Commissioner was keen to keep Magnus well away from. While Magnus had many strengths that the Commissioner professed to admire, political tact wasn't one of them.

They had found the black Suzuki Vitara that had been rented by the mysterious Dutchman parked in the suburb of Árbaer. Forensics were all over it. If a fingerprint from the vehicle could be matched to one of the many sets found in the church, that would point strongly to a link between Nico's and Ásta's murder.

But Magnus was tired and frustrated. He wondered what to do about the information from Apex about Dieter and Erika. He would like to get some corroboration from someone else before confronting them, but from whom? Nico might have known, but he was dead. Dúddi had not been involved in Freeflow for long enough. Perhaps Ásta had discovered something about it, which was why she had died? Was that why she knew the Israelis weren't responsible?

Possible? Just. But there was clearly someone else involved outside Freeflow, the man who had killed Nico, who had attacked Erika, and who had presumably murdered Ásta. Why would he care about Dieter's jealousy of Nico?

It didn't add up.

'Magnús?'

It was Vigdís. She was holding a loose page torn from a spiral reporter's notebook. She was wearing gloves.

'Yes?'

'Look at this. We found it in Ásta's bag. It's her writing, by the way.'

It was a kind of to-do list. Seven single words in a column. Top of the list was the word 'Scanning'. It was obvious what that meant. Fourth on the list was 'Dumont?'.

'Dumont?' said Magnus. 'That's something to do with the Belgian scandal, right? Wasn't that the name of the Finance Minister?'

'That's right. In 2008 Sabine Dumont became Finance Minister in the Belgian government. Two weeks later, Freeflow published details of an internal investigation into her time as an economist at the European Monetary Institute in Frankfurt in 1998.'

'What's the European Monetary Institute?'

'It doesn't exist any more. It was the predecessor organization to the European Central Bank.'

'OK.'

'Anyway, Dumont had an affair with a German banker called Helmut Bernecker. The investigation was launched in 2000 and it uncovered evidence that suggested Bernecker had traded on inside information about European monetary policy from Dumont. But the evidence wasn't conclusive and the report was shelved.'

'Not good for Madame Dumont.'

'No, but what was worse was that in 2005 Bernecker, who was now working for a fund manager, was found guilty in a totally separate case of insider trading. But no one went back to look at the old Dumont investigation until Freeflow put it up on the web for all to see.'

'I'm guessing that didn't do Dumont's career a whole lot of good.'

'She resigned the next day. Three days after that she killed herself in a hotel room in Antwerp.'

'So Freeflow got its scalp,' said Magnus. 'But why would Ásta be interested in that case in particular?'

Vigdís shrugged. 'I don't know. There was a big sheaf of paper she had printed out next to her computer: downloads from the Freeflow website and press comment on their various leaks. The Dumont scandal was in there, but so were all the others: Gruppo Cavour, the German bank in Luxembourg, the Icelandic bank, all of it.'

Magnus stared at the piece of paper. 'Belgians speak Dutch, don't they? Flemish is more or less the same as Dutch, right?'

Vigdís shrugged. 'I'm not sure. I've never been to Belgium. You mean you think our friend who rented the Suzuki Vitara was actually Belgian?'

'I don't know.' Magnus sighed. He was tired. It was getting late. The investigation was charging off without him. 'You've had a bad day, Vigdís.'

She nodded.

'Want a beer?'

Although it was nine o'clock on a Friday evening, 46 in Hverfisgata was only half full. It was still early for Reykjavík, which didn't really get going until midnight.

Magnus carried a beer and a large glass of wine back to Vigdís. She was sitting on a high stool at a small table in front of a large abstract painting. 46 liked to call itself 'Gallery 46', but the crowd included a number of the regular drinkers from the Grand Rokk, which had closed a couple of months before. It had been Magnus's regular haunt in Reykjavík. 46 wasn't as cosy, but it would do.

'What a day,' he said. 'You know, I liked Ásta.'

'Me too. From what I saw of her.'

'I prefer it when I haven't had time to get to know the victims.'

Vigdís sipped her wine. 'Do you really think someone in the Church shut her up?'

Magnus gulped his own drink. That felt good. 'No,' he said.

'Because clergymen don't kill people?'

'Actually, I think they probably don't,' said Magnus. 'But that's not it. It's too much of a coincidence for Ásta and Nico's death not to be connected. And I can't see why anyone trying to protect the Bishop's reputation would want to kill Nico and Erika.'

'But isn't it also too much of a coincidence that Ásta had such explosive information?'

'Not really,' said Magnus. 'In fact that's the whole trouble with this case. Freeflow deals in information that people want to cover up. That's what it does. And it's why every time we pick up a stone we find something new and nasty underneath.'

'That video was nasty,' said Vigdís. 'I hope they get to publish it.'

'If it's genuine,' said Magnus.

'What do you mean?'

Magnus didn't reply. He drank his beer.

'Magnús?'

'The CIA thinks it's a fake.'

'The CIA? How do you know what the CIA think?'

'Because I've spoken with someone.'

'Magnús!' Vigdís looked genuinely shocked. 'Don't tell me you work for them after all?'

'No,' said Magnus. He saw the doubt in Vigdís's brown eyes and it disturbed him. He didn't want to lose her trust, or Árni's. They were unfailingly loyal to him. 'No. A couple of days ago a CIA agent approached me. He wanted me to tell him what Freeflow was working on. I told him to piss off.'

'Good.'

Magnus smiled quickly. 'Then I saw him again today.'

'Árni said you had been talking to strange men.'

'He knew about the Gaza video. He didn't know for sure that Freeflow was working on it, but he said there were rumours about a video going around and that it was faked.'

'How could it be faked?'

'Strictly speaking the audio is faked.'

'Why?'

'The CIA agent said to disrupt the peace process. He said it might be the Palestinians. Or it could even be the Israelis themselves. A lot of the hard right in Israel don't want to give the Palestinians anything in peace negotiations. The CIA wants me to tell Freeflow this.'

'And have you?'

'Not yet.'

'Will you?'

'I don't know,' said Magnus.

Vigdís frowned. Magnus wasn't sure if it was disapproval at him talking to the CIA, or if she was thinking. He waited.

'You know they could be bullshitting you,' she said.

'The CIA? Why?'

'Isn't that what the CIA do?'

'I suppose so. But why would they make something like that up?'

'So that you tell Freeflow and Freeflow don't publish it. The video is genuine after all, but the CIA buy some more time. The spook asked you to shut down publication the first time he saw you. He's just asking you again, but in a different way.'

Magnus could feel himself blushing. Why hadn't he thought of that?

'Of course, it *might* be fake,' Vigdís said. 'We just don't know.'

'Screw it,' he said, draining his glass. 'I need another drink. You?'

'Sure,' said Vigdís, emptying hers.

It didn't take long to return with refills. Gunni, a big tug-boat captain Magnus knew from the Grand Rokk, was trying to chat Vigdís up, but she brushed him off expertly.

He winked at Magnus as he stumbled back towards the bar.

'One of your buddies?' Vigdís said.

'He's OK,' said Magnus.

'He needs to work on his chat-up lines.'

'I'll give him some lessons,' Magnus said.

'No offence, but I think he's going to need more than that.'

At least she smiled. Vigdís was quite attractive when she smiled. She had big brown eyes and a long, sculpted face with angular cheekbones. Her habitual expression was cool and detached, but when she smiled or laughed, her teeth flashed and her eyes danced.

Plus she had a great body.

'Magnús, you're leering.'

'Am I?' said Magnus, trying very hard not to blush again. He groped for a smart rejoinder, but failed, and drank his beer instead.

Vigdís flashed him another good-humoured smile, knowing she had caught him, but it didn't last long. The silence started off a little awkward, but then became gloomy.

'Hey, I'm sorry about Paris,' Magnus said.

Vigdís shrugged.

'Have you spoken to Daníel?'

'Davíd. Yeah. I spoke to him. He's pissed off. Very pissed off.'

'That's stupid,' Magnus said. 'It's not your fault.'

'Now he's stuck in Europe. He has some big meeting in Chicago he can't afford to miss on Monday. I think he's planning to go to Madrid or somewhere and try to get a flight to the States from there. So even if I can get to Paris he won't be there.'

'It's still not your fault.'

'Maybe not this time. But the other three times were. And Davíd did point out that if I'd left here on Wednesday as planned, I would be in Paris right now.'

'Ah.' There wasn't much Magnus could say to that.

Vigdís looked Magnus in the eye. 'The thing is I really like him. I mean *really* like him.'

'Well, then, take some vacation and fly over to New York in a couple of weeks.'

'He won't let me. He said this was the last time.'

'Then don't tell him. Just show up.'

'I could,' Vigdís said, averting her eyes from Magnus. 'I've thought of that. But I don't know what I would find. What he would say when I got there.'

Magnus thought of Ingileif and Hamburg and what might happen if he were to fly over there to visit her unannounced. 'I see what you mean.'

'How's Ingileif?' Vigdís asked, as if reading his mind. 'Aren't you seeing her tonight?'

'Er, no,' said Magnus.

'That doesn't sound good.'

Magnus told Vigdís about his conversation with Ingileif the night before. It was good to talk to his colleague. Ingileif was right; he didn't really have any close friends in Iceland, now she had gone.

'I think she's jerking you around,' said Vigdís, when he had finished.

'She says that I am just an uptight American.'

'You may be an uptight American, but that's who you are. She should accept that. She shouldn't just get to do things her way.'

What Vigdís said sounded right. 'So what do you think I should do?'

'Tell her how you feel about her. Tell her you want to see her in Hamburg. Tell her to dump this Turkish guy.'

'But what if she doesn't?'

'Then you're better off without her.'

'I guess I am,' said Magnus, but he knew his voice lacked conviction.

'There are plenty of other women in Iceland, you know,' said Vigdís.

Magnus looked at her. 'I guess there are.'

Vigdís drained her drink. 'OK, I've got to go. Thanks for the drink, Magnús.' She gave him a peck on the cheek and she was gone.

Magnus had another beer in 46. It tasted good. When he had first arrived in Iceland the year before, he had obliterated long hours in the Grand Rokk, and he really felt like doing it again. He knew it was dangerous: he had had problems in the past in the States, especially right after his father had been murdered. His mother had died an alcoholic. And there was something about Reykjavík which welcomed heavy drinkers.

A crowd of a dozen kids entered the bar at the beginning of their Friday night out, laughing and shouting, already well oiled. The bar was filling up rapidly. His mood contrasted sharply with the increasingly upbeat crowd, so he left. He grabbed a large hot dog on the walk home.

There was a note waiting for him on the kitchen table. *Hey Magnus. Gone to Faktory to see Katrín sing. Meet us there. Ollie*

Magnus certainly wasn't in the mood for that. Although Katrín had a certain dramatic presence on stage, her voice was mediocre, and Magnus found it embarrassing to watch her. And even if she were Björk, Magnus wouldn't want to go out to see her that evening, especially at Faktory, the bar that had taken over the site of the good old Grand Rokk. But he felt guilty that he hadn't seen his brother since the previous lunchtime at the Culture House. He pulled out a pen and scribbled: *Sorry, long frustrating day and I'm beat. See you tomorrow morning. M.*

But as he wrote it, Magnus knew he wouldn't. He would be up early to go into the police station, and Ollie would be tucked up with Katrín. Ollie was supposed to be going back to the States on Sunday, volcano permitting. Magnus would have to find a way to spend time with him before then.

He went up to his room, pulled out a half-full bottle of J&B and poured himself a drink. He thought about what Vigdís had said about Ingileif. She was right. She was dead right. He should tell Ingileif what he thought of their relationship, what he expected of her.

He pulled out his phone and dialled her number. She didn't pick up.

Of course she didn't. Good thing really, his thoughts weren't coherent enough to have a serious conversation with her.

He flopped back on his bed and stared at his wall. He had more to add to it after his conversation with Jóhannes Benediktsson the day before. More importantly, he needed to speak to the Commissioner about the similarities between Benedikt's case and his own father's death. But that would have to wait. Both he and the Commissioner had a busy few days ahead of them, what with Freeflow and the Church of Iceland.

He undressed and crawled into bed. It had been good to talk to Vigdís. He liked her. Suddenly he was struck by a thought. What had she said? *'There are plenty of other women in Iceland, you know?'* Was she coming on to him?

He smiled at the idea. She was cute. Very cute.

He imagined what she would do if he brought her back to his room. How she'd take the wall.

Actually, she would take it very well. She understood him, she wouldn't be surprised, she wouldn't ridicule him. In fact she would be right in front of it asking him questions, shifting things around.

His brain stopped whirling and he fell asleep, thinking of long black limbs.

CHAPTER TWENTY-SEVEN

Saturday 17 April 2010

THE OH-SO-FAMILIAR images shuffled in front of Erika's eyes. She recognized every building, every vehicle, every figure as it jumped and danced under the fire of the Israeli soldiers. She knew the Hebrew words as spoken by the Israelis, she knew their chuckles, she knew every comma and period of the subtitles. Yet the video still moved her. The callousness of those doing the firing, the innocence of their victims, and in particular the bullets thudding into the body of Tamara Wilton, still shocked her.

The three minutes were up, the credits rolled and her screen went black.

She sat back. It was good. It was very good. It was the best thing that Freeflow had done.

The bastards in that helicopter would pay. Their superiors who tried to pretend that what she had seen had never happened would pay. And perhaps the next time that the soldiers of a civilized nation decided to do something barbaric, they would think again.

Perhaps. That was the best Freeflow could hope for.

She leaned back. Everyone in the house was gathered around the computer. Their eyes switched from the screen to her.

She closed her eyes. Opened them. And smiled.

'We're done,' she said. Then she leaned forward and typed: *okay apex we're done.*

Franz and Dúddi whooped and gave each other high fives.

Dieter grinned broadly. She leant over and hugged him. She hugged all of them.

She glanced down at the words that had appeared on her screen.

i'm not sure we are. i'm still not sure about the helicopter noise.

She groaned and typed: *enough, apex. just be quiet. and consider yourself hugged.* Then she minimized the screen. 'Well done, guys,' she said. 'That was really good work. I'm proud of you. The whole world should be proud of all of us.'

'And so they will,' said Viktor. He had arrived at the house an hour or so before. He wanted to be there at the end.

'And thanks for all your help, Viktor,' Erika said.

'The Modern Media Initiative didn't work quite like it should,' said Viktor. 'Once it's on the statute books later this year, things will be better.'

'Given what happened to Nico, I'd say it was very useful in protecting us,' said Erika. 'Anywhere else we would have been shut down while the police trampled all over us.'

'Yeah,' said Viktor. The atmosphere in the house was deflated, as they were reminded of their former colleague. And in Viktor's case, his niece.

'So what happens now?' asked Zivah, after a pause.

'Dieter and Apex send the video out to our partners: the *Washington Post*, Reuters, the *Guardian*, *Der Spiegel*. And to Tamara's sister. I fly out to Glasgow and we give the press conference tomorrow morning in London.'

'That's when we publish?' Zivah asked.

'That's when we publish.'

'And when do *we* get out?' Zivah's voice quivered. Erika had spoken to her at length the night before, tried to calm her down. She thought she had succeeded, at least partially.

'As soon as flights open up,' said Erika. 'And I've no idea when that will be. Sorry, Zivah.' Apex had refused a wholesale assault on Icelandair's reservation system to grab seats for the three other foreign members of the team: Franz, Zivah and

Dieter. Erika knew it was unfair, but now everything was done, she couldn't wait to get out of the house herself.

'You sure we don't have to tell the cops I'm leaving the country now?' Erika asked Viktor.

'I'm sure they'd like to know. They won't be expecting it with the ash cloud. Give me a call when you are boarding the plane, and I'll inform them. But there's nothing they can do to stop you.'

'Thanks, Viktor. I know my flight's not till two o'clock, Dúddi, but do you think we could leave earlier? Maybe go to the Blue Lagoon? I could use a long hot soak.'

'Sure,' said Dúddi, with a broad grin. 'And don't worry, guys, I'll look after you until you can escape. We'll go out tonight. You guys deserve a Saturday night in Reykjavík.'

'Do you think it's safe, Erika?' asked Dieter.

For a second Erika hesitated. But she was too tired to worry. 'Of course it's safe, Dieter. I've got to get to the airport somehow, and this Blue Lagoon thing will be full of tourists. I'll be fine.'

The conference room was full. The Commissioner was even present this time: the involvement of the late Bishop had raised the political stakes to the point where he had to keep himself informed. But Chief Superintendent Thorkell ran the meeting.

Magnus started off going through new developments in the Nico Andreose investigation. The ruling out of some of the Canadian and Italian tourists, the introduction of a possible Dutch and Belgian angle through the Suzuki Vitara and Ásta's to-do list. He mentioned for the first time that he had had a message from Apex which suggested Dieter might be jealous of Nico.

Edda presented some of the evidence from the Vitara found parked in Árbaer, the same one that had been rented for cash by the Dutchman. There were plenty of fingerprints, and they had made a match with one of the many sets in the church. They were still analysing fibres from the driver's seat to see if they matched the single fibre found on the stone by the volcano. But they couldn't get DNA samples to Sweden for analysis until the ash cloud died down.

'The prints sound like a pretty conclusive link to me,' said Magnus. 'The assailant rented a car similar to that seen on the volcano, and was in the church the night Ásta died. Did you check for a Jaap Peters on the Icelandair flight on Sunday, Árni?'

'Yes. No luck.'

'But none of that explains the link with the Bishop,' said Baldur.

'Perhaps that was just another leak,' said Magnus. 'To add to the long list of people Freeflow has pissed off.'

'Can you bring us up to date with your investigations into that?' Thorkell asked Baldur.

Baldur spoke for fifteen minutes. No one in the Church had admitted anything, but it was pretty clear that the late Bishop had done quite a lot of things that he shouldn't have done to quite a lot of women. Magnus could see the Commissioner frowning. This was going to be a major political headache for him. Magnus hoped to God that he wouldn't try to tell the police to look the other way. Nothing screwed up a murder investigation more than powerful people trying to shut down particular lines of inquiry, and succeeding.

Except that in this case, Magnus had the feeling Ásta's leak had nothing to do with her death. He tried to make the point, but Baldur was having none of it.

As Magnus and Baldur left the meeting, a uniformed constable was waiting for them. 'We've got someone to see you downstairs,' he said. 'A pastor.'

Egill looked distinctly uncomfortable as they led him into an interview room.

'Had a bad night's sleep?' asked Baldur.

Egill nodded nervously.

'What do you want to tell us?'

Egill ran his fingers through his thinning hair. He looked at Magnus. 'You remember that you asked me yesterday whether information given to a priest should remain confidential even if it relates to a crime, and I told you it should?'

'Yes, I remember that,' said Magnus.

'It's been a central tenet of all Christian sects for centuries, as I'm sure you are aware. The Catholics have the sanctity of the confessional, but the principles apply more widely.'

'I see,' said Magnus.

'Well, this business with our former Bishop made me think overnight about the rights and wrongs of keeping quiet when you see something illegal – not that I know anything at all about him.'

'No,' said Magnus. Baldur was sitting in silence, although Magnus was sure he would have his own views on the matter. The important thing now was to let Egill talk, and Baldur knew it.

Egill smiled. 'Ironically, that was exactly what Ásta wanted to ask me about. Whether she should talk to you about what someone had told her.'

'What did you say?

'I advised her not to. Especially since the person who had spoken to her was doing so in the belief that because she was a priest the knowledge would go no further.'

'Did she take your advice?'

'She seemed to disagree with it. She wasn't sure. Although she didn't tell me she was going to, I am not at all surprised that she went into the church to pray for guidance.'

Why the hell did you not tell us this yesterday? was what Magnus wanted to shout at the priest. But he didn't. 'How much did she tell you about this . . . individual?' he asked calmly.

'Very little. She told me very little on purpose. It sounded like this person had made some kind of confession to her.'

'Did she give you any clue what about?'

'No. Not at all. But she did say that the crime was a serious one.'

'What about the sex of this person? Did Ásta use the words "he" or "she"?' Baldur asked.

'Good question,' said Egill. He closed his eyes, trying to remember. 'She said "he". I'm sure she said "he" just once, as in, "He asked me for my assurance that I wouldn't tell anyone."' He nodded, more firmly this time. 'It was definitely a he.'

'Was there any indication that this person might have been involved with the Church in any way?' Baldur asked. 'A fellow clergyman, perhaps?'

'No,' Egill replied firmly. 'None at all.'

They spent ten more minutes asking the same questions in different ways, but without getting any different answers. Both detectives refrained from yelling at their witness. Magnus badly wanted to, and he was sure Baldur felt the same way.

'That bastard should have told us this right away,' muttered Baldur as they left the interview room. 'All this crap about confidentiality of the confession. What about "Thou shalt not kill"? And "Thou shalt help the police find the killer"?'

Magnus sympathized. 'I wonder who it was who confessed to Ásta?' he said.

'And what they confessed,' said Baldur. 'I'll bet you it had something to do with that pervert the Bishop.'

'I'm not so sure,' said Magnus.

'Baldur!' Árni was approaching them along the corridor, looking flushed.

'What is it?' asked Baldur.

'We've found the murder weapon. The candlestick.'

'Where?'

'Right next to Raudavatn.' Raudavatn, or Red Water, was a tarn about a kilometre from the church in Grafarholt.

'Things are beginning to move,' said Baldur. 'Are you coming, Magnús?'

'No, I'll stay here,' said Magnus. He appreciated Baldur including him, but although things were moving he wanted to stop rushing around.

He wanted to think.

Once Baldur had gone, he too left the building and walked down towards the bay. The sky was clear and it was cold, with a gentle breeze blowing in off the water from the north. He crossed the busy Saebraut and walked a little way along the shore to the Viking ship sculpture. He sat down, hunched in his jacket against the cold, and stared out over the bay.

The Snaefells Glacier way in the distance was hidden in its own little cloud, but Mount Esja was clear. Its upper reaches were daubed in a dribbling of white snow, and the cliffs below glowed a pale yellow in the low morning sunlight. A hundred and fifty kilometres over to the east, beyond the mountains, lurked Eyjafjallajökull, lobbing ash miles up into the sky and over towards northern Europe.

There was no sign of it at all in Reykjavík. The air was fresh and clear and crisp.

Magnus took a deep breath, and let his mind drift back to the case. There were so many lines of inquiry and they all pointed in different directions. He went back through them. The unknown assailant on the volcano; the black Suzuki Vitara rented to a non-existent Dutchman; Mikael Már and his French business associate; the Heathrow café receipt; the Gaza video and the Israelis it would annoy. Then there were all the other people Freeflow had antagonized: the Chinese; the Zimbabweans; the Belgians; the Italians; the German bank; the American college fraternities and God knew who else. Then there was Nico and his various betrayals, to his wife and to his mistress. Dieter's supposed infatuation with Erika. The Italian, Israeli and Canadian tourists they had tracked down. And finally there was Ásta's note about Dumont, and her threat to reveal a scandal at the Church of Iceland.

The whole investigation hadn't been a process of elimination; it had been a process of multiplication.

But why had Ásta died? It seemed she had heard what amounted to a confession. From whom?

It could, of course, be someone the police didn't know about yet, a member of the Church of Iceland, perhaps. Much more likely, it was someone involved in Freeflow. The list wasn't very long: Franz, Zivah, Dieter, Dúddi. Viktor perhaps.

Or Erika. Erika was interesting. She was right at the centre of all the betrayals.

But she was the target. Erika was always the target.

A pair of terns wheeled and dived a few yards ahead of Magnus, sleek and graceful.

OK. So which of the Freeflow team could be linked to the tangle of leads that had emerged over the previous few days? A link that Ásta had possibly noticed.

He stared out across the bay into the cool breeze.

Then it came to him.

He stood up and turned back to the office. The more he thought about it, the more sure he was. His steps quickened until he broke into a run.

He burst into the Violent Crimes Unit and dived for his phone.

'Magnús,' Vigdís began. 'Baldur wants to talk to you about the murder weapon—'

Magnus held up his hand to silence her as he checked his notes for Mikael Már's phone number. He dialled it.

'Hello.'

'Mikael Már, it's Magnús from the Metropolitan Police. Do you have your friend Monsieur Joubert's telephone number in France?'

'Er, OK,' said Mikael Már, clearly taken aback by the urgency in Magnus's voice. 'It's right here. One moment.'

He took less than twenty seconds to find it, but Magnus's fingers were drumming. Vigdís and Árni stared at their boss.

'Here it is.' Mikael Már read out the digits and Magnus wrote them down.

A moment later, Magnus was dialling France.

'Joubert,' said a voice.

'*Monsieur Joubert? Parlez-vous anglais?*' asked Magnus.

'Yes, yes, I do,' said the voice uncertainly, with a heavy French accent.

'My name is Sergeant Magnus Jonson. I am with the Reykjavík Metropolitan Police and I would like to ask you one quick question. It's about the man that you and Mikael Már spoke to on the Fimmvörduháls volcano last Monday.' Magnus forced himself to speak slowly so that the Frenchman would understand him.

'Ah, yes. Mikael Már told me there had been a murder at about the time we were there.'

'That's right. I believe the man you talked to spoke French?'

'That is correct.'

'Did he have an accent?'

'Er . . . yes. Yes, he did.'

'And could you tell where he came from?'

'Oh, yes. The accent wasn't very strong, but it was quite obvious he was not French.'

'Was he Swiss?'

'No. No, not at all. The Swiss accent is very distinctive.'

'I see, Monsieur Joubert. So which country did the man come from?'

'Belgium. I am quite certain he was Belgian.'

CHAPTER TWENTY-EIGHT

'OK, DÚDDI, LET'S go,' said Erika.

'What about the police?' said Dúddi. 'There's still a car parked right outside. Will they stop us?'

'Oh, God, I forgot about them,' said Erika. She *was* tired; she was usually alive to who was watching her. 'It would be best if the police didn't realize I was leaving until Viktor called them.' Viktor had left the house earlier for his office, where he was preparing his arguments in case there was trouble at the airport.

'You could hop out a window at the back,' said Dúddi. 'You can cut through the garden of the house behind us. I could drive around to Lokastígur and pick you up?'

'Good thinking,' said Erika.

'Hey, Dúddi, shall I take her?' said Franz. 'I think the other guys need you here, and when I'm at the airport I can try to figure out flights for the rest of us.'

Erika glanced at Dúddi. 'It might make sense,' she said. 'If you don't mind Franz driving your car.'

'Never had an accident so far,' said Franz, holding his hands up.

Dúddi hesitated. 'Better not,' he said. 'You wouldn't be insured. And however good a driver you are, there's nothing you can do if some other idiot drives into you. But you can come with us, if you want to sort out your flights. It probably would be better to do that at the airport.'

'I think I will, actually. The Blue Lagoon sounds cool.'

'Can we rent suits there?' Erika asks.

'Suits?' Dúddi frowned. 'Why do you want a suit?'

'*Swim*suits,' said Franz.

'Oh, yeah. No problem. But don't wear them in the shower before you go in, otherwise you'll get yelled at.'

Dúddi left by the front door and Franz and Erika opened a window at the back of the house. Erika had her backpack: all the luggage she ever took anywhere.

'Bye, Dieter,' she said, hugging him. 'And you, Zivah. You've done a great job. I know it's been hard.' She hugged her too.

'I'm sorry I got scared,' said Zivah. 'It's been a wonderful experience.' Erika noticed there was a tear in her eye. 'I believe in what you're doing.'

'What *we're* doing,' said Erika. 'I hope we'll see you again?'

Zivah smiled. 'Oh, yes,' she said. 'Definitely.'

With that, Erika hopped over the sill and into the garden, Franz dropping down behind her.

'Árni!' Magnus turned to the detective. 'Do you have the manifest for that Icelandair flight that took off from Heathrow on Sunday just after the time on that café receipt?'

'I do.' Árni reached for a pile of papers by the side of his desk and extracted a couple of pages. 'Here it is.'

Magnus scanned it quickly. 'I knew it!' he exclaimed, glaring at Árni. 'Why the hell didn't you read this more carefully?'

'I did,' Árni squeaked.

'Then why didn't you spot that?' Magnus slammed the manifest on to the desk and thrust his thumb halfway down the list of names. 'Tell me what it says.'

'Sébastien Freitag. Belgian,' Árni read.

'Freitag? Freitag!' Magnus shouted. 'Didn't that ring any bells? Like maybe he was related to François Freitag, otherwise known as Franz, who has been sitting in the house on Thórsgata for the last week!'

'But Franz Freitag is Swiss.'

'No he's not, Árni. He might have a Swiss passport, but he speaks French with a Belgian accent. I bet this guy is his brother or something.'

Árni's Adam's apple bobbled. He looked as if he was about to burst into tears. Magnus didn't care.

'OK, Franz Freitag is Belgian,' Magnus said. 'His brother Sébastien was up on the volcano when Nico was killed. He had rented the Suzuki Vitara under a Dutch name because imitating a Dutchman was easy for him. He attacked Erika when she went out for a run, and he was also in the church where Ásta was found murdered. Perhaps it was Franz who confessed to Ásta? Maybe she discovered something to do with the Dumont scandal and she asked him about it? We need to figure out the connection between Dumont and the Freitags.'

Magnus was staring at Árni, but Árni's brain had turned to jelly.

'There's an easy way to find that out,' said Vigdís, turning to her computer. Magnus looked over her shoulder, with Árni hovering too close behind him. Vigdís called up Google and typed in two words: *Dumont* and *Freitag*.

The first answer was in French. Vigdís clicked on it and brought up an article from the Belgian newspaper *La Libre Belgique*. Magnus couldn't read French very well, but he did understand the word *mari*, which was next to the name Ernst Freitag, and the *deux fils*, Sébastien (26) and François (22). Ernst seemed to be a *citoyen suisse*.

'Come on, you two. We're going to Thórsgata. Now.'

The door of the house in Thórsgata was opened by an exhausted-looking Zivah.

Magnus rushed past her into the living room, ready to make an arrest. Only Dieter was there, headphones on, tapping on his keyboard. No sign of Franz.

'Upstairs, Árni,' said Magnus. 'Where's Franz?'

'Why do you want to know?' said Dieter, straightening himself up and facing Magnus.

Magnus took three strides over to him, grabbed him by the T-shirt and lifted him out of his chair. 'I've had enough of you people not telling me the truth! I want to know where Franz Freitag is and I want to know now! And please don't tell me he is with Erika.'

Dieter swallowed. 'Why do you want to know?' he repeated.

'Because Franz is trying to kill her, that's why. Is that good enough for you?' He threw Dieter backwards so that he tripped over a bin and fell on to the floor.

'What!'

'I know you care about Erika, Dieter,' Magnus said, standing over him. 'So if you want her to stay alive, tell me where he is.'

'OK, OK. They've gone to the airport. Dúddi, Erika and Franz. But they are stopping at the Blue Lagoon first.'

'Have you got Erika's cell number?'

'No,' said Dieter. 'She uses pay-as-you-go phones. She doesn't keep them switched on.'

'What about Dúddi?'

Dieter shrugged.

'When did they leave?'

'About a quarter of an hour ago.'

Sébastien Freitag sat in the café in Hafnarfjördur, nursing his second cup of coffee, and stared out over the harbour. Lying on the table next to the cup was his phone.

It was nearly over, one way or the other. In five hours either Erika Zinn would be in a plane over the North Atlantic, or she would be dead. Where Sébastien would be, he had no idea.

After the Italian, killing the priest hadn't been so difficult. And it had had to be done. François had been such a fool to tell her everything when she had confronted him with her discovery that he was Sabine Dumont's son. Of course, in typical François fashion, he had thought he was being clever, ensuring her silence through the seal of confession. But confession only applied in the Catholic Church; François should have known that. They couldn't risk Ásta talking, just couldn't risk it, at least not until after they had got to Erika.

So she had had to die.

Sébastien didn't feel any regrets about Nico. The Italian was an integral part of Freeflow. Although he hadn't been around when Freeflow had published the investigation, he was just as guilty as the rest of them. Just as guilty as Erika.

Freeflow had destroyed their mother.

Sébastien would never forget that week in the summer of 2008 when his family had been blown apart. They were all so proud of his mother's achievement in becoming Finance Minister. It was so unexpected and yet it seemed to her family that it was nothing less than what she deserved. Then, two weeks later, Sébastien had noticed on his way to work the headline on the morning paper: *Dumont affair with German Fraudster*.

He couldn't conceive of his mother having an affair with anyone, let alone a German banker. A corrupt German banker who was in jail.

He had called François in Zurich and told him. The newspaper story referred to an organization named Freeflow, of which neither brother had heard. As soon as Sébastien got in to work he had checked out their website and seen all the squalid details.

He was furious with his mother. He called her the next day and had a bitter conversation with her on the phone, which ended with her hanging up in tears. A day later she was found swinging in a hotel room in Antwerp.

Their father, a mild-mannered Swiss economist who had followed his wife from Frankfurt to Belgium, was bewildered and then devastated. He left his job at a think-tank in Brussels and returned to Zurich. But no one there wanted to hire him – he was old, washed out, miserable. So he drank.

He blamed himself, he blamed her, he blamed everyone but the people who had really caused his wife's death: Freeflow.

Specifically Erika Zinn. He might not have blamed her. But his sons did.

It was when they read Erika's justification in an interview in *Der Spiegel* about her decision to put the investigation up on to the Freeflow website that the two brothers had decided they must take action. The arrogance, the sanctimoniousness, the assumption of role of judge – no, worse that that – of God, in the life of their mother. And in her death.

Erika claimed that transparency of information was of paramount importance. That Sabine Dumont had deserved the scandal that she had found herself in when everyone in Belgium discovered what she had done. That if she chose to take her own life, that was up to her. It was a consequence of her actions ten years before, not Freeflow's.

That was unfair and untrue.

Erika Zinn had as good as killed Sébastien's mother.

And Sébastien owed his mother a lot. She had always believed in him – when he had been expelled from high school for breaking the leg of that jerk Marcel with a hammer, when he had been arrested for getting his own back on the kid who accused him of cheating at university. It was down to her that he had eventually graduated as an engineer, and that he now had a good job with the electricity company.

No one else had cared.

He had given her a hard time when she was alive, a very hard time, secure in the knowledge that she loved him unreservedly. He regretted that now. He would make up for it.

The anger and the hatred that he had nurtured for nearly two years flared up again. Erika was going to die. She deserved to die. Of that, Sébastien was sure.

The idea that he should do something tangible to avenge his mother's death had come to him after his mother's funeral, during a long night of drinking with his brother. At first François hadn't thought he was serious, but the more

Sébastien thought about it, the more it seemed the right thing to do, the only thing to do. And he could persuade François. His younger brother was if anything more devastated than he was by what had happened, and, as always, he followed Sébastien's lead. Sébastien knew he would have to do the actual killing himself, but he could rely on his brother to help. And it had been François who had thought of infiltrating himself into Freeflow.

If only Sébastien had been slightly quicker on the volcano, Erika would be dead and he would be back in Belgium. But it hadn't worked out that way.

François had suggested bagging the whole plan, lying low until the ash cloud lifted and trying again somewhere else. But that didn't make sense, and Sébastien had told him so. They didn't have much time. They simply had to do what they had set out to do: kill Erika Zinn. Sure, there was an ever-increasing chance that they would get caught, but Sébastien really didn't want to risk getting arrested *before* they had achieved their objective. Killing Erika was all that mattered.

François had understood. They had gone into this together; they would finish it together.

Hafnarfjördur was on the way to the airport from Keflavík. François had said that Erika wanted to spend an hour at the Blue Lagoon before the airport. Plan A was for François to drive her by himself towards the lagoon, and meet up with Sébastien on a quiet track Sébastien had checked out earlier. Plan A was good. Plan B, if someone else drove her, wasn't quite so good, but still might work.

Plan C, if she changed her mind and was driven directly to airport, didn't really exist. There was no Plan C. They would just follow her and take any opportunity they could.

They might be lucky, but frankly, under any of the three plans, there was a chance they would get caught. However, they were committed now. They had to finish what they had come to do, and take the consequences.

Sébastien's phone buzzed and a text message came through.

Plan B

Sébastien took a deep breath. He left some krónur on the table, and hurried outside to his car.

CHAPTER TWENTY-NINE

IT WAS WONDERFUL to be out of Reykjavík and on the open road. Once Dúddi had driven past the town of Hafnarfjördur, they were into a bleak, brown landscape of rock and dirt. No trees, just a light dusting of green moss. On the right was the sea, and on the left, in the distance, a low ridge of jagged mountains. They passed a perfectly conical miniature mountain, like the volcano in a child's drawing, and then turned off the main airport road following signs to the Blue Lagoon.

It was a cold clear morning; the temperature could not have been much above freezing. Erika could see steam rising up in great billows from the foot of the range of mountains. 'Is that it?' she asked Dúddi.

'Yep.'

'But what are all those buildings next to it? It looks like a power station?'

Indeed there were lines of pylons running across the lava field towards the steam.

'It is. The lagoon is totally artificial. It's made up of heated water from the geothermal plant.'

'That's a bit disappointing.'

'Oh, don't worry. I'm sure you'll like it.'

They passed a line of racks on which what looked like brown rags hung. 'What's that?'

'Drying racks for cod. Stockfish, I think you call it.'

'Do we?' said Erika. She had never heard of them. They looked disgusting.

They were now very close to the power station, which was beginning to look like some exotic Cold War base from an old James Bond movie. Metal domes, wires, black rocks piled in puzzling directions and steam spewing out of the ground. They rounded a corner and were soon in a kind of stone amphitheatre, which doubled as a parking lot. One bus and a dozen or so cars were parked there.

'We're lucky,' said Dúddi. 'This place can get crowded, but it doesn't look too bad this morning.'

They walked through a pathway cut into the rock and into a modern glass and wooden building. The entry ticket price was high. Franz took very little persuasion to pay for Erika. Dúddi said he would wait for them both in the café.

Erika went into the changing rooms and showered. She stripped off the dressing on her cheek; she was sure the water would do her wound good. She put on her rented swimsuit and went out to the lagoon.

The cold air bit her exposed skin, but it was only a few steps into the water, which was an unnatural bright milky blue. She closed her eyes as she lowered her body down to her neck and felt the warm soft liquid embrace her.

In the cold air, steam rose from the water and she couldn't see how far the lagoon stretched. Underfoot was a soft white mud. She noticed a couple of women had smeared it on to their faces. Maybe she would try that later.

It was crowded near the entrance to the pool, and so she waded out deeper. She wasn't looking for Franz and hoped he wouldn't find her. She wanted to be alone.

The steam hovered just above the water, dampening sound as well as obscuring vision. Yet she could see upwards to the cold clear sky. It was a very strange sensation, to be surrounded by warmth and yet to see rock cliffs rising just a few hundred feet beyond the lagoon. The pool turned out to be quite large and she began to swim a gentle breaststroke. Eventually she reached the far side: a perimeter of rocks piled high. She could see no one through the steam.

She lay on her back and floated: it was easy to float in that mineral-rich water. She closed her eyes. She could hear the murmur of voices in many languages: English spoken with an Irish accent; Spanish; some kind of Scandinavian language with a different rhythm to Icelandic.

It felt good. It felt *so* good. There was something soft and invigorating about the water beyond just its temperature.

She had a lot to do once they reached the airport. She hadn't yet thought how she would run the press conference, what she would say. She would decide that later.

She was proud of what they had achieved in Iceland, but the cost had been too high. Although she was angry at the way Nico had betrayed her, she was deeply sad about his death. She had enjoyed being with him.

And Ásta. Someone with so much promise ahead of her should not have died.

She thought about the man who had twice tried to attack her. Why couldn't the police figure out who he was? Erika's instinct was that he was Israeli. But there was something familiar about him. She was pretty sure that she had never seen him before, but he did remind her of someone.

Out of the corner of her eye she saw a figure wading through the steam. She turned to look. A wisp of steam blew away so that she saw the profile.

It was Franz.

No, the man was bigger than Franz.

Oh God! She recognized him.

She stood up straight. The man saw her and increased his stride towards her. There was no one else in sight.

Beneath the ripples she saw a dancing rod of grey steel. He was going to stab her, drop the knife and disappear into the steam.

He was only a few yards away now. Behind her was the rough rocky edge of the lagoon. She could never climb out that way in time. She was trapped.

She screamed.

*

Magnus drove fast. As they reached the turn-off from the airport road, he saw the lights of two police cars coming the other way from Keflavík.

'Keep an eye out on the lava field,' he said to his colleagues.

Although the terrain was basically flat, there were slashes across the landscape: gullies and fissures into which a vehicle could be driven or a body hidden. And, of course, there was the shoreline on the other side of the airport road. But they couldn't see anything driving along the tracks that criss-crossed the lava field, nor the tell-tale cloud of dust that a vehicle would kick up.

They reached the parking lot for the Blue Lagoon. There was already a police car there with its blue light flashing, probably from Grindavík, the fishing village just over the low ridge of mountains. Magnus, Vigdís and Árni jumped out of the car and ran along the path to the entrance. A policeman was talking to the woman at reception.

'Sergeant Magnús,' Magnus said, identifying himself. 'Has she seen them?'

'Yes,' the officer replied. 'The woman and one of the men went to change. The other said he was going to the café.'

'How long ago?'

'Ten minutes,' the woman at the reception desk said.

'Vigdís, take the changing rooms. Árni, come with me. You too,' he said to the constable.

They ran through the changing room to the edge of the pool. Magnus scanned the thirty or so swimmers he could see. No sign of anyone who looked like Erika, Franz or Dúddi. But with the steam, it was difficult to be sure.

'Árni, take the perimeter. You stay here,' he said to the constable. And with that he jumped in and waded fast into the steam.

The water was warm, but dragged at his sodden clothes. People stared at him. The wrong people. Not Erika.

He saw the back of a dark-haired woman swimming away

from him and called Erika's name. The woman turned around. It wasn't her.

Then he heard a scream. It was close by. He tried to quicken his step, the water up to his chest. The steam cleared and he saw a tall broad-shouldered man moving towards a smaller figure in a black swimsuit.

'Hey! Police!' he shouted in English. 'Stop!'

The man turned to face him. It was the guy who had grabbed Erika by the Saebraut. Sébastien Freitag.

Freitag was only a couple of yards from Erika, who was backed against the rock edge. He raised a knife. There was no way Magnus could get to him before he plunged it into her.

'Cowabunga!'

A figure flew through the air from the rocky edge, screaming as it did so, and landed on Freitag's upraised arm.

Both bodies plunged under the water. Magnus was on them, looking for the knife.

Árni screamed, in pain this time. He had his arms around Sébastien's chest and neck, but Sébastien's knife arm was free and was stabbing down on Árni's back.

Magnus grabbed the arm and pulled it back. Sébastien was big, but Magnus was bigger. He banged Sébastien's hand against the rocky wall of the pool, but Sébastien wouldn't let go of the knife. The fingers of Sébastien's other hand clutched at Magnus's face, reaching for his eyes. Magnus jabbed at Sébastien's throat with his elbow, and the knife finally slipped out of Sébastien's grasp. Magnus wrapped his arm around Sébastien's neck in a headlock and plunged his face under water.

Árni let go. There was a streak of red in the milky blue.

The uniformed constable jumped in next to them, handcuffs at the ready. It took them a minute but finally Sébastien was cuffed and subdued.

'Are you OK, Árni?' Magnus asked.

Árni flexed his shoulders. 'It hurts, but I think it's a scratch rather than a hole.'

'Cowabunga?' Magnus raised his eyebrows.

Árni shrugged, embarrassed. 'I wanted to distract him. It was the first thing that came into my head.'

'Nice one, Árni.'

CHAPTER THIRTY

Sunday 18 April 2010

MAGNUS'S ALARM WENT off: 7.50 a.m.

He rolled out of bed, padded over to his desk and powered up his laptop.

Freeflow's press conference was at nine o'clock British time, eight o'clock in Reykjavík. Erika had told him how to watch it live on his computer.

After discussions with the Commissioner, Magnus had taken a written statement from her about the attack in the Blue Lagoon, and then let her get on her flight to Glasgow, with the promise that she would return to Iceland within three days, ash cloud permitting. It had taken two hours to find Franz, who had never actually gone into the lagoon himself, but was waiting outside with clothes for his brother. He had escaped into the nearby mountains, where a police dog had eventually tracked him down.

Both he and his brother had given lengthy statements about what they had done and why they had done it. They showed no remorse for trying to murder Erika, just regret that they had not succeeded. Magnus doubted that Franz had the guts to kill anyone himself. But even now he seemed to be under the influence of Sébastien: he was adamant that what his elder brother had done was right and that Erika had deserved to die. Reality had not sunk in. Yet.

But Sébastien had known what he was doing all along. He

was a cold-blooded, calculating killer. His own grief had not given him the right to ruin the lives of all those who knew and loved Ásta and Nico. Very few people who were prosecuted in the Icelandic justice system were acquitted, and Magnus was pretty sure that Sébastien and François Freitag were going down. Which was a thought that gave him pleasure.

Árni's knife wound was more than a scratch, but less than a hole – more of a slice, really. He had been stitched up at the hospital in Keflavík, but would be off work for a couple of days. Magnus had agreed to keep the 'Cowabunga' out of his report.

The computer settled down and Magnus typed in the relevant website address. A picture of an empty lectern appeared, somewhere in London. A crowd of journalists murmured out of shot. After a minute or so, the hubbub died down and two people appeared: Erika and a blonde woman of about twenty-three with a fresh rosy face.

Erika approached the microphone. 'Good morning, everybody,' she said. 'And thank you for coming at such short notice. We are going to show you a video of an event that happened on 14 January 2009 in Gaza. With me is Samantha Wilton: her sister, Tamara, is one of the people you will see on the video. The video lasts three minutes, and is an edited-down version of the full sixteen-minute footage that was given to Freeflow. The unedited version is on our website, should you wish to view it.'

She paused, looking around the audience. 'I will not tell you what we at Freeflow think of what you will soon see. That is not our role. It is up to you to interpret. But I will ask Samantha to say a few words afterwards.'

The camera switched to a projector behind the lectern where a grainy black-and-white video ran. There were subtitles as the Hebrew was translated into English. Also the names of the victims were captioned as they spilled out of their vehicle.

Magnus had seen the unedited version before, but it was just as horrifying the second time around. Worse, given the translations of the Israeli soldiers' comments as they were firing.

The screen went black. There was a long silence, broken only by a cough from one of the journalists. Then Samantha Wilton approached the lectern and began to speak haltingly. It was disconcerting to see the identical twin of the figure that a moment earlier had been writhing in the dirt in Gaza. She was brave, she was beautiful and she was angry.

She only spoke for two minutes. Her words were understated, but they were powerful. What had just been shown was immoral, unjust, criminal. And the criminals should be made to pay.

Magnus watched Erika take a couple of questions from the journalists, and then he shut down his computer. He planned to go into the station later that morning to plough through paperwork. Murder always generated paperwork: fortunately there was less of it in Reykjavík than he was used to in Boston. But before he did that, Magnus wanted to speak to Ollie. Presumably Ollie's flight was still scheduled to leave that afternoon – flights from Reykjavík to the States had mostly been uninterrupted. In fact, Magnus should take his brother to the airport.

There was yet another difficult conversation to be had with him. Jóhannes was right; Magnus had a duty to tell Snorri about the similarities between Benedikt's murder and his own father's. Perhaps on Monday. Ollie wouldn't like that, but he had a right to know what Magnus was planning.

It was Sunday, and Ollie's last morning, so Magnus waited an hour or so before going downstairs to wake his brother up. There were signs someone had already had breakfast.

He went through to Katrín's bedroom and knocked on the door. Twice. Three times.

Eventually she appeared, blinking. 'What is it?' she asked.

'Have you got my brother in there?'

'No. He left early this morning. He says he's going for a drive with a friend?'

'A friend?'

'Some schoolteacher he met.'

Schoolteacher? That must be Jóhannes. 'Did he say where he was going?'

'Yeah. Back to the farm where he grew up.'

Magnus drove fast, his hands gripping the steering wheel so tightly they were white. He should have been pleased that his brother was finally taking an interest in their grandfather and their father's death, but he wasn't. He was furious.

The only reason that Magnus could think of for Ollie and Jóhannes to drive up to Bjarnarhöfn was to confront the old man. And if that was going to happen, Magnus wanted to be there. It was out of consideration for Ollie that he had held off asking his own questions about the two murders. And now Ollie was blithely blundering in by himself.

Sure, there was emotion involved in Magnus's frustration, but the policeman in him knew that Ollie's action was a really bad idea. If anyone was going to ask Hallgrímur questions, it should be Magnus. He knew what to ask, and he would know what to do with the answers. Magnus couldn't trust Ollie to do that.

Jóhannes seemed an intelligent man. Maybe he could be trusted at least to remember the answers.

It was weird that Ollie had teamed up with Jóhannes. Who had contacted whom? Magnus wondered. It must have been Ollie who had made the first move. Jóhannes's disapproval of Ollie had been obvious at lunch, and Magnus would naturally be the brother he would call.

But why would Ollie talk to Jóhannes and not Magnus? Perhaps he had tried to, but Magnus was too busy chasing homicidal Belgians.

Strange, very strange.

Magnus was skirting the flank of Mount Esja. The sun glinted off the grey Faxaflói Bay, and Reykjavík was gleaming in the distance. It was a little less than two hours to Bjarnarhöfn from Reykjavík. Magnus had forgotten to ask Katrín what time Ollie had left, but he guessed it was early: Magnus hadn't heard his brother leave the house. So it was unlikely he would catch them up.

He picked up his phone and called in to the station to tell Baldur he wouldn't be in until late afternoon. He made an excuse about how it was Ollie's last day and a problem had come up with his flight home. Which was true; Ollie would be hard pushed to get to Bjarnarhöfn and back in time to catch it.

Baldur didn't complain. He still had his work cut out. Although the Church wasn't implicated in Ásta's murder, Soffía's allegations were out in the open, or at least halfway out. It was going to be a rough summer for the Church of Iceland.

The car radio cut to the news. The Freeflow video was given prominence and they played a clip of Samantha Wilton's plea for the criminals responsible to be brought to justice. There was already a comment from the Israeli government, who said that the video was a fake. That was quick, thought Magnus. An Icelandic correspondent speculated that the peace process would be delayed yet again.

Was the video a fake? Magnus had no idea. But it seemed to him that Freeflow was wide open to misinformation, no matter how carefully it said it vetted everything it received. And he wasn't convinced by Freeflow's protestation of neutrality. Although it wasn't overtly commenting on the evidence, the video had been edited and presented for maximum emotional impact. What Magnus didn't know was whether Freeflow was the manipulator or the manipulated.

The road plunged into the deep twisting tunnel under Hvalfjördur and the radio cut out. As he emerged on to the other side, he switched to a CD. It was a Brahms cello sonata that Ingileif used to play all the time. She had introduced Magnus to classical music and the sonata had become one of his favourite pieces, inextricably mixed up in his mind, in his soul, with her.

Just when he thought he had got used to being without her, she had burst back into his life. For a couple of days, a couple of nights, he had remembered why he loved being with her so much. Fooling around with her was fun, but she meant so much more to him than that, and he couldn't pretend to himself or to her that she didn't.

Which was why Kerem pissed him off so badly. She was jerking Magnus around and he didn't like it.

Presumably she was still in Iceland somewhere, trapped by the ash cloud, staying with her friend María probably. The sooner she was back in Hamburg with her Turk the better.

He ejected the cello, and replaced it with Soundgarden. Much better.

He approached the Snaefells Peninsula along an empty road. While the sky above him was clear and the sea over to the left sparkled, the mountains that formed the knobbly backbone of the peninsula were shrouded in a layer of dark cloud. He climbed the Kerlingin Pass and plunged into the moisture. The cloud pressed down on the north side of the mountains; visibility was poor, and he could see no more than about a mile ahead. He turned left along the main road towards Grundarfjördur, and then right again, through the Berserkjahraun, the Berserkers' Lava Field. Stone twisted and twirled on either side of the car. Mysterious figures lunged out of the mist to left and right. He had to slow down as he made his way on the rough track cut in the lava field towards the farm.

Cold fingers of long-repressed fear clutched at Magnus's chest, making it difficult to breathe. The memories reared up like the congealed lava. The beatings that his grandfather had given Magnus and his brother; the humiliation, the loneliness, the desperation. The four years spent at that place from the age of eight to twelve were without doubt the worst of Magnus's life. And of Ollie's.

Things had been so much worse for Ollie. He was younger, and not as tough as Magnus. Their grandfather had picked on him. Ollie had slid into a never-ending cycle of bedwetting at night and punishment during the day.

That was why Ollie had vowed to blank those four years out of his life, and why Magnus was amazed that he should venture back here with a stranger.

Come to think of it, why had Ollie come to Iceland at all? Magnus had asked him the question and he hadn't really answered it. Maybe it did have something to do with his past after all.

Magnus himself had returned to Bjarnarhöfn six months before, just after he had discovered the similarity between the murder of his father and of Benedikt. He had confronted his grandfather for the first time in thirteen years. It was nothing more than an exchange of threats, but even though the old man was at least eighty-five, Magnus had felt the chill of his power and authority.

Visibility was only a couple of hundred yards as he pulled out of the lava field and up a low hill to the small complex of buildings between a fell and the sea that was Bjarnarhöfn.

The farm was still. Beside the track leading to the farmhouse itself was a small single-storey dwelling with white concrete walls and a metal roof. This is where Hallgrímur now lived with his wife, Magnus's grandmother: the main house was occupied by Hallgrímur's son Kolbeinn.

There was an old blue VW Passat station wagon parked just outside the house. Magnus had no idea if it was Hallgrímur's or Jóhannes's. He pulled up next to it, and jumped out.

He rapped on the door. No answer. There was no sound of farm activity, but he could hear the noise of the waterfall tumbling off the fell behind the farmhouse. A raven croaked.

Magnus knocked again.

No reply.

He tried the door. It was open. He walked in.

'Hello!' he shouted. 'Grandpa!'

No response. Tentatively at first, and then more quickly, he moved from room to room.

No one. There was a half-full cup of coffee on a table by the sofa in the living room. Magnus stuck his finger in it. Tepid. A Sudoku puzzle book lay open and face down on the table.

He left the building and stood outside the house, wondering where to go next. The farmhouse itself was about fifty yards away. As he walked towards it, he looked down towards Breidafjördur but couldn't see it in the mist.

What he could see was the tiny black chapel, in its little graveyard. The door was open.

That door was never left open.

He turned and jogged down towards it, opening the gate to the churchyard. He slowed as he approached the entrance to the chapel itself.

'Grandpa?' he called. 'Ollie?'

No reply, save for the croak of a raven.

He pushed the white door more firmly open, and entered the little building, which was not much more than a hut. Inside the walls were freshly painted, a bright shade of light blue. Six short rows of yellow pews led down to an altar fenced in by an ornate white communion rail beneath an ancient painting of Jesus and two of his disciples. All this, Magnus took in in an instant. But his eyes were drawn to the floor in front of the altar.

There lay his grandfather, Hallgrímur, face pressed against the wooden floor, eyes shut. A trickle of fresh blood ran down the old man's face from his temple, forming a small pool on the wood.

'Oh, my God,' said Magnus. 'Ollie, what have you done?'

AUTHOR'S NOTE

THERE MUST BE dozens of authors who have looked to the *New Yorker* for their inspiration, and I am one of them. An article appeared in that magazine on 7 June 2010 entitled 'No Secrets' by Raffi Khatchadourian. It described the visit of Wikileaks to Iceland in March of that year, while the volcano was erupting, to prepare for publication a leaked video of the accidental shooting of journalists by US forces in Iraq.

Freeflow is a similar organization to Wikileaks, but the Freeflow team portrayed in this book do not represent individuals who worked with or for Wikileaks. Neither are Freeflow's leaks real scandals. While there were a number of controversial incidents in the 'Gaza War' of the winter of 2008–9, the shooting depicted in this book is fictional. Controversy also surrounds the late Bishop of Iceland, but Soffía and her experiences are invented. Belgium has its scandals, of course, but my Finance Minister and her past are entirely fictional.

My thanks are owed to the following: Pétur Már Ólafsson at Verold, Superintendent Karl Steinar Valsson, Chief Superintendent Sveinn Runarsson, Audur Möller, Alda Sigmundsdóttir's Iceland Weather Report blog, Michael Olmsted, Deborah Gavish, Michael Kram, Kim van Poelgeest, Oli Munson at Blake Friedmann, Richenda Todd, Liz Hatherell and Nic Cheetham, Rina Gill, Becci Sharpe and Laura Palmer at Corvus. As always, I am grateful to my wife, Barbara, and my children for their patience and support.